Stealing Hope

ALSO BY BARBARA L. CLANTON

THE CLARKSONVILLE SERIES
Out of Left Field: Marlee's Story (Book One)
Tools of Ignorance: Lisa's Story (Book Two)
Going, Going, Gone: Susie's Story (Book Three)
Stealing Second: Sam's Story (Book Four)
Out at Home (Book Five)
Tools of the Devil (Book Six)
Going Under (Book Seven)
Stealing Hope (Book Eight)

THE WHICKETT SERIES
Art for Art's Sake: Meredith's Story (Book One)
Dani's Story (Book Two) … <Coming Soon>

THE GRASSE RIVER SERIES
Quite an Undertaking: Devon's Story (Book One)
Rebecca's Story (Book Two) … <Coming Soon>

THE GIRLS' SPORTS SERIES (Children's Books Ages 9-12)
Bases Loaded
Side Out
Live, Love, Lacrosse

Stealing Hope

BOOK EIGHT IN THE CLARKSONVILLE SERIES

BARBARA L. CLANTON

eBook ISBN   978-1-953734-27-3

Revised First Edition 2022
9 8 7 6 5 4 3 2 1

Cover design by Sarah (Forcoverservice)

Published by:
Bibi Books Publishing Company, LLC

Dedication

To my fabulous fans and dedicated readers of the Clarksonville series. I appreciate your notes and comments through email and social media. I love your questions and our (sometimes) in-depth discussions about Sam and Lisa and Marlee and Susie. It's very clear that you are invested in them as much as I am.

Acknowledgments

Thanks go out to my cheerleading friends and family, who continually ask wide-eyed, "You wrote another book?" Yes, I did. A big collective hug and big thanks go out to Angela Muir, Andrea Danak, and Erin Saluta, who were my Beta readers extraordinaire. You guys each give me something different and continually make the stories better. I am grateful for your continued support and tough love. Thanks to the folks at Regal Crest who encouraged me to do what I do! And, finally, thanks to my wife, Jackie, for her continued support.

Table of Contents

Author's Note to the Revised Edition

I'm almost sad that this is the last book I get to revise and update in the young adult Clarksonville series. "Stealing Hope" is Book Eight in the series, initially published in 2019. This one is from Samantha Rose Payton's point of view. Or should we just call her Sam? She's the one that has to somehow merge both of her personas and let us know.

Naturally, the entire gang appears in this book centered on Sam. The Fam Four, consisting of Sam, Lisa, Susie, and Marlee, are ready to back each other up in their often confusing and challenging worlds.

Back in 2019, when this book originally came out (pun intended), a reader sent me a very nice email. And in it, she said, "You will be taking these girls to college." I had to read the sentence a few times because my mind kept trying to make her (now-obvious) statement into a question. No, she wasn't asking me IF I would continue the series with them in college. Nuh-uh. She was TELLING me I was going to do this. Will I? Perhaps. You, dear readers, will let me know if you want that—although I already know what happens during Marlee, Susie, and Sam's first year in college (and Lisa's senior year in high school). Just sayin'.

And just a note that this is a *revised* edition, not a second edition. Nothing major has changed in the story plot. Only the grammar, punctuation, and awkward stuff (to my current eyes and ears) have been changed, updated, or eliminated. I'm confident that the emotions and situations will stand the test of time and that you will enjoy more of Sam's life story.

Cheers,
Barb
Central Florida (November 2022)

Chapter One
Because I Know

Sam Payton dove into the driver's seat of her Mercedes and checked her reflection in the rearview mirror. Her blonde hair was pulled back in a functional ponytail, but there was no time to stop home for a shower or any kind of wardrobe change, so she was heading to Clarksonville as is—East Valley softball sweatshirt on top of a long-sleeved t-shirt and sweats. She wished she could take the time to at least touch up her eyeliner. Lisa loved it when she wore eyeliner. It made Sam look sexy, she'd said once. Sam didn't feel sexy at the moment, though. She was sweaty and grimy from practice. Thank God Coach Gellar made it a short one.

"You look *gorgeous*, Sam," Susie Torres teased as she plopped into the passenger seat. "Let's go already."

"Shuddup, Sus." Sam opened her mouth to check her teeth in the mirror.

"What, did you eat salad after practice?" Susie gave Sam a light backhanded smack on the arm. "You're acting like this is a first date or something. You and Lisa are hitting eleven months on Saturday."

"I know. I know." Sam started the engine and backed out of the parking spot at Sandstoner fields, home of their East Valley softball team. "I think I'm nervous because it's Lisa and Marlee's home opener today and...."

1

"And what?" Susie waved to one of their teammates as they sped out of the parking lot. "Are you nervous because we're going to be late for their first game? Or that you might not be getting *any* tonight?"

Sam squealed with laughter. "Shut up, Sus. You're not 'getting any' either. It's a school night, in case you've forgotten."

"*Dios mio*, I can't wait to be out of high school," Susie said.

"Ms. Armstrong said we have exactly four weeks until the AP Enviro exam, so the end may be closer than we think."

Sam pulled her two-seater convertible onto County Road 62. One day soon, she hoped to be able to put the top down, but not today. Oh, no. The second week of April in the north country of New York State still held the threat of snow.

She accelerated to five miles over the speed limit on the road that led Sam to her girlfriend Lisa and Susie to her own girlfriend Marlee. It sucked that their respective girlfriends went to a rival high school, but love conquered all, Sam always thought, and she never once minded the forty-five-minute drive. The four friends kept the road hot between East Valley and Clarksonville for almost an entire year.

Susie pulled her sun visor down and checked herself in the vanity mirror. Her long dark, auburn hair was pulled back in a ponytail, which she usually kept tucked under her hat on the field, but the hat had been tossed in her bag after practice.

"Don't worry, Susie. You're *gorgeous*," Sam mimicked and gave her friend a return backhanded smack to her bicep. "Ow," Sam held out her limp hand, feigning injury. "Your biceps are like granite."

"My woman likes me that way."

"A lot of women seem to like you that way," Sam teased but

instantly regretted it. "I'm sorry, Sus. Sometimes when I try to be funny...."

Susie sighed and then said, "I still don't see what the big deal was. I told everybody that kissing Alivia meant absolutely nothing to me. She was the one who kept cornering me. It's been four weeks since Ronnie's stupid party."

Irritation shot right from Sam's heart out of her eyes. She knew Susie saw the fleeting anger. "I don't think you get it, bestie," Sam said. "Your girlfriend was in the front yard crying her eyes out because you were shit-faced drunk. And you? You were in a dark back room kissing another girl. What's not to understand?"

"How long do I have to pay for this, Sam?"

"I don't know," Sam said, the irritation clearly showing in her voice. "I don't know." She focused her attention on the old-growth forest on either side of the highway and counted birch trees. It was her way of calming down. Once they passed through the oak tunnel where huge branches met overhead, the road opened up, and she hit the accelerator.

"I had my second meeting yesterday," Susie said meekly.

"AA?"

Susie nodded.

"How'd it go?"

"Okay, I guess." Susie's head dropped, and she picked at the cuticle on her thumb. "I don't like sitting there hearing about everyone else's shit. It just makes me think about drinking again." Susie looked up. "You know?"

"Maybe you're supposed to identify with their stories or something."

"*Madre de Dios*, I do. That's the problem. I just want to forget that stuff, not relive it weekly." Susie was quiet for a moment and then said, "They have these steps, you know? You're supposed to 'work them.'" Susie put up air quotes.

"Like what?"

"Like the step that says you have to admit that life became unmanageable with alcohol."

Sam looked at her friend, and her heart softened. Susie was desperately trying to get her act together. It wasn't easy with her parents in the middle of a knock-down, drag-out divorce, and then there was the whole Alivia kissing her thing. "You tried to hide from your life by being drunk a lot."

"Yeah, I did." Susie looked out the passenger window for a moment and then said, "Lisa says I have the power inside me to change."

"My Lisa?"

Susie nodded.

"She told me you guys had been talking on the phone," Sam said. "Just don't get any funny ideas, Torres." She trusted Lisa, and she wanted to trust Susie, but....

Susie groaned. "Sam, c'mon."

"I'm sorry," Sam said. "I think that was me being passive aggressive. Lisa has such a big and caring heart." But, Sam thought, Lisa did give Susie a neck and head massage recently during one of Susie's nastier hangovers.

"She does have a big heart," Susie said. "She's helping me learn how to calm myself with breathing techniques. She says I have this inner strength I haven't tapped into yet. She says meditating will help me let go of the anger I have toward my stupid parents." Susie laughed at her own words. "I guess it's not working."

"Not yet. Give it time, Sus."

Susie pointed out the window. "Look there. See that?"

"The convenience mart?"

"Yeah, see all those beer signs?" Susie counted them out loud. "Six! And there were probably more."

"Oh, oh, oh. This is that alcohol versus candy advertising game you and Marlee are playing?"

"Yeah, I think I may be winning this round." Susie did a happy dance in the passenger seat. "Free backrub for me."

Sam simply smiled at her friend.

"What? Why are you smiling?"

"Because you have an amazing girlfriend who would give up sugar, candy, and soda just to try to experience what you're experiencing."

"I'm so lucky she took me back after that whole Alivia misunderstanding."

Sam blanched at the word. Susie still had no clue. Is that how Susie thought of it? As a misunderstanding? "Um, yeah." Sam nodded. "You *are* lucky."

Sam pulled the Mercedes into the Clarksonville High School parking lot behind the school. There wasn't a single spot left.

"What's going on here?" Sam said and headed toward a parking lot in front of the school. "There must be a baseball game today, too."

"I don't know, but this is crazy."

Once Sam parked, they half-walked, half-ran all the way back around toward the field.

"They're playing Racquette, right?" Susie said.

"Yeah, the game's probably almost over."

"If it isn't already. They might have mercy-ruled them by now." Susie held the walk-in gate open for Sam.

They crested the rise from the parking lot, and Sam's jaw almost hit the ground. "Holy crap! Look at this." People two-deep filled both sidelines. The two small bleachers couldn't accommodate the huge crowd.

"And look, Sam," Susie pointed to the empty baseball field. "There's no baseball game today."

"All these people are here for the girls' game? Humph, what d'ya know?"

"Apparently, this is what happens after you win a state championship," Susie said.

As they walked up, the Clarksonville team was running onto the field. Obviously, no mercy rule had been affected. It also meant it was the top of the inning, and Racquette would be coming up to bat.

"Aw, crap, Sus," Sam said. "We've got our East Valley stuff on."

"We're gonna get booed for sure," Susie said. "*Dios*, look at the little league softball team."

"How cute. They wore their little uniforms and everything. Our girlfriends are celebrities, Sus." Sam craned her neck to try and see the scorer's table behind the home-team bench. Clarksonville High School was one of the county's poorest schools, and the softball field didn't have much beyond the basics. Unlike the more affluent East Valley team, the Clarksonville field didn't have dugouts or even a fence separating the field from the sidelines. There was no electronic scoreboard, no water fountains, no anything. "Hey, Sus, can you see the score?"

"*Dios* freakin' *mio*," Susie said with a groan. "It's tied."

"Tied? No way," Sam said. The manual tabletop scoreboard

came into view. "Holy crap, you're right. Four to four. And it's the top of the seventh inning. How is that even possible? This is powerhouse Clarksonville versus no-name Racquette. What is happening here?"

"Hey, there's Alivia," Susie said. "C'mon, let's go ask her what's going on."

Sam did a mental eyeroll. Susie still saw Alivia as a friend. Eating lunch with her every day in the school cafeteria probably didn't help. She wished Susie would get some quick perspective on what everyone else, except maybe Alivia, understood.

Sam's heart did a flip when she spotted Lisa behind the plate. Lisa rifled Marlee's last warmup pitch down to second base. Lisa was almost six-feet tall and built like an Amazon warrior, with her long black braid cascading down her back. Lisa splayed her hand across her chest protector and adjusted it. Sam sighed. She loved Lisa's hands, how they cradled her face, and how they made Sam's body feel so good. She loved everything about her girlfriend.

"Yo, lover girl," Sus called with a laugh. "Get over here."

Sam felt her cheeks flush as she made her way through the crowd. She muttered to Susie, "Can't help it. All I have to do is look at her, and I melt."

"I know what you mean," Susie said.

Shit, what did Susie mean by that? Was she talking about Marlee? Or was she agreeing with Sam that Lisa was attractive? Sam sighed mentally. Susie's infidelity was still throwing Sam for a loop. Sam could only imagine what it was doing to Marlee. Trust. There had to be trust. But how do you get that back once it had been compromised?

Sam squeezed in on the far side of Susie. If she could have found a smooth way to get in between Alivia and Susie, she would have done it. And Susie? She should know better than to go anywhere near Alivia when Marlee was around. But for whatever reason, Susie just didn't understand. Alivia had recently dumped her boyfriend Karl and completely shocked everyone by switching teams, kissing Susie, and then seducing Jessica, one of Lisa and Marlee's teammates. Alivia and Jessica had been seeing each other for a little over three weeks now, and all seemed to be going strong with them.

"Hey, Alivia," Sam said in greeting. "What's going on? Why are they not blowing out Racquette?"

Alivia grimaced and said, "I don't know anything about this sport, but these people," she gestured to the Clarksonville fans around her, "say that the umpire isn't giving Marlee a fair strike area or something."

"Strike zone?" Sam offered.

"Yeah, that's it." Alivia pushed a lock of her chestnut hair behind her ear. Sam had always admired the color. "But when the other pitcher is up there, they say his strike zone is as wide and high as a barn door."

There was a definite hostile feel to the crowd as Sam watched Marlee throw her first pitch of the inning. The umpire called it a ball. Sam exchanged a glance with Susie.

"That was definitely a strike," Sam said.

"I would have swung at that," Susie said.

"Ball two," the umpire called on the next pitch. He was a short, stout man, and Sam resented how close he leaned into Lisa as she squatted behind the plate.

"I don't know how Marlee is staying so calm and cool," Sam said, pointing out Marlee's neutral expression.

"She's got one of the best poker faces I know," Susie said.

"These people," Alivia whispered, "said Marlee is the best pitcher in the state. Is that true, you guys?"

Sam and Susie nodded in unison. "Pretty much," Sam said.

"Wow." Alivia seemed impressed. Alivia did have a big heart. She just had no boundaries. "Did you guys see my sweet thing in the outer field?"

"Outfield," Susie corrected. "Center field, to be exact. And, yes, we saw Jessica out there."

"That uniform, not the best style, but the fit is mmm...." Alivia said in a low tone. At least she had some decorum while ogling her first-ever girlfriend in a public place.

"You've got it bad, Alivia," Susie said.

Alivia looked up at Susie, one devilish eyebrow raised. "Jealous?"

That was all Sam could take. She smacked Susie on the arm and said, "I see Lisa's family. I'm heading over there." Yep, neither of them had a clue.

Sam greeted Lisa's mother and father. They had obviously gotten there early enough to get prime bleacher seats. Lisa's father pulled Lisa's four-year-old sister Bridget onto his lap to make room for Sam.

"Hi, Samtha," Bridget said and immediately crawled off her father's lap into Sam's. Her mop of dirty-blonde curls was sorely in need of some hairbands or something, but she didn't seem to mind, so neither did Sam.

"How's my favorite Sweetpea?"

"Good. Lisa's angry." She pointed to where Lisa stood with the ball in her hand, watching the second Racquette batter walk on four pitches. The home crowd was loudly booing its collective disapproval. There were now runners on first and second with no outs. At least Clarksonville would get a chance to get up to bat in the bottom of the inning. Lisa threw the ball back to Marlee and then put both hands out to either side as if to say she had no idea what to do to get the idiot behind the plate to call strikes.

"This is a nightmare," Sam said.

"Oh, honey," Lisa's mother said and patted Sam's thigh, "it's been like this since Marlee's first pitch."

"It's not going to be a pleasant evening in the Brown household tonight," Lisa's father added.

"I think you're right." Sam's heart clenched. At least Lisa had a family to be in a bad mood with. Sam often found herself alone in the big mansion she called home. Even when her parents were home, she was by herself. Her parents probably didn't even know where she was at the moment unless her father had put another tracking device on her phone. Or her car. Either was a definite possibility. Yeah, what was she thinking? He knew exactly where she was.

The next Racquette batter stepped into the batter's box and did the unthinkable. She actually swung the bat. A pop-up soared high above Marlee's head. The umpire called the batter out by the infield fly rule, but then Marlee did the most brilliant and amazing thing imaginable. She didn't catch the ball on the fly and let it drop to the ground. She scooped it up on the first bounce. The runners, not understanding that they were not forced to run because of the infield fly rule, ran. Marlee threw the ball to her shortstop, who tagged out the runner heading toward third. The shortstop then rifled the ball to her second baseman, who tagged out the runner heading her way. And just like that, Clarksonville had turned a triple play and was out of the inning.

"Way to be smart, Marlee," Sam called out, her voice one of many cheering for the home team.

Marlee finally broke a smile as she sat down on the team bench.

"That was fucking brilliant, Marlee," Lisa said, obviously not caring that she had just dropped an f-bomb in front of the entire home team crowd mere feet behind her.

Marlee just rolled her eyes and blew out a sigh.

"Batters three, four, five," Coach Spears called out. "It's now or never. You can't be picky. Everything seems to be a strike when we're up." The frustration was clear in the Clarksonville coach's voice. Sam shook her head. That stupid troll of an umpire was playing favorites.

"Maybe the Racquette pitcher is his niece or something," Sam whispered to Lisa's parents and pointed toward the umpire.

"Could be," Lisa's mother said.

"The prevailing theory in the stands here," Lisa's father said, "is that the umpire is helping out the underdog."

The man seated in front of them turned around and said. "Everybody's gunning for the state champs."

"It's not fair," the woman sitting next to him added. "Oh, honey, look. Jessica's up. Come on, baby," she yelled toward Jessica. "Get a hit."

Holy crap, Sam thought with wide eyes. She was sitting right behind Jessica Myers's parents. They were really young. But then again, so were Lisa's parents.

"Keep that elbow up like we practiced," Jessica's father called out. Sam glanced over at Alivia. Her eyes were positively riveted on her girlfriend heading to the batter's box. With satisfaction, Sam

11

was glad to see that Susie had walked over to talk to Jeri, Marlee's friend and former teammate who had graduated the year before. Sam couldn't help thinking Susie should have gone over to sit with Marlee's mother and her new boyfriend. A strikingly handsome boyfriend, Sam noted with a little smile.

Apparently, Jessica had learned to keep her elbow up and smacked a double into the left-center field gap.

Sam cheered with the crowd.

"C'mon, Lisa, get a hit," Sam called out. Heat swam through Sam's core as she took in Lisa's tall, strong body, her sure and confident movements, and her polyester uniform pants showing every muscular curve. Maybe they could find alone time after Sam's game in East Valley tomorrow.

Lisa stepped in the box and was usually a careful hitter, letting a pitch or two go by to get the feel, but apparently, there was no time for that sort of thing with a strike zone as wide as a barn door. The Racquette pitcher put her hands together and then whipped her arm in a circle. The pitch wasn't fast and wasn't even a strike, but Lisa swung anyway. She didn't get much power in her stroke, but it dropped in for a base hit right behind the shortstop. Unfortunately, Jessica had to stop at third base since the shortstop had fielded the ball quickly.

"That's okay," Sam called. "There are no outs."

Her heart clenched as she watched Marlee head to the batter's box. This had to be so hard for her.

Marlee let the first pitch go by. It was clearly a foot outside the strike zone, but the troll called it a strike anyway.

Jessica's father bellowed, "Yeah, that ball caught the corner, alright. The corner of Fourth and Main."

Sam burst out laughing. Jessica's father was funny.

"The on-deck circle is not the strike zone, blue," someone else yelled.

The second pitch came in, and Marlee waited just the right amount of time. She swiveled her hips, moved her weight forward, and swung the bat with a fierceness Sam had never seen before. The crowd leaped up and held its collective breath as the ball sailed higher and higher and higher. The crowd erupted when it cleared the left-field snow fence and smacked into the school building. Marlee had just hit a three-run walk-off homerun to win the game by a score of 7-4.

Sam hugged Lisa's parents and then watched Marlee do her homerun trot around the bases. All class, Sam thought. She never once raised a fist in triumph. Jessica and Lisa were waiting for her at the plate. Jessica patted Marlee on the back, but Lisa picked Marlee up in a bear hug and twirled her around a couple of times. The rest of their teammates swarmed them, and they all fell to the ground. After a while, they picked themselves off the ground and headed to the high-five line to congratulate the other team on a well-played game, even though it hadn't been.

Sam wondered what the Clarksonville team was going to say to the Racquette team. "Good game" didn't seem appropriate.

Sam told Lisa's parents she'd see them at their house when she dropped Lisa off later. She made her way down the bleachers to find Susie, who was still talking with Jeri.

Sam stopped dead in her tracks when she caught a longing, love-struck expression on Alivia's face. And she wasn't looking at her girlfriend, Jessica. She was looking at Susie. Thank God Susie was oblivious.

"I'm going to kill her," Sam heard Marlee growl.

Sam whipped around to see Marlee's fists balled up, an expression of rage on her face. Sam followed Marlee's glare. Damn it. Marlee had seen Alivia ogling Susie.

Sam ran toward Marlee to try and stop her from making the biggest mistake of her life, but Lisa beat her to it. Lisa grabbed Marlee from behind and swung her backward. Their momentum caused them to crash on the ground together.

"What are you doing?" Marlee spat at Lisa. She wriggled away from Lisa's grip and leaped to her feet. Lisa did the same and positioned herself between Marlee and Alivia. Sam moved in beside Lisa, not sure how to help.

Marlee tried to move around Lisa, but Lisa pushed her back physically.

"Get out of my way," Marlee said through clenched teeth. She put both hands on Lisa's shoulders and shoved. Lisa stumbled back a few steps.

"Marlee, stop this." In a surprise move, Lisa lunged forward and wrapped Marlee tightly in another bear hug. Marlee squirmed to get away. "Hey, I saw it, too," Lisa said softly in Marlee's ear. "I saw the look she gave Susie."

"Me, too," Sam said.

"Did Susie see it?" Marlee struggled to get loose.

"No," Sam said. "She was talking to Jeri. She was facing away from Alivia. I promise, Marlee. She didn't see it."

Marlee relaxed and stopped fighting.

"If I let you go, will you stop being insane about this?" Lisa held on.

Marlee nodded and then burst into tears.

"Oh, no, no, no." Lisa held on and rubbed Marlee's back. "You're okay. It'll be okay. I promise."

"How can you promise that?" Marlee said, trying to catch her breath.

"Because I know. I just know," Lisa said with so much conviction that even Sam believed it.

"C'mon, Marlee," Lisa said softly. "All those little girls are waiting to meet Marlee the great. For some reason, they all want your autograph."

Marlee scoffed and wiped at her eyes. "Okay, but Alivia better not come anywhere near me."

"I'm on it," Sam said and headed straight for Alivia. Finally, there was something she could do to help.

Chapter Two
Until You Get It

"**N**ight games in April," Sam said with a shake of her head. "Who thought that was a good idea?" She pulled the strings of the hood tighter on her East Valley sweatshirt.

Susie jogged in place to keep warm. They were waiting for their coach to call them onto the field for their pregame warmup. It was their first game of the season, and they had been unlucky to get powerhouse Southbridge as their first opponent.

Sam looked past her teammates getting ready for the game. The parking lot was busy, but she didn't see Lisa's Sebring yet.

"They'll be here," Susie said. "They probably went home to shower and stuff after practice."

"We're hanging in your room tonight, right?"

"Yep." Susie didn't sound that excited.

"Your mom's okay with that?"

Susie laughed. "She doesn't really care about anything anymore." She rolled her eyes. "I just hope Marlee...." She didn't finish her thought.

"What's up, Sus?" Sam said in a whisper.

"To be honest, I'm not sure. I still don't really understand why Marlee flipped out at the game yesterday. I mean, I saw you guys holding her back. She looked so pissed. Jeri and I thought she was mad at that stupid umpire. You know? But then you told me the real reason."

"Only the four of us, and Alivia, know the truth. I'm pretty sure everybody else thinks Marlee was upset about that asshat of an umpire."

"Marlee was a little reticent today," Susie said quietly. "She didn't use any emoticons any time she replied to one of my texts. She usually sends at least three."

Sam nodded, not knowing what to say to reassure her friend. She looked into the East Valley stands and got instantly pissed. "I'll be right back."

Sam marched toward the stands where Ronnie and his boyfriend, Jordan, were making their way to sit with Jessica, Alivia, Karl, and a few of their theater friends. Jordan's bright red hair and fair skin complemented Ronnie's black hair and olive-toned skin. They were a cute couple, but Sam had no time to think about that.

"Oh, so you are alive," Sam spat at Ronnie. "Where were you today?"

"What? No hello kiss?" Ronnie feigned innocence. He stepped down from the bleachers and stood face-to-face with Sam but on the other side of the fence.

Sam reached out and hooked her fingers on the chain link separating them. She almost wished she could get her hands around his throat. "Mr. Auerbach kicked you out of the quintet today. Did you know that? I'm now in a quartet doing last year's music. Thank you so much, Ronnie."

"Really?" The disappointed expression on Ronnie's face seemed sincere enough, but Sam was still pissed.

"And we were also supposed to learn Eleanor Rigby by the Beatles. We can't do that without the double bass." Sam stamped her foot. "You need to come to school, idiot." She didn't wait for a reply as she spun on her heels and stomped back toward the dugout.

"Hey, East Valley," a melting voice called.

Sam's body relaxed instantly. She couldn't help the insta-smile that sprang up on her face. She headed to the fence near the dugout and put two fingers through one of the holes. "Hel-lo, Clarksonville."

Lisa smiled, her eyes conveying everything Sam wanted them to.

"It's nice to see you again," Sam said.

Lisa grasped Sam's fingers firmly. "It must be something about these East Valley lights because I'm getting sucked into your blue-gray eyes again," Lisa whispered. She still held onto the fingers.

"Funny that. Because your brown eyes swallow me up. Every time."

"Sam, c'mon!" Abby, the East Valley shortstop, yelled over. "Coach wants us on the field."

Sam looked apologetic. "Gotta go. Infield warmup. Get ready to watch Southbridge kick our asses." Sam pulled her hand back and waved at Marlee, who sat alone on the bleachers. Marlee nodded back, but there was no smile. Lisa leaned forward against the fence. Sam felt her warm smile follow her.

Sam ran to her position at second base. She inhaled the familiar smell of damp clay from the freshly watered infield. For Sam, even though the temperature was in the forties, that smell was a sure sign of spring.

The game started without any fanfare or speeches. Just the usual recorded national anthem and a simple "Play ball" from the umpire, who was a woman and obviously not the troll from the Clarksonville game. Sam figured Southbridge would get on the board right away in the first inning, but that's not what happened. The first three batters never reached base at all. Either the Southbridge team was having an uncharacteristically slow start, or Mary had better pitching stuff than Sam thought.

Sam ran off the field after the third out. She pulled her batting helmet out of her assigned cubby and threw her glove in. She headed toward the on-deck circle with her bat and took a few practice swings.

Thank God Bree wasn't pitching for Southbridge. She and Sam had a tussle during a summer game when Bree slid in hard at second base. Sam came out of it with a black eye, and Bree ended up getting sent back to Juvie. Sam was glad Bree wasn't the pitcher, but then again, she wasn't glad. This Southbridge pitcher was fast, and Coach Gellar told them she had an effective drop ball. Great, Sam thought, the stands were full of spectators, and Lisa was there, and she was going to strike out every turn at bat. Fun.

Sam groaned when Rachel struck out on three pitches. Sam headed toward the batter's box. Rachel said, "Just keep your head in there, Sam."

Sam stepped into the box and dug an anchor hole with her cleats. She stepped out with her left foot to check the sign from Coach Gellar. Fake the bunt, then swing for a hit. Got it. She turned back and reached her bat across the plate. The pitcher put her hands together and leaned forward. She pulled the ball out of her glove, swung it back, and then exploded forward with a more than three-hundred-and-sixty-degree circle whip.

Sam showed bunt but then pulled back, ready to swing. It was too high.

"Strike," the umpire called.

Dang. It *was* a strike. That sneaky drop ball broke down into the strike zone.

On the second pitch, Sam showed bunt again. A fastball was headed right down Broadway, but Sam swung so far behind it that the ball was probably in the catcher's mitt before Sam's bat had even moved.

"Strike two," the umpire yelled so loud everyone in Clarksonville County probably heard it.

Sam checked the sign from Coach Gellar. Hit away. Sam almost laughed. *Easier said than done, Coach.*

Sam dug in and got ready for the next pitch. Ack! She'd been waiting on another super-sonic fastball, but it wasn't. It was an off-speed pitch, and she couldn't pull the trigger.

"Strike three!"

"Shit," Sam muttered under her breath. Damned change up. She hustled off the field and said to Abby, heading toward the plate, "She'll get tired eventually."

"Doesn't do me any good right now," Abby muttered.

Abby fared no better than Rachel or Sam, and the East Valley Panthers were held scoreless in the first inning.

Things didn't improve much for the East Valley team, except for Susie's line drive single to right field in the second inning and then her towering double over the center fielder's head in the fourth. None of the East Valley batters could get Susie any further along either time, so the score stayed tied at 0–0 after four innings.

The pitchers for both teams didn't seem to be tiring, but the fielders did, and the error count increased on both sides. Despite the errors, no one scored for Southbridge, and, unfortunately, no one scored for East Valley either.

By the time the top of the seventh inning rolled around, Mary was still pitching strong, and the Southbridge batters went down one, two, three.

Sam ran into the dugout and grabbed Susie's helmet from her cubby. She bowed low and held the helmet out in front of her. "Susie Wan Kenobi," Sam said, "you're our only hope."

Sam's teammates laughed, and Susie said, "Give me that." She grabbed the helmet from Sam's outstretched hands and pulled her bat off the rack. She headed toward the batter's box and yelled back to Sam, "Thanks for the added pressure, dork."

"Anytime, Sus! Anytime."

Every single one of Sam's teammates was up and smacking the chain link fence of the dugout, yelling for Susie to save them.

Susie dug into the batter's box and waited for the pitch without moving. There was no practice swing and no helmet adjustment. Nothing. Her eyes were locked onto the pitcher.

The pitcher went into her wind-up and fired. Susie didn't waiver and swung the bat like Sam had seen her do a thousand times before. She sent the pitch rocketing into the gap in right-center field.

"Yeah," Sam yelled at the top of her lungs. "Go, Susie, go." The East Valley crowd roared its excitement as Susie hit first base and then headed for second. She didn't stop there and went for third. The throw from the outfield came in. The second baseman took the relay throw and rifled it to third. Susie slid. The third baseman put on the tag.

"Safe!" The umpire in the field yelled.

"Yes, yes, yes!" Sam jumped up and down, holding onto Abby.

"No outs! No outs! No outs!" Sam prayed to every god there was for Keisha to get Susie in. She looked at Abby and said, "Susie's the first runner to reach third in this game."

"I know," Abby said. "Holy crap, Sam." She pointed to their coach. "Did you see Coach Gellar's sign?"

"Yes," Sam said. "I'm just glad it's not me up at bat right now."

The Southbridge pitcher went into her windup as Susie rocked back on the base. As the pitcher released the ball, Susie exploded toward home plate. The suicide squeeze play was on. Keisha squared around to bunt and pushed her bat toward the ball.

"Yes!" Sam shouted as the ball bounced into fair territory.

The pitcher seemed caught off guard and was late breaking from the circle. She picked the ball up with her bare hand and shovel-passed it to her catcher. Susie slid.

The umpire stood there but didn't make the call.

"What's the call?" Sam muttered. "What's the call?"

The ball trickled out of the catcher's glove and rolled toward the backstop.

"Safe!" the umpire yelled. This time Sam was okay with all of Clarksonville County hearing her. Sam raced out of the dugout toward Susie, who hadn't had a chance to get up. Too late, friend. Sam jumped on the pile forming with Susie at the bottom. Instead of getting trounced by Southbridge, East Valley had just beaten them by a score of 1–0.

~~~

After the high five-line, a quick team meeting, and an even quicker raking of her second base territory, Sam grabbed her gear and followed Susie into the parking lot to greet all their friends.

Marlee, Lisa, Jessica, Alivia, Karl, Ronnie, and Jordan gave congratulatory hugs and high-fives. Sam was pleased to see that Susie practically ignored Alivia and maneuvered so that Alivia wasn't able to give her a hug or even a high-five. Maybe Susie understood it after all. Sam's heart broke a little because Marlee didn't smile the entire time Alivia stood among them. Thank God the two groups parted ways fairly quickly.

"Hey, Ronnie," Sam called back over her shoulder. "Be in school on Monday, or I will personally kick your ass."

"Now that I've got to see," Jordan said with a laugh.

"Yes, Mom," Ronnie said and then bowed toward Sam.

She waved him off and followed her friends toward Lisa's Sebring.

As they talked about the game, Marlee finally smiled and complimented Sam on her diving back-handed snag of a line drive. Sam found herself blushing for some reason. When Marlee complimented you, it was definitely genuine. Sam thanked her and waited for Marlee to say something to Susie about her amazing triple and then her gutsy sprint home to score the winning run. When she didn't, Sam cleared her throat and said, "Hey, guys, why don't you head back to Susie's first, and Lisa and I will pick up snacks."

"Nothing sugary," Susie reminded. "Right, *mi vida*?"

Marlee simply nodded. The lack of joy in Marlee's entire body language made Sam want to hug her and tell her the world would be okay.

"I'll shower first, Sam," Susie said.

"Sounds good." Sam's heart broke again when Susie reached for

Marlee's hand, but Marlee evasively put her hand in her front pocket instead.

Once the doors to Lisa's Sebring were closed, Sam blew out a big sigh. "I hate this." She grimaced at Lisa.

"I know," Lisa said. "Marlee was really quiet all the way out here, and when she saw Alivia sitting in the bleachers, I don't know, she shut down even more."

"What can we do?"

Lisa started the engine and backed out of the spot. "Short of sending Alivia to Siberia, I don't know."

Sam chuckled. "That would solve a lot of problems, but I'm afraid your new awesome center fielder might go with her."

"That's true," Lisa said. "Jessica is head over heels in love. She can't believe that such a pretty girly-girl like Alivia was interested in her."

"Let's change the subject. The last thing I want to think about is Alivia's love life."

"Ditto. Come on, let's get those snacks." Lisa pulled onto the main street that would take them to the Stewart's in town. "You guys must be starving."

When they walked into Susie's room in what used to be a caretaker's apartment over the garage, Sam was happy to see Susie and Marlee engrossed in Marlee's favorite PlayStation game, "Jungle Party." Marlee even giggled a few times as they played. The game was designed for ages ten and up, and it was a fun and easy game for the four of them to play together, and Marlee, in particular, loved it. Sam was one-hundred percent positive that Susie put the game on as soon as she and Marlee got in the room.

"I'm gonna take a quick shower, you guys," Sam said and

headed to the small bathroom. She took one step and stopped. "What was I thinking?" She dropped her bag on the floor and walked back to Lisa. She put her arms around Lisa's neck. "I love you, baby." She reached up and let Lisa kiss her senseless.

"There," Lisa said. "That oughta hold you."

"Phew," Sam said. "Is it hot in here, or what?" Floating, Sam grabbed her bag and headed into the bathroom. She cleaned up as fast as she could, not wanting to waste any time. It was bad enough that she didn't get to see Lisa much during the week, and now that softball season was upon them, it would be less than that. Sam didn't even want to think about what was going to happen when she went away to college in the fall.

Sam stepped out of the bathroom feeling fresh and ready for some quality nooky time with Lisa.

Lisa had joined Marlee and Susie in the Jungle Party game, but they were talking about Mary, the East Valley pitcher.

"Mary's not a flashy pitcher," Marlee said. "She's not crazy fast like the Southbridge pitcher or Christy—"

"Or you," Susie added.

Marlee scoffed but didn't smile. Normally a compliment like that would have earned Susie a smile at least.

"Anyway, her pitches have a lot of movement on them."

"And I was impressed at how well she hit the corners," Lisa added. "All four corners. She can pitch up in the zone and then fool you down. You know she didn't walk a single batter tonight."

"Nope," Marlee said. "I think she threw a one-hitter."

"Uh, Sus?" Sam said.

"Yeah? Oh, do you want in?" Susie gestured toward the game.

"Sure, but I think we have a problem here." Sam put both hands on her hips.

"What's that?"

"I think these two Clarksonville spies just scouted us. I think we're sitting here calmly giving them all of our East Valley secrets."

"Speaking of secrets, Susie," Lisa said. "How did you hit so well tonight? I mean, no one else on your team…." She gave Sam a boo-boo face. "Sorry, Sam." She turned back toward Susie. "No one but you got a hit off that pitcher."

"I don't know if I should tell you," Susie said and waggled her eyebrows. She successfully added Sam to the video game and settled back.

Sam crawled in the well between Lisa's knees and then leaned back against her. Sam's whole body smiled when Lisa kissed the crown of her head. "Hey, no fair," Lisa said to Sam. "You're distracting me. Susie?"

"I probably shouldn't tell you two," Susie gestured to Lisa and Marlee, "especially because you'd figure it out on your own anyway, but I picked the pitcher. She has that double-pump arm motion, you know? Where she starts with a backswing before coming forward again and then circling around?"

"Yeah," Lisa agreed.

"So, if you just watch the hip, she pretty much shows you the pitch. She shows it to you twice. Once on the way back for that weird backswing and then again as she whips her arm forward."

"Oh, geez," Lisa said. "The grip. Right? You watch for the grip, which tells you the pitch."

Susie's face-splitting grin answered the question.

"So, what did she throw when you hit your triple?" Lisa asked.

"Fastball all the way. I get credit for the hit, but that pitcher supplied most of the power." Susie nudged Marlee with her arm. "Right, *mi amor*?"

"Yeah," Marlee said without much emotion. She didn't take her eyes off the video game playing on the screen in front of them.

Sam exchanged a concerned glance with Susie and then said, "Oh, shoot, Lisa, where are the chips?"

"On Susie's desk, I think."

Sam put her game controller down and scrambled to her feet. She brought the assortment of chips back to her friends and, this time, sat behind Lisa. "Can I braid your hair?"

"Mmm," Lisa purred. "Sure. I don't have a hairbrush, though."

"I'll use my fingers. They're clean." Sam sighed. The sigh wasn't meant for Lisa; it was for herself. She raked her hands through her girlfriend's long tresses and made three loose strands. The first two overlays were the key to getting it right. After a few up-and-over movements, Lisa's neck was exposed. Aha. Just what she wanted. Sam leaned forward and softly kissed Lisa's neck, earning a soft moan in response. "I love your hair, baby."

"Mmm," Lisa moaned again in response.

Sam finished the braid and reached into her own bag for a hairband to finish it up.

"Hey, baby," Sam whispered in Lisa's ear, "do you want to move to our private corner?"

"Yeah," Lisa said quickly.

"Hey, guys," Sam said huskily, "Lisa and I are gonna go to our assigned sector by the weight bench."

"Cool," Susie said. "Turn the radio on. I don't want to hear whatever's going to go on in that dark corner. My ears might combust."

"Shuddup, Sus," Sam said with a laugh. "I'm hitting the lights, too."

"Good, that way my eyes won't–"

"Shuddup, Susie," Lisa said, making everyone laugh, including Marlee.

After shutting off the lights, Lisa lay down on the mat and pulled Sam on top of her. A slow top-forty love song was playing on Susie's clock radio and set the mood perfectly. Lisa positioned Sam so there were many delicious points of contact. Sam leaned down and brushed Lisa's lips lightly on her way to her neck. Lisa sighed in frustration. She obviously hadn't wanted Sam to move on so soon, but Sam knew how to stir Lisa up. Sam nuzzled Lisa's neck and then undid the buttons on Lisa's blouse. Her lips moved down to Lisa's bra line. If they were alone, the bra would soon be gone, but they weren't, so she could only go so far.

Sam kissed her way down one side of Lisa's body, feasting on Lisa's tightening ab muscles, and then worked her way back up. Devouring Lisa's smooth, strong body made Sam tingle all over. God, she wished they were alone. Like really alone. Alone at the lake house alone, not in a stupid car or on the floor of her best friend's bedroom.

Sam lingered at Lisa's bra line, and she had just started to pull a cup off to expose one of Lisa's breasts when Lisa grabbed Sam's hand.

"No, Sam. They're right there. I can't."

"Okay." Lisa was right. Sam worked her way back up to Lisa's neck and then to Lisa's lips. The light kisses turned more fervent as Lisa moaned and then started her own exploration of Sam's body. Sam shifted above Lisa so that Lisa could reach all the important spots. After a while, she settled her full weight on Lisa's body, making sure her hip bone hit Lisa in just the right place.

Sam applied a little pressure, but Lisa put her hands on both of Sam's shoulders to stop her.

"C'mere," Lisa said, easing Sam off her and to the side. They lay face to face.

"What's the matter?" Sam whispered.

"Listen." Lisa sighed.

Sam craned her ears to hear over the radio. Marlee and Susie were talking.

"I'm okay right here," Marlee said.

"You sure? My bed is kind of lonely right now," Susie said in temptation.

"I'm sure," came the cold reply.

Sam groaned into Lisa's shoulder.

"Can they hear us talking?" Marlee asked Susie.

"Nah," Susie said. "They're too involved with each other over there."

Marlee didn't hesitate. "I saw the way she looked at you yesterday."

Susie groaned.

Sam and Lisa groaned too, but quietly.

"It keeps replaying in my mind," Marlee said.

"But it wasn't me looking at her, Marlee," Susie said quietly. It sounded like she knew she was losing again.

"Did you sit with her at lunch today?"

Sam didn't hear anything. Susie must have nodded because they did sit with Alivia at lunch.

"You know," Marlee continued, "I really thought I was okay

with the shit that happened, but I thought it was in the past. Apparently, it's not. And now, I don't know. I saw Alivia kiss Jessica after the game, and I couldn't help picturing her kissing you."

"It didn't mean anything."

"But you see her every day. Every day, Susie," Marlee's voice was rising. "You eat lunch with her every day. She probably sits next to you, too."

"She doesn't," Susie defended.

"Okay, then she sits across from you so that she can gaze lovingly into your big brown eyes," Marlee spat.

There was no longer any pretense that Sam and Lisa weren't hearing every word. They sat up and buttoned up their respective shirts. Their alone time was over.

Sam heard a controller hit the floor and then somebody stand up.

"I have to go," Marlee said.

"*Mi vida*," Susie pleaded, the emotion evident in her voice. "C'mon."

"No. I can't. I can't right now."

Susie groaned, and then there was the distinct sound of Marlee putting on her coat and walking toward the door.

"Marlee," Susie called and stood up, "don't go. I love you."

Marlee stopped walking. "I know," she said simply. She cleared her throat and said, "Lisa, take your time. I'll be outside." The last word was high and tight with emotion.

"Okay, Marlee." Lisa waited until Marlee left and then said to Sam, "Baby, I gotta go. We'll finish this tomorrow. Happy almost anniversary."

"I love you," Sam said. "Let me walk you out."

"No, I think you're needed here." Lisa gestured toward Susie, who now sat on her bed with her head in her hands. She was crying softly.

Sam nodded and reached up to kiss Lisa quickly. "Text me when you get home, and drive carefully, baby."

"I always do."

Sam waited until Lisa had gone out the door and heard the car engine start.

Susie must have been listening, too. She looked up at Sam for the first time. "How long do I have to pay for this?"

"Until you get it, Susie. Until you get it."

Chapter Three

Lonely

Sam held Lisa's hand as they walked in the woods at Lake Birch Park. The leaves underfoot were slick from that morning's rain, but even though it was an overcast Sunday, it was still perfect. She was with Lisa.

"It's beautiful out here." Sam breathed in the damp leaves, loving the earthy smell.

"I know." Lisa squeezed her hand. "Marlee suggested it when I said we were looking for a place to be alone. She said that she and Susie came here a couple of times, but did you know that her ex-boyfriend, Bobby, used to bring her here, too?"

Sam shook her head. "I can't picture Marlee with a guy."

"I can't either," Lisa said with a laugh. "In fact, I can't see her with anyone other than Susie."

"Me, neither," Sam said somberly. She stopped when they reached a fork in the path. "They've got to figure this out. But baby?"

"Yeah?"

"This is you and me time. Can we not …." Sam didn't want to seem insensitive to her friends' problems, but sometimes she needed a break.

"I know what you mean," Lisa said. "Hey, let's go back to the car so we can, um, be closer for a while. Okay?"

"Great idea, Ms. Brown. Great idea." Sam turned and practically dragged Lisa back to the Sebring. "Back seat, my love. Back seat."

Lisa raised her eyebrows. "Are you sure? What if other people drive up?"

"Then we'll stop what we're doing. Until then, let's have some fun."

Lisa hesitated.

"C'mon, chicken," Sam said.

Sam dove into the backseat as soon as Lisa unlocked the doors. Lisa landed on top of her and covered her face and neck with kisses. Sam grabbed Lisa by the hips and pulled her down hard. She moaned when Lisa's lips touched her own, lightly at first but then with more intensity causing tingles to settle low in Sam's belly. Her toes practically curled when Lisa brushed a lock of hair off her forehead and said thickly, "You're so beautiful, Sam. I love you."

Sam drank in Lisa's love. "I love you, too, baby. I wish we were at the lake house or somewhere else worthy of you. The backseat of a car isn't what I want for you."

Lisa kissed Sam again, and then they heard a car approaching on the gravel. Lisa groaned and sat up. "My arms were getting tired holding myself up anyway. I didn't want to squish you."

Sam laughed and sat up. The car had parked in the farthest corner of the lot. It was so far away that Sam felt safe enough to crawl into Lisa's lap. She wanted to keep contact.

"I feel safe in your arms," Sam said.

Lisa held her tight. "I've got you."

"Let's never do what they're doing."

"We won't."

"Promise?"

"Yes." Lisa sealed her answer with a kiss. She reached up, undid the buttons on Sam's shirt, and pulled Sam's bra back slightly, exposing the soft flesh underneath. Cool lips explored Sam's skin; it wasn't long before she'd left Sam with a souvenir to get her through the week. She settled the bra back in its proper place and then kissed her way up Sam's chest and neck, finally settling back to her lips.

Things heated up to the point of ultimate frustration.

"Baby, baby," Sam said. "We have to stop, or else I'm going to compromise your reputation right here in the backseat of this Sebring."

"Now, who's the chicken?" Lisa quipped.

"I know, but it's daylight, and I don't feel one-hundred percent comfortable here, and someone else could drive up, or the people in that car could go for a walk, and I can't, I won't do that to you," Sam said in a rush. "I want this to be different. You're better than this, Lisa. I want to make love to you, not just f—" Sam couldn't say the word. It was too debasing to say to Lisa.

"Thank you, Sam. But I don't care. When I'm with you, I'm home. I'm a princess when I'm with you."

Sam stroked Lisa's cheek. "You are a princess always. But I want to make love to every part of your body. I want to take my time worshipping every inch of your skin as I peel your clothes off. I want to feel your naked body against mine. I want to make you float in bliss for hours, not just a few stolen minutes in the backseat of a stupid car." Sam swiped at the tears in her eyes. "Gah," she groaned. "Sorry, I didn't mean to get so emotional."

Lisa kissed Sam's forehead. "I want those things, too, Sam. And

I'm kind of turned on by all those things you just said, I have to admit."

"Mmm, you are?"

Lisa nodded. "Hey, I wasn't supposed to say anything, but we might have a place next Saturday. Marlee's mom might be going on an overnight trip to Burlington with that Bob guy she's seeing. Marlee said her mother doesn't want her to stay home alone and suggested we stay over."

Sam raised her eyebrows. "They have that spare bedroom."

"With a queen-size bed," Lisa added. "But you can't mention this to Susie. Not yet."

"Is Susie not invited? Because if Susie's not going, then we shouldn't go, either. Marlee can stay at my house that weekend."

Lisa was quiet for a moment and then said, "I know. I know. I hope those two figure it out soon. Their one-year anniversary is in a week. Did you know that?"

"Holy!" Sam said. "I forgot about that. Okay, here's what I propose. On the drive back to Marlee's later, we brainstorm ways to get those two back together. But for now...." Sam crawled off Lisa's lap and guided her down on the backseat, "let's focus on our own love life."

"Here, here," Lisa said and pulled Sam on top of her.

~~~

The dreary, drizzling Sunday evening fit the mood in Susie's Honda CRV idling in Sam's driveway. Sam should have been opening the door and heading inside the house, but it was hard to leave her friend.

"How was Lake Birch?" Susie asked and waggled her eyebrows.

Sam shrugged. "Trying to be intimate in public is wearing thin, you know?"

"Yeah, it sucks," Susie said. "I may never get another chance."

An uncomfortable silence filled the car.

"Did you get a lot of calculus done at Marlee's?" Sam asked, trying to change the mood.

"Yeah," Susie said, but her expression was one of utter defeat. "Marlee's a good tutor, a really good tutor, but that's all we did. We never left the kitchen. She didn't kiss me or hug me or even hold my hand. She didn't touch me. Not once. Not even accidentally."

Sam's heart went out to her friend. She was sure Marlee still loved Susie, but Sam wasn't sure how to help her friends get beyond Susie's huge mistake. And Marlee wasn't the only thing Susie was dealing with. Susie's father had basically abandoned them, and Susie's mother had checked out of the equation, making Susie the acting head of the household. Susie made dinners for the family and made sure Miguel had lunch for school and that he did his homework.

"I'm sorry, bestie." Sam patted Susie's hand. "Marlee's in a funk about this, but I know she'll come around. She does love you."

Susie groaned. "I'm not so sure about that." She had a faraway look in her eye as she stared out the front windshield. After a moment, she turned to face Sam and said, "What did you mean the other day when you said I didn't 'get it?'"

"I don't know. I mean, you're telling Marlee you love her with words. You have to show her somehow."

"I'm trying. I don't know what else to do." Susie rolled her eyes. "I mean, should I send her flowers or something?"

"That wouldn't hurt. What about writing a letter?" Sam suggested. "I mean, I know that'll be more words, but you've written to her before."

"That's not a bad idea." Susie sighed. "Hey, listen, I have to get home. I have chicken quarters in the crock pot, and I have to get the rest of dinner going."

"Hang in there, Sus." Sam opened the car door. Her heart clenched as she looked back at her friend. Susie looked gaunt. Defeated. Life was definitely throwing her some serious challenges.

Sam walked up the steps to the mansion and opened the front door. The melancholy sounds of the piano filled the foyer. Sam hung up her coat and opened the conservatory door. Sure enough, her mother was sitting behind the Steinway concert piano, playing a piece Sam wasn't familiar with. All she knew was that it was in a minor key, C-minor to be exact, and was seriously adding to her melancholy mood.

Sam sat down quietly in one of the high winged back chairs to listen to her mother play. Her mother wasn't a virtuoso or anything, but she had a nice touch on the keys. Sam took in her mother's pale face. Lisa had been right, Mother looked tired and, as always, too thin.

Her mother finished the piece, and Sam jumped up and clapped. "Bravissima, Mother. Bravissima." Sam wanted to ask her mother how she was feeling but didn't know how. "Would you like to play something together? Pachelbel's Canon in D, maybe?"

"That would be lovely, Samantha Rose. Yes, thank you." Sam's mother scooched over on the piano bench to make room for Sam to sit on her right side.

Sam rifled through the catalog of sheet music and found the

piece. Sam didn't think she'd need it, but her mother surely would.

Sam's mother played the first few measures before Sam joined in above. Sam felt herself relax as she played the notes and listened to the soothing melody. It was nice sharing this with her mother. Her mother hit a few wrong notes but kept a steady tempo. When the song wound down and they hit the last note, Sam said, "That was nice, Mother. Your tempo was perfect."

"Thank you, Samantha Rose. Yes, that was lovely indeed." Her mother's hand went up to her throat as it usually did when she was embarrassed about something.

"Would you like to play another piece together?"

"Oh, dear, I know you have homework to do. And, besides, you need to eat your dinner. Mrs. Tardelli probably left something for you in the refrigerator."

Clearly dismissed, Sam stood. "Yes, Mother. Thank you." She turned to go but stopped and turned back around. "I enjoyed playing with you. We should do that again sometime."

"That would be nice." Her mother shuffled the sheet music and started playing the mournful song she'd been playing when Sam first got home.

Sam turned and left the room. She clicked the door quietly behind her. Since her father was still in Albany, she couldn't visit him in his study. And she didn't head toward the kitchen, either. She had already eaten at Lisa's house. Before leaving for Clarksonville with Susie that morning, she'd left notes for her mother and Mrs. Tardelli, telling them both when she would be back and that she would eat with the Brown family. Her mother either forgot or never read the note.

The melancholy music from the conservatory followed Sam

from the foyer down the hallway, and she soon found herself unlocking the door to Helene's old apartment. She turned on the lights and took in the emptiness of it. The furniture was still there, but everything had been draped with dust covers. Helene had always filled the space with such a vibrant sense of life, but now it was hollow and cold. Sam pulled the corner of the sheet back on the couch and sat down. She closed her eyes and imagined that Helene still lived there and was simply in the small kitchen making tea. Sam imagined they were settling in to watch a hockey game, one of Helene's favorite activities. Sam had become a Montréal Canadiens hockey fan because of her.

Sam felt her chest tighten. She missed Helene terribly. It was already April, and Helene had left in January. That was four months ago. Sam had promised to visit her in Montréal but hadn't gotten around to it so far. Soon, Sam vowed. Soon.

Helene had been her nanny for eighteen years, and if she had stayed, Sam would have unloaded all her worries about Susie's home life and Susie and Marlee's flailing relationship. She'd cry to Helene about how Ronnie was ruining the quintet. And just that afternoon, after making love with Lisa, an even newer worry cropped up. Lisa told her that some stupid kid at her school was getting overly attentive. Apparently, some guy named Alexander sat next to or behind her in every class they had together. He had recently traded with some other kid to get into Lisa's history review group. She said he was kind of a weird and creepy kid. Sam told her to be careful and never be alone with him. She said the situation was okay for now, but it was annoying that he was everywhere she was. He had even been at the softball game on Thursday. Too bad Sam hadn't seen him, or she would have kicked his ass far into next week. Or she would have had Susie do it, anyway.

Helene would know what to say about Lisa's situation and all the others, too. Of course, she would probably tell Sam that her friends could handle their own problems, and perhaps Sam should butt out. Maybe imaginary Helene was right. Maybe Sam should back off. Ahh, but everything happening to her friends affected her, too, so she couldn't butt out.

Sam rubbed her right temple. The familiar pressure of a migraine had begun. In the past, she would have run up to her room and downed a few pain pills, but Lisa wanted her to back off the pills and relax in a more natural way. Sam took a deep breath, held it, and then let it out slowly. She did that a couple more times and then began a systematic massage of her head and neck. It was so much better when Lisa did it, but Lisa wasn't there. Neither was Helene. And her mother? Her mother wouldn't know the first thing about it, so forget that. She'd just tell Sam to see Dr. Boyle, the family psychiatrist, for another prescription of painkillers.

Thinking of her mother made Sam wish they were closer. She wished she could tell her mother things about school, her friends, and Lisa. Did her mother even know that she and Lisa had celebrated their eleven-month anniversary the day before? No, she didn't. Or if she did, she didn't care. Helene had at least sent a congratulatory text message. That had been nice.

With a heavy sigh, Sam pushed herself off the couch and replaced the dust cover. She ran a hand along the kitchen table. This was the table where Helene had counseled her on so many different life issues over the years. They had shared stolen late-night moments at that table, mainly because Sam had been lonely, and maybe, Sam realized, maybe because Helene had been lonely, too.

Up in her room, Sam sat at her desk and opened her AP Environmental Science textbook to the chapter on global changes. She had started the homework problems during her free period at the end of the day on Friday, but she still had three more questions to go.

"What are the causes of ozone depletion?" Sam read out loud. She laughed and said, "The ozone gets completely sucked out of my world when Lisa wears her hair up, and I kiss every square inch of her exposed neck." Warmth flushed through her as she said the words out loud. She read through the chapter to find the real answers and wrote them on her paper. The next question read, "How are Greenhouse gases created?" Sam burst out laughing. "When Susie eats burritos from the school cafeteria," she said, but instead wrote, "The main sources are using fossil fuels, destroying forests, too much livestock farming, too many synthetic fertilizers." There were others, but she figured Ms. Armstrong would think those were enough. She hoped so, anyway.

"Okay, last question," she said out loud to no one. "How are you personally going to make the world a better place?" She wrote the cliché answers of recycling, driving an electric car, and using solar panels and then threw her pen down and slammed the book shut. "You know how I'm going to make the world a better place? By absolutely butting into my friends' businesses and being a pest until all their problems are fixed, that's how. And number one on the list is helping Susie and Marlee get back together."

She pulled her practice violin out of its case, rosined the bow with two strokes, and pulled out the quartet music Mr. Auerbach had given them because Ronnie hadn't shown. She knew the piece by heart, but Helene would tell her to practice it anyway, being ever-mindful of form. It would do no good to get sloppy, especially if she hoped to major in Music Performance in college.

She sat up straight, bow raised, ready to play the first note, and hesitated. "Damn it, Ronnie," she blurted and put the bow and violin down. She yanked her cell phone out of her pocket and texted Ronnie.

> SAM: Be in school tomorrow! Or else! (skull and crossbones emoji)

His reply came back instantly.

> RONNIE: Aye, aye, Captain! (heart emoji)

> SAM: You'd better because I'm going to practice Carbajo's third movement from *Antigona*. The one written for a QUINTET!"

She typed the word *quintet* in all caps, so he would know she was shouting at him and that she wanted him to take a major hint.

> RONNIE: Ahh, *Canto al Amor*. The Song of Love. It makes you think of your tall Amazon princess, doesn't it?

Truth be told, Ronnie was right. The soulful melody stirred her soul and made her think about Lisa every time. Sam sometimes got tears in her eyes when she played the piece.

SAM: Just be at school tomorrow!

She turned off her phone and stood up. She stared at the closed door to her suite. She wanted to open the door and play so loudly that her mother would be forced to come in and ask her what she was playing. She wanted her mother to sit on the couch and ask Sam to play something else. Or even ask Sam how her life was going. She wanted her mother to … notice her.

Sam turned from the closed door and headed to her bedroom, the violin practice abandoned. It was only seven o'clock, but the migraine pressure was back, and she was suddenly so tired she could barely breathe.

Chapter Four
Off the Hook

"I hate Mondays," Susie said to Sam and threw her lunch bag on the table.

Sam patted her on the arm and nodded toward the cafeteria door with her chin. Alivia was just entering.

Susie groaned. "And now I hate Mondays even more."

They both followed Alivia's path, and Sam breathed a sigh of relief when she got on the back of the long hot-lunch line.

"Oh, thank God," Susie said. "We get a few minutes of me not feeling guilty for eating lunch with her."

"We could move to another table."

"I know, but won't that hurt Alivia's feelings?" A worried expression crossed over Susie's face.

Sam silently stewed. She couldn't believe that Susie was so goddamned worried about hurting Alivia's feelings. Alivia was the one that had single-handedly wrecked Susie and Marlee's relationship. "Susie, can I set up an analogy for you?"

"About what?"

"Just bear with me for a second. I don't have a lot of time to get this out." Sam looked toward Alivia on the line.

Susie nodded her understanding. "Okay, go."

Sam sighed. This was going to be hard. "Okay, say that Marlee kisses, um, who? Oh, I've got it. Jessica Myers. Say that Marlee kisses Jessica Myers."

"She wouldn't," Susie said firmly.

"Maybe not, but I never thought you'd kiss Alivia."

Susie seemed to think about it for a second and then said, "Point taken. Go."

"Marlee tells you that Jessica kissed her. Marlee says she has no feelings for Jessica."

"And I'd believe her because the same thing happened to me. I don't see how this is helping, Sam."

"Wait, wait." Again, Susie wasn't getting it. Susie wasn't allowing herself to see through Marlee's eyes. Feel what Marlee felt. "Let me start again. Describe Marlee to me."

"Why? You know what she looks like."

"Through your eyes, Sus," Sam said softly.

"She's five foot six, short blonde hair the color of corn silk with dyed black tips. It's so soft. I love running my fingers through her hair."

"You're digressing. What else?"

"She has smooth, clear skin. She's lean but strong, especially her abs and her hands. I love her hands. And her lips. They're so soft and supple and—"

"You're losing focus."

"Sorry."

"Now describe Jessica."

Susie sighed and said, "Fine. Jessica is tall. She's strong. She has long light brown hair, pretty green eyes, a chiseled chin, pouty lips, small chest but big enough."

"You've really looked at her, Sus, haven't you?"

"When she first started coming to the youth group meetings, I was sizing up the competition."

Sam laughed. She had done the same thing. "Okay, but you'd agree that Jessica is attractive, right?"

"Yeah, I guess."

"So, picture this. Let's say Marlee and Jessica are both in the Clarksonville locker room, and everybody else has gone home. They're alone. Jessica moves in closer and plants a kiss right on Marlee's lips. Picture it, Susie."

Susie's brow furrowed. "It sucks."

"It does, doesn't it? Okay, so Marlee tells you it meant nothing. But then it happens again. Jessica kisses Marlee again."

"Again?" Susie said. "No way."

"Yes way. Maybe the next kiss happened at Lisa's house, in the back room where Lisa's mother cuts hair. Maybe you, Lisa, and I were on her front lawn looking at clouds. Marlee was in that back room alone with Jessica. And they were kissing each other."

"Stop, Sam. Come on. They can't do that."

"It's exactly what happened with you and Alivia, isn't it?" Sam asked. "Jessica's on Marlee's lap in that back room. She's kissing Marlee's lips, her face, her neck."

Susie smacked the tabletop with her open palm. "I'll kill her." She stared at the table, her breathing short and angry.

"Kill who? Jessica or Marlee?"

Susie's eyes darted up and searched Sam's face. "Both of them."

Sam stayed silent, praying that Susie would finally understand things from Marlee's point of view. Finally understand the anger and sorrow that Marlee was feeling.

Susie put her head in her hands. "*Mierda*, Sam. Is this what

Marlee's been going through?"

Sam nodded. "But that's not all. Even after she tells you what happened and vows that she has no feelings for Jessica and that it will never happen again, even though it happened twice already, she continues to eat lunch with Jessica in the school cafeteria."

"Every day?" Susie looked stricken.

"Yes, and then one day you catch Jessica staring at Marlee, her unrequited love obvious to anyone who sees her face."

Susie stood up abruptly. "No, no. She can't do that. Marlee's mine. She can't move in on Marlee like that."

"But Marlee sees her every day, Susie. Marlee eats lunch with Jessica every single day. How do you feel about Marlee now, Sus?"

"I can't breathe."

"That's how Marlee feels," Sam said softly. "She can't breathe when she thinks about you and Alivia. Susie," she said carefully, "this is what you did to Marlee."

Susie looked miserable. She stabbed at the tears in her eyes. Maybe she was finally 'getting it.' Maybe she was finally getting some perspective.

Sam looked up to see Alivia making a beeline for their table. Susie must have seen it, too, and said, "Sam, I can't stay here. I can't sit with her. I gotta go." Susie turned to leave.

"Wait, I'll go with you." Sam stood up and said to Alivia, "Hey, sorry about this, but we have to head out. Ronnie's not in school, and we are going to drive to his house and drag his ass here personally."

"Ooh, can I come, too? I want to see this."

"No," Susie said abruptly. "I think it's better if we create some distance between us. I'm trying to patch things up with Marlee. I can't hang with you."

"Are we not friends anymore?" Alivia's hurt expression tore at Sam's heart.

"I don't know," Susie said. "We crossed some major boundaries, Alivia. Both of us. I have to draw a line somewhere." Susie took a breath and said, "We can't eat lunch together anymore, either."

Alivia's bottom lip started quivering. "Okay, fine. Whatever." She turned around and stomped toward the table where Karl was sitting with a couple of theater kids.

"Oh, shit, Susie," Sam gushed once Alivia was out of earshot. "I didn't know you had that in you."

Susie was wide-eyed. "I didn't either, but some things are more important, you know?"

"C'mon, we only have thirty-five minutes left to haul Ronnie to school."

They grabbed their respective lunches and hustled out the side door of the cafeteria in record time.

~~~

Sam and Susie picked up their softball gear after practice and headed toward their cars in the parking lot.

"I can't believe how hungover Ronnie was," Susie said with a shake of her head.

"And I can't believe he and Jordan are still drinking like fishes," Sam said. "He was of no use in Strings today. He didn't know any of the music in the *Antigona* piece, and Mr. Auerbach was practically growling the entire time."

"But I think maybe we got in Ronnie's head today," Susie said.

"You know? By physically going to his house and driving him to school?"

"Maybe," Sam mused. "He did seem pretty repentant. I don't know, Sus. I'm worried he never learned his lesson when you guys got caught drinking after the youth group meeting."

"I didn't learn my own lesson right away, either." Susie hung her head.

Sam put a reassuring hand on Susie's arm. "You're doing all right now, aren't you?"

"I'll be one month sober on Wednesday." Susie smiled sheepishly.

"Sus, that's fantastic." Sam wrapped her friend in a hug. "I'm so proud of you." She pulled back and added, "You're doing this even with all the other shit going on in your life."

"I'm trying," Susie said. "Hey, Sam?"

"Yeah?" Sam unlocked her trunk and threw her softball bag in.

"I wrote Marlee a letter."

"You did?"

"Yeah," Susie said. "I have it right here. Can you read it? Tell me what you think?"

"Right now?"

"Yeah, I want to drive to Marlee's and give it to her tonight."

"Hop in." Sam unlocked the doors and sat in the driver's seat.

Susie unzipped her softball bag and pulled out a multi-page letter written on notebook paper. She sat in the passenger seat and handed it to Sam.

"Sus, when did you write this tome?" Sam laughed to let Susie know she was teasing.

"During sixth period Enviro, seventh-period Ethics, and eighth

49

period free in the locker room. You saw me."

"I thought you were doing homework." Sam chuckled.

"Nope, I was doing save-my-relationship work. There's some really personal stuff in there. You can read it, skip it, or whatever. I don't care."

Sam read Susie's words written in blue gel pen on lined notebook paper. The writing looked rushed, as if Susie had been trying to get all of her thoughts out at once. "Ooh, this part's good."

"What part?"

"Well, all of it so far, but I like this. 'I want to be happy. I want to be happy with you. Don't you want to be happy with me? You feel more right for me than anything I've ever had in my life.'" Sam looked at her friend. "That's nice."

"It's true."

Sam read some more. "Nice. 'I'm going to fight for us. I'm not going to let you give up on me or give up on us. When you touch my body, I—'" Sam looked at Susie with wide eyes. "I'm going to read this part, but to myself. Okay?"

Susie nodded.

Sam relaxed once she got past the intimate stuff and read on. Susie's following thoughts were similar to ones she'd voiced to Lisa many times. Thoughts about picturing them being together for the rest of their lives. "This part's really deep, Sus. 'In my AA meetings, there are steps I'm working through. One of them says I need to do a moral inventory, while another says I have to admit my wrongdoings. I did you wrong, Marlee. I put myself first. I had no freaking clue how much I hurt you. Sam helped me see that today. She helped me get perspective about what you're feeling. I couldn't breathe when I thought about what it would be like to find out that you had kissed someone else. I'm so very ashamed of what I did, Marlee.'" Sam clapped her hands. "Yay, Sus. You finally get it."

"I think so."

"And I love this part about how you can't picture a future without Marlee in it, how no one would ever be able to take her place. I mean, Sus, this part's a little bit rambling, but I think you're trying to find a million different ways to convey that. It's good, though."

Sam quoted the next few lines, "'There is no one else. There is only you standing right here in front of me. You are all I want, Marlee. All I need.'" Sam made a boo-boo face at her friend. "This is so nice, Sus. And this ending part about working through it together and coming out the other side stronger? That's good. Poetic even." She read the last part. "Oh, Sus. You're wearing your heart on your sleeve with this last line. 'I'm kind of lost without you, Marlee. Are you missing me? Missing me at all?'"

"Is the letter okay?"

Sam nodded and folded it up and handed it back to her friend. "I would just hand it to her and leave. She needs to process this by herself without your sad face watching her expectantly."

Susie smacked her friend on the arm. "I don't have a sad face."

Sam scoffed. "Yeah, you do. You've been wearing it for four days now."

"I'm gonna go before I lose my nerve." Susie opened the car door and climbed out.

"Good luck, bestie," Sam called after her. "I'm rooting for you guys."

"Me, too," Susie said and hopped into her own car.

Sam sighed. She knew what she had to do, and she had forty-five minutes tops in which to do it. Sam pulled out her phone and said, "Call Marlee." Within seconds Marlee answered.

"Hey, Two," Marlee said, using the nickname she had for Sam. "What's up?"

"Nothing much, P." Sam watched Susie back out of her parking space. "You just seemed kind of down on Friday. And Saturday. And Sunday. This is me checking in with you."

"Did Lisa make you call me?" Marlee's tone was suspicious. "She's already given me two earfuls about Friday."

"No, she didn't," Sam said. "I'm just worried about you."

"You know, Sam, I thought I was getting over the sting of it. Susie and I had an amazing time at the lake house. I won't give you details, but we didn't get much sleep either night. I thought it was enough to jumpstart my trust, but then I saw that bitch looking at Susie in a way that only I'm allowed to, and I got so mad and confused all over again."

"You should have seen Susie tell off Alivia today."

"She did? Oh, man, I wish I could have seen that," Marlee said.

Here was Sam's chance to put in a good plug for Susie. "You should have seen how mad Susie was, Marlee. She wasn't mean or anything. Just really forceful. Ask her."

Marlee didn't say anything.

"So, tell me how you're doing," Sam said.

Marlee sighed into the phone. "My shoulder's hurting again."

"From last year's injury?"

"Yeah, I think so. And I strained a groin muscle which takes forever to heal, so Coach wants me to baby it. It's kind of awkward putting ice on your crotch after practice. And my mother isn't home. She's out with Bob again. Anyway, I have cramps to beat the band, and…." Marlee sniffed loudly as if holding back tears. "And worst of all, I hit a bird with my car on the way home. A sparrow. I put it in the woods on the side of the road. I don't know if it'll recover or not." She sniffed again. This time Sam heard the telltale sign of tears.

"Marlee, Marlee, Marlee," Sam said, "you're having a crappy day, aren't you?"

"Yeah, and I'm really bummed that the Petrovs next door might lose their house and have to move."

"The Petrovs. They're that nice older couple that let us park in their driveway for Susie's surprise party?"

"Yeah."

"Tell me what's going on with them," Sam asked.

Marlee said she wasn't exactly sure, but her mother had said something about a second mortgage with an astronomical balloon payment. Sam was surprised that she actually understood the problem the Petrovs were having. Maybe she'd absorbed more of the Payton family business than she'd realized.

"Marlee, I'm so sorry to hear about that. They're such nice people. I hope things work out for them."

"Thanks, Sam. I've known them my whole life." Marlee groaned and said, "And I don't know what to eat for dinner. I'm so sick of spaghetti."

"Do you have any potatoes?"

"Yeah."

"Last time I was at your house, I saw a can of chili in your pantry. Do you still have it?"

"Uh, hold on." Sam heard the sound of Marlee's pantry door opening. "Yep."

"Okay, let's make you a baked potato topped with chili. It's really filling."

"Sam?"

"Yeah?"

"How do you know how to make this? You have chefs."

"Lisa's mother makes this all the time. Do you need me to walk you through it?"

"Nah," Marlee said. "But thanks for the idea. Sometimes I can't think." Marlee was quiet for a minute and then said, "Sam, I'm so confused about Susie. I can't think straight about her. I let her off the hook that night at the youth group meeting because, because…."

"Because you love her," Sam said quietly.

"Yeah."

Sensing that Marlee was ready to talk, Sam said, "Put me on speakerphone while you cook."

"Okay."

"Why do you love Susie, Marlee?"

There was silence on the other end until Sam finally said, "Marlee, are you still there?"

"Yeah, I'm here." Marlee sighed loudly into the phone. "I love how she smiles at me, even when she's tired. The way she lights up when she talks about clouds or science or whatever. I love when she sings along with the radio. I love that Patches loves her so much. Susie didn't even like cats before she met Patches. And I love that she insists I look good in pink—"

"You *do* look good in pink," Sam said with a laugh.

"I hate pink, and she knows that but teases me anyway. I love the way she touches me, Sam. You know, when we, uh, you know. You know what I'm saying, right?"

Sam chuckled. "Yes, Marlee, I do."

"And then after? She gives me these little kisses that tell me she's not done loving me, that she'll never be done loving me. She holds me in her arms, and it feels…."

"Safe?"

"Yeah. It feels safe. It feels right." There was a distinct sound of banging pots, and then Marlee said, "Hey, Sam, do I have to have green beans?"

Sam laughed. "No, Marlee, you don't have to have green beans if you don't want to."

"You know what I really want? I want chocolate, but I can't."

"Your no-sugar thing," Sam said simply.

"Yeah. This is really hard."

"How are your headaches?"

"Gone, gone, gone. Except for right now, but I think that's because of tension. Other than that, I feel so much better."

"You're doing the no-sugar thing to help Susie, aren't you? In solidarity? So, you know what withdrawal and cravings are about?"

"Yeah," came the one-word answer.

"You know what that is, Marlee? That's your heart talking."

"Right now, my ovaries are doing all the talking!"

Sam burst out laughing. "Ask Susie about chocolate-flavored protein shakes. I don't think they have a lot of sugar."

"I don't know, Sam. I know you're trying to help and all, but I'm not in any shape to think about or talk to Susie right now."

Too late, Marlee, Sam thought wryly. Susie should be knocking on your door in less than thirty-five minutes.

Chapter Five
What's Important

S am dropped her overnight bag on the dresser next to Lisa's in the guest bedroom in Marlee's house.

"Look at that bed, baby," Lisa said. Her clear excitement mirrored her own.

"And it's all ours for one whole night." Sam pulled Lisa into a hug. She put her arms around her girlfriend's neck and pursed her lips, waiting.

Lisa ever-so-slowly brushed her lips across Sam's and whispered directly in her ear, "I don't plan on getting any sleep tonight, Ms. Payton."

Sam moaned as tendrils of desire spiraled through her.

Lisa planted a big sloppy wet kiss on Sam's lips and then pushed her away playfully. "Hey, what're these?" She picked up three envelopes. "They have your name on them."

Sam took the envelopes Lisa handed her. "I don't know. Let's see." She opened the envelope marked with the number one. She chuckled, "It says, 'This is my final payment for the Neiman Marcus clothes you helped me buy.' There's a check inside." She opened the second envelope, "And this is Marlee's first check toward her bass equipment."

Lisa put both hands on one of Sam's shoulders from behind. "She's a good one, that Marlee."

"Yeah, she is." Sam opened the third envelope. There was only a simple note inside. "It says, 'Sam, thanks for helping me remember what's important.'" Sam smiled.

"What does she mean by that, baby?"

"I called her the other night. The night Susie drove over here to give Marlee that letter."

"Judging by this note, it sounds like you helped the situation. I know they've been talking for a few days, but Marlee didn't say they were fully back together. Do you think this means…?"

"God, I hope so. Come on, let's go back down." Sam stuffed the envelopes in her bag and then noticed a small white box on the bedside stand next to a small ice-filled cooler of bottled waters. "Hey, baby, look. This box says, 'Open Later. At all costs, do not share with Marlee!!!'"

They laughed, and Lisa said, "With three exclamation points, she must mean that. Let's open it when we come back up, okay?"

"Sounds good." Sam linked arms with Lisa and pulled her toward the door. "C'mon, let's go downstairs. I'm starving."

Sam paused at the closed door to Marlee's room. "Susie's going to stay in Marlee's room with her, isn't she?"

"Last time she stayed over, she slept on the couch downstairs."

"She was blacked out drunk last time," Sam said quietly.

"Yeah, things are different now."

"Race you." Sam pushed Lisa back down the hall before taking off for the stairs.

"Cheater!" Lisa called after her.

Sam hit the kitchen floor first and dove into a seat at Marlee's kitchen table.

"You are such a cheater, Sam," Lisa accused again once she got to the bottom of the stairs.

"Yep." Sam grinned. "Hey, Marlee, those steaks smell so good. Thanks for feeding us tonight."

"I'm happy to, Sam." Marlee pulled the baked potatoes from the oven. "I've got my helper making broccoli."

Susie turned from the stove and grinned. Normally at that point, Susie would have quipped something about Marlee and green vegetables mixing like oil and vinegar, but she didn't. Susie had been kind of quiet on the drive over, too. It was weird, and Sam didn't like it, not one bit. Things obviously weren't fully patched up in Susie/Marlee land.

Susie turned away from them and pulled the pot of vegetables off the stove. She placed it on the table wordlessly.

Marlee pulled the steaks out of the cast iron skillet and put them on a large platter. She placed it on the table and said, "Does everybody have what they need?"

"Yeah," Lisa said. "Everything looks so good, Marlee. I know you don't usually, but would you mind if I said Grace?"

"Sure," Marlee said and sat down. "That would be nice."

Lisa reached for Sam's hand and held her other out for Marlee, who took it and then reached for Susie's. Sam completed the circle by taking Susie's offered hand.

Sam clamped her lips tight to hide her smirk. Lisa had found a sneaky way for Susie to make contact with Marlee.

Lisa bowed her head. "Heavenly father, please bless this food we are about to receive and bless the hands that prepared it." She paused for a moment and then added, "And, Lord, please help the

East Valley softball team not be too sad when Clarksonville kicks their butts in Monday's game." She quickly added, "Amen."

"A-men," Marlee said loudly.

"I am not 'Amen-ing' to that," Sam said.

Susie chuckled but didn't add anything. She was so not herself that evening. It made Sam sigh.

"Okay, let's eat," Marlee said with a growl making everyone laugh.

The next half hour was dedicated to filling plates and then filling bellies.

Sam took her last bite of the ribeye steak and melted again. "So good, P. So good."

"Yeah, everything was great," Lisa added.

"Thanks, you guys," Marlee said. "It's Angus beef. Grass-fed, no hormones, all-natural. I did a pepper and spice dry rub."

Over the past year, the four friends had developed a natural rhythm, a natural ebb and flow to their conversations, and Sam fully expected Susie to say something at that moment. When she didn't, Sam was kind of thrown. She looked up. Susie was smiling, but her smile was tight-lipped. It looked as if she didn't want to jinx her chances of getting back with Marlee. She didn't want to say or do anything wrong. Maybe they were taking baby steps toward repairing their relationship.

Having Susie sit there silently was way too awkward for Sam, so she said, "Susie had a big day on Wednesday, didn't you, Sus?"

Susie almost looked surprised to be invited into the conversation. "Uh, yeah. I guess."

Sam stared at her friend. "I don't think these guys realize what milestone you reached."

Susie's cheeks tinged pink. She cleared her throat and said, "On Wednesday I hit one-month sober." She reached into her pocket, pulled out a coin, and held it up. "They give you this one-month coin to celebrate, but I don't think it really means anything. When I first met Marlee, I went longer."

"That was then, Susie," Lisa said. "Your life is different now. I'm proud of you."

"Me, too," Marlee said.

Susie looked at Marlee. The need for approval in her eyes was both obvious and heartbreaking.

Susie cleared her throat again as if uncomfortable being the center of attention. "Guess who showed up at that AA meeting."

"Who?" Sam said.

"Ronnie."

"No shit."

"Yeah, I told him about the meeting at lunch that day. He said he'd think about going, and I was surprised when he actually showed up. One of those AA steps I'm working on says I should try to help other alcoholics."

The room got stock still. Sam said quietly, "Susie, that's the first time I've heard you label yourself like that."

"It's taken me a while to be able to do it." Susie looked down at her plate, her cheeks turning bright red. "The label fits."

The look on Marlee's face was full of love and hope. Unfortunately, Susie didn't see it.

"Ronnie was quiet during the meeting, though," Susie continued. "And you guys know he's never quiet. He sat there listening, and I think he even had tears in his eyes at one point. When I walked him to his car, he said, 'That was enlightening, Susie.

Thanks for letting me attend.'"

"'Letting' him attend," Lisa repeated. "Does that mean he thought he was there to support you or something?"

"Maybe, but I hope he does better than that. I hope he goes again next Wednesday. He has to want to change, though." Susie looked directly at Marlee. "He has to understand what's at stake if he doesn't." Her gaze never left Marlee's.

Marlee looked down. The intensity must have been too much for her.

"So, Susie," Lisa said, "Sam got her acceptance to Rockville University. Did you hear yet?"

Susie's face brightened. "Yeah, I got in. It feels so good knowing that I'll be going somewhere for college. I got into Brockport, too, but Coach Greer at Rockville got me a little bit of money to play softball."

"Fantastic, Susie," Sam said.

"I wasn't expecting anything. That will really help."

"I wish I could say I was going to Rockville with you," Sam said with a frown. "At first, my parents were excited about the Wright School of Music there, but now Mother is all about her alma mater, Wellesley in Massachusetts."

"Where Hilary Clinton went?" Marlee was wide-eyed.

"Yeah, even though Rockville wants to give me the Frankl Prize for the most promising musician, Mother thinks being near Boston will be better for me. They haven't told me where I'm going yet." Sam shrugged.

"Baby," Lisa admonished. "Really? Your parents would force you to go somewhere you don't want to go?"

Sam nodded in answer. The dutiful daughter must do as bidden.

A bit of an awkward silence followed for two reasons. One because Sam wasn't allowed a choice in her own future, and two because it was Marlee's turn to talk about her college plans, but she hadn't opened her mouth yet. They all knew that Marlee had gotten into Cornell, so she must have gotten into Rockville, too. Coach Greer had been heavily recruiting Marlee, so money wouldn't be as much of an issue at Rockville.

Come on, Marlee, Sam willed with her mind. Talk to us. Talk to Susie.

Marlee must have heard her silent plea because she said, "I got into Rockville, too." Marlee smiled briefly at Sam and Lisa and then settled her gaze on Susie. Susie lifted her chin expectantly. Questions seemed to be silently shooting back and forth between them, and Sam felt bad observing their very private moment but couldn't look away. Lisa must have felt it, too, because she grabbed Sam's hand and squeezed.

Agonizingly slowly, Marlee pushed her chair back and stood up. She moved behind Susie's chair and slid it back with Susie still in it. Susie looked startled by the sudden movement but didn't say a word. Marlee moved to Susie's side and, in one swift move, straddled her lap. She placed both hands on either side of Susie's face and said, "I'm going to follow my heart, Susie. I'm going with you to Rockville."

Susie burst into tears. Tears of relief, no doubt.

"You are?" Susie said once she had caught her breath.

"I can't live another minute without you, sweetie. I love you." Marlee stroked Susie's face and then kissed her gently. Susie groaned and then crushed Marlee to her.

"Yay," Lisa said quietly to Sam. She waved an imaginary flag in victory.

"Finally," Sam whispered back.

Marlee and Susie kissed each other hungrily as if they hadn't seen each other in years. Sam and Lisa seemed long forgotten.

Sam quipped, "Break it up, you two!" Her comment earned her a backhand in the bicep from Lisa. "Never mind. I meant, keep it up, you two."

Marlee smacked Susie with one final noisy kiss and then stood up. She reached into her back pocket and pulled out two tickets. "Susana Torres, would you do me the honor of going to the Clarksonville prom with me?"

Susie leaped to her feet and kissed Marlee again. "Of course, mi vida. Of course." She twirled Marlee around the kitchen and said, "I don't have tickets. I didn't presume, but will you go to the East Valley prom with me?"

Marlee nodded. It was so good to see the two of them lovey-dovey again.

"Good," Sam said. "Order is finally restored. Lisa already said 'Yes' for the East Valley prom."

"And Sam said, 'Yes' to Clarksonville's prom," Lisa added.

"Far out," Marlee gushed. "Let's rent Cassie for both nights."

Susie burst out laughing, which was the best sound of the evening. "We should rent her limo, too," Susie quipped. "Don't you think?"

Marlee laughed. "Okay, just for that, wise guy, you get to dry while I wash."

Sam stood up. "And we'll clear the table. Right, baby?"

As they cleaned up the kitchen, Marlee said, "I had a couple of movies for us to choose from, you guys, but...."

"But you're really tired," Sam blurted quickly, "and really really really just want to go upstairs to your bedroom. Is that it?"

Marlee nodded her head vigorously. Her grin and blushing cheeks told the whole story.

~~~

After washing up for bed, Sam and Lisa said their 'goodnights' to their friends and headed to the guest bedroom for the night.

Lisa threw her toiletry kit into her bag and spun around. "I can't believe we play you guys on Monday. I almost don't want to."

"I know. It's going to seem so rude when I hit a double off Marlee."

Lisa burst out laughing and said, "I am so happy Mrs. McAllister decided to spend the night in Vermont."

"Oh, me, too, baby. Me, too. This way, I can sleep with the enemy." Sam growled low in her throat.

"Before you guys picked me up tonight, my mom pulled me aside, you know."

"Why?"

Lisa laughed. "She had the safe sex talk with me."

"Oh, my God." Sam grimaced and put her hand over her mouth. "Does she think this'll be our first time?"

"I guess." Lisa blushed and added, "Sam, it was so awkward."

"She was just doing the parenting thing, right?"

"Yeah." Lisa turned away and lit the candles that Marlee had left for them. "Are we?"

"Are we what?"

"Are we practicing safe …." Lisa looked back at Sam. "You

know?" Her cheeks were tinged pink.

"I guess so," Sam said. "If we had sex toys or something, we would use condoms, but we don't use toys." Sam sat down on the edge of the bed.

Lisa's blush intensified.

"And, I mean," Sam continued, "they say that when you sleep with someone, you're also sleeping with everyone they've ever slept with, but neither of us has ever had another partner like that, right?"

"No. Much to Tara's irritation, she never got past second base with me."

"Good. We hate Tara," Sam said with a grin to soften her very real animosity about Lisa's first girlfriend.

"That we do." Lisa laughed and then turned off the overhead light. The flickering candles made a soft sensual glow creating the perfect mood. "Ooh, that's nice." Lisa turned on the clock radio. The four friends had agreed to play music to lessen the chance of overhearing what was happening in each other's rooms.

"But if we'd had other partners," Sam said, "then I guess we'd want to use dental dams for, uh, for...." It was so much easier just to have sex than to talk about it.

"Oral stuff?" Lisa offered. She looked down, clearly self-conscious.

"Yeah, for that," Sam said with a sheepish grin.

"So, what about you and Susie?" Lisa asked, looking up shyly.

"You know all about that already, baby."

"I know, but tell me again." Lisa pulled Sam to her feet and wrapped her arms around Sam's waist.

Sam threw her arms around Lisa's neck, enjoying the strength of Lisa's strong body. "Okay, but I have to start way before that."

"Okay."

"Let's slow dance to this song while I tell you this story."

Lisa leaned down and kissed Sam eagerly and then pulled her close.

"The story starts in the spring of my sophomore year. A certain Clarksonville softball team came to East Valley for a game during the very first week of the season. We won that game, by the way."

Lisa swatted Sam on the butt. "A fluke, of course."

Sam laughed. "Of course. Anyway, before the game started, I was stretching with my team, and this really cute Clarksonville catcher caught my eye. She had this long black braid, you know? It swung behind her when she walked. She and her pixie-cute pitcher were headed out to the warmup pitching area behind left field, and I could not keep my eyes off you. I mean *her*." Sam smiled. "She had this commanding walk and the way she took charge of the game and took charge of her pitcher? Yeesh, I was mesmerized. I could barely breathe when I got up to bat. I fouled off one of Marlee's pitches, and it went straight up in the air behind you in foul territory. You threw your mask down and looked up to find the ball, but it had sailed back over the fence into the stands. I picked up your mask and held it out for you to take. You seemed surprised by that and smiled at me, and it was a genuine smile. You made eye contact, and your 'thanks' came from every part of you. Lisa, it was right then, at that precise moment, that I fell hard and fast for you."

Lisa kissed Sam gently.

"And then I went and struck out on Marlee's very next pitch," Sam said with a laugh. "But I didn't even care. After that, I had to find a way to see you again."

"That was when you drove your driver's ed teacher all the way

66

to Clarksonville for one of my games?"

"Yep," Sam said. "I paid him three hundred dollars extra for that. I even made him watch the entire game with me. As I sat there in those tiny Clarksonville bleachers, my heart hoped you'd remember me. I hoped you'd remember me picking up that mask for you, but you didn't even see me. Nothing. My heart broke a little that day, but then I remembered we had one more game against you guys that season. We were going to play you again."

Sam paused in telling her story to brush her lips along Lisa's neck. She left a trail of tiny kisses from one side to the other.

"I counted the days, Lisa. Every day that went by meant I was one day closer to seeing you."

"All this, and I didn't even know. I'm so sorry, Sam."

"And then, during that next game, there was no opportunity to pick up your mask for you. And I couldn't figure out what to do to get your attention."

"You guys won that game, too," Lisa said with a frown.

"Yeah, another fluke. But I almost passed out in the high-five line because you slapped my hand. You had actually touched me. I have to admit that I went into a little bit of a funk after that. Susie sensed that something was up, that I was miserable and needed a friend. That's when our real friendship kind of started. After a while, I took a big risk and finally confessed to her that I liked girls. She came out to me seconds later. I didn't tell her about my attraction to you, though. Not right away. I didn't want to get teased. She hadn't been with anybody either, and it was that summer when we started our mutual exploration. We were fumbling around for a little under two months, but we never got up the nerve to touch each other, you know, intimately. We almost got to second base, but Helene walked in on us."

"Helene interrupting you makes me very happy."

"Yeah," Sam said with a chuckle. "It's better that nothing ever happened. We both agree on that now. So, there you go. There's my story about how Susie was never an intimate partner to me."

"Except maybe a partner in crime," Lisa said with a chuckle.

"Yeah, no kidding. But it's also my story of how I almost let you get away from me. Thank God you finally noticed me the next season."

"I did. It was your eyes. I got caught in their vortex. And, you know what?"

"What?"

"Good things come to those who wait," Lisa said. The message her eyes sent could have caught the room on fire. She leaned down and kissed Sam passionately. There was nothing else in their world but each other.

Gah, Sam needed Lisa's skin on hers and began a slow and luxurious removal of Lisa's clothing. The soft candlelight intensified the mood. Whenever new skin was exposed, Sam lavished the area with kisses or tiny strokes from her fingers or both. Not a single square inch went unworshipped. Lisa's heavy breathing told her all she needed to know. Demanding equal clothing removal, Lisa performed the same ritual but at double the speed. Her need was obvious.

Sam needed Lisa's weight on top of her, so they moved to the bed. She needed Lisa to touch her body—to find the sensitive spots she knew so well. "Yes, baby, yes," she said in encouragement as she melted under Lisa's touch.

Sam strained against the hands that held her arms pinned over her head while Lisa feasted on her body. She loved the power Lisa had over her. Lisa leaned down and gave Sam a slow and lingering kiss on the lips. Sam's breathing was labored. They had all night, but she needed Lisa's touch elsewhere immediately.

"Baby," Sam murmured. "Baby, please."

Wordlessly, Lisa released the arms she held overhead and began an agonizingly slow journey south.

Chapter Six
Cold and Forgotten

Sam woke. The early morning sun illuminated the room with soft pastels. One of Lisa's arms was loosely draped over Sam's waist. Sam melted as she remembered the strong, safe, secure hold Lisa had on her throughout the night, even when they weren't touching.

Lisa stirred behind her. Sam rolled over to face her lover. She waited until Lisa's eyes opened and smiled before touching her cheek tenderly.

"Mmm," Lisa murmured. "I love waking up next to you."

"Same." Sam leaned in and kissed Lisa once. Her ears perked up when she heard an odd sound disturbing the peaceful Sunday morning stillness.

"What is that?" Lisa asked with a yawn. They had gotten some sleep, but not a lot.

Sam's eyes shot open wide when she realized what it was. She covered her mouth with a hand.

Lisa must have realized it, too, because she said, "Oh, geez, Sam. They're still at it."

"Who's moaning like that?"

"I think it's Marlee," Lisa said.

Marlee's clear and audible rising passion could be heard through the walls of the two rooms.

"What do we do, Sam? What do we do?"

"Don't panic," Sam said, trying not to panic. She hit the switch on the clock radio, and the music perfectly drowned out the sounds of their friends making love in the room next door.

Sam looked at Lisa. "Do we have time for…?"

Lisa thought about it for a moment. "We'll just make it in time for church if we don't eat breakfast."

Sam's grin almost split her face. She threw herself on top of Lisa and said, "Breakfast. The least important meal of the day." She made a meal of Lisa's neck, and then they relived a few of the delicious moments from the night before.

~~~

Sam pulled Susie's car into Marlee's driveway after reluctantly leaving Lisa and her family after lunch. The church service that morning had been blessedly short. The new pastor, Reverend Cross, had been wonderfully brief and to the point. Lisa seemed to enjoy showing off Sam to the new pastor, and Sam was delighted to know the pastor had no clue who Sam was. Most people knew Sam as Samantha Rose, the wealthy heiress to the Payton family fortune whose family owned and operated much of Clarksonville County.

What Sam seriously needed now, though, was a long afternoon nap. That morning, she'd left Susie and Marlee a note because they still weren't up when she and Lisa left for church. She thanked Marlee for letting them stay over and reminded them that Sam would be back after one o'clock to pick up Susie and head back to

East Valley.

Marlee's mother was home from Vermont, so Sam turned the car around on the gravel driveway making sure she didn't block Marlee's mother's car in. She also wanted Susie's car pointed to the street, so they could make a fast getaway. Sam had a serious nap to take and a ton of homework to finish.

Sam hopped up the steps. The kitchen door opened before she had a chance to knock.

Marlee held it open, a forced grin on her face. The smile disappeared quickly, though, and her lower lip trembled. She started to cry, and Sam pulled her into her arms.

"What's wrong, P? What happened?"

Marlee just groaned and then pulled away. She stubbornly brushed the tears off her cheeks. At just that moment, Susie came bounding down the stairs, two overnight bags in hand. Her hair was wet from an obviously recent shower.

Marlee's face scrunched up at the sight, and she started crying again in earnest.

"Uh, oh." Susie dropped her bags on the kitchen floor. "*Mi vida*, what's wrong? Why are you crying?" Sam stepped aside so Susie could whisk Marlee into her arms. Susie held Marlee close but mouthed wordlessly to Sam, "What happened?"

Sam shrugged and mouthed back, "I have no idea."

Marlee's mother came down the stairs and popped into the kitchen carrying a laundry basket of clothes. She was obviously on her way down to the basement to wash them. She took in the scene before her and gently set the basket on the table. Marlee's back was to her mother, and she didn't see the look of concern Susie exchanged with Marlee's mother. The exchange was touching.

Marlee pulled back and wiped at her eyes again. "Don't go," she said quietly to Susie. "I just got you back." With a moan, Marlee leaned forward and kissed Susie passionately and squarely on the lips. Panicked, Sam tried to look anywhere but at her friends. Marlee's mother looked down, giving them a small amount of privacy.

"You're sweet," Susie said after a moment, "but I have to go. I have dinner to cook at home. I have homework, and I have to make sure Miguel does *his* homework."

Marlee groaned into Susie's chest and then started crying again. They were mournful sobs that positively broke Sam's heart. No one in the kitchen knew what to do. Susie pulled Marlee's head tighter to her chest and wrapped her in her arms. Susie looked like a deer caught in the headlights.

After a few moments, Marlee caught her breath and said, "It's our one-year anniversary."

"I know, *mi amor*," Susie said low. She exchanged quick concerned glances with both Sam and Marlee's mother. "I...I can stay," she said tentatively. "I'll stay," she said again with more conviction.

Marlee's eyes were closed, her head still lying on Susie's chest. "I love you." She pulled back from Susie but slid her arm around Susie's waist and turned around. She brushed her tears away and then noticed her mother. "Oh, Mom. Hi. How long have you been standing there?"

Her mother simply smiled and said, "Long enough. Are you okay?"

Marlee looked over at Susie at her side. "I am now."

"Okay, then. I'll be in the basement doing laundry."

"Have fun," Marlee said.

Marlee's mother laughed. "Oh, sure. It's my favoritest thing to do." She picked up the basket of clothes and headed for the basement door.

"Are you okay, Marlee?" Sam asked.

"I think we didn't get enough sleep last night," Marlee said quietly.

"*Enough* sleep?" Susie said. "How about *no* sleep." She laughed, and Marlee's face lit up into a devilish grin. Oh, yeah. Her friends had had about as much fun, if not more than she and Lisa had.

"Uh, Sus?" Sam said.

"Yeah?"

"I, unfortunately, *do* have to get home."

"Oh, right," Susie said. "You already have the keys, so just drive my car home. I'll pick it up later."

"How are you going to get home? Why don't I call my car service to pick me up, and then you can drive yourself home later."

"Nope. I don't want to inconvenience you or your family," Susie said. "Really. Just take my car, and I'll figure something out."

By this point, Marlee had let Susie go and was rooting around in the refrigerator. Her back was to them.

"Not Alivia," Sam mouthed wordlessly and shook her head for emphasis. There was a very high probability that Alivia was in Clarksonville visiting Jessica. Sam wasn't sure if the year-younger Jessica had a driver's license yet, and if not, then Alivia most certainly would be in Clarksonville.

Wide-eyed, Susie vehemently shook her head. "I'll figure something out, Sam."

"Okay, well, call me if you can't find anybody. I'll either come back or send my car service to get you. Okay?"

"You got it." Susie smiled. She then glanced at Marlee and sent a look of concern Sam's way.

Sam reciprocated the look. "Call me when you're coming for your car so I can open the gate for you."

"You got it, *gringa*."

"Marlee," Sam said, "I love you. Please feel better." She pulled Marlee into a healing hug and said low, "Get some sleep."

"Yeah," Marlee agreed. "After sustenance, then maybe a nap."

"Ooh," Susie said. "I second that motion."

"All in favor?" Sam said.

"Aye," they said in unison and laughed.

"Thanks for a great evening, you guys," Sam said. "Oh, and thanks for the chocolate-covered strawberries in our room, Marlee."

"You didn't leave any, did you?" Marlee's voice held the slightest tinge of real panic.

"No, no. Lisa took the rest home for the three musketeers. Her sisters and brother devoured them after lunch."

"Good."

~~~

Sam did her best to keep her eyes open during the forty-five-minute drive home. Her only goal once she got there was to crawl up the stairs to her rooms to take a glorious Sunday afternoon nap.

She parked Susie's car on the driveway behind the garage that housed her Mercedes and grabbed her overnight bag from the passenger seat. Her legs felt like lead weights as she lumbered up the stone steps.

To her surprise, there was a bustle of activity inside the mansion. Confused, Sam followed the sound. Her heart leaped to her throat. The door to Helene's apartment was open, and people were inside. Sam dropped her bag and took off in a run. "Helene?" she called, hoping beyond hope.

She went into the apartment to see a team of maids dusting and cleaning. What was happening? The maids never came on Sunday.

"What's going on?" Sam asked the closest worker. "Is Helene here?"

"I don't know, Miss," the maid said with a curtsy. Sam hated that her mother made them do that. "Miss Mimi has us cleaning and getting these rooms ready."

"Ready for what?" Sam asked, knowing the poor woman wouldn't know. "Sorry, I know you don't know."

She headed into Helene's old bedroom and found two more maids putting fresh sheets on the bed. The blinds were open, and the dust motes floated freely in the sunbeams. "Is Helene coming back?" She asked the two working women.

More curtsies. The older of the two women said, "We don't exactly know, Miss. I believe we are getting the rooms ready for someone, though."

Sam wanted to ask more questions but settled for, "Do you know where Mother is? Or Daddy?"

"No, Miss. I'm sorry."

"Thank you." Sam wished she knew the woman's name so she could address her properly, but she didn't. And she *should* know her name, damn it. The woman had worked for them for a couple of years now. She was kind of in charge of the rest of the maids or something. Sam had never really paid attention to that stuff before.

Strangers in Samantha Rose Payton's home were a regular thing.

The nap momentarily forgotten, Sam headed to her rooms and threw her overnight bag on her bed. She pulled out her phone, punched a few buttons, and the phone dialed Helene. Sam hung up immediately.

What if Helene wasn't really coming back? Of course, she wasn't. Helene had moved on. Permanently. She had taken all of her stuff. But why hadn't anyone told her what was happening in the apartment? Crap, what if her mother had hired another nanny? Or a new house manager or live-in cook? Helene had done all those jobs and still had time to teach Sam how to speak French, play the piano, and check your opponent against the boards without getting called for a personal foul. Sam felt her blood pressure decrease as she remembered all the good times she'd had with Helene.

Sam's cell phone rang in her hand. She looked at the display. It was Helene calling her back. Sam didn't answer. She didn't want Helene to find out that she had almost sent herself into a panic attack over strangers touching Helene's stuff, especially because that *stuff* wasn't Helene's anymore.

She sat down hard on her bed, leaned back, and kicked her overnight bag to the floor. She flicked her shoes off and was out the instant she closed her eyes.

~~~

Sam felt better when she woke but was not exactly refreshed. She wondered if her parents had come home yet. She desperately didn't want to go back downstairs if the maids were still there, but she had so much nervous energy that she had to do something. She decided to head out for a run and threw on sweats and a good pair of running shoes. The sounds of the maids greeted her as soon as she opened the door to her wing of the house. Steeling her nerves, she bolted down the stairs and then out the front door.

She headed down the long sloping driveway toward the gate at an easy warmup pace. She wished she could smash through the steel-reinforced gate, turn right and head back to Clarksonville. She'd scoop up Lisa, and they would run away together where no one and nothing would bother them. Ever.

Instead, she turned left inside the gate and headed toward the woodsy part of the walking trail her parents had constructed years ago. The late-afternoon April air was chilly, but it felt good to fill her lungs and move her muscles. She picked up the pace when she hit the far corner of the property near the stand of birch trees. A few years back, as a newly-minted teenager, she used to peel the bark and scratch 'I love you' declarations to whatever girl she was attracted to at that moment. Back then, Helene was the only person in the entire world she'd told that she liked these girls. Sam knew enough not to spill the beans to her parents or anyone else. The perfect Payton princess would never do anything so unseemly.

Sam increased her pace. She didn't want to think about Helene. It made her too sad. Maybe she'd take a trip to Canada once softball season was over. Montréal wasn't that far away. When Sam reached the next corner of the property, she turned left and put on speed in an out-and-out sprint. She emerged from the woods gasping for breath but didn't stop. She ran past her mother's gardens. She ran past the pool house and pool that no one swam in. She ran past the gardener's shack and finally slowed her pace when she reached the southeast corner of the Payton family estate. She slowed to a jog until she finally came to her favorite spot. An old, dilapidated swing hung from a low branch. She breathed in deeply while catching her breath and then climbed onto the swing. She was surprised that the ropes didn't snap.

No one had been out there in years. When she was younger, she would sit in the swing and face the ivy-covered stone wall surrounding the estate. She'd imagine ways to magically shimmer through the wall and emerge on the other side free. Sometimes she imagined swinging up so high that she could leap off and fly over the fence. Of course, in this version of her fantasy, she always landed on a cushiony pile of leaves. When those ideas waned, Sam took to throwing rocks at the stone wall. If you looked closely, you could see the pockmarks where she'd chipped the stone. Maybe that's how she'd developed her good throwing arm.

Sam turned to look at the lonely mansion behind her. She always thought it looked cold and forgotten, just like the people in it. She rocked back and forth on the swing for a while until she felt her legs cramping up. Knowing she had to go back inside eventually, she hopped off the swing and headed directly back to the house and the sanctuary of her rooms.

Chapter Seven
It Was a Start

After a quick shower, Sam's second one that Sunday, she pulled out her first-period French textbook and read the short story her teacher had assigned. Ten *critical thinking* questions later, Sam shoved the book into her backpack and pulled out her Precalculus text. She wished Susie or Marlee were there to help with this stuff. The topic was probability. It always made sense when Mrs. Hanson went over it, but it made absolutely no sense when it was her turn to try it. Sam wrote something down for each of the twenty-five questions but reasoned that the probability she had gotten any of them right was close to zero. Whatever. She'd tried.

She took a quick trip to the bathroom, grabbed another bottle of Perrier from the mini-fridge in her room, and settled in for a rousing round of history homework. She had to read the article "A History of Missteps: Why Good People do Bad Things" and then answer two pages of questions about the article. "Hmm," Sam mused out loud. "This is Susie. She's a good person, but she just went down a bad path for a while."

Forty minutes later, Sam put the period at the end of her last sentence and fell back, exhausted. She put her history notebook in her backpack. Dutifully, she pulled out the next subject on the homework hit parade – AP Environmental Science.

She sighed when she thought about doing her AP Enviro reading. No, she'd had enough. Maybe she could do it during lunch tomorrow. Or, better yet, Susie could give her a summary. If Susie had even done the reading, that is. Susie kind of had her hands full at the moment. She checked her phone for a text from Susie. Nope, nothing. She'd either found another way home or was still at Marlee's.

Sam wanted to call Lisa and tell her about Marlee's mini-meltdown, but Lisa was studying with Missy Matthews for some big Anatomy test on Monday. They were at Missy's house all afternoon, and Sam didn't want to interrupt. She decided to go for something that usually calmed her and grabbed her practice violin and a stack of sheet music. She made sure the quintet music was right on top and then headed out of her suite and down to the conservatory. She hoped her parents would come home from wherever they had gone and would hear her practicing. Maybe they'd come into the conservatory to listen or sit down and talk. Blessedly, the maids were done and gone.

She played the *Antigona* piece first. Her brain supplied the missing viola, cello, bass, and second violin parts as she played. Thoughts of her amazing night with Lisa filled the space. Losing herself in the emotion, she played it again. After two full run-throughs, she was satisfied with her interpretation and moved on to the Beatles song. While practicing a particularly tricky run high on the neck, she heard her parents enter the house.

"I'll be in my study," her father's authoritative voice said from the foyer. She heard his quick footsteps head down the hallway toward his office.

Sam didn't hear her mother's response. Hoping her mother was still in the foyer outside the conservatory, Sam started playing the Beatles piece again, hoping to attract her into the room. Sam's heart fell when she played the entire piece, and no one came in. Frustrated, she gave up. She packed up her violin, stacked up her music, and headed out of the room.

Sam's cell phone dinged as a text came in. She set her violin and sheet music down on the marble foyer table. It was Mother's expensive showpiece to impress guests. The oversized ornate vase in the center was filled with fresh-cut flowers, as it always was. Sam pulled her cell phone out of her pocket. The text was from Susie. She was at the gate. Sam hit the button in the security panel near the front door to open the drive gate at the bottom of the hill.

Sam opened the front door, curious to see how Susie had gotten back to East Valley. It had already started getting dark, but she immediately recognized Mrs. McAllister's old Cadillac. Sam wished she could have been a fly on the wall inside the car for that forty-five-minute drive. Sam couldn't wait to tease Susie about it.

Despite the growing cold, Sam didn't put a jacket on as she stepped onto the front landing. She pulled Susie's car keys from her pocket and headed down the steps.

Mrs. McAllister pulled her car in front of Susie's. Susie got out of the passenger side and headed toward the trunk just as Mrs. McAllister stepped out to unlock it.

"Hey, Sam," Susie called as Sam walked over.

"Hi," Sam said back. "How was the drive?" She said it enough, but her eyes sent a dying-to-know message to Susie, which was deflected by a roll of Susie's eyes.

"Fine," Susie answered succinctly. She pulled her bags out of the trunk.

"You know, the North Country on a Sunday evening," Mrs. McAllister said. "We roll up the sidewalks when it gets dark."

Sam chuckled. It was kind of true. "So," Sam said pointedly, "how is our Marlee doing? I was surprised by the waterworks."

Marlee's mother sighed. "That kid keeps it all in until the dam bursts."

"And burst it did," Susie added.

"For the last week or so, she's been down in that basement playing her guitar to loud rock music." Marlee's mother looked playfully at Sam as if she were to blame. "She's been stuck on Effervescence? Something like that."

Sam thought for a second. "Oh, Evanescence. Great band. Their songs are pretty rocking."

"I know she's troubled when she gets quiet and doesn't talk to me," Marlee's mother said. She pulled her sweater tight around her. "It was obvious that she was working something out in her head."

"I think we finally worked it out," Susie said quietly in her own defense. Sam hoped it was true.

"Is she home alone now?" Sam asked.

"No, no. I asked our neighbors, the Petrovs, to come by for a visit. They're saints. They helped me out so much after Marlee's dad died. They stayed with Marlee while I tried to find work. They're like surrogate grandparents."

"That's sweet," Sam said. "And Marlee was okay having babysitters at age seventeen?"

"Oh, yes. She loves them. They turned on the Mets game right before we left."

"Uh oh," Sam said. "Was that a good idea? You know how

passionate Marlee gets about her Mets."

"She got that from her father. He used to throw things at the TV when the Mets were losing. Every Mets fan's lot in life, I'm afraid."

Susie chuckled and added, "The Mets were winning when we left."

"Phew," Sam said dramatically. "But she was okay, otherwise?"

"Yes," Marlee's mother said. "She was doing her math homework."

"And we all know how happy Marlee is when she's doing math," Susie said with a laugh.

"Okay, girls," Marlee's mother said. "I need to get home." She put a hand on Susie's shoulder and reached over to touch Sam's forearm. Touching them both, she looked Susie directly in the eye and said, "Take care of my baby." Her voice choked up on the last word. "She's all I've got."

Sam's heart flew out of her chest and wrapped itself around Marlee's mother.

"I will," Susie said, tears gleaming in her eyes.

"We both will, Mrs. McAllister," Sam said quietly. "She's like family to me now."

Marlee's mother smiled. The security lights outside the mansion reflected off the sheen of tears in her eyes. "Thank you." She gave each of them a final pat and headed back to her car.

Sam and Susie watched silently until the car had gone out the gate and turned back toward Clarksonville.

"Oh, my God, Susie." Sam couldn't contain herself. "Forty-five minutes with your mother-in-law? How was that?"

"I was so frickin' nervous, Sam, but she was cool. She told me she knows Marlee and I have been working through some stuff, but she said I made Marlee happy and I was good for Marlee."

Sam scoffed. "She doesn't know you at all, does she?" Sam laughed and then felt bad. "I'm sorry. I didn't mean that, Sus."

"I know. You're just being you. A dork."

Sam laughed.

"So, anyway," Susie continued, "we talked about my AA meetings and how that was going. She asked if my parents were drinkers."

"They're not. Not really."

"No, they're not," Susie agreed. "I think she was trying to get a feel for my 'home life.'" Susie made air quotes around the words. "To make a long forty-five-minute conversation short, she basically praised me for getting my shit together—"

"She didn't use those words, did she?"

"No." Susie laughed. "It's just the best way to summarize it. She said she was proud of the strong person she saw before her. One that took responsibilities seriously – like taking care of my brother and my mother."

"So, she understands that you're the only adult in residence at home."

"Yeah." Susie sighed. "She also said she was sorry that Isabella and Eduardo were getting divorced. She could only imagine how hard that must be on me."

"I think she gets it, Sus. I think she gets *you*."

"I wasn't sure she was ever going to forgive me for driving over there drunk out of my mind that time. And it wasn't the first time I did that either."

"It wasn't?" Sam's eyes grew wide. Just how long had Susie been hiding her drinking?

"Another day, Sam, okay?"

"Another day," Sam agreed and wrapped her arms around her friend for a healing hug. "I love you, Asswipe. I'll see you tomorrow morning."

"See ya." Susie took her car keys from Sam's hand and headed to the driver's door of her car.

"Hey, Sus?" Sam called after her.

"Yeah?"

"Happy Anniversary."

The satisfied smile on Susie's face made Sam happy.

"Thanks. One whole year. I didn't think we were going to make it."

"I had faith in you guys," Sam said. "Oh, and when you get home, do the AP Enviro reading first. Give me a summary tomorrow."

Susie laughed. "Do your own homework, *gringa*." She smiled, which let Sam know she was teasing. "I'm kidding. You know I always do Enviro first. See you tomorrow."

~~~

Sam ran up the steps and into the house. She grabbed her violin and sheet music from the foyer table and dashed to her room to put them away. Her stomach growled, reminding her that her after-church lunch with the Brown family was long gone. It was time to head down to the big kitchen to see what Mrs. Tardelli had left for her in the fridge.

Sam opened the door to her wing just as her mother was doing the same from hers.

"Mother," Sam said, "I'm just heading down to eat dinner. Will you join me?"

"No, dear. Your father and I ate earlier."

Normally, Sam wouldn't press it at that point, but something shifted in her, and she said, "Please come sit with me, Mother. I'll make you a cup of tea or coffee."

Her mother looked startled by the request.

"Oh, all right, dear. I guess this can wait." She held up her datebook, the one that held the various calendars of all her charity events and committees.

Sam's spirits soared. She had no idea what she and her mother would talk about, but they did have some common interests – music, for sure. Okay, maybe that was all, but it would be a start. Oh, wait, she could ask about Helene's old apartment and find out why the maids were there.

Sam's mother made herself a cup of green tea using the hot water dispenser near the farmhouse sink and joined Sam at the formal dining room table. Mrs. Tardelli had laid out a place setting in Sam's usual spot. Sam set her reheated plate of pork medallions with an apricot glaze on the placemat. The singleness of her place setting against the enormity of the table made Sam a little lonely. She was grateful her mother had agreed to join her. She took a bite of her Caesar salad just as her mother asked a question.

"How was your overnight trip, Samantha Rose? Did you enjoy your time with your friends?"

Sam almost choked. Enjoy? Mmm, yes, she most certainly did enjoy her time alone with Lisa. She chewed as fast as she could, lamenting the big bite she had taken, wishing she hadn't. She'd been hanging out with Lisa and her friends for so long that she'd forgotten how a female in the Payton household was supposed to eat—demurely, taking the tiniest of bites and then pushing the rest of the food around without eating. She took a sip of water and practically swallowed her mouthful whole.

She cleared her throat and said, "It was lovely, Mother. Marlee cooked ribeye steaks with a side of roasted broccoli with a garlic-lemon sauce." Okay, she embellished a little, but it didn't matter. She had to speak her mother's language while reassuring her that she was not becoming one of the 'public' as her mother often referred to anyone without means or high standing.

"That sounds interesting. Marlee is the one with the short hair?"

"Yes, Mother. My softball team is playing hers tomorrow evening. Maybe you and Daddy could—"

The door to the dining room crashed open, and her father stormed in, waving a stack of papers toward Sam. "Samantha Rose Payton, you must stop buying things for your friends. Your expenses have shot way up over the past few months, far exceeding the cap I've put on your accounts."

At first, Sam was stunned. First of all, she never knew she had caps on her accounts, and secondly, he'd never scolded her about spending money before, not that she'd ever spent that much. He was right, though. Lately, she'd been buying a lot of things for her friends.

"Daddy, my friends have been paying me back for the most part. Certainly, you've noticed some deposits going into my account regularly."

"For the car you sold to Lisa, yes. What are the others?"

"Marlee is paying me back for some Neiman Marcus clothes I helped her pick out. That's done as soon as I deposit her last check, and now she's on a payment plan for some music equipment."

"I certainly hope you're charging this girl interest."

"No, Daddy. I can't do that to my friends."

He harrumphed and said, "You are not their personal bank, Samantha Rose. Put a lid on this."

Sam knew better than to defend herself than she already had, but she liked helping her friends get the things they needed. Things she could blink for and get instantly. Instead, she said, "Yes, sir. I will."

Her father turned to leave when Sam blurted, "Daddy, there's an investment opportunity I might be interested in."

"For you or for me?"

"Uh, kind of for me, I think."

His raised eyebrows almost made Sam laugh.

"I never knew you were interested in business, Samantha Rose," her mother said.

"Marlee's neighbors, The Petrovs," Sam explained, "took out a second mortgage on their house, but apparently, they're upside down on it and can't seem to make the payments. It's a white clapboard house over 6000 square feet on one hundred acres. It has a banquet hall, a conservatory, an exercise room, pool. The works."

Her father laughed and said, "It almost sounds like you want to buy this for yourself.

She hadn't thought about it that way, but escaping the mansion suddenly made her happy. "Um, not that I want to cheat them, but I think I can get the home and land for a song, Daddy."

His face was beaming. "What about the family? The Petrovs?"

"Oh, they'd stay. I'd collect rent."

"Sounds like risky business, Samantha Rose. If they can't pay their own mortgage, what makes you think they'd be able to pay rent?"

"I guess I have a few things to think about."

"Yes, you do, young lady," her father said. But he had that look that said he was taking her idea seriously. "I'll tell you what, if the Petrovs are amenable, I'll send Marla to assess the property and the viability of your plan." Marla Cohen was the county's leading real estate agent because her firm handled most of the Payton family real estate purchases and sales in East Valley, Clarksonville, Southbridge, and Northfork.

"Thank you, Daddy." Sam smiled. She was happy. She wanted desperately to ask about Helene's apartment but decided not to ruin the moment. The three of them were in the same room together. Maybe they could act like a real family. It was a start, anyway.

Chapter Eight
Pick a Side

It was the first time in a long time that Sam had gotten a case of nerves this bad before a game, but as she stepped off the East Valley bus and walked toward the Clarksonville softball field, her nerves jerked into overdrive. She hated that she and Susie had to compete against their girlfriends. It was too stressful.

"Breathe, Sam. Breathe," Susie said with a laugh. "Whether we win or lose doesn't affect our relationships."

Sam scoffed. "How do you always know what's going on in here?" Sam smacked her own forehead with an open palm.

"I know you, dork." Susie made a funny face at her and then said, "C'mon, co-captain, let's find our luxurious non-dugout and get ready."

"Yep," Sam said, half-listening. She was actively looking for Lisa. There she was by the visiting team's bleachers. She was talking to someone that looked just like—

"Holy shit," Sam screeched and took off. Her softball bag bounced against her back as she ran. She dodged a few teammates and spectators and then flew into Helene's arms. She hung on tightly as tears flew from her eyes.

"I can't believe you're here." Sam felt strong, nurturing hands

91

go around her back. "*Mon petit hibou, tu m'as manqué,*" Helene said.

"I've missed you, too." Sam pulled back but kept one hand on Helene's arm. She drank in Helene's warm smiling face, familiar pale skin, and blonde hair streaked with natural gray.

Sam reached over and grabbed the sleeve of Lisa's sweatshirt. "Hi, baby."

"Hi. You didn't tell me Helene was coming for a visit." The happy smile on Lisa's face made Sam smile even more inside.

"I didn't know." Sam turned to face Helene. "Why are you here? Why didn't you tell me you were coming?"

"And ruin the surprise?" Helene tousled Sam's hair as if she were three years old.

"What are you doing here? How long can you stay? You're staying at the house; I hope you know that." Sam scowled at Helene as if daring her to object.

"Thank you, Samantha Rose. I already dropped my things off there."

"Aha!" Sam said, still holding on to both Helene and Lisa. She was almost afraid they might disappear if she let go of either one of them. "I knew it. I saw them cleaning your apartment." Mother hadn't said a word about it. She must have wanted it to be a surprise.

"Hey, Sam?" Lisa said. "I need this arm." A teasing grin lit her face.

"Oh, sorry." Sam let go of Lisa's sleeve. "Have a good game but not *too* good!"

"Same." Lisa winked at Sam and then said to Helene, "It's nice to see you. Sam's been missing you."

"I'm sure I'll see you again while I'm here," Helene said with a smile.

Helene, watching Lisa return to her home team set of benches, said, "All is well there?" She had a mischievous grin on her face.

"All is more than well there," Sam said and felt her cheeks get warm.

"*Je suis content pour toi*," Helene said and gave Sam another hug.

"I'm happy for myself, too," Sam said with a grin.

"Sam, c'mon," Abby called from the visitors' side of the field. "We have to throw."

"Yeesh," Sam said, "I have to go, but everything's okay with your sister? Your new niece?"

"Everyone there is fine, Samantha Rose. We'll catch up later." Helene sat down on the lowest bleacher seat. "Go on. Have a good game."

Sam turned to go but then rushed back to give Helene one last hug. She wanted to hang on longer but abruptly released Helene and sprinted to the rickety visitors' bench.

"You didn't tell me Helene was coming," Susie said as she finished tying her cleats.

"I didn't know." Sam plopped on the bench and pulled her cleats out of her bag.

"It was a nice surprise then."

"Yeah. Surprised the hell out of me." Sam finished putting on her cleats and pulled her glove and batting glove out of her bag. She hated the Clarksonville field. There were no dugouts, bat racks, or cubbies for your gear. You had to keep everything on or near your bag on the ground. There weren't even water fountains. And, to add insult to potential injury, they still had those stupid dilapidated splintery wooden benches for the teams to sit on. You didn't dare slide on them unless you wanted splinters in your butt. She looked over at the Clarksonville side of the field and was surprised to see two sturdy metal benches on their home team side.

She pointed out the benches to Susie and said, "This amazing team wins the state championship, and all they get are two new benches?"

"I know. It sucks," Susie said. "I have to try not to kill myself on that crappy snow fence in the outfield."

Sam shook her head. The whole thing just wasn't right. Something nagged at her. "Oh, shoot, I didn't say hi to Marlee. How is she?"

"She's good."

Both heads turned toward the pitchers' warm-up area behind the home team bleachers, where Marlee was warming up with Lisa.

"Not *too* good, I hope," Sam mumbled, referring to Marlee's pitching prowess.

"We're going to get our asses handed to us, Sam."

Sam blew out a sigh. "You're probably right, friend. You're probably right." She leaped off the bench. "But let's not let these guys know that." She nodded her head toward her teammates. "C'mon, let's get our *powerhouse* East Valley team warmed up."

~~~

Sam stood in the on-deck circle, trying hard not to focus her attention on Lisa squatting behind the plate. Sam's heart had already skipped a few beats when Lisa threw down to second base after Marlee's last warmup pitch. Lisa's explosion of power made her weak-kneed every time. And she definitely couldn't look over to where Helene sat alone on the visitors' bleachers. There was way too much emotion for her there. She couldn't wait to tell Helene everything that had been going on with her and her friends, like all of Susie's stuff, and her deeply-seated suspicion that Lisa had grown another inch or more and had surpassed the six-foot mark. But all that would have to wait about two hours – or less if Clarksonville mercy-ruled them. Life would be hell with Coach Gellar if that happened.

Rachel Jacobs, the East Valley center fielder, was the first batter up. Marlee needed only three pitches to strike her out and send her back to the benches. It looked like she had thrown three straight fastballs.

"Good luck!" Susie said as Sam headed up to bat. "You'll need it. I know you."

Sam tried not to laugh but looked back at Susie with a smirk. Yeah, she was going to need all the luck in the world to get her bat to even touch one of Marlee's fastballs. She wished she was good enough to read pitches like Susie and Lisa were. Marlee was probably good at it, too. Marlee wasn't just an amazing pitcher.

Sam's heart swelled when she saw Lisa's mask lying on the ground, dead center in the batter's box. Sam's smile almost split her face. She reached down, wiped the mask on her clean uniform pants, and handed it back to Lisa. Lisa locked eyes with her and sent so much love that Sam wanted to drop her bat and kiss her girlfriend right there in front of everybody.

"Thank you, Ms. Payton," Lisa said without shifting her gaze. She had no clue what the umpire thought about their exchange and found that she didn't care.

Sam nodded. "You're welcome, Ms. Brown." Sam broke contact and looked away. Gah, Lisa's eyes had been sucking her in. She had to focus. She dug into the batter's box and took a practice swing. Marlee was in an all-business mode in the circle. You could never tell what was going on behind her always-calm and always-collected expression. That's why Marlee bursting into tears on Sunday morning had been so surprising.

"Fastball," Lisa said quietly.

Oh, wow. Lisa was going to help her.

Sam dug in while Marlee started her motion. The fastball screamed its way toward them. Sam swung so late that she almost fell.

Lisa stood up and said, "Time," to the umpire who granted it. She leaned toward Sam and whispered, "Go get a lighter bat," and then trotted toward the pitching circle to talk to Marlee.

Sam didn't have to be told twice. She scurried to the sidelines, knowing exactly which bat to grab. She ran back to the box and took a practice swing. Yeah, this ought to do the trick.

Lisa trotted back behind the plate and said, "Fastball."

The fastball headed straight down the middle of the lane, and Sam swung and fouled it off. She almost jumped up and down. She had actually made contact with Marlee's new-and-improved and way-faster-than-last-year pitch.

"Fastball," Lisa said again. There was a time when Sam might have been suspicious that Marlee would throw an off-speed pitch or something, but Sam truly believed her girlfriend. They had established that much trust.

The third fastball came screaming toward her. Sam swung and was amazed at the line drive rocketing off her bat. Julie,

Clarksonville's first basemen, dove to her right and snagged the ball out of the air for the second out of the inning.

Sam groaned. She hadn't made it very far out of the box and was already out.

"Almost, baby," Lisa said. "Almost."

"Next time," Sam said quickly and returned to her team's splinter-hazard bench.

"Nice catch, Julie," Sam called as she went by. Julie was one of Lisa's good friends and had become a friend to Sam in the process.

Julie smiled and nodded her head once toward Sam in greeting.

Sam sat down and cheered on Abby, their shortstop, who was digging in at the plate. Sam looked to her left and smiled at Helene. Helene lifted her hand and put her thumb and index finger an inch apart. "So close," she mouthed.

Sam grimaced and nodded her head.

"Hey, Sam," Ronnie shouted from the stands, "good try."

Whoa, she hadn't known they were coming. Ronnie sat with Alivia and Karl. Alivia was there to cheer on Jessica, but she wasn't sure why the two guys were there. She waved back but then looked away quickly. She didn't want to chance a reprimand from Coach Geller. She'd spent almost one entire summer season in Coach Gellar's doghouse, and she didn't want another.

Abby struck out on three pitches leaving the East Valley Panthers not only scoreless but hitless and base-runner-less in the first inning. That was a rare event for the Panthers, but Sam figured it wouldn't be the last time it happened in this game.

The Clarksonville shortstop was the first batter up in the home half of the first inning, and she hit a little flair just over Sam's head in shallow right field. There was no way Sam could reach it. So, just like that, Clarksonville had a base runner. Julie was up next for Clarksonville and bunted her teammate over to second base. Sam took the throw at first base for the out from Mae, the East Valley first baseman, who had charged in for the bunt. Up next was Jessica Myers. Sam groaned because Jessica was a strong hitter, and then after that, Lisa and Marlee would be up. East Valley wasn't going to get out of this inning unscathed. Sam just knew it.

Jessica stepped into the batter's box, and Alivia stood up and screamed wildly from the stands. "Go, Jessica. Hit the ball out there."

Sam was a little hurt by Alivia's switch in allegiance. After all, Alivia went to East Valley, and here she was, rooting for Clarksonville.

"C'mon, East Valley," Karl yelled in response. "Easy out."

Doing the complete opposite of Karl's prediction, Jessica sent a well-placed line drive into the left-center field gap. From her position in left field, Susie turned to run after it. Knowing she couldn't get the runner at third, Susie fired a line drive to Sam covering second base. Jessica slid in safely a split-second before Sam put the tag on her. Sam leaped up and ran toward the runner who had rounded third. Certain the runner wasn't going anywhere, Sam tossed the ball back to her pitcher, Mary.

"Big hitter up next," Sam said to her. Lisa was heading into the batter's box.

Mary did her best to try and pitch around Lisa, giving her pitches on the edge of the strike zone, but the count was soon three balls and one strike. A hitter's count, for sure. As soon as the ball left Mary's hand, Sam knew they were in trouble. A big fat meatball pitch was heading right toward Lisa's weapon of destruction. Lisa swung, and there was no question that it was heading over the fence. It was simply a matter of how far it was going to go.

The Clarksonville side of the field burst into cheers and hoots and hollers. Lisa's family members were probably the loudest of all. And just like that, Clarksonville was up by a score of three to nothing.

Sam held her hand out for Lisa to slap as she ran by on her homerun trot. "Nice one, Ms. Brown," she said as Lisa ran by.

"Thank you, Ms. Payton." Lisa hit the bag at second and then looked back over her shoulder, sending Sam a devilish smile. Sam melted in her cleats. Maybe one day, Sam would get to call Lisa Mrs. Payton, or better yet, Lisa would call her Mrs. Brown. Sam flushed at the thought.

Marlee was up next, with only one out. Marlee completely had the power to send one over the fence but hoped she wouldn't. That would make East Valley even closer to losing by the mercy rule.

Marlee got herself set in the batter's box. Mary put her hands together and whirled her arm around for the pitch. Sam was surprised when Marlee shifted her feet. Sam knew what that meant and took two steps toward first base. True enough, Marlee sent a hard grounder toward the right side of the field in what had been a gap between second and first, but because Sam had moved, she was well-positioned to snag the flaming-hot grounder and threw Marlee out quickly.

"Sorry, P," Sam called to her friend, who was now heading for the home team bench.

"I'll get you next time, Two," Marlee called without breaking stride.

The next Clarksonville batter had the decency to strike out, and it was East Valley's turn to get up to bat again.

"C'mon, Susie," Sam called, "stay focused out there." It was one thing to try and concentrate with your girlfriend squatting mere feet behind you, but it was another thing entirely having to stare at your girlfriend while she threw fireballs at you. Sam didn't envy Susie at that moment.

"C'mon, stud," Ronnie yelled toward Susie good-naturedly, "get a hit or something!"

"Yeah, c'mon, Susie," Alivia yelled from the stands. "I'm cheering for you."

Sam whipped her head to see if Marlee had heard. If she had, she didn't show it. Marlee's poker face was intact and strong. Sam let herself relax. Alivia seemed to be rooting for both teams at the same time. Interesting.

Susie dug in the batter's box to get set.

"Nothing up here. Just a whiffing bag of wind," Lisa quipped to Marlee.

"Hey," Susie said as if hurt, but Sam knew her besties were just teasing each other. Susie was one of the best, if not *the* best, hitters in the county.

Sam was always amazed to watch Susie up at bat. A serious focus overtook her as she settled in to hit. Marlee's pitch came in fast and furious. Susie's swing matched the intensity but ticked just underneath the rise ball, sending a screaming foul ball back into the backstop. Lisa hopped up to get it and tossed it back to Marlee.

Unfortunately for Marlee, Susie kept getting a piece of every pitch and fouling off each one. Sam got concerned when at one point during Susie's at-bat, Marlee reached up and rubbed her shoulder. Ten pitches in, Marlee completely fooled Susie with an off-speed pitch. She missed for strike three and the first out of the inning.

"Dang it," Susie said as she headed back toward the bench. Susie wasn't really mad, Sam sensed. She was just a little frustrated that she'd gotten fooled by the super-sneaky change-up.

"That's all right, bestie," Sam said. "Next time."

"Yeah," was all Susie said.

Keisha and then Mae fared no better than Susie, and each struck out in turn, ending the inning.

Clarksonville managed to get three more runs over the next few innings, while East Valley continued not only its scoring drought but its hitting drought as well. At the top of the seventh and potentially last inning, Clarksonville was leading by a score of 6–0, and not only did Marlee have a perfect game going, but she had also struck out every batter except for Sam.

Coach Gellar called them into a team meeting by the visitors' bench. "Don't let them psyche you out," she said to the East Valley players surrounding her. "This home crowd is their tenth player. Tune them out, then get up there and do what you do."

"It ain't over 'til it's over," Sam said.

"She's right," Coach Gellar said. "Hits, on three. One, two, three!"

"Hits," the East Valley players yelled in unison.

Sam understood. Coach Gellar had adjusted their team goal. They truly had no chance of winning against the powerful Marlee McAllister, but at least they could try to save some dignity by disrupting her no-hit, perfect-game bid. Sam understood the need to change focus, but she would be getting up that inning, and although the odds were a million to one against Sam actually getting a hit off of Marlee, she didn't want to be put in the position to possibly do it.

As Sam walked to the on-deck circle, she heard the small East Valley contingent cheering for her teammate Rachel, heading up to the batter's box. She recognized Ronnie's low tenor, Alivia's high-pitched cheers, and Karl's somewhat shaky voice in the sea of shouts and cheers. A brief worry about what was going on with Karl flashed through her mind but put the thought aside. Right now, she had business to attend to.

Rachel struck out on three pitches and said, "Good luck, Sam," as she lumbered by, completely dejected. Lisa didn't say a word to Sam as she stepped up to hit. Sam didn't make eye contact, either. The time for teasing and playing around was over. These were high stakes for Marlee. Sam briefly thought about striking out on purpose but knew Marlee wouldn't want that. Marlee wouldn't want a hollow victory if her friends just gave up. She'd want to earn it.

Sam stepped her left foot out of the box and looked down for Coach Gellar's sign. What else could it be but hit away or slap? Sam raised an eyebrow when it wasn't. Coach was right. For Sam, it was probably the best option for getting on base. But then Sam felt guilty immediately. What if she actually *did* get on base? Marlee's perfect game would be ruined. In an instant, Sam knew what she had to do. She decided that turnabout was fair play, and since Lisa had helped her during her first at-bat, she was going to help Lisa. And Marlee, by extension. Without overtly tipping Lisa off to the play, Sam shifted her feet and lowered her bat ever-so-slightly.

"C'mon, Lisa," Sam willed with her mind, "see it."

A funny little noise escaped Lisa's throat. Yes, apparently, the message had been received. Hopefully, no one else was wise to her ruse.

As the pitch came in, Sam shifted her feet even more and lowered her bat to bunt. She made contact and tried to soften it enough so that Lisa could get to it easily. Sam sprinted out of the box, not seeing but picturing Lisa springing up from her squat and turning her body in such a way as to pick up the ball with her bare hand and firing a bullet to first base. Sure enough, Julie stretched for the throw, and Sam was called out.

Sam raced off the field to cheers for a valiant effort from her teammates and the small contingent of East Valley fans. Susie nodded at her knowingly as she stepped into the on-deck circle. She must have seen Sam's giveaway. Sam hoped Abby didn't suddenly figure out how to hit Marlee. She also hoped that Marlee wasn't getting tired. Nah. Never happen. Marlee was a machine.

Luckily Abby didn't have any miraculous epiphanies about hitting the New York State champion pitcher and struck out as predicted.

Sam cheered quietly to herself as the home team crowd went berserk. Sam walked up next to Susie and watched the Clarksonville players mob their pitcher. They had to mob both Lisa and Marlee because Lisa had trapped Marlee in a bear hug. Sam had seen Lisa do that before and now understood why she did it. Lisa was protecting Marlee from her well-meaning teammates. Sam smiled. She didn't know it could be possible, but she loved Lisa a little more that day.

The East Valley team had to wait a while for the high-five line since the Clarksonville team didn't seem ready to stop celebrating. When Sam finally got to Marlee, she hugged her and said, "That was freakin' inspired pitching, P!"

"Thanks, Two. You're the only one who put the ball in play, you know." Marlee wagged her finger. "I predict you'll get that hit you want next time."

"Yay," Sam said and high-fived her girlfriend next.

"Thanks for the tip," Lisa said in Sam's ear.

"Don't tell."

Lisa smiled wordlessly and let her penetrating gaze do the rest of the talking for her. The late April afternoon had suddenly gotten very warm.

Alivia descended on Jessica as soon as she emerged from the high-five line. She threw her arms around Jessica and kissed her hard.

Sam's eyebrows reached the sky. She had no idea if Jessica was out of the closet, but apparently, she was now. As she observed, Sam realized that Jessica seemed to kiss Alivia back without worrying about what anyone else thought. "Good for her," Sam mumbled as Lisa's hand slipped into hers.

"Get a room," Ronnie said to the two girls kissing in front of him.

"Pick a side," Karl slurred. "Boys or girls, 'Livia? Boys or girls?"

Sam's heart dropped. Now she understood why Karl's voice had been shaky in the last inning. He held an oversized plastic to-go cup in his hand. Sam would bet money it was filled with alcohol of some kind.

Susie must have seen it, too, because her cheeks had gotten red, and there was a scowl on her face. Marlee followed Susie's gaze. "What's up, sweetie?"

Susie nodded her head toward Karl, who was still badgering Alivia verbally. When he started in on Jessica, that must have been too much for Marlee. She marched over to them and got in between Karl and Alivia, who was still clinging to Jessica.

"Hey, Karl," Marlee said.

"Hi, Marlee," Karl said, his expression softening. "Great game, friend." Sam's anger softened. Karl truly was a good guy, but going down the wrong path. Like Susie had.

Susie hung back, tears welling in her eyes. "Is that what I looked like?" she asked Sam softly.

Sam pursed her lips together and nodded slowly. Better that Susie knew the truth. Susie's eyes squeezed shut against her misery. She headed over to Marlee.

"Hey, Karl?" Marlee said.

"Yeah?" He swayed on his feet. He was definitely hammered.

"Can I show you something?"

"Okay."

Marlee reached into the back pocket of her uniform pants and pulled out a laminated photograph. Sam exchanged a look with Lisa. Lisa shrugged as if to say she had no idea Marlee carried a picture in her back pocket.

"Do you see the man in this picture?" Marlee asked. By then, their East Valley friends and Helene had crowded around the scene.

Ronnie said, "Who is that, Marlee? That guy is hot." He fanned himself and acted like he was going to swoon.

Marlee spoke directly to Karl. "That man was my father."

A lump grew in Sam's throat. Lisa squeezed her hand harder.

"He's dead," Marlee said simply. "He was killed by someone like you, Karl."

Karl inhaled sharply. "Like me?" He put his hand to his chest and frowned.

"Yes," Marlee continued. "Someone like you had a few drinks for fun and then decided to get in a car and drive. He killed my father. That man has to live with his guilt for the rest of his life. And me?" Marlee looked straight into Karl's eyes. "I never got to see my father again. Not for one minute. Not to say goodbye. Not anything. My father never got to see me play softball on a school team. He never got to see me fall in love. He won't see me graduate, go to college, get married. None of it."

Karl started crying and sat down hard on the first bleacher. Alivia sat down and put an arm around him. Jessica didn't seem phased by her girlfriend's sudden show of affection toward her former boyfriend. She just watched the drama unfold like the rest of them.

By this time, Susie had put a loving arm around Marlee's waist. Marlee patted the hand that held her but didn't take her eyes off Karl.

"Stud muffin," Alivia said, using her nickname for her former boyfriend, "we used to drink so much because we didn't know what else to do with ourselves. Didn't we?"

Karl wiped at his eyes and nodded.

"We weren't in love, were we?"

He shook his head.

"And the drinking was a way to fill the space between us. Something we could do together and have fun."

Karl nodded.

"But you don't have to keep drinking, Karl," Alivia said softly. "I found someone amazing, and she doesn't drink, so neither do I." She looked up lovingly at Jessica, who patted her heart twice in response.

At that point, everyone turned and looked at Sam. Once again, this seemed like the natural ebb and flow of the relationship she had with these particular friends. They looked for her to lead. And lead she did. "Who drove here today?" Sam asked.

"He did," Ronnie answered, "but I'll drive us home."

Sam raised her eyebrows in question.

Ronnie didn't seem offended. "I'm clean, Sam." He lifted his arms out wide to show that he didn't have a secret stash of alcohol hidden on him. "I promise, promise, promise." He shifted his gaze to Susie and said to her specifically, "I promise."

Susie nodded at him. It was all she could do. Everyone could see how choked up she was about Marlee's blunt story about her father's death.

"All right," Sam said. "Call me when you get home. Okay, Ronnie?"

"Will do."

"And Karl," Sam said, "you and I are going to have a heart-to-heart talk tomorrow at school during lunch."

"Okay, Sam." Karl looked at Marlee. "Sorry 'bout your dad." His words seemed to be even more slurred than before.

Marlee nodded once to him and then pulled a now-weeping Susie in her arms for comfort. The two of them walked away for a much-needed private moment.

Ronnie and Jessica helped Karl stand up, and with Alivia holding Jessica's hand, they headed toward the parking lot.

Before Sam could greet Helene, Lisa muttered, "Oh, geez," and turned away quickly.

"What, baby?" Sam said. "What's wrong?"

"Alexander's here again."

"That weird kid you were telling me about?"

"Yeah. Black hair, bottom bleacher."

Sam and Helene turned to look. There he was, disheveled greasy black hair, sweatshirt tucked into his belted pants, sitting all alone. The stands were completely empty, but he didn't seem to be going anywhere. It definitely looked like he was waiting for something. Or someone.

"He's waiting for you, isn't he?" Sam said.

Lisa nodded and groaned. Sam exchanged a glance with Helene.

Sam weighed her options and said to Helene, "Don't leave. I'm driving home with you." And then, instead of marching straight over to Alexander and punching him in the nose, she pulled Lisa behind her and headed toward Lisa's coach to fill her in.

Chapter Nine
Numb

Karl placed soggy crinkle cut fries and greasy cheeseburger on the cafeteria table. Sam grimaced at his choice. He seemed to rethink it and pushed the tray far away from himself.

"Hey, Susie," Karl said quietly, "when's your next AA meeting?"

"Tomorrow," Ronnie answered for her.

"Every Wednesday at five o'clock at the Civic Center," Susie added.

"Don't you have practice?" Karl held his temple. Sam had seen Susie do that on many occasions and slowly realized how often her best friend had had hangovers during school. Why hadn't she recognized it?

"Coach lets me leave practice early on Wednesdays."

"I'll drive you," Ronnie said to Karl. Susie smiled at his words. Sam smiled at all of them.

Karl looked down at the table and sighed. He seemed to want to be alone with his thoughts.

Sam said to Susie, "So, what's going on at home these days, Sus?"

Sam was glad when Susie didn't hesitate. She wasn't sure if she was opening up another can of worms, but Susie seemed ready to talk.

"My mother is fine with me taking over the kitchen. We've only eaten together as a family a couple of times since my father left. Mami and Miguel seem okay with whatever I've got cooking in the crockpot or with leftovers."

"That's a tough gig," Ronnie said. "I have two loving parents that I've completely disrespected." He sighed and then looked down at his half-eaten lunch.

"Like all things in nature," Susie said, "I have to adapt."

"Has your dad been back to see you and Miguel?"

"Just that one time when he brought me my car. Maybe he'll come to one of our games." Susie's voice had a hopeful tone, and Sam sent a quick plea to the universe to make it happen. "Oh, hey, Sam, I wanted to ask you something."

"What's that?"

"My mother doesn't get the mail out of the mailbox these days, so I do it, and we're starting to get envelopes stamped 'Final Notice.' I told Mami about them, but they're still sitting on the mail table in the living room. Should I open them or what?"

"Open them immediately," Sam said quickly. "And then call your father and find out what you should do. It looks like you'll have to be your family's accountant, too."

"Mmm," Susie groaned, not sounding happy about this new development.

"Your mother's either depressed or in denial, Susie," Ronnie said. "Maybe she needs to talk to someone."

Susie burst out with the most sarcastic laugh Sam had ever heard. "My mother? Take advice from anyone? Never going to happen. You know, guys," Susie added, "the other day, my mother told me to stay home and clean the house. You know what I told her?"

"What?" the three friends said simultaneously.

"I told her, 'no.' I told her I was going to Clarksonville to visit Marlee and that I'd find time to clean the house over the weekend. I even suggested that we do it as a family, Miguel included."

"You actually stood up to your mother?" Sam said, her mouth hanging open.

"Even I know how impossible that is for you," Ronnie said.

"Mmm," Karl said behind closed eyes. Apparently, he wanted to be helpful but wasn't in much shape to contribute. Sam had wanted to have a heart-to-heart talk with him but decided to postpone it. Karl wasn't in any shape to deal with anything at the moment.

"So, what did your mother say?" Sam asked.

"She said I was selfish like Papi, doing things my own way without regard for others. Then she went up to her bedroom and didn't come out."

Sam was outraged. "You're the only one in that house that's doing anything. This reminds me of that summer you slaved for Mrs. Johnson. You made, what, twelve cents an hour for cleaning, cooking, laundry, gardening, mowing, and weeding, all while taking care of her two children?" Sam shook her head. "I'm glad you stuck up for yourself, Sus."

"Yeah and get this. I've got this thought in my head that wants me to tell Mami that because I'm eighteen years old, I will be allowed to have Marlee stay over with me in my room anytime I want."

"Overnight?" Sam said, her eyebrows shooting high.

"Yep." Susie's cheeks tinged red.

"Wow, you're either really brave, Sus, or really crazy." Sam moved her index finger around in a circle near her ear.

"A little of both, I'm afraid."

The group of friends laughed, and Ronnie said, "Speaking of parents, my mother was so happy to hear me practicing last night." He turned to Sam and said, "That *Antigona* piece is nice. My part isn't as intricate as yours, though, Sam."

"Yeah, I know, but the double bass adds just the right flavor at just the right times," Sam said. "I think we're going to practice it in Strings today."

"Look," Karl said, coming out of his coma. He pointed to the table of theater kids. Alivia turned away suddenly when all eyes at their table looked over. It was obvious she was respecting Susie's wishes, but it was also obvious that she desperately wanted to be sitting back with her friends.

Ronnie quipped something about being completely outnumbered by lesbians if Alivia came back to the table. Sam didn't think Alivia was a tried-and-true lesbian. She might be wrong about that, but maybe Alivia was bisexual and simply followed her heart wherever it led. And this time, it had led directly to Jessica Myers.

Sam's phone rang in her pocket. She smiled, thinking it was Lisa. They had lunch at the same time, although thirty-five miles apart. Sam was glad she looked down at the caller ID because it wasn't Lisa.

A shot of adrenaline hit her as she stood up. She indicated to her friends that she was going to take the call in the hallway.

"Hello, Mother," Sam said as she walked to the cafeteria door. "Is everything all right?"

"Hello, Samantha Rose," her mother said. "How is your school day going?"

Sam had reached the hallway. Luckily no one was around, and she could hear much better. "Fine, Mother. I was just eating lunch in the cafeteria with a few friends."

"Oh, good. I caught you at the right time.

There was a bit of silence until Sam said, "Mother, is everything all right? You don't usually call me at school." *You don't call me…ever*, Sam thought. "Is Helene all right? Daddy?"

"Yes, Helene is settling in fine, and your father is off somewhere checking out a new property."

Sam's nerves jangled. Why was her mother calling? "Did you need me to do something for you, Mother?" Maybe she wanted Sam to pick up some particular sheet music or something from the music room. Her mother had been playing a lot of piano lately.

"No, nothing like that, dear. I wanted to…I just wanted to…."

Sam waited, hoping her mother would finish her stuttering thought.

"Oh, dear," her mother said. "Stefan is here for my workout."

"Oh, okay, Mother," Sam said. "I guess that means you have to go?"

"Yes." Just one simple word.

"I will let you go then," Sam said as if she had been the one that had initiated the phone call.

Her mother's goodbye was succinct and without fanfare, as if she had been hanging up with the dry cleaner or something.

Sam hung up and muttered, "What was that all about?" She went back inside the cafeteria. Thrown off balance, Sam joined her friends. She didn't feel like talking anymore.

~~~

After her AP Enviro class, Sam headed to her beloved Strings class. This was the class she could really unwind and dig into something she was good at, something she was genuinely interested in. She put her backpack in her assigned cubby and pulled out her practice violin and sheet music. Noticing the racks of sheet music, she rifled through the piano music but didn't find anything interesting for her mother. On the other hand, she found several new ones that Helene might like. Anything on the racks was fair game to borrow as long as you checked with Mr. Auerbach first.

Sam left her violin on her usual chair and went over to her teacher.

"Oh, hello, Samantha Rose," Mr. Auerbach said. His wrinkled white dress shirt was rolled up at the sleeves as if he'd had an arduous day. He noticed the sheet music in her hand and nodded, waving her off as if it was silly of her to even ask if she could borrow it. His eyes narrowed as he spotted Ronnie. "Ah, good. Quintet then. Antigona, third movement, please." He adjusted the glasses resting on the bridge of his nose and added, "Violins and viola must get bow strokes synchronized. Get that done today, please." He turned away from her.

Before Sam had a chance to reply, he walked away to work with some of the younger students on the far side of the room. On any given day, you could hear Vivaldi on one side of the room and Schubert on the other. How Mr. Auerbach kept all his students working and focused was beyond her. She wouldn't have been able to do it.

Sam headed back to the quintet. "Okay, you guys," Sam said.

114

"*Canto al Amor.*"

"*Antigona*? Third movement?" Maddie asked as she quietly tuned her violin.

Sam nodded.

"Oh, good," Dominique said. "I like that one." She held her viola in one hand and flipped through her sheet music.

"Let's start at the top," Sam said, "and then whenever somebody wants to go over a part, we'll stop. Okay?"

Everyone nodded, and then, tuning out the younger quartet on the other side of the room, her quintet began playing.

Caleigh stopped playing her cello and waited for the rest to stop. She tucked a wisp of her dark brown hair behind her ear and asked, "Can we go back to thirteen? I'm getting jarred out of my place when Ronnie doesn't come in on time."

Ronnie's right eyebrow had a life of its own as it shot skyward. Sam agreed with him. He had come in on time.

"Sure," Sam answered, not allowing any kind of judgment in her voice. She turned her sheet music back one page.

"Oh, wait," Caleigh said. "I see it now." She looked up at Ronnie. "Sorry, I thought you were supposed to play that quarter note in every measure, but now I see that you don't."

"You were cueing off Ronnie?" Sam said.

"I guess so," Caleigh said. She didn't know how to explain to Caleigh that she needed to own her part and *feel* her own points of entry. Did others cue off of her? Yes, she knew they did because in every strings group she'd been in, many of the musicians watched her. Maybe because she was always the lead violin.

They played for a few more measures until it became obvious that Sam, Dominique, and Maddie had to work out their up/downs through a particularly busy section filled with long runs of quarter notes. After a while, they felt good about the technical side of things.

Sam, feeling antsy, said, "Hey, guys, can we play the whole movement through entirely once? No stops, no pauses. No worries about up strokes or down strokes. Just make a mental note of anywhere you want to go back to, but let's keep going all the way through, okay?"

"Sounds good," Ronnie said. He often grew restless when other instruments were working something out. "Especially the part about strokes."

The others groaned, but Sam simply rolled her eyes at him and flipped her sheet music open so she could see all the pages. She waited until she intuitively knew the others were ready and then tucked her violin under her chin. She waited a moment more and then raised her bow in an exaggerated motion to signal the start to the others.

The notes flowed freely from her instrument. The other instruments added texture and nuance. It wasn't long before she was lost in the love song. Her senses flooded with thoughts of Lisa's smile, the exact moment she'd fallen in love with her, their first kiss, and their first real lovemaking at the lake house. Her heart swelled along with the music. Her eyes were open, but they did not see the present. They were reliving private moments from the past. Connecting with Lisa in fiery embraces, each hungry for the other. Lisa strong and sure, finding ways to delight Sam's body. Sam caressing Lisa passionately in ways known only to her. Lisa arching up under Sam's well-placed kisses, crying out passionately under well-timed strokes. And then, finally, basking in the warm pastels of their peaceful reconnection with the earth.

The movement ended, and Sam finally returned to reality when she heard the sound of many bows tapping furiously on music stands. She blinked to let the classroom back in and looked around the room. The entire Strings class was giving her their version of a standing ovation.

"Samantha Rose," Mr. Auerbach said with a choked voice. He took off his glasses and wiped at his eyes. "That was inspired. That was ethereal. You *are* the music." He turned away and said to his younger charges, "Now, that's how it should be, people. You don't *play* the instrument. You *are* the instrument."

Sam felt her neck and face burning in embarrassment. Gah, if they only knew what she'd been daydreaming about.

Ronnie leaned forward and said softly, "One day, I hope to be that much in love, Samantha Rose."

Sam blew out a small sigh and closed her eyes. Too bad she had softball practice that afternoon because she wanted to drop everything, fly to Clarksonville, whisk a certain probably-taller-than-six-feet junior off her feet, and let her know how much she loved her.

"She knows," Ronnie said quietly.

"How do you and Susie always know what's going on in my head?"

"It's your heart, honey. It shouts." He smiled and said, "Okay, women of this quintet, can we go back to sixty-nine?"

Caleigh gasped. "Ronnie!" She whacked him with her bow.

~~~

After a long soaking shower, Sam felt somewhat refreshed. She got dressed in sweats and a t-shirt and stretched her aching muscles. Softball practice that afternoon had been grueling. Coach Gellar understood that Clarksonville was the better team this season, they all understood that, but Coach wasn't going to let the embarrassment of getting beaten in a perfect game stop her from killing her own players. Sam dreaded the blowing of the whistle. It meant they had to line up on the foul line and run sprints until Coach felt like stopping. And whoever came in last had to run more. Unfortunately, Susie was one of those dead-last runners more often than not. Sam was afraid her bestie was heading into another funk, but this time Sam knew what signs to look for and absolutely would not let her start drinking again. She texted Marlee and Lisa and let them know her worries. Both Marlee and Lisa said they were already on guard, and each one of them had reached out to Susie already.

Sam loved her friends and wondered what life would bring all of them. She hoped they would somehow be able to be in each other's lives for a long, long time. Nah, she wanted them forever. She wanted them around her always. She truly did think of Marlee and Susie and Lisa as family. Sometimes you made your own families when the ones you were born into didn't quite satisfy your needs. Sam sighed when she thought about her distant and aloof mother and her all-business father. It is what it is, Sam thought with a mental sigh.

She pulled out her homework binder. She planned on doing her first-period French essay and then running down to visit Helene for a while, just like old times.

She picked up her book and read the title out loud, "*L'école des Femmes*," and thumbed through it. "The School for Women," she translated. "Or did Molière mean Wives?" Sam wondered. As she perused the book, she mused on the plot. A creepy old guy trying to groom an adolescent girl to fall in love with him? That part was kind of disturbing, and she was definitely glad his plans had been foiled.

"Nope, I've got it," Sam said out loud and tapped her pen on her desk. She lifted the lid on her laptop and started a new Word document. After typing her name and class period on the top of the page, she typed the heading, "*L'amour Conquiert Tout*." She pressed the enter key a few times and then let her stream of thoughts pour out in french. She'd tidy them up into a cohesive essay once the ideas hurtling around her head were down on the page. She thought of Susie and Marlee's recent test of their relationship. "Yep," Sam mused out loud, "love does, indeed, conquer all." She referenced different passages in Molière's play and backed up her assertion that because the heart wants what the heart wants, it recognizes the kindred spirit it was destined to be with. For the young girl in the play, it certainly wasn't the creepy old guy. For Sam, it certainly *was* Lisa.

A soft knock on the door startled Sam out of her reverie.

"Come on in," Sam said, knowing it would be Helene. No one else ever came to her rooms. Her heart felt warm and gushy at the thought of Helene being home.

Sam stood up and gave Helene an all-consuming hug. "I love that you're here."

"Me, too," Helene said. "I'm not interrupting, am I?"

"Nope. Your timing was perfect." Sam reached for Helene's hand and led her to the couch in her suite. "Now tell me everything you haven't already told me about Chantal and her sweet baby, Alicia." Sam plopped down on the other side of the couch, her heart full.

Helene showed her pictures on her phone and told a few stories about the precious new life her sister had brought into the world. She said she tried to help her sister not freak out about the slightest little thing.

"You have experience by raising me, don't you?" Sam said.

"Your parents raised you, Samantha Rose."

Sam scoffed. "All three of you raised me."

Helene seemed to muse on Sam's statement for a moment and then said, "My sweet, sweet, sensitive girl, you're right. And you were a dream to raise. I was happy to be a part of your life for so long."

Sam looked down for a moment and then said, "How long are you staying?"

"I'm not sure. A couple of weeks to start, I think."

"Doesn't your sister need you?"

Helene hesitated.

"What, Helene? Did something happen?"

"No, but it was time for me to leave. I think Chantal would like me to stay, but her husband—"

"Antoine?"

"Yes, he was more than ready for me to go. *C'est le vie,*" Helene said with a wistful smile.

"Oh, Helene, I'm sorry. Where will you go?"

"I have some options. Don't worry about me. But that's not why I came up here tonight."

Alarm bells jangled along Sam's nerves. She searched Helene's face and saw a mixture of worry, love, and compassion.

"Helene, what is it? Are you okay?" Sam was thinking the worst.

"It's your mother, Samantha Rose."

"What about Mother?"

"She found a lump."

"A lump?" Sam couldn't comprehend what Helene was trying to tell her.

"A suspicious lump in her breast," Helene continued. "Your father took her to Dr. Gold's office for an immediate mammogram and ultrasound."

"When? Where was I? Why don't they tell me anything?" Pressure built up in Sam's right temple, but she refused to acknowledge it.

"They wanted to have more information before they told you anything," Helene said softly.

Sam sighed. "So, what...." She didn't know what to ask. "So, what now?"

"Dr. Gold referred your mother to an oncologist, Dr. Salazar. He said they needed more information. Your mother is scheduled for a biopsy on Saturday at the hospital."

"I'm going," Sam announced and stood up. Pacing seemed like the best thing to do at the moment. "Why can't she go tomorrow?"

"Everything that can be done is being done in its time, Samantha Rose."

Sam stopped in her tracks and jerked her head to look at Helene. "Biopsy. That means cancer, Helene. Doesn't it?"

"Nothing is certain until we get the results."

"But it *could* mean cancer. It *could* mean that Mother has breast cancer," Sam said, not liking the words at all. She held her breath, waiting for Helene to confirm what she didn't want confirmed.

Helene tipped her head once in affirmation. Sam groaned and closed her eyes. Numb, she reached for the back of the couch and held on as a wave of dizziness overcame her.

"Come sit, *mon petit hibou*," Helene said after a moment. She patted the couch.

Sam did as bidden, and for the next half hour, the words tumor and biopsy and cancer infiltrated her sanctuary, her safe haven.

"Mother called me at school today," Sam said after a particularly long silence.

"She wanted to tell you herself," Helene said. "She wanted to tell you when she knew you would be surrounded by your friends who would take care of you."

"That's why she called me during my lunch period."

Helene nodded.

"Helene, are you here to take care of Mother?"

Helene nodded. "And to take care of you."

Sam, at eighteen years old, fell into her nanny's arms and sobbed.

Chapter Ten

Not Right Now

Sam's parents and Helene walked several steps ahead. Lisa leaned over and whispered to Sam, "I'm surprised they let me come today."

Sam smiled at Lisa, knowing Lisa could read the worry in her expression. "I think they want you here for me." At Lisa's puzzled expression, Sam added, "In case I have a breakdown or something."

"Hmm," Lisa said with a raised eyebrow. "Is this likely to happen?"

Sam shrugged. "I'm trying to be strong, but a biopsy...." She paused to gather her thoughts. "The results of Mother's biopsy will give us answers."

Lisa nodded while she took Sam's hand, and Sam was okay with that. Since Sam had been publicly outed in the local newspaper six months before, she decided that she might as well stay out. And, besides, it took a lot of energy to be in the closet. Sam needed to reserve her energy for what might lie ahead with her mother.

"I didn't know that East Valley Hospital even had a cancer wing," Sam said, pointing to the bold black letters over a wide hallway off the big lobby.

After entering the hallway, Lisa slowed down and read "The

Rose Salon." She had a perplexed expression on her face. "Why do they have a hair salon in the hospital?"

Sam shrugged. It did seem kind of weird. "Look, it says 'Free Head Shaves.'"

A woman walking behind them said, "The chemo messes with fast-growing cells. It makes your hair fall out." They had reached the open door to the salon, and the woman went in. She pulled the wig off her head. "See?" She turned and smiled a resigned smile at them. Her head was partly shiny bald and partly stubble. "Shaving is the only way to manage it. The wigs fit more comfortably that way, too." She pointed to a display case full of wigs in all colors, shapes, and lengths.

Neither Sam nor Lisa had a clue what to say. The woman probably knew they'd be awkwardly speechless and turned away from them and went over to hug one of the stylists.

A middle-aged receptionist standing near the entrance to the salon said, "When you have cancer, hair loss is a harsh and rude reminder that your body is in a fight for its life."

"I can imagine," Lisa said. Sam nodded.

"Before chemo, some women even donate their own hair and have a wig made for themselves."

"Mmm," Lisa said, clearly moved. Sam, though, was paralyzed. That balding woman could be her mother soon.

The phone rang, and the receptionist turned away.

"C'mon." Sam pulled Lisa along behind her. "They're already at the elevators. Sam didn't want to hear scary words like chemo but knew that she might hear a whole lot worse before their afternoon was through.

Alone with their own thoughts, the elevator ride to the third floor was quiet. Once the door finally opened, Sam was content to let her father lead.

"Here it is," Sam's father said. He read the sign on the door. "East Valley Oncology Group." He opened the door for the four women to go through first.

Sam's mother and father sat down at one of the registration check-in booths. Helene herded Lisa and Sam to a group of isolated chairs in the large waiting area. Sam was surprised to see about a dozen people waiting. She had no idea so many people in her hometown were battling cancer. A woman wearing a scarf around her head was sitting at a table doing a puzzle with a young boy about eight years old. His mother had cancer. What a thing to go through at that age, Sam thought. "My own mother might have cancer," she mumbled quietly to herself. At eighteen years old, she didn't want to go through it either.

"Thanks for letting me come to this," Lisa said to Helene as they sat down.

"It was Sam's mother's idea, actually."

"It was Mother's idea?" Sam said. "Huh." That was interesting.

After a long fifteen minutes or so, her parents came and sat with them. Bless Helene for trying to keep some kind of conversation going. She asked both Sam and Lisa about their schoolwork and softball schedules. Lisa, taking up the cue, amiably asked Helene about her new niece in Québec.

After a while, they settled into an unsettled silence, and Sam started to get antsy. They had a ten o'clock appointment, and it was already ten-thirty. Sam stood up to get a drink of water. There were conical paper cups, and she couldn't help thinking how Marlee would have calculated the volume of the cone or something. She smiled as she thought of her friend.

Sam gestured to the water cooler, silently asking if anyone else wanted water. When they didn't, she walked over to a display case of colored ribbons. Pink, the sign said, was for breast cancer awareness, purple for pancreatic cancer, and orange for leukemia. The list went on. The ribbons were free, but Sam didn't take one. Taking one would mean it was true, and she didn't want it to be true.

At long last, Sam's mother was called in. The entire group of five stood up and followed the young-looking nurse behind the double doors.

"I'm Becca, Dr. Salazar's head nurse." Becca looked to be in her mid-twenties. Her hair was pulled back into a tidy ponytail, and her turquoise nurse's uniform was cheery. Sam couldn't deal with any of Becca's cheeriness. Didn't she know why they were there? Her mother might have cancer.

Lisa squeezed Sam's hand. She glanced over, and Lisa mouthed, "Breathe." Sam nodded and did as told.

Becca stopped before a room marked number seven, and Sam couldn't help thinking that was Susie's uniform number. Damn, with these reminders, she might actually remember more about this doctor's visit than she wanted to.

They went into the small meeting room and sat at a round table. There was room for three or four more people, but it was definitely *not* an examining room. It was probably the room where all the bad news was given out, the kind of news that shattered families. Sam wondered how many other families had sat in these same seats and been dealt life-changing news. Sam found herself sitting between Helene and Lisa.

Sam was impressed with Dr. Salazar when she walked in a few

minutes later. She looked to be in her early- to mid-forties and wore a rust-colored turtle neck sweater under a brilliant white lab coat with her name stitched in dark blue on the upper left chest. Her black slacks looked functional and fit her well. She wore dark-rimmed glasses and had her auburn hair pulled up into a business-like no-nonsense bun.

"You must be Mimi?" Dr. Salazar shook hands with Sam's mother, who nodded.

Sam's father stood up and said, "Gerald Payton." He put out his hand like Sam had seen him do a million times before. The doctor nodded and shook his hand warmly. Sam wondered how many times Dr. Salazar had to tell someone they had cancer. That must suck.

The doctor then reached across the table, shook hands with Helene, and said, "I'm Dr. Mariana Salazar."

"Helene Bouchard, caregiver. And this is Samantha Rose, daughter. And Lisa, Sam's girlfriend."

Dr. Salazar shook hands with Sam and Lisa in turn. "It's wonderful to meet you all. I'm pleased that Mimi has a good support team. That's important for what may lie ahead."

The doctor sat at the table and said, "Now, before we get into specifics, I'm assuming it is okay to talk freely and candidly with everyone in this room?" Her gaze settled on Sam's mother.

"Oh, yes, of course," Sam's mother said quietly.

Becca, who had remained standing behind the doctor, handed her a form. "This HIPAA form tells us who we are legally allowed to talk to about your diagnosis and treatment." She slid the form over to Sam's mother, who slid it to Sam's father. "Just put the names here, sign, and then we'll be able to talk freely."

Sam's father set to work.

"Now, while we're waiting, let's talk about good practices." She looked at all the women in turn as she said, "If you're not already doing so, a breast self-exam is essential once a month. Your aim is to become acquainted with how your breasts normally look and feel. As you become familiar, you can better discern if something is different. The woman herself finds many lumps, but it is often a partner who finds an abnormality." The doctor looked right at Sam when she said the words. Sam couldn't help the blush she knew was spreading across her face. Lisa reached under the table and squeezed her hand. There was going to be a lot of hand squeezing that day.

"Now, if you find a lump like Mimi did, don't panic. About eighty percent of lumps are non-cancerous."

Inside her own head, Sam said, "Which means twenty percent *are* cancerous."

Her mother signed the HIPAA form, and Becca put it on a small table Sam hadn't noticed before.

"So, Mimi, tell me your story," Dr. Salazar said. "Why are you here?"

"I hadn't been feeling well for some time. I thought it was the winter doldrums, that lack of sunlight thing. And then, last week, I felt something odd in my breast while taking a shower. We went to Dr. Gold immediately, and he sent me for a mammogram and an ultrasound. He confirmed it was a tumor and then passed me along to you."

"Dr. Gold's a good one, and he'll still be a big part of your care. We won't leave him out of the loop."

Sam's father cleared his throat and said, "I called Helene immediately and asked if she'd be able to get her affairs in order and come back to help in case…." His voice caught with emotion. He tried again, "In case we needed her help."

"We're grateful to have Helene in our lives," Sam's mother said, her expression softening.

Helene nodded. Her smile was sympathetic.

"Excellent," Dr. Salazar said. "Again, I'm happy to see such a good support team." She patted the table once and said, "Okay, so here's what's going to happen today." She turned toward Becca, who handed her a laminated sheet entitled "Core Needle Biopsy of the Duct." Becca passed three more laminated copies around the table. If the sheets had to be laminated, that meant they did this kind of thing often.

"As you can see here," Dr. Salazar pointed to one of the bullet points on the laminated sheet, "approximately ninety percent of women with breast cancer are diagnosed based on a needle biopsy. The biopsy we will do today removes a small bit of breast tissue. This will go to the lab, where a pathologist performs tests to give a detailed diagnosis. We should have the pathology report by mid-week."

Sam groaned. Damn. She naively thought they would get the results today.

"There's no way to speed up the diagnosis process?" Sam's father asked.

"No, and we don't want to," the doctor said, unfazed by Sam's father's hinted at request. "We want the lab to do its normal thing. We don't want to rush them into a wrong diagnosis."

"Sounds logical." Sam's father sat back in his seat. Sam wished he would take her mother's hand. It was so comforting having Lisa hold hers.

"Over the last twenty years, the chances of making a complete recovery from breast cancer have greatly improved, so if it does turn out to be a cancerous tumor, we are not going to panic." The doctor spoke directly to Sam's mother, who nodded. What else could she have done except say, "No, doctor, I fully intend to panic"?

Becca leaned over and handed the doctor another laminated sheet. Becca's shrug and raised eyebrows were sending the doctor a question. The doctor looked directly at Sam for a moment and then nodded. Becca passed around several laminated sheets titled "BRCA Gene Testing."

"I highly recommend, Mimi, that you also take this simple blood test to identify the BRCA genes. BR stands for breast, and CA stands for cancer."

"There are genes that test for cancer?" Lisa asked wide-eyed.

"Yes, we can test to see if there is a genetic predisposition to breast, colon, and ovarian cancer. We use DNA analysis to identify mutations in either one of the two breast cancer susceptibility genes — BRCA1 and BRCA2. Having a BRCA gene mutation is uncommon, though. Still, women with inherited mutations in these genes are at an increased risk of developing cancer, which is thought to be responsible for up to ten percent of breast cancers. Mimi, your daughter, should also be tested to see if she inherited the gene."

"She's not my biological daughter," Sam's mother said simply.

Sam forgot to breathe. Lisa did not know that. Sam's parentage was one of the Payton family skeletons, and she herself had been on the strictest of orders not to tell anyone that her former nanny Helene was her true biological mother. She hadn't told anyone. Not even Lisa.

Sam felt, rather than saw, Lisa's eyes on her. Lisa's hand pulled away slowly. Sam's nerves sparked at the sudden lack of contact.

"I see," the doctor was saying somewhere in the background of Sam's brain. "She can still have the test done, but it's up to you. Or her, I suppose." Becca gathered up the laminated sheets, and then the doctor said, "What other questions do you have?"

Sam's father said, "What happens if we do the biopsy on the tumor and it's negative?"

"We will still need to remove the tumor surgically," Dr. Salazar said.

"I have a hypothetical question," Sam's father continued. "What might this cancer do if we leave it alone?"

"Well," the doctor said, her fingertips steepled, "left untreated, the cancer cells would most likely continue to grow. They would spread to other parts of the body. Cancer likes to attack soft tissue like the liver and the lungs. These compromised organs will first result in discomfort, then real pain until the ,organs ultimately fail and the body stops working."

"And the patient dies," Sam said in her head, knowing everyone else at the table was thinking the same thing. Sam couldn't help it. She started crying. She couldn't stop her tears. They were coming from somewhere deep inside the depths of her heart. It wasn't fair. Cancer. Why? Why her mother? Why now? With both arms, Lisa pulled Sam close and stroked her back. Helene rubbed her arm. With a strength she didn't know she had, Sam stopped her tears from becoming full-on sobs.

Dr. Salazar stood up and said, "I'll give you all a moment, and then Becca will be back to get Mimi for the biopsy." She and her head nurse left the room quietly.

Helene said, "We will do what we have to do, Samantha Rose."

"I know," Sam managed to say. "But I'm quitting softball."

"You are not going to quit softball," Sam's mother said quietly.

Sam scoffed and looked up. "I thought you hated me playing softball, Mother."

"You love it so much. How can I keep that from you?" Sam's mother's face softened. "I never want you to say that I stopped you from living your life, Samantha Rose."

Sam looked down.

A full minute later, cheery Becca returned to bring Sam's mother to the room where she would get her biopsy.

"I love you, Mother," Sam said as she leaped up and hugged her mother. Sam's mother hugged Sam stiffly and followed Becca out the door. They turned to the right.

Sam said to Lisa. "Come with me to the bathroom?"

Lisa nodded and followed Sam out the same door. They turned left. "Turn left you live," Sam mumbled sarcastically and couldn't finish the thought.

Once inside the restroom, Sam led Lisa into the large accessible stall and slid the latch closed. Lisa pulled Sam into a healing hug. Sam nuzzled into Lisa's warmth wishing she could stay there forever. Lisa kissed her on the forehead and pushed Sam's head down to rest on the cushion of her breasts. It felt like home.

After a few minutes, Lisa said, "How are you?"

Speaking into Lisa's chest, Sam said, "My mother might have cancer, so I'm not all sunshine and roses." She pulled back and looked into Lisa's eyes. Lisa gently brushed away Sam's tears and caressed Sam's face with delicate fingers. Sam caught Lisa's hand in her own and kissed it. "Who gets cancer? Why does anyone get cancer? Why do some people have to die?"

"We don't know that she has it yet."

"I know," Sam said and wiped at her eyes again. "Aren't you going to ask me about ...?" Sam couldn't finish the question. The cat was out of the bag about Mother not being her biological mother.

"Yes, I am." Lisa stood up taller. "But not right now."

Chapter Eleven
Other People

"We'll find out either today or tomorrow," Sam said to Susie from the passenger seat. She rechecked her phone—no text from Helene, who'd promised to let her know as soon as Dr. Salazar called.

Susie reached over and squeezed Sam's hand. "This is a tough one, Sam. I'm sorry."

"Cancer sucks."

"It does."

They rode along C.R. 62 in relative silence. Susie was doing slightly over the speed limit so they could catch the tail-end of their girlfriends' game in Clarksonville. Susie was also probably speeding because it was kind of hard talking about cancer. What did you say to someone whose mother might have it? It had already been three days since the biopsy, and it seemed like all of Clarksonville County had heard about her mother's illness. Nothing any member of the Payton family did went unnoticed. And she knew people meant well, but if one more person said the words, "Your family is in my thoughts and prayers," she was going to choke.

Sam watched the forest go by as Susie drove. She tried to distract herself by counting the birch trees whizzing by.

"How many so far?" Susie said with a laugh.

"Fifteen, sixteen, seventeen," Sam said and then looked over at her friend who knew her so well.

Susie glanced back and threw her a quick tight-lipped grin. Yeah, Sam was lucky to have such a good friend.

"Can I ask you something, Sam?"

"Sure."

"Your call Saturday night was, uh…." Susie pantomimed that her mind had been blown.

"I know. Sorry. It was a huge Payton family secret. I wasn't allowed to tell anyone. Ever. It could hurt the family or something. I was shocked when Mother just came right out and said she wasn't my biological mother in front of Lisa, the doctor, and the nurse. A little while later, Daddy told me to tell you guys."

"Your mother probably thought Lisa knew already. But *Madre de Dios*, Sam, that's a huge detail to omit from your life."

"I know." Sam shrugged.

"But your father is still your father. I mean, he's your biological father, right?"

"Yep."

"And Helene really is your mother? I mean, your full-on biological mother?"

"Yes, Helene Bouchard is my biological mother."

"You know, it's kind of super-obvious," Susie said. "You and Helene look so much alike. Same hair color, same facial features. You didn't suspect anything growing up?"

"No. Isn't that ridiculous? We believe the lies we're fed." Sam scoffed. "But like I told you guys, I didn't even know until four months ago. Last October, in Helene's hospital room after the accident. That's when I found my birth certificate in her purse and read it. My brain overloaded when I saw Helene's name listed as my biological mother."

"And that's why you fainted that day," Susie said, putting two and two together. "*Gringa*, I wish you had told us." Susie frowned at her friend.

"I wasn't allowed to tell. The Payton family name must not be tarnished. To be honest, the fact that my parents allow me to have a relationship with Lisa still boggles my mind."

"Even if they *didn't* allow it," Susie said, "I think you would have found a way."

"Maybe. But probably not. You don't know my father. He always gets what he wants."

"Is Lisa still pissed at you for not telling her about Helene?"

"Yes, but she's holding back her feelings because of Mother's situation. She said that I could have confided in her, that she would have kept the secret. She said we had agreed to trust each other and not keep anything from each other. She said I violated that trust."

"Violated?"

"Yep. That was the word she used."

"Ahh," Susie said with a knowing smirk. "You, too, Samantha Rose Payton, are not immune to the angry girlfriend syndrome, are you?"

Sam chuckled. "Nope. Apparently not."

~~~

Susie pulled her Honda into the Clarksonville lot, and they were lucky enough to get a parking spot near the field. They jumped out

136

of the car and hustled toward the gate. Sam was surprised that the game was still going on. Clarksonville should have mercy-ruled Northwood by now.

Sam's jaw dropped open when they crested the rise. Not only was the game not over, but Clarksonville was losing by a score of 11–7 in the top of the sixth inning. Kerry was pitching for Clarksonville, and Marlee, unthinkably, was sitting on the bench. Sam noticed a giant bag of ice on her shoulder, and another nestled at the top of her leg, obviously for her troublesome groin muscle.

"Sam, what the hell?" Susie said, her mouth hanging open. They slowed down their walk, trying to make sense of it.

Sam just shook her head. "Looks like Marlee's hurt."

"I know," Susie said. Her tone was one of concern and worry. "I'm going to find out what's going on. I'll see you up there."

Susie made her way through the crowd and, going against team rules, sat on the Clarksonville bench next to Marlee. Marlee was startled and turned to face Susie. Sam's heart broke when she saw the defeated expression on Marlee's tear-stained face. Tears filled Marlee's eyes as Susie threw an arm around her and pulled her close. She murmured something to her, and Marlee just nodded.

Sam stole a glance at Coach Speers, the Clarksonville coach, who was watching Susie and Marlee. She could have kicked Susie off the bench, she had every right to, but she didn't. She simply winked at Susie to let her know her presence was okay and turned back to her scorebook.

Sam made a beeline toward Lisa's parents. After giving a round of hugs, she pulled Bridget onto her lap and said, "What's happening here? They should be killing Northwood."

Lisa's mother rolled her eyes and pointed.

Sam groaned. She hadn't noticed. It was that troll umpire again. The one that didn't give Marlee any kind of strike zone to pitch in.

"Is Marlee hurt?"

"We're not sure, but we don't think that was why she was taken out of the game," Lisa's father said. "She walked fourteen batters—"

"Fourteen?" Sam was incredulous.

Lisa's mother nodded. "Coach Spears had to pull her out at the top of the fourth. Marlee had reached her pitch limit."

"A hundred pitches in four innings? How is that even possible?" Bridget squirmed in Sam's lap, so Sam pulled out a tiny book of stickers she'd stashed in her sweatshirt pocket for just such occasions. "Here you go, Sweetpea. Pick out a sticker, and I'll put it on you, okay?"

"What do you say, Bridget?"

"Thanks, Samtha." Bridget wrapped her arms around Sam's neck for a hug and then kissed Sam on the cheek.

"You're welcome," Sam said, her voice thick with emotion. Lisa's family was so loving and accepting.

Lisa's mother said, "During the first two innings, Northwood was swinging their bats. That's why the score isn't worse than it is. Once that barbarian of a coach over there figured out the umpire wasn't giving Marlee any strikes, he ordered his players not to swing."

"So, every four or five pitches," Lisa's father took up the tale, "Marlee would walk a batter and then another and another."

"She walked in runs," Sam said with a grimace.

"Yes," Lisa's mother said. "Not all the runs but most. That umpire makes me so angry." She growled in frustration.

"Don't be angry, Mama," Bridget said and placed a hippo

sticker on the back of her mother's hand.

"Thank you, Sweetpea." Lisa's mother gave her youngest daughter a big sloppy kiss on the forehead, causing Bridget to giggle and squirm in Sam's lap.

"Luckily," Lisa's father said, "some of the girls on the Northwood team figured out what was going on and are blatantly defying their coach by swinging their bats."

"It's nice to see young people who understand the difference between right and wrong," Lisa's mother said. "Coach Speers has done her fair share of protesting. Just enough not to get thrown out of the game."

Sam shook her head. Poor Marlee. This wasn't fair to her or the rest of the Clarksonville team. Stupid umpire. Sam wished she could do something but didn't know what.

Sam looked over at Lisa squatting behind the plate. Her black braid was hanging down her back. Marlee's replacement threw a pitch that was close on the corner, and the umpire called it a strike.

"He called that a strike for Kerry," Sam said.

"Yes," Lisa's mother said, "but not for Marlee. The Northwood pitcher's strike zone is even bigger."

On the next pitch, the batter swung but fouled the ball off. Lisa threw her mask down and turned toward the backstop. Sam cringed as Lisa reached out with her bare hand to find the backstop while looking up high for the ball. The ball thwacked into her outstretched mitt for the third out of the inning.

The crowd cheered for their Clarksonville team. Apparently, Kerry had held Northwood to only one baserunner over the last two innings. Sam tried to make eye contact with Lisa, but Lisa was all business as she stripped off her catcher's gear and headed to the on-deck circle.

Sam cheered loudly along with the Clarksonville fans as first Julie and then Jessica hit singles to left field. Sam was on her feet stomping the bleachers when Lisa's double to right-center brought in two runs making the score 11–9 but still in Northwood's favor. Unfortunately, the next few Clarksonville batters couldn't bring Lisa in, and the bottom of the sixth inning ended with Northwood still leading by two runs.

In the top of the seventh inning, Kerry held Northwood scoreless, which brought hope, but the bottom of Clarksonville's order couldn't get the job done. In a stunning upset, Northwood beat Clarksonville by a final score of 11–9. The only sounds that could be heard were the Northwood team celebrating. They had beaten the undefeated State champions.

Sam sidled up next to Lisa after the game. "How in the world does Marlee walk fourteen today when she pitched a perfect game against us last week?"

"Nothing was different today," Lisa said as she angrily stuffed her equipment in her bag. "Marlee was on. It was that idiot." Lisa looked up at Sam. "I don't understand why he's allowed to do that. Coach Spears is going to look into him. Maybe she can get him disbarred or fired or whatever they call it."

"Why doesn't the field umpire intervene?" Sam said.

"I don't know, Sam. It's just not fair." Lisa looked toward Marlee, standing near the bleachers with her mother. Susie stood protectively next to them, holding Marlee's softball bag over one shoulder. "Look at that," Lisa said and pointed. Lisa's youngest sister, Bridget, was holding Marlee's hand.

"That's so cute," Sam said.

"Bridget is such a tender heart," Lisa said. "She probably saw that Marlee was hurting."

"Yeah." It was all Sam could choke out over the lump in her throat.

There was a line of people going by Marlee shaking her hand or patting her on the arm. Each one gave her some kind of cheer-up advice or commiserating sentiment about how unfair it was.

"I'm sure she's absolutely hating that," Sam said, referring to all the attention Marlee was getting.

Lisa nodded in agreement and resumed her angry bag-stuffing.

"Baby," Sam said, "we don't have to go to the youth group meeting tonight if you guys aren't up for it."

"No, I want to go," Lisa said and latched her bag shut. "That self-defense instructor's going to be there, and well, I think I should know something about that." Sam followed her gaze toward the bleachers. "Alexander's here again."

"Are you kidding? I thought…." Knowing Coach Speers had her hands full, Sam said, "I need to make a quick phone call." She walked toward the bleachers and took a covert picture of Alexander. He was watching all the players, not just Lisa. Sam walked to a quiet spot behind the pitcher's warm-up area and punched in the numbers. "Daddy, I may have a problem, and I was wondering if I could get your help."

~~~

Lisa stepped behind Sam and wrapped her arm around Sam's neck in a back choke hold. She pulled Sam closer to her. "Give me your candy, little girl," Lisa growled low in Sam's ear.

Even though they were simulating an attack from behind, Sam didn't mind being pressed back against her girlfriend at the youth group meeting.

"Captives," the cute, incredibly in-shape female self-defense instructor said, "remember to reach up and hold onto your attacker. Right hand goes just above the elbow at the bicep, and the left grabs the wrist. Step to the right, drop the left fist, and swing back hard. You're hoping to hit him in the groin, but whatever you hit, hit it hard. As soon as your assailant bends over, bring your elbow up hard into whatever body part you happen to catch. You're hoping to catch his chin but take whatever you can get."

The instructor walked around the room as they tried it. Even Anne was trying it with one of the Southbridge girls that didn't have a partner.

"Good, good," the instructor said. "Don't hurt your partner now," she said with a laugh when Alivia squealed at Jessica's aggressive moves.

Ronnie quipped, "I thought you liked Alivia's hold on you, Jessica."

"I do. I do," Jessica said. "But she was really choking me."

"I was?" Alivia let go completely. "Sorry, sweet thing. I was taking my bad guy role too seriously."

The instructor chuckled again, saying, "Practice a few more times and then switch places."

"I can't believe this works," Sam said.

"I know," Lisa said. "And I had a good hold on you."

They switched positions, but at 5' 4", it was hard for Sam to get a good choke hold on Lisa because she was so tall. One of these days, she was going to muster up the courage to ask Lisa just how tall she really was now.

After a few more minutes and a few adjustments, the instructor said, "Great job, everyone. That's it for this evening. Thanks for inviting me, and if any of you want a fuller self-defense course, please consider taking one of our courses here at the college. Any age can join, and you don't have to be enrolled at the college."

The group clapped, and several youth group members swarmed the cute instructor. Sam and Lisa walked over to Marlee and Susie, who were talking to Anne.

"Thanks for making this happen, Anne," Susie said.

Anne smiled and said, "I don't know if this training would have helped you with your attacker...." She was obviously referring to Susie's recent sexual assault when she'd been blitzed-out drunk.

Susie simply shrugged.

Anne's cheeks were turning red. She patted Susie's arm and then said to Sam, "Your family is in my thoughts and prayers, Samantha Rose."

"Thanks, Anne," Sam said, numb to the pat phrase.

Anne walked over to talk to the self-defense instructor.

Marlee gestured toward the instructor. "She *is* kind of cute." She was obviously trying to lighten the mood.

"You're the only girl I see," Susie said.

Before Sam could make a sarcastic comment, her cell phone rang. Her heart jumped into her throat. She read the caller ID wide-eyed. "It's Helene."

"C'mon," Lisa said, "let's go in the hallway." She pulled Sam by the arm toward the door.

"Hello, Helene," Sam said and let Lisa guide her to a dark, deserted stairwell. She leaned back against the cinderblock wall. Lisa had an arm loosely wrapped around her waist.

"Is Lisa there with you?" Helene asked.

"Yes, she's right here." Sam felt Lisa's arm tighten around her. "You're on speakerphone."

"The biopsy came back positive. It's cancer."

Sam cried an agonizing moan as she slid to the floor, taking Lisa with her. Cancer. Her mother had cancer. Lisa was her rock, but Sam needed a mountain at that moment.

"Is Sam okay, Lisa?"

"Not really," Lisa said, "but I'm right here with her."

"Good. Samantha Rose?"

"Yes?" Sam said, her head leaning on Lisa's arm.

"Are you okay?"

"Yes." It was a valid question. Sam had had a few panic attacks when she was younger.

"Okay, I'll give you some details, but stop me if it's too much. Ask any questions you have. I may not know the answers yet, but I'll do my best to find out. Okay?"

"Okay." Sam's eyes were closed.

"Dr. Salazar called just now and said your mother has Stage 0 Ductal Carcinoma in situ. She referred to it as DCIS."

"Ductal Carcinoma means the tumor is within the milk ducts?" Lisa asked.

"Yes."

"Stage 0 sounds promising," Lisa added.

"Yes, Dr. Salazar was optimistic. Stage 0 means the cancer hasn't spread outside the milk duct into the surrounding breast tissue, lymph, or blood systems."

"It's contained, Sam," Lisa said. "This is good. Really good."

144

Sam nodded once. Her mother had cancer.

"The tumor is relatively small and slow growing," Helene continued. "Dr. Salazar said that if you had to have cancer, this was the type to have."

"Okay," was the only word Sam could manage. Her mother had cancer.

"Your mother will have to have a lumpectomy. It'll be a short overnight stay."

"Okay."

"Your parents and I will meet with Dr. Salazar and a surgeon tomorrow to discuss options and schedule surgery."

"I'm going with you," Sam said, finally getting out more than one word.

"Your parents and I knew you would say that, and they're fine with it. Your mother wanted me to tell you that she's going to bed and you shouldn't rush home. She wants you to stay there with your friends this evening."

"Okay," Sam said. She had been ready to grab Susie and rush back to East Valley.

"She'll talk with you in the morning, but you can visit me tonight if you want."

"Okay."

"Goodnight, girls," Helene said.

"Thank you, Helene," Lisa said. "Goodnight."

"Okay," Sam said.

To Sam, Helene's news was somehow not real. Cancer happened to other people, not her family, not her mother.

Chapter Twelve
Live Your Life

Most kids would have been happy to have a day off from school, but most kids weren't on their way to the hospital to meet with a surgeon because their mother had cancer.

Sam was between her mother and Helene in the backseat while her father sat in the passenger seat. Rolando, her father's driver, sat behind the wheel of the town car as they made their way to East Valley Hospital on a dreary Wednesday morning.

"Daddy?" Sam addressed her father from the backseat.

"Yes, kitten," he said and turned to face her. His blue eyes were cloudy, and he looked pale. The stress of her mother's situation was undoubtedly taking a toll on him like it was on the rest of them.

"Were you able to look over the Petrov family situation? You know, that big house next to my friend Marlee's house?"

"Oh, yes. A great investment, Samantha Rose. According to Marla Cohen, the land alone is worth making an offer on, and that house is in great condition."

"Marlee told me that Mr. and Mrs. Petrov take amazing care of the place. So, does that mean I can buy it?"

"Green light, as far as I'm concerned. I think my daughter has a real nose for business." His smile was genuine. "Let's set up a meeting with Ms. Cohen, and we'll hammer out an offer."

"Thanks, Daddy." Sam was excited. She hoped to be able to help Marlee's neighbors. They had been so good to Marlee's family. And, by finding this steal of a deal, Sam hoped her parents would think her capable and mature. So capable and mature that they would let her go to Rockville University with Susie and Marlee in the fall.

Helene patted Sam on the knee and smiled at her. Yes, Helene probably understood her motivation. Helene always understood. Sam wondered if one day she could call Helene "*Maman,*" the French word for mother. That was too much to ask at the moment. There were other things to deal with.

"Rolando," Sam addressed the man who had been her father's driver longer than Sam had been alive.

"Yes, miss?" Rolando glanced at her in the rearview mirror, his crinkled eyes twinkling.

"Is this really your last day with us?"

"Yes, miss. I'm sorry to be leaving your family."

"Is Arizona going to be better for your wife?"

"I hope so, miss." His face held a sad smile. "Her rheumatoid arthritis is excruciating for her. The North Country cold is pure agony."

"We're going to miss you," Sam said with a frown.

"Yes, we are," Sam's mother chimed in.

"Indeed," Sam's father added.

"You'll keep in touch, Rolando," Helene said and leaned forward to touch his shoulder.

"Yes, miss. Of course. You've all been so wonderful and supportive of my family."

"The same could be said for your family," Sam's father said.

They rode along in silence until the hospital came into view. Rolando pulled the car into the circular drive at the front entrance and opened the door for Sam's mother.

"Thank you, Rolando," Sam's mother said. "Gerald will call you when we're ready to go home."

"Very good," he said and bowed his head slightly.

Sam was taking mental notes. She'd have to tell Cassie, the new driver Sam had convinced her parents to hire, all these little things her parents expected from their employees. Opening the door and bowing your head respectfully was one of them. And, oh yeah, there was one more thing.

Sam walked right up to Rolando and put her hands on her hips. She cleared her throat loudly, "Ahem."

"Yes, miss?" Rolando said, looking up at the sky, purposefully not making eye contact. "May I help you with something?"

Sam stuck out her lower lip.

Rolando looked down. "Why the big frown, little one?"

"You know why."

"Ahh, you got me." He smiled and reached into his jacket pocket. He pulled out a shiny butterscotch candy and held it out to her. "I have one just for you."

In one smooth motion, Sam snatched the candy and flew into Rolando's arms. With emotion in her voice, she said, "I'm going to miss you, sir."

"You are a beautiful young woman, miss. It was an honor and a privilege to watch you grow up." He wiped at the tears in his eyes.

Sam pulled back and wiped at the tears in her own eyes. She turned from him just in time to see a smile lighting up her mother's face. Even though it was a sad and scary day, Sam's heart was full.

"You'd better keep in touch, or else."

He laughed and said, "I will."

Sam turned away and wished Lisa could be there for this meeting with the surgeon. But Lisa was in school, and this was just a meeting anyway. On the day of the actual surgery, Sam would ask Lisa to go with them whenever that was.

~~~

The meeting room in the surgery center was much smaller than the one where they'd met Dr. Salazar, but the size of the room didn't matter. The information was what mattered. Sam, her parents, and Helene sat at a rectangular table with Dr. Salazar and the surgeon, Dr. Myra Kulkarni. Dr. Kulkarni gave the impression of a woman in charge. She wore her short dark hair loose and looked to be in her mid-to late-fifties. With her wire-rimmed glasses, Dr. Kulkarni had an older sexy librarian thing going on. Sexy surgeon, maybe?

After introductions and a summary of Sam's mother's case, it was obvious that the two doctors had worked on many cases together. Dr. Kulkarni took the helm and said, "We'll go in and remove the DCIS with enough healthy breast tissue around it to be sure that the tumor has been completely removed. We want to clear the margins making sure we've got it all. If the margins are positive, though, we'll have to go back in for a second surgery to excise them. The patient remains open on the operating table until the pathology results come back. That takes about forty minutes. This could go back and forth several times. And every time we go back in, this increases the chances for needing to do a full mastectomy."

Before anyone could ask, Dr. Salazar said, "A mastectomy

means the entire breast is removed. Breast reconstruction is typically done after that." After a moment, she added, "As I've said before, caught early enough, there is a very high cure rate. Breast cancer does not necessarily mean a death sentence."

"You think we've caught this early enough?" Sam's father said.

"Yes, I'm optimistic."

Sam couldn't wait to fill Lisa in. Lisa told her to call or text as soon as the meeting was over. Sam's mother sat there stone-faced, and Sam wasn't sure her mother was fully aware of what was going to happen next. Sam wondered what Lisa would ask in a moment like this. Lisa was a year younger physically, but she often seemed older, wiser, and stronger than Sam and all their friends.

"So, Dr. Salazar," Sam said after clearing her throat, "after the surgery, my mother will have time to recover, and then we'll regroup to come up with a plan for further treatment, right?"

"Yes, and that will most likely involve treating the breast with radiation. Radiation after a lumpectomy remains the standard care. We'll do a regimen of five days per week over three to seven weeks. We also can't rule out the possibility of chemo, but let's not get ahead of ourselves."

Sam hoped her mother was listening because it seriously looked like she had checked out. Her mother's eyes were open, but they didn't seem to have much life.

"After surgery," Dr. Salazar continued, "Dr. Kulkarni and I will bring Mimi's case to the cancer team, and together we'll agree on the best course of action."

Sam liked that a bunch of doctors would be involved in her mother's care. That sounded like a good thing. It was strange how she could think clearly and ask sane questions during this bizarre and unbelievable situation. At the last meeting, she was a blubbering crying fool. What helped immensely was that both Dr. Salazar and Dr. Kulkarni showed compassion and treated them like intelligent human beings.

"What exactly is radiation?" Sam asked, willing her mother to at least look up. She didn't.

"Low doses of x-rays," Dr. Salazar said. "We hope they will destroy any abnormal cells that may be left in a woman's breast after surgery."

Dr. Kulkarni chimed back in and said, "After all the radiation is finished, we'll have another consultation about breast reconstruction surgery. Silicone implants may be used, depending on the disfigurement. This is optional, of course. Many women choose not to have reconstructive surgery and simply wear a padded bra with a prosthesis that gives a natural shape under the clothes."

"And after that," Dr. Salazar said, "we'll talk about possible hormone therapy."

Sam's mother took an audible breath and let it out with an overwhelmed sigh.

"It's a lot," Dr. Salazar said softly to Sam's mother, who looked up at the doctor. "My advice to you, Mimi, is to control what you can. Keep your life as normal as possible. Eat well. Exercise. Love your family." She smiled. "Letting go of your fears is impossible, but please know that you have experts on your side. Dr. Kulkarni is one of the best and will take good care of you."

Dr. Kulkarni pushed her chair back. "I do have an appointment I must get to, but are there any other questions?"

Sam shook her head and watched the rest of her family shake theirs.

Dr. Kulkarni shook hands with everyone at the table and left for her appointment.

"Mimi," Dr. Salazar said softly, "you're in good hands."

"Thank you," Sam's mother said as if trying to believe the doctor's words.

"I'll leave you all to talk for a while–"

"There's no need," Sam's mother interrupted. "Let's get this thing out of me as soon as possible."

Dr. Salazar nodded. "Good. I'll show you where surgical scheduling is, and then I'll see you on the day of the surgery."

"Thank you, doctor," Sam's father stuck out his hand and gripped the doctor firmly in handshake.

"You're welcome." Dr. Salazar then shook everyone else's hands in turn and led them to the scheduling desk on the opposite side of the registration area, where they had checked in earlier.

~~~

Once they were back in the town car, Sam's father turned in his seat and said, "We're going to be open and honest about your mother's situation, Samantha Rose."

"Okay," Sam said, not quite knowing what he meant.

"That means we're not going to hide the severity of the situation from the public."

There it was. Those words – the public. It was all about perception and what other people thought about the Payton family.

"What about Helene?" Sam asked. "Are we going to be open and honest about that to *the public*, too?" Sam had no idea where her brashness came from. She could feel Helene's glare but couldn't look away from her father. She wasn't picking a fight, not exactly, but she wanted answers.

"Too many people know at this point," her father said. "We have to get ahead of this before it gets beyond our control, so to answer your question, yes, we are letting the cat out of the bag, so to speak."

"What's the spin?" Sam asked, knowing there would be one.

Her father laughed at Sam's bold question. "The *spin,* as you call it, will be that we've always been an extended and welcoming family. Helene graciously offered to carry my child. We'll be open about your mother being unable to conceive and that Helene got pregnant in the *new*-fashioned way by artificial means."

"People will talk, Daddy. They'll want to know where Helene came from."

"Canada," Helene said with a grin. "We think it's best to say that my family and your mother's were old family friends."

Old family friends, Sam mused. That's interesting, seeing as they found Helene waitressing in a diner in Montréal. And since the family had already been tarnished with a gay daughter, why not expose this family skeleton, too?

"Daddy? Mother? May I have permission to call Helene, *Maman?*"

Helene made a small noise as her hand flew over her heart.

All eyes went to Sam's mother, who said, "She is your true mother, so I naturally understand that you would want that. I...." Sam's mother looked down and picked at a thread on her spring jacket. She was obviously thinking it over. She looked up, locked eyes with Sam, and said, "Yes. Yes, of course, you should be able to call your mother, *Maman.* Will you still want to call me 'Mother'?"

Sam wanted to embrace her mother in a reassuring hug, but hugs were a rare thing between them. Instead, she said, "Yes, of course, Mother. That hasn't changed. I love you, as always."

Her mother nodded and then exchanged a tight-lipped smile with Helene.

Sam turned, grinned at Helene, and then mouthed silently, "*Bonjour, Maman.*"

Helene beamed back.

Sam couldn't help thinking about what Rolando thought about the conversation in the car around him. He had been keeping Payton family secrets for over twenty-five years, though, so he probably already knew about Sam's real parentage.

"And Mother," Sam said boldly, "since your surgery is on Monday, in five short days, I want to spend every minute with you, so I'm not going to the East Valley prom this Saturday." Lisa would be disappointed, for sure, but it had to be that way.

"Oh, yes, you are, Samantha Rose," Sam's mother said sternly. "And I insist that you bring your friends here for pictures. I want to see you live your life. Cassie can drive you and your friends to the prom."

"Let your mother have this, kitten," Sam's father said.

"Yes," Sam's mother agreed. "Let me see you happy."

Sam wanted to dig her heels in and knew at some point on this cancer roller coaster she would have to but decided against it for the moment. Her mother flashed her a genuine, relaxed smile. It was a rare glimpse of her real mother—the mother she desperately wanted to know.

Sam nodded her acquiescence and leaned back into the seat for the rest of the quiet ride home.

Chapter Thirteen
It's Prom Night

Sam watched from inside the stretch limo as Marlee and Susie gave another round of hugs to Marlee's mother, Bob, and Mr. and Mrs. Petrov before getting in the back with her and Lisa.

"Bye," Marlee called again and waved through the rear window to her people. They were still waving at her.

"To the prom, my good woman," Sam said to Cassie through the open window to the driver's area up front.

"Yes, miss," Cassie said with a grin.

Susie burst out laughing and smacked Sam in the arm.

Sam groaned. "Oh, God, Cassie, do that in front of my parents, not here."

"Yes, miss," Cassie said again and lifted the bill of her chauffeur's cap, revealing her short-cropped flaming-red hair. "Just kidding. It's fun to tease you, Sam."

"Speaking of teasing," Marlee said devilishly to Cassie, "your dad filled me in on a little secret."

"Oh, no," Cassie groaned as she turned out of Marlee's gravel driveway onto C.R. 62. "He didn't."

"He did. You guys," Marlee gushed to her friends, clearly excited to tell Cassie's secret, "Cassie has a girlfriend."

The back of the limo erupted in cheers.

"Details," Susie demanded.

"Who is she?" Sam asked.

"Yeah, who is she?" Lisa echoed.

"Oh, no, no, no," Cassie protested, embarrassed. "It's still new, and I don't want to jinx it."

"Aww," Sam groaned. "You spoil the fun."

"Where'd you meet her?" Lisa asked.

"At a mutual friend's party a few weeks ago."

"A few weeks," Marlee mused. "Hmm, that means more than two, so let's say three weeks then."

"You guys are relentless." Cassie glanced at them in the rearview mirror. "Yes, I met her three weeks ago."

"What does she do?"

"Not gonna say," Cassie said.

"Okay, then where does she live?" Sam asked. She felt like a junior detective trying to get information from a difficult subject.

"East Valley."

Sam laughed. "I didn't think you'd give that up so fast."

"Yeah, really," Marlee said. "Are you going to her house after you drop us off at the prom?"

Cassie nodded, causing another round of cheers in the back. "Well, I will after I go to my aunt Doreen's house to drop off some books for my nieces."

"Aww," Lisa said. "I didn't know you had nieces. How old are they?"

"They are the cutest. Bethany is ten, I think, and Emma will turn two this summer."

"Hey, Cassie?" Susie said. There was a serious tone to her voice.

"What's your aunt's last name?"

"Same as mine. Johnson. She married my Uncle John, Dad's younger brother."

Sam put it together instantly. "Holy shit, Susie. Cassie's aunt is Mrs. Johnson, that jerk you babysat for. Isn't she?"

Susie nodded. She had a stricken look on her face.

"Cassie," Sam said, "I'm sorry. I shouldn't have called your aunt a jerk."

Cassie scoffed. "Personally, I would have used the word *bitch*, so don't be sorry." She glanced at Susie. "Susie, if it helps, no one in the family likes Aunt Doreen. Not even my dad, and he likes everyone."

When Susie didn't speak, Sam said, "She didn't treat Susie or Susie's mother very well, I'm afraid."

"I can imagine," Cassie said with a frown. "Just don't judge me, okay? She married into my family."

"You two are night and day," Susie said, finally finding her voice. "She still owes me money for my last week there."

"And that would be about a buck eighty-nine, right?" Cassie quipped.

Susie laughed. "Yeah, I guess I'll just forget about it. Don't bother telling her I said hello."

"I won't. If those kids weren't there, I'd probably never see the woman." Cassie cleared her throat. "Okay, listen, you guys, I put some sparkling waters in the cooler back there for you. Help yourselves. I'll put the window up to give you lovely ladies some privacy."

"Thanks, Cassie," Sam said.

"Yeah, thanks," the others chimed in.

After the window went up, Marlee said quietly, "We have to

find out who Cassie's going out with. This is so exciting."

"I never took you for a gossip queen, Marlee," Sam said. It was a little bit out of character.

"Well, her dad kind of hinted that he wanted me to find out."

"Oh, that's right," Sam said knowingly. "You work with her dad at Aldwell's Auto on Saturdays."

"Yep. Big Joe. He's like an uncle to me," Marlee said with a smile. Marlee had an attractive smile and looked stunning in her black pants suit. The sleeveless top was adorned with a low-cut ornate neckline, and the jacket she wore on top had sheer sleeves showing off Marlee's toned arms. It was definitely a new look for Marlee but suited her well.

"And the Petrovs are like grandparents to you," Lisa added. "Aren't they?"

"Yeah, they are," Marlee said and sighed. "Sometimes you make your own family." The smile she shot her friends melted everyone's heart, Sam's for sure. "And, Sam? That's a nice thing you're doing for them. Thanks."

"It was an obvious solution to their problem," Sam said. "And you know what, you guys? The house will be in my name."

"Just you? Not your parents?" Lisa asked.

"Nope. Daddy said it's up to me to make sure the rent is collected and the house and land stay in good shape."

"The Petrovs will see to it," Marlee said with authority.

"The deal is that they'll pay rent to me, and then I'll pay Daddy back. It's scary how much I had to borrow from him to buy the house and land."

"How much?" Susie leaned in close.

"That's between me and the Petrovs," Sam said. "We go to

closing in a couple of weeks."

"You know what, you guys?" Susie said. "I feel like we haven't seen each other in forever. I mean, I see this *gringa* all the time," Susie nodded her head toward Sam, "but...."

"I know," Marlee said. "We don't get to hang out much because of school, softball, and weekend jobs."

"Well," Lisa said, "we've got tonight's dance and next weekend's Clarksonville prom, so we're gonna see each other a lot this weekend and next."

The ride from Clarksonville to East Valley went rather quickly as they chatted amiably in the back of the limo. They collectively wondered what Cassie's new love interest was like and schemed about ways to get her to tell them more about her. They talked about lots of other things, too, but Sam noticed that they specifically avoided talking about Sam's mothers. Yes, plural. The word cancer never came up once, and neither did the words biological mother. She was sure her friends were trying to give her privacy, but she also knew they would be ready to listen when she was ready to talk. For now, she wasn't.

Cassie pulled the limo up the circular drive to Sam's house, and the four girls went in for pictures. This time Sam insisted her parents pose with them for a few. There was one slightly awkward moment when Sam insisted that both her mothers pose with her, but Sam acted like nothing was weird. Hey, she'd had two mothers growing up, and she was going to celebrate it. The cat was out of the proverbial bag, anyway, right?

Once the photo session was finished, Sam ushered the group back into the limo, and they headed to the Payton Arena on the north side of East Valley, where the prom was being held.

"I still can't believe your family owns the arena, Sam," Marlee said wide-eyed as the limo pulled in behind the long line of cars. "I mean, wow, look at the lights strung over the entryway. It's like at Le Bistro when they open the back patio in the summer. It's magical."

Sam just smiled at her friend.

The window between them and Cassie went down about six inches. "Girls, sit tight, this is a long line, and it looks like it's going to take a while."

"That's okay, Cassie," Sam said. "We like each other."

Cassie laughed and put the window back up.

The wait wasn't that long, and Cassie pulled up to the entrance and put the limo in park. Several police officers looked up at the limo and pointed. Sam recognized them from the winter formal in December. This was her father's doing, of course. He was still being cautious. Sam didn't mind, especially now that her friends were getting used to the extra attention Sam always received when she was in public.

Marlee started to reach for the door handle, but Sam stopped her. "Cassie likes this part."

Cassie opened the door, and Marlee stepped out and then reached back in to help Susie out in her flowing floor-length dress. "Man, you look amazing," Marlee gushed and blew out a sigh.

"Thank you," Susie said. "You're not too shabby, yourself."

Cassie reached her hand in the back to help Lisa out. "Hey, Cassie," Lisa said, "can you give us a minute."

"Absolutely," Cassie said and shut the door.

Lisa put her hand on Sam's arm. "Sam?"

"Hmm?"

"Anytime you want to leave or whatever, we can go. Okay?"

Sam melted at her girlfriend's obvious empathy. "Thank you, baby. I love you." She leaned in and hugged Lisa. She would have kissed her, but she didn't want to ruin Lisa's carefully applied lipstick or her own. "I love when you wear your hair up like this," Sam moaned into Lisa's ear. "You take my breath away, baby."

"Stop." Lisa pushed Sam away gently. She locked eyes with Sam. "I've never made love in the back of a limo, but if you keep looking at me like that…."

Sam grinned. "Can't help it." She curled her fingers in a come-hither fashion and opened the car door. Once they were out, Sam let Cassie shut the car door behind them.

"Text me whenever you're ready, girls. I can be here in fifteen minutes."

"Have fun at your hot babe's house," Susie teased.

Cassie didn't respond to the teasing, but the blush on Cassie's face said it all. "Hey, girls, send me some pictures if you can. I want to show my new, uh, friend."

"We will," they all called back simultaneously and then laughed.

After dropping off their jackets at the coatroom, they stopped for pictures with the official prom photographer, and Susie insisted they take a few with the four of them together. She said she needed pictures of her new family, her *real* family. Sam's heart broke a little for her friend at that moment.

Once they were finally inside the reception hall, Sam's breath caught in her throat. The prom committee had outdone itself. The Paris at nighttime theme might have been a bit cliché, but the decorations were breathtaking. The brilliantly lit twenty-foot Eiffel Tower was the centerpiece of the room. There were stone benches and three-tiered streetlamps near faux cobblestone paths. A working fountain and lights strung from every corner of the hall completed the romantic feel.

"I can't get over the budget you guys have at East Valley," Marlee said. "This is incredible. Don't expect anything close to this at Clarksonville next weekend."

"Hey, you guys," someone inside the hall called. "Over here." It was Alivia. She was pulling Jessica by the hand behind her. "Ronnie and Jordan are here. Come sit with us?" The excited look on her face was priceless.

Susie looked down, obviously wanting no part in the decision. All eyes went to Marlee, the de facto decider.

"Sure," Marlee said. "As long as you keep your hands to yourself." Her request was not in jest and was surprisingly passive-aggressive. Marlee was usually easygoing.

"I will. I will. I will," Alivia said with a squeal. "Does that mean you forgive me?"

"I'm pretty sure that's going to take a lot more time, Alivia," Marlee said evenly. "But I'm willing to honor a truce this evening."

"And next Saturday, too? Because I'm going—"

"Yes, sure. Next Saturday, too," Marlee said.

"Yay," Alivia cheered demurely. Sam was happy that Alivia seemed to understand how badly she'd messed up by getting in between Susie and Marlee. "And I am sorry, Marlee. Really."

Marlee nodded once but never smiled. No, Alivia was never going to be a friend to Marlee. Sam was sure of that.

Jessica looked confused as hell at the exchange between Alivia and Marlee.

"Come on," Alivia said and led the way back to the large table where the boys sat.

"Oh, no," Sam whispered to Lisa. "Jessica doesn't know."

"I never brought it up with her."

"That's gonna suck big time for Alivia when she tells her what happened between her and Susie," Sam said as they followed Alivia toward the table.

"Technically," Lisa said slowly, "Alivia wasn't with Jessica when she kissed Susie. Either time."

"You're right. Could be a loophole."

"Hey, baby," Lisa said and stopped walking.

"Yeah?"

Lisa stepped closer and put a hand on Sam's shoulder. "Baby, I want …."

When Lisa didn't continue, Sam pulled her closer and said, "What's up? Are you okay?"

"Yes. I just wanted to thank you for helping me with my Alexander problem. I know it was you. He got transferred out of every single one of my classes and wasn't at my game yesterday."

"I hope that was okay. Daddy made some calls." Sam searched Lisa's face. It seemed like there was more Lisa wanted to say. "Was there something else?"

Lisa didn't answer right away but then said, "No, come on. Let's join our friends."

"All of my women look ravishing this evening," Ronnie gushed as he and Jordan stood up to hug Sam and Lisa.

Sam hung on a little longer when she embraced Ronnie. He smelled of cologne, nothing else. "I'm clean, Sam," Ronnie said and pulled back.

Jordan smiled. "We're turning over a new leaf."

"Glad to hear it," Susie said from her seat next to Marlee.

Ronnie bowed and then said to Lisa, "You are particularly gorgeous this evening, Lisa Brown. You have been from the moment I met you, my Amazon queen. Almost out of Sam's league." He winked at Sam, but she knew he was teasing. "Do you remember when we met?"

"How could I forget?" Lisa said. "It was pre-Jordan at the Stewart's in East Valley. You, Alivia, and Karl were singing songs from Fiddler on the Roof." She sat beside Ronnie in the chair Sam had pulled out for her.

"I remember that," Alivia chimed in from the other side of Jordan, far away from Susie. "We were trying to recruit Sam for the play."

"Which you finally did," Sam said with a grin.

"And," Lisa said to Ronnie, "you practically accused me of giving Sam a black eye."

"Oh, right," Ronnie grimaced. "But I didn't know you then. Sorry."

"Ahh, my black eye," Sam said. "From that whacked-out creep, Bree."

"My wonderful stalker," Marlee said with bugged-out eyes. "Thanks for bringing that whole thing back up, Ronnie." She twitched one eye but couldn't keep it going and broke down laughing.

"I'm glad that's behind us," Susie said. "Okay, who wants punch or whatever?"

"Water for me, please," Marlee said.

The others gave their orders, and Ronnie, Susie, Jordan, and Jessica headed for the refreshment table.

"I love Susie's dress," Lisa said as she watched them walk away.

Susie's crimson chiffon floor-length dress with a scoop neck top and no sleeves complemented Marlee's black outfit perfectly. "Of course, the East Valley red color is somewhat annoying." Lisa grinned.

"She does look amazing," Marlee said wistfully. "I can't believe how lucky I am."

Alivia had the decency to keep her eyes down but then said to Sam and Lisa, "Girls, I love your matching dresses. Silver-gray is perfect for you both. The asymmetry of your dress, Sam, complements Lisa's floor length. The V-neck of Lisa's complements your scoop neck. Just beautiful."

"Thanks, Alivia," Sam said. "Love your dress, too."

"And those earrings," Lisa added.

Alivia reached up and touched her ear. "A gift from my bae. But I'm going to have to get creative for next Saturday's prom at Clarksonville. I didn't know I'd be going to two."

Sam wasn't sure why she blurted out what she did, but she said, "Why haven't you told Jessica about you and Susie?"

Marlee looked up with interest.

Alivia looked down. "I don't want to ruin it. I love Jessica, Sam. I've never felt like this about anyone ever before. She makes me feel like a princess. Like I'm the most important person in the world. And she's so strong. I get shaky when I look at her. A good, really good, kind of shaky."

"Does she think she's your first?"

"My first girl?" Alivia asked.

Sam nodded.

"Well, she is, really." Alivia glanced at Marlee and said, "She's the second girl I kissed, but the first one I had any real feelings for." Alivia looked down again.

Sam hoped that Marlee was buying the load of crap coming out of Alivia's mouth because Sam wasn't. Good on Alivia for trying to repair things with Marlee, though.

"Well," Sam said, playing along, "when you do tell Jessica, make sure she understands all that. And make sure she understands who started it." Sam locked eyes with her friend. "Be honest."

"I will." Alivia looked at Marlee again. "Honest. I'll tell her later tonight. She knows something's going on, I think."

"You think?" Sam said sarcastically. Her eyebrows were raised to the sky.

Susie and the gang came back with the drinks and sat down.

"Hey, guys," Susie said, "the next good song that comes on, we're dancing, okay?"

"You got it," Ronnie said, and there was general agreement all around.

"Incoming." Jordan pointed toward Freddie and Rebekah heading toward them. "Hopefully, they didn't backslide into their old bible-thumping ways."

"Shh," Sam hushed Jordan and glared at him in a friendly way. And actually, Sam wished the same thing. About five months earlier, at the winter formal, Freddie, Rebekah, and a few of their other friends had harassed them by spitting out Bible verses and unfiltered hate. It wasn't until Lisa helped Freddie while he was having a seizure later that same night that they started to see Sam and her friends as actual non-demonic people. Sam stood up. She would take the brunt, just in case they had done some backsliding.

"Hi, you guys," Freddie said and hugged Sam quickly. Sam noticed that he had grown his strawberry-blonde hair out a little bit. It looked good on him, not as severe. "Glad to see you're all here in force. Good for you." He nodded at everyone at the table. "How are you, Lisa?"

"I'm fine, thanks," Lisa said.

Before Lisa could say anything more, Ronnie blurted out, "Where's your entourage?"

"We, uh, parted ways," Freddie said.

"It's a good thing," Rebekah added.

"I want to thank you guys again for opening my eyes," Freddie said. "I was blindly following some wrong, really wrong, information coming from the pulpit of my church."

"We're going to the Unitarian Church now," Rebekah said, reaching for Freddie's arm.

"Yeah, my parents hate it."

Jordan laughed. "Your parents hate that you're going to church. That's a new one."

Freddie grimaced. "They hate that I'm going to the *wrong* church."

"Well," Lisa said, "I, for one, appreciate your open-mindedness."

"It's mutual, Lisa," Freddie said, his face showing real emotion.

Lisa stood up and gave them both a hug. "Thanks for being a couple of good ones, you guys."

They nodded and headed back toward their table, clearly moved by the exchange.

"People can change, can't they?" Lisa said and sat back down.

Just then, two girls in the junior class came up to Sam.

"Samantha Rose," the taller of the two said, "we want to thank you and all of your friends for being so brave and out and open." She reached for the other girl's hand. "We're going to be out and open, too, from now on."

The table erupted in clapping and cheering.

"Good for you," Sam said and hugged them both. "It's a little scary, but it's much harder to stay in the closet."

The shorter girl rolled her eyes and said, "Tell me about it."

"Do you want to join us?" Sam said, even though there wasn't much room at their full table.

"No, no," the taller girl said. "Thank you. We're with some friends who are here for support." She pointed to a table near the DJ booth. Their friends waved at Sam's table, and they all waved back.

"Well, good luck, and if you ever want to talk or whatever, let us know." Sam's gesture included Susie and Ronnie. "Okay?"

"That's sweet, Samantha Rose. Thank you." They returned to their table, and Sam sat down wide-eyed.

"Wow," was all Sam could say. "I don't even know their names. Do any of you know who they are?"

Everyone at their table shook their heads. "I'm clueless as usual," Ronnie quipped. "But, apparently, they know who *we* are."

A new song blasted from the DJ's speakers. "That's us." Susie leaped up from her chair. Marlee was right behind. Sam chuckled. Those two loved to dance.

"Dance?" Sam said to Lisa.

"But of course." Lisa stood up and said to the rest of the table, "Come on, everybody."

"Ha ha," Ronnie laughed an evil laugh. "It's time for the queers to show these people how it's done."

~~~

Sam was tired on the ride to Susie's house after the prom but not exhausted tired. She looked forward to spending some quality time with just her core friends. The four friends said their goodnights to Cassie and headed up the stairs to Susie's room over the garage.

"Are you sure your mother doesn't mind?" Sam sneaked a peek toward the main house.

"She doesn't know I exist anymore," Susie answered matter-of-factly. "I think she wrote me off like she did my father."

"I'm sorry, sweetie," Marlee said and hugged Susie from behind as Susie unlocked the door to her room.

"It is what it is," Susie said.

Sam frowned. It sounded like Susie had given up.

"Okay," Susie said once they were all inside. "Let's all change."

They took turns using Susie's bathroom to change. Sam came out of the bathroom feeling so much more comfortable in sweats and a t-shirt. Marlee was just getting off the phone with her mother.

"She said I could stay!" Marlee squealed. She and Susie jumped around excitedly.

Sam's eyes bugged out. "Sus, you're positive you had that Marlee-staying-over talk with your mother?"

"Yep," Susie said. "She said I was eighteen and welcomed me to do whatever I wanted. Something like that."

"Finally," Marlee gushed. "A real sleepover in East Valley."

"Whoa, you guys," Sam said. "This is life-changing. So, how about you give me your car keys, Sus, and I'll drive Lisa home. I'm not saying we won't stop somewhere along the way to, uh…."

"Watch submarine races," Lisa finished.

Marlee snorted at Lisa's joke. "My catcher is a comedian."

"Uh, no, you guys," Susie said. "Marlee and I are the ones going for a drive. You two are going to stay right here and…."

"Watch submarine races," Marlee finished.

"Yes," Susie agreed. "My bed has fresh sheets, or you can go to your usual corner. If you want, I have extra pillows, sheets, and a blanket in the closet."

"Susie," Sam said, "we don't want to put you out."

"It's prom night, bestie," Susie said. "And, besides, you guys would do it for us."

"We would," Lisa said. "Sam, if we're relatively quick, I'll still make it home in time for my curfew."

Sam's eyes grew wide. "Why are you two still here?" Sam said to Susie. "We'll take our usual corner, you guys. That way, you'll have the green light as soon as you get back."

"Text me when we can come home," Susie said, slipping on shoes. She threw Marlee a pair of Crocs.

"You got it, bestie."

As soon as Susie and Marlee left and they couldn't hear Susie's car anymore, they scurried around, setting up a makeshift love nest in their usual corner near the weight bench.

They lay down together and kissed each other gently. Before it escalated, Lisa pulled back and brushed a lock of hair off Sam's forehead. She had to do it three times until it finally stayed put. Sam chuckled.

"I have to be honest, Sam," Lisa said. "Hearing you guys talk about college makes me feel a little empty. I want to spend every moment with you before you have to leave in August."

"I'm going to miss you something fierce," Sam said, "but I'm going to get home as often as possible. And, I'm telling you right now that I'm not going to give you a speech about how if you meet someone new, you can be with that person. Hell, no, Lisa."

"I won't want to meet anyone new, Sam. I worry about you, though, surrounded by all those college babes."

"Not going to happen. Ever," Sam said emphatically and meant it. Lisa was her world.

"I'm happy to hear you say that, Ms. Payton."

Sam found herself hypnotized by Lisa's simmering gaze. She lost all her breath in one feverish moan as Lisa kissed her passionately. Lisa pulled back, her brown eyes lusty. She moved back in for a quick brush of her lips on Sam's. Sam touched Lisa's face softly, still feeling Lisa's kisses on her lips. The desire in Lisa's eyes was intoxicating. Lisa sat up, rolled Sam on her back, and kissed her again.

"That's it," Sam said, gasping. "I'm not going to college."

"Shh." Lisa put a finger over Sam's lips. "It's prom night." She kissed Sam once and began a tantalizing exploration of Sam's body.

Chapter Fourteen
Notre Petit Ange

Sam and Lisa sat in the waiting room of the surgical wing at the hospital. They had both taken the day off from school for Sam's mother's lumpectomy. Sam was antsy. All this waiting and not knowing what was going on was the worst.

Sam chewed on her nails. It had already been an entire hour. Was everything okay? Were they going to have to do a second or even third procedure to clear the margins? Sam's breath shortened as she thought of all the possibilities, but then a strong arm went around her.

"Hey," Lisa said, "let's get a soda from the vending machines down the hall."

Sam looked up, seeing love and compassion on Lisa's face. She didn't want to do something as trivial as buying a soda when her mother was undergoing life-altering surgery and was about to say so when Lisa pulled up on her arm. "C'mon. You need to walk."

Lisa told her mother, Helene, Sam's father, and Sam's mother's friend Mrs. Worthington where they were going and asked if anyone wanted anything. No one did, so she ushered Sam by the elbow down the hall.

"I'm glad my mother let me take today off from school," Lisa said.

"Me, too," Sam said. "I'm happy your mom came. That support is nice."

"Bridget goes to preschool two days a week now, and Mama made today one of those days. Of course, once summer's here, I'll be watching the kids full time."

"We'll watch the kids together. I'm spending every minute with you."

"And you'll be spending time with your mother, too," Lisa reminded.

"Yes, of course," Sam said. How in the world had she forgotten that fast? "I'm just going to split myself in two. Hey, I have an idea. What if you bring the kids out to the house to go swimming?" They had reached the alcove where the vending machines were. Neither of them made a move to put money in any of the machines.

"Ooh, I have another idea," Sam said excitedly. "We can hire a swimming instructor and teach the kids how to swim over the summer."

"See?" Lisa said and ran a hand down Sam's cheek. "That's why I love you so much."

Sam felt her cheeks burning.

"So, we've never had that, uh, in-depth conversation." Lisa looked down at the concrete floor. "There's never been a good time."

"Yes, Helene is my biological mother," Sam said, knowing precisely what conversation Lisa was referring to. She explained how her mother couldn't have children, so they'd hired a surrogate, even though it was illegal in New York state.

"That's why you were born in Arizona," Lisa said, nodding.

"Everyone back home thought mother was actually pregnant,

but when they couldn't pull off the ruse any longer, they all went to Phoenix and hid out."

"Hmm," Lisa said, "how are they going to explain that lie?"

"The Payton family knows how to spin things," Sam said with a shrug.

"So, Helene is your *real* mother," Lisa said as if she were still trying to wrap her head around it.

"Mother is also my real mother," Sam said softly.

"Oh, believe me, I know how that goes," Lisa said. "I never call Lawrence Brown, Sr. my step-father, even though he is. I just called him Papa. And William is my bio-dad. They're both my fathers."

Sam wrapped Lisa in a hug. "We have three fathers and three mothers between us. We are overrun with family."

"And Helene's niece, Alicia, is really your first cousin," Lisa said excitedly. She must have been realizing it for the first time. "And Helene's sister Chantal is your aunt."

"Yeah, I only met Chantal once."

"I told my mom, you know, about Helene," Lisa said. "I hope that was okay. She got it out of me the day I found out. I was kind of quiet when I got home."

"That's fine. Daddy said we're being open and honest now. That's a real change for us Paytons."

"Girls," Lisa's mother called from down the hallway. "The surgeon will be out in a minute."

"Yikes." Sam reached for Lisa's hand. "C'mon. Hurry." They practically ran back to the waiting room.

As Sam and Lisa walked up, Dr. Kulkarni was just coming out from behind the electronic sliding doors.

Sam was holding her breath.

"Breathe," Lisa said softly.

Sam breathed, but shallowly.

"Mimi is doing fine. We removed the tumor and were able to clear the margins in the first go around."

"Fantastic," Helene said.

"You got it all?" Lisa asked.

"Yes," Dr. Kulkarni answered. "In a few minutes, Mimi will be heading to her assigned room for a one-night precautionary stay. But you can go up and visit right away. She might be a little out of it and disoriented from the general anesthesia, but that will pass. I expect a good recovery if she follows up on her aftercare. I fully expect all of you to assist in that." She took a step back as if to go and then said, "Questions?" She looked at the six faces in front of her.

"Not yet," Sam's father said. "I'm sure we'll have a ton later."

"My head nurse will meet you in the room with a list of post-surgery instructions."

Sam's father stuck his hand out and said, "Thank you, doctor."

"Of course," Dr. Kulkarni said. "Now, if you'll excuse me, I need to finish up my notes on this case."

"Thank you," Sam called after her. The others echoed her thanks.

They headed to the assigned room and found Sam's mother sleeping peacefully in the oversized private room. Dr. Kulkarni's head nurse was a no-nonsense woman in her forties with short salt-and-pepper hair. She ushered them to a corner of the room away from Sam's mother, hoping not to wake her, and gave them the post-surgery instructions. The nurse quickly figured out who would be the primary caregiver and handed the printout to Helene as they read them over together.

"Her shoulder will be stiff after surgery, so don't let her get upset about that. During the first week, you need to baby her. Make sure she lays low. No excessive activity, which means all hands are on deck helping." The authoritative nurse looked every one of them in the eye when she said that, and Sam found herself nodding. "She'll need physical therapy to increase her range of motion and to strengthen her muscles."

"We've already informed Stefan," Sam's father said. "He is a licensed physical therapist and has been Mimi's personal trainer for years."

"Oh, good," the nurse said. "He's someone she already knows. The trust is there. I recommend that she sleep clutching a pillow, and I would get a surgical bra that closes in the front. This way, she won't have to lift her arms or strain anything. Some women simply go without a bra for a while if they're small enough. They let the girls hang free, so to speak."

Sam exchanged a smile with Lisa but didn't dare look at her father. No, that would have been too awkward.

The nurse then gave Helene another printout about wound care and a card with Sam's mother's follow-up appointment.

"What else can I answer for you?" the nurse asked. When there weren't any questions, she showed them where the nurse call button was if they needed anything and reiterated that they could call her with questions anytime. She said she would get back to them within a twenty-four-hour window. She reminded them to call 9-1-1 if there was a true emergency.

Sam's blood pressure spiked at the nurse's last comment. Would they need to call 9-1-1? Was there a chance of an emergency?

Lisa reached for her hand and squeezed. It was her signal that

Sam needed to stop the panic in her head and breathe. And then something weird happened. Sam caught an exchange of glances between Lisa and her mother. They were communicating something. Oh, no, was Lisa going home?

"Um, everybody," Lisa said quietly to the group, "I have an appointment downstairs, so my mother and I are going to leave for a little while."

"What appointment?" Sam said. "Is everything okay?" Did Lisa have a medical problem? Is that why Lisa's mother was here, too?

"Sam, Sam, Sam, don't panic." Lisa squeezed the hand she was still holding. "I have an appointment at the Rose Salon downstairs."

"You're going to get your hair done?" Sam was really confused. "Right now?" Lisa's mother did hair. Maybe Lisa was going to get her split ends cut off or something.

"Sam, I'm donating my hair."

Sam blinked, not comprehending the words Lisa had spoken.

"Oh, Lisa," Helene said, pulling Lisa away from Sam and engulfing her in one of her famous hugs. "That is so wonderful, but are you sure?" Tears were filling Helene's eyes.

"I am," Lisa's own eyes were tearing up.

Sam looked around, and the only dry eyes in the room were hers.

"That is a wonderful gesture, Lisa," Mrs. Worthington said, giving Lisa a hug of her own.

"What's happening?" Sam asked, clearly confused.

"*Mon petit hibou*," Helene said, "Lisa is going to have her ponytail cut off so it can be made into a wig for cancer patients."

"Your hair?" Sam said, looking at Lisa's long tresses. This was the hair that Sam loved running her hands through and braiding and unbraiding, the hair that was almost a third person in their relationship.

Lisa nodded, and then Sam finally understood. Lisa was going to have her long hair cut off to donate it. Sam swallowed hard as emotion closed her throat. "Your hair." Sam reached over and petted Lisa's ponytail. "Can I—" Sam cleared her throat and tried again. "Can I talk to you first?"

Lisa nodded, and Sam pulled her out of the room and didn't stop until they were in the large accessible stall in the bathroom by the elevators.

Wordlessly, Sam wrapped Lisa in a hug and cried into her chest. "Baby, your hair. It's a part of you."

"I know." Lisa rubbed Sam's back and kissed the top of Sam's head. "I know."

"Are you sure?" Sam pulled back and searched Lisa's eyes for meaning.

"Yes, I am," Lisa said. "My parents and I discussed it, and they're okay with it. Your family, Sam, can donate money and things. My family doesn't have money or things. We have each other, but I'm not donating Bridget."

Sam chuckled. "Yes, please don't."

"But the one thing I *can* donate is this." Lisa pulled her long black ponytail from behind her and stroked the ends. "My hair will help someone, Sam."

Sam sighed and smiled as more tears welled up in her eyes. Sam stroked the hair Lisa was holding. She pulled the ends up to her face and rubbed them against her cheek. "I'm going to miss this thing."

"I know."

Sam kissed Lisa once and then laid her head back down on her chest. "I love you, Lisa Anne Brown."

"I love you, too, Samantha Rose Payton."

~~~

Lisa sat in the chair in the Rose Salon, surrounded by Sam, Lisa's mother, Helene, the stylist they had seen their first day at the hospital, and the receptionist. A dozen or more pictures had already been taken of Lisa pre-cut, and it was time for the actual deed.

The stylist explained the donation process to them. "We use the Pantene Beautiful Lengths program because they donate the wigs to the American Cancer Society Wig Bank. They service both adult cancer patients and kids with cancer."

Sam's heart swelled that Lisa was making such a noble gesture.

"There are other donation programs like Locks of Love and Wigs for Kids, but we've had great success with the Pantene program. Now, the hair must be at least eight inches–"

"No problem there," Lisa's mother interrupted with a laugh.

"None," the stylist said with a smile, clearly impressed at the length. "And it must be free of bleaches, dyes, or other chemicals. There must be no hair product or sprays in it." She ran her hand down the length of Lisa's hair. "This is perfect. And because this is so long, I'm going to put a third band in the middle, just to make sure it all stays together."

She put the hairband on and picked up a hefty pair of scissors. "I understand that Mom is doing the honors?"

Lisa's mother nodded and took the scissors. "Unless Samantha Rose wants to?" She held the scissors out toward Sam.

"Oh, no, no, no, Mrs. Brown. Not me." A chuckle went around

the circle of women at Sam's wide-eyed expression. "You do it." Sam looked at Lisa. "Ready, baby?"

"As I'll ever be. Go ahead, Mama." Lisa swallowed hard.

Lisa's mother sighed, held onto the ponytail with one hand, and placed the scissors above the highest hair band. The receptionist took pictures with Lisa's phone. "One, two, three," Lisa's mother said in warning. She had to cut four times until the ponytail came loose. She held it up to a rousing round of cheering and applause.

Sam's breath caught in her throat just as Helene's strong arm went around her waist. Bless Helene for knowing she'd need her strength at that exact moment.

"Are you okay, Sam?" Lisa said from the chair.

"I don't know," Sam walked over and ran her fingers through Lisa's now short-cropped hair. "It's so short, baby."

"I know," Lisa looked at herself in the mirror.

"It was like watching your mother cut off your arm or something."

A collective chuckle reminded Sam that they weren't alone. She cleared her throat and stepped back.

"But you know what?" Lisa turned and faced Sam. "It'll grow back."

Sam breathed easier. "Right. I hadn't thought of that."

"Now we measure this bad girl," the stylist said and laid the length of the ponytail against a permanently affixed yardstick. "It's a record. I knew it would be. Twenty-four inches."

There was a collective "Wow" from the group, and then the stylist said, "So, now I'll place the ponytail in a zipper-locked bag, seal it tight, and ship it off to Minnesota."

"I've never been to Minnesota," Lisa said.

"And now part of you will," the stylist said with a chuckle. "Thank you for trusting us with this amazing gift, Lisa. You are a generous soul."

Lisa's cheeks tinged red as she acknowledged the compliment.

"Okay, daughter," Lisa's mother said. "Early American bedhead?"

"Go for it."

Lisa's mother cut and styled Lisa's hair, and Sam was amazed at how different Lisa looked. Lisa almost looked older with her tousled just-out-of-bed look. Her high cheekbones stood out more prominently, and her luscious lips begged to be kissed. Tingles were forming deep in Sam's core just looking at her transformed girlfriend.

At this point, there wasn't a dry eye in the salon. A small crowd had gathered around them. Lisa stood up and hugged her mother. Helene then pulled Lisa into another one of her motherly hugs and cupped her chin. "You are special, *mon petit ange.*"

Lisa smiled, probably having no clue the pet name Helene had called her, but Sam thought it was true. Lisa was a little angel.

Helene released Lisa, who then flew into Sam's arms.

"You look so sexy," Sam micro-whispered in Lisa's ear.

"Really?" Lisa said.

"Mmm," was all Sam could manage. She had to pull out of the embrace because all she wanted to do was kiss Lisa senseless. She reached down to hold Lisa's hand and turned just in time to catch their mothers talking.

Helene said to Lisa's mother, "That's a beautiful daughter you have there."

Lisa's mother smiled knowingly. "I was thinking the same about your daughter. Yes, your *daughter*, Helene. I saw the resemblance immediately when I met you at that summer softball game last August. I knew the word *nanny* wasn't right for you. I kept it to myself and just wondered."

"I'm glad it's out now," Helene said. "It was hard being in the closet for so long."

The two women smiled at each other and exchanged a meaningful look.

"Let's have tea sometime," Helene said.

"Yes, let's." Lisa's mother let her gaze settle over Lisa and Sam. "I believe we have a lot in common."

"Yes, we do."

~~~

They hurried back to Sam's mother's hospital room to find her somewhat awake. Sam's father and Mrs. Worthington stepped back to let the four women get closer. Sam and Helene gave Sam's mother hugs, and Helene asked her how she was feeling.

"So far, so good, I imagine," Sam's mother said and then closed her eyes momentarily. It was obvious that the anesthesia hadn't quite left her system.

"Mother," Sam said, "the surgeon said she got it all. I'm so pleased."

"Good, good."

"Mother?"

"Hmm?" Sam's mother squinted to focus on her daughter. She, clearly, wasn't quite awake.

"Mother, I want you to see what Lisa did." Sam gestured for Lisa to come closer so her mother could see her. "Lisa donated her long hair to make wigs for cancer patients."

Sam's mother looked confused at first, but then her eyes widened as they focused on Lisa. "You...." Sam's mother reached out for Lisa, who moved closer to the bed. Sam gladly stepped back to give her access.

Just as Sam's mother touched Lisa's cheek, the sun peeked out from behind the clouds flooding the room with light. "You are a veritable angel." One of Sam's mother's genuine smiles emerged. She lowered her hand from Lisa's cheek and grasped Lisa's hand. "You're an angel. An angel sent down to me." Sam's mother sighed and closed her eyes.

Once again, everyone, including Sam and Lisa, teared up.

Sam's mother said, "Take care of Samantha Rose. She is a sensitive child."

"I will," Lisa said and wiped at her tears with her free hand. "I already do."

"And tell her I love her. I don't think she knows."

"I will," Lisa said, her voice choked with emotion.

Sam's mother clung fiercely to Lisa's hand. A small contented sigh escaped, and then, with her eyes still closed, she said, "Remind Gerald to eat. He gets so busy, he forgets."

"Okay, I will." Lisa grinned at Sam's father, who smiled back warmly.

"And, Helene," Sam's mother said sleepily. "She is a godsend. She has always been Sam's true mother. Tell her it's okay to be that." Sam's mother's eyes opened, and she looked straight at Lisa. "Will you tell her? Tell her it's okay."

"Yes, of course, I will," Lisa said, her voice soft but choked with emotion.

"Thank you, my angel." Sam's mother released Lisa's hand and closed her eyes and slept.

"Yes," Helene said to Lisa. "*Notre petit ange,* thank you."

Chapter Fifteen

Neanderthals

Ronnie grabbed Sam's cell phone across the lunch table. "Let me see those pictures again." He scrolled through the photos of Lisa before and after her hair donation.

"She looks so hot with this uber-short hair, Sam," Ronnie said. "I don't know why you're even in school today."

"I can't wait to see her in person," Susie said. She opened her lunch bag and then opened her AP Enviro notebook. With the AP Enviro exam two days away, Susie had taken to studying any moment she got. "Too bad we've got three games this week, not to mention my two AP exams."

"I know," Sam said. "I can't believe we have an away game at Southbridge today. I wanted to be there when my mother got home from the hospital."

"Helene will text you, won't she?"

Sam grinned. "You mean my *maman* will text me about how my 'mother' is doing?"

"This is really going to get confusing, isn't it?" Susie said. "You're sure you don't want to stick to calling her Helene?"

"I'm sure. She and I were both denied the title for eighteen years, Sus. I want that for us now."

A silence settled over the lunch table for a moment until Sam said. "Are you ready for your AP Calculus exam tomorrow morning, Sus?"

"Marlee's the most amazing tutor, so yeah."

"I'm sure a lot of 'tutoring' went on Sunday," Sam teased. She used air quotes around the word tutoring.

"Tutoring in the ways of love, maybe," Ronnie teased.

"We did math. Just math," Susie insisted. When both Sam and Ronnie shot her doubtful expressions, she confessed, "Okay, okay, we went down in the basement for a while, but we just made out. I promise. Her mother and Bob were right upstairs."

Ronnie high-fived Sam, who then took out an imaginary bill from her imaginary wallet to pay Ronnie for an imaginary bet.

"You guys suck," Susie said.

"Who sucks?" Karl asked and plopped his lunch tray on the table.

"You do," Sam said. "For not going to the prom."

"Phht," Karl spat. "And watch Alivia fawn all over her new gal-pal. No thanks."

"I'm sorry, Karl," Sam said. "I didn't know you still had feelings for her."

"I don't. Not really, but it's a big blow to a guy's ego to get dumped for a girl. Like I wasn't man enough or something."

"You'll find somebody new," Susie said. "Someone who's gonna see how awesome you are."

Sam's phone chimed an incoming text. She grabbed her phone from Ronnie's clutches before he could read the text, which she knew would be from Lisa. Sam maturely stuck her tongue out at him.

"Not your most attractive gesture, Samantha Rose," Ronnie said.

Sam stuck her tongue out at him again and read her text. "I woke up in the middle of the night," Lisa texted, "and couldn't figure out what was wrong. I had to wake up completely to remember that I had no hair. My head feels so light. It's weird."

"It looks sexy," Sam texted back.

"Thanks! Everyone, even people I don't know, are freaking out about my hair. Mostly good."

"That's great, baby. What bad things?"

After a moment, Lisa's return text chimed in. "Some whispering behind hands. A couple of junior girls made faces and pointed."

"Sorry, baby. Ignoramuses."

"Exactly."

Susie nudged Sam on the arm. "What's up?"

"Just some assholes at Lisa's school. They don't like her haircut."

"Do they know why she cut it?" Karl asked. "Because it's kind of epic."

"They probably don't," Sam said. "People just want to criticize or kick you when you're different. Assholes."

Sam texted back. "Assholes."

"No kidding."

"Stay strong, little angel."

"Don't call me that," Lisa texted. "It makes me uncomfortable."

"Sorry. I won't. But you are."

Sam texted back and forth with Lisa throughout the rest of the lunch period despite Susie's best efforts to get Sam involved in studying for their big AP Enviro exam in two days.

187

On their way to their AP Enviro class after lunch, Susie said in all seriousness, "Sam, are you up to speed on the natural biogeochemical cycles?"

Sam burst out laughing.

"Why are you laughing?" Susie asked, a confused look on her face.

"Because you're an adorable nerd." Sam held the classroom door open for her friend and then scurried in before the other students could take advantage of her door-holding generosity.

"Thank you?" Susie said, the confused expression still etched in her features.

They sat in their usual seats, Sam in the front, Susie right behind her, and Karl behind Susie. Susie turned in her seat and said to Karl, "I have a game tomorrow, so I won't be at the meeting."

Karl didn't respond right away. "I know what you're hinting at, but I'm not going back to AA. I don't think I'm like you. I'm just going to slow down. You know? I'm only going to drink on the weekends. And I definitely won't drive drunk or even buzzed. But I, uh, I like drinking, Susie."

"Me, too," Susie said quickly. "But I have to respect what you want to do. Just know I'm here if you want to talk about anything."

"Cool," Karl said with a nod. "Thanks for being concerned about me. I think I'm okay."

Ms. Armstrong called the sixth-period class to order by flicking the classroom lights. It was an effective way to get thirty teenagers' attention without having to shout over them.

Ms. Armstrong pushed her glasses back up the bridge of her nose and said, "You have all the tools you need to do well on Thursday afternoon. I've taught you the entire curriculum in depth.

And remember, if it says to explain or justify your answer, then explain using concepts from class. Don't merely state your opinion. Back it up with facts. And speaking of facts…." She turned on the projector, and the title page to a PowerPoint quiz popped up. "This is not for a grade but will give you an idea of what topics to review. But before that, I want to send each of you a personal message."

She started with Sam. Ms. Armstrong used no words, only kind but firm eyes telling Sam to take this exam seriously. When she moved on to Susie, their teacher's eyes conveyed a kindred spirit vibe—almost like Ms. Armstrong knew Susie would ace the exam. Sam looked down and vowed to put some real studying time in. When and how she would do that was a mystery, but she would try.

Sam hadn't ever looked at her teachers in a personal way before, but as Ms. Armstrong continued her silent messages to each student, Sam's heart filled. Ms. Armstrong exuded confidence and strength from her smooth honey-brown hair pulled back into a ponytail, glasses, and poised demeanor. But at the same time, she also exuded a vulnerability that Sam had never picked up on before as she broadcasted her emotions to each one of her advanced placement students. It was a powerful few minutes. Sam hoped that one day, she, too would find a career that would make her feel the way Ms. Armstrong must be feeling at this moment.

"Get out some paper and a writing instrument," Ms. Armstrong instructed once she finished her silent messages. "There are twenty questions. Let's see how you do."

Her teacher waited until the paper shuffling and can-I-borrow-a-pen moments were complete.

Susie smacked Sam on the shoulder when the first slide read, "Explain the Ammonification process in the natural biogeochemical cycle."

"See?" Susie whispered to Sam. "It's important."

"Okay, okay," Sam said and put both hands up in defense. She vaguely remembered that ammonification had something to do with nitrogen and microorganisms, but she couldn't put it together. Now she knew what Susie would be doing on the bus ride to Southbridge that afternoon. Yep, she would be tutoring Sam in AP Environmental Science. Hopefully, it wasn't a case of too little, too late.

~~~

Sam's head was spinning with environmental science facts when she stepped off the bus at Southbridge High School. It was only a forty-minute ride, shorter than her usual drive to Clarksonville, but Susie had filled her head with so much science that Sam was positively overflowing. One thing she realized as Susie helped her was that Susie positively loved science. She loved thinking about it and talking about it, just like Sam loved playing the violin and learning new music. Sam couldn't believe Susie's mother had never taken the time to understand Susie's passion for all things science. No, Susie's mother wanted her to become a nurse. Nursing was a noble profession, for sure, Sam thought, but it wasn't for everybody, and Sam didn't think it suited Susie at all.

"You'll be lucky if coach starts you today," Susie said as they walked to the visitors' dugout.

"Why?" Sam said.

"You weren't at practice yesterday."

"Oh, right. My mother having surgery was infinitely more

important." Sam kicked a pebble across the parking lot.

"You know that, and I know that, but does Coach Gellar?"

"It'll be whatever it'll be, Sus." Sam held the door to the dugout open for her teammates.

"You sound wise today or something, Sam," Abby, the East Valley shortstop, said.

"Must be her alter-ego," Susie joked.

"Shut up, Sus," Sam said and laughed.

They sat down on the bench in the dugout to put on their cleats.

"Now, don't get mad at me, Sam, but I think you've just been going through the motions in that class. You've been doing your homework but not absorbing it."

Sam wasn't mad. She was just surprised at her friend's frank assessment. She nodded her agreement. "You may be right. I've been doing it to get it done, so I can move on to the next class and do the same thing."

"I bet cash money that you don't do that in your Strings class."

Sam laughed. "No, and I hate when other people do."

Susie looked at Sam with a grin. She raised her eyebrows, asking if Sam understood the point she was making.

"Got it, friend," Sam said. "I got it. Now let's go kick some Southbridge butt."

Susie growled and said, "We beat 'em once, and we can beat 'em again."

Abby groaned, "Maybe not. That Bree girl is back."

Sam's eyes grew wide as she looked up to see Bree warming up in the bullpen. Her dyed-blonde hair was pulled back into a tight ponytail, and she was pitching as fast as ever. "How did she ever get out of Juvie?" She turned to Susie. "Don't tell Marlee."

"I have to," Susie said equally as wide-eyed. "But after the game. I'll call her on the way home. *Dios mio*, I can't deal with this right now."

Damn. Just when Susie was feeling strong about something in her life, Bree had to show up again.

The top of the East Valley order was up in the first inning, and Sam stood on deck watching Rachel, the East Valley center fielder, take ten pitches to finally work out a walk from Bree. Bree seemed calm and cool and collected. Maybe her stint in Juvie had changed her. Lisa did say, just the other night, that people could change.

Without a hopeful heart, Sam stepped up to the plate and took the sign from her coach. Sam's instructions were to slap it in the five-six hole. Sam understood why. The shortstop seemed more interested in covering second base if Rachel tried to steal. Rachel was a definite threat. Sam and Rachel were always neck and neck when it came to the number of stolen bases they had each season.

Sam stepped back in the batter's box just as the catcher said, "Heard your father knocked up his mistress. Is that true, princess? Heard you were the result of that."

Sam stepped back out of the box to stop the swirls of anger and confusion going around her head. Suddenly dizzy, she squatted so she wouldn't fall.

"Time," Coach Gellar called and ran over. "Are you okay? What happened?"

Sam stood up. "Yeah, I'm okay."

"Maybe I shouldn't have started you today. Maybe your mother's situation is too much for you to handle."

Sam snapped her head up and looked her coach in the eye like she'd seen her father do to so many of the people he dealt with and said firmly, "I'm fine, Coach." No bitch behind the plate was going to get under her skin. Oh, no. She was a Payton, groomed to hide all emotion and pain. She had just been surprised by the catcher's taunt. The smallest inkling of doubt tried to creep in about the story Helene had told her about her conception, but she refused to let it grow and definitely would not in front of that cretin catcher.

Without another word, Sam stepped back in the box and completely ignored the catcher and everyone else. She even ignored Bree, the one throwing pitches at her. Sam chopped the very first pitch into a perfect high-bouncing slap into the infield gap between shortstop and third. When both she and Rachel made it safely to their respective bases, Sam did an internal happy dance. Abby was up next and would, hopefully, get Rachel in to score. It would be nice to go onto the field with the lead.

Sam stood on first base, watching Coach Gellar for the signs. Abby got the hit-away sign, so that meant Sam was in react mode. She had a runner in front of her, so she needed to watch what Rachel did. She had to make sure she didn't get doubled up on a caught line drive. She had to remember that she did not have to run in the event of an infield fly rule call. All these things and more were ticking through her head when the Southbridge first baseman said, "We heard you look like your father's whore. Is that true, Samantha Rose?"

In true Payton fashion, Sam did not react, but it was hard. That asshole had just called Helene a whore. Who does that? Who does that and gets away with it? Sam looked for Susie in the on-deck circle and focused on her friend. Susie must have sensed her laser beam stare and turned. Susie raised her eyebrows in question, asking if Sam was okay. Sam pressed her lips together and nodded once, indicating that she was okay, even though she was far from it.

Abby sent a shallow pop just over the second baseman's head for a base hit. The ball was too close to the infield to send Rachel home from third, but all runners were safe, allowing Susie to get up to bat with the bases loaded.

"Is it really true that your father has a harem?" the Southbridge shortstop said to Sam as the ball came back in the infield.

Somehow, Sam managed to relax. If this was the Southbridge team's strategy for beating East Valley today, they would have to try harder. The bases were loaded. There were no outs. Their strategy wasn't working.

It took one evil smile and one obviously intentional pitch from Bree to hit Susie in the back and force in East Valley's first run. Susie was brave and didn't rub the spot, but she looked over at Sam on third base with more questions in her eyes. Sam just rolled hers to say that Bree hadn't changed one iota. Susie just shook her head, indicating, "No, she has not."

The third baseman stepped over, and Sam cringed, waiting to hear what filth she would spew. She looked Sam right in the eye and said, "I'm sorry about my teammates, Samantha Rose. They're Neanderthals, and I don't know why they listen to Bree. I tried to stop them, but they started making fun of me, too. I'm sorry to be part of this team, and I want to quit, but that means they win. I love softball. You know?"

"Me, too. And thanks," Sam said and wasn't sure why she even bothered to confide in this stranger, but added, "For the record, my biological mother was a surrogate, not a mistress, not a—" She couldn't say the other word. "Not anything else."

"I know. And, again, I'm sorry." The third baseman backed up into her position and pounded her glove.

Keisha smashed a double, clearing the bases with no outs. Southbridge's hate-campaign strategy wasn't working, and by the time the first inning ended, East Valley was leading by a score of 5-0.

Back in the dugout, Susie asked Sam what was happening, but Sam innocently said, "Nothing. No worries." Another Payton trait. Lying. Sam wasn't good at it at all, and she knew that Susie was on to her, but Susie left it at that and ran out to left field. Sam ran to her position at second base and took a moment to breathe.

Although Sam was surrounded by her teammates on the field, she enjoyed the relative solitude her position afforded her. There was no one nearby to whisper crap in her ear. There was no one to tell her what to do or think. She was her own person in total control, commanding her exclusive second base territory.

That is until the players on the opposing team made it to second base, which many of them did throughout the next few innings. Some either ignored Sam or offered her an apologetic glance. A few others, though, offered up some more choice words. Sam did her best to ignore the words 'two mommies,' 'gold digger,' 'bastard,' 'illegitimate,' and one she'd never heard before that almost made her laugh—'born on the wrong side of the blanket.'

Abby overheard one of the comments and walked up to the girl, and said something to her that wiped the smile right off the girl's face. Abby didn't look at Sam or even acknowledge that she'd heard, but Sam was grateful for her shortstop's support.

The bottom of the seventh, and hopefully final, inning arrived, and Sam could not have been more grateful. Not only had the game been physically grueling, but it had been emotionally grueling, especially when she thought about her mother coming home from the hospital that afternoon. She'd had strict instructions from both Helene and Susie not to check her phone during the game, and she honored that. But the second the game was over, she was going to power that thing on and call Helene.

The East Valley Panthers were leading by a score of 12-8 when Bree stepped into the batter's box for the third time in the game. Sam had gotten lucky the first two times since Bree hadn't reached base at all. Bree was probably chomping at the bit to comment on Sam's parentage, and Sam was just fine not hearing it. In fact, Sam had already decided to sit out the after-game high-five line altogether. There would be no telling what else those assholes from Southbridge would say, and she didn't want any of her teammates to hear a word of it. It wasn't fair to lay the Payton family baggage on her teammates.

Bree stood in the batter's box, looking like any other batter. But Sam knew better. The girl mimicking an athlete was pure evil. From her position in the field, Sam scoured the stands for the parole officer that had hauled Bree away the last time. No matter how many times she scanned, she didn't see the burly woman. Sam also noticed that not a single one of the people in the home stands cheered for Bree when she was at bat. Only a handful of teammates in the home dugout cheered. The rest looked at their feet or were busy retying their cleats.

Mary's first two pitches were in the dirt for balls one and two. No, no, no, Sam pleaded in her head. Don't walk her. Bree rested the bat on her shoulder, clearly sending the message that she wasn't going to swing until she got a strike. Sam's stomach clenched when Mary walked Bree in four pitches.

Sam wasn't sure why she did it, but she turned to look at Bree standing on first base. She shivered at the purely evil grin Bree shot her. All at once, Sam was sure that Bree's sole agenda was to wreck Sam somehow. Bree had punched her the last time they tangled, resulting in a black eye for Sam, but this time Bree had taken to sneaky verbal warfare. Sam hoped beyond hope that Bree never made it to second base.

Her hopes were dashed when Abby signaled for Sam to cover second base in the event the runner on first tried to steal. It quickly became a slow-motion bad dream from Mary's pitch to Bree exploding off first base to the batter swinging late, trying to ensure a successful steal. Sam was having an out-of-body moment when she ran over to cover second base. She put her glove up big as a target for Baxter, her catcher behind the plate. Baxter rifled the ball toward Sam. Sam distantly watched herself catch the ball and apply the tag on Bree's foot. Bree was out by a mile, and the umpire called it so.

Sam was about to step back, but a hand reached up and grabbed her glove arm. A well-placed kick connected with her shin, and Sam went down on top of Bree. Despite the piercing pain in her shin, Sam didn't make a sound. It was as if none of it was really happening to her. It wasn't real.

Bree held on to her and growled in Sam's ear, "I heard your giant girlfriend was a gift from Daddy's harem. Did he get tired of fucking her? Gave you his sloppy seconds? Does she fuck you as good as she fucked your fath–"

Sam shot back into her body as her right fist connected with Bree's face. She pulled her other arm free and pummeled Bree with punch after punch after punch. Left, then right, then left. Bree didn't stand a chance. Even when Abby pulled her off and Susie held her arms behind her, Sam struggled to break free and finish the job.

Bree was still breathing.

A sharp slap to her face knocked her out of her fury. "What the fuck, Susie?" Sam rubbed her cheek.

"Hey, bestie?" Susie said, her dark eyes glaring. "I'm going to keep holding you because I think you've lost your mind."

"Let go."

"No," Susie said. "You're not thinking right."

"Why did you hit me?"

"To knock sense into you."

Coach Gellar bellowed, "Get her off the field."

"C'mon." Susie pulled Sam toward the dugout.

Reality crashed in as she let Susie guide her. "Oh, shit. What did I do?" She stopped abruptly, and Susie almost lost her grip on her. Sam turned toward Bree, who was now standing up and holding a towel to her bloody nose.

"She'll be all right," Susie said. "I heard her coach say nothing was broken. She just has a bloody nose and will have some bruises."

"A black eye, maybe?" Sam asked with a hopeful grin. When Susie didn't reply or even smile, Sam added, "Ahh, well, a girl can dream."

Susie scoffed. "C'mon, I have to deliver you to the dugout. You're playing time today is over. The umpire threw you both out of the game."

"Good." Sam was relieved.

Chapter Sixteen
Fam Four

It had been four whole days since Sam had taken her rage out on Bree. And during those four days, Sam carried around a mixture of shame, embarrassment, and even fear about her uncontrolled fury. Everyone kept trying to get her to talk about it, but she didn't know what to say. She didn't even know what to say to Dr. Boyle, her on-again-off-again psychiatrist. All she told him was that when you reach a breaking point…you break.

She wanted to forget about it, but the kids at school kept asking her, and once again, Samantha Rose Payton was the center of attention at East Valley High School. Some people thought she relished the spotlight and did things, even whacky things, to stay in it. These people didn't know her at all, did they? No, not at all. They believed what they wanted to believe. She was not the "badass" that Ronnie now referred to her as or a vigilante, as some of the other kids said. The only one who could empathize was Karl. He was the only one who said, "It's not going to be easy to live with it, Sam." He would know. He beat up his cousin, Dirk, after discovering that Dirk had sexually assaulted Susie.

But she had to stuff all that deep down because it was prom time again. She put on her best smiles at Lisa's house and was glad when the picture-taking and hugs with Lisa's family were finally over. They could finally retreat into the back of Cassie's limo. Sam did not feel like making a public appearance that evening. Far from it. And if she really thought about it, she barely wanted to be with her friends. Besides sleep, all she wanted to do was sit in one of the Tivoli chairs in her parents' bedroom and talk to her mother. Her parents, as far as Sam knew, knew nothing about the altercation. Oh, Helene knew, of course. Coach Gellar had called Helene as soon as they got back to the school. Sam had had to endure a long sit-down with Helene that very night and another the next night. Helene was worried. Obviously. Sam knew that, but really, she just wanted to be left alone.

"Samantha Rose?" Lisa's mother called her away from the group.

Sam cringed when she heard her name. Damn. She had almost gotten away.

Sam walked over to where Lisa's mother stood alone in the driveway. It was far enough away from the others that Sam knew they were about to have a heart-to-heart. There were tears in Lisa's mother's eyes as she pulled Sam into a firm hug. "I meant what I said to your mother. Your mother, Helene." She chuckled. "You have a beautiful soul, Samantha Rose, and you don't have to keep things bottled up."

Sam nodded and then felt Lisa's mother step back. Sam accepted the tissue and dabbed at her tears. Sam wanted to rub the tears away, but she couldn't ruin her mascara and eyeliner. It had taken too long to put herself together for the evening. Sam let out a sigh trying not to cry at Lisa's mother's kindness.

"You are very much a part of this family, warts and all," Lisa's mother said with a grin, "so please know that if you need to let off steam, we'll listen. We'll help in whatever way we can."

Sam nodded again, feeling like the dam that had been threatening to burst was somewhat under control.

"And if you haven't noticed, Lisa's not the only one who loves you. This whole family does."

"I know." Sam swallowed hard against the emotion threatening to come bursting back up. "Thank you." She chuckled at the insane thought percolating in her head. "I think I have three moms now."

Lisa's mother chuckled and threw a guiding arm around Sam's shoulder. "I believe you do. Now go join your friends."

Sam took a step toward the limo but stopped and lunged back to hug Lisa's mother one last time. "Thank you," she said without looking her in the eye.

Sam said goodbye to the kids and Lisa's father and got in the limo where her friends were waiting.

Cassie shut the door, and they were finally alone.

Lisa was wide-eyed. "What was that all about?"

Sam dabbed at her tears and laughed. "I have three moms now."

"Ahh," Lisa said. "No doubt."

"No Doubt. Good band," Marlee said, making everyone chuckle.

The window to the driver's section lowered a couple of inches. "To the prom, my good women?"

"Actually, Cassie," Lisa said, "can you find a quiet spot so the four of us can talk for a while?"

Sam winced. It wasn't over. How could it be?

"Your wish is my command," Cassie said. "I've got a good spot by the Gengo River. It's kind of hidden, and no one's ever there."

"Ooh," Susie teased. "Have you brought your new girlfriend there?"

"I can neither confirm nor deny anything," Cassie said with a grin. "It's right on the edge of Clarksonville. It'll take about five minutes." She pulled the limo away from the curb at Lisa's house. They all waved and called their goodbyes to Lisa's family. Lisa's seven-year-old brother, Lawrence Jr., ran alongside the car until it pulled out onto the main street.

"Lisa," Cassie said through the still-open window, "your hair looks lovely. I am beyond words for your selfless…what? Donation? Act? Gift? Yes, your selfless gift. Sam, you've got a good one."

"I know."

"Don't ever let her go."

Sam just smiled at Cassie, but in her heart, she said, "I won't."

"Oh, girls, by the way, my girlfriend–"

"What's her name again?" Lisa asked with a smirk.

"Good try," Cassie said. "She loved the pictures you sent me from the last prom. She especially liked the one of you guys on the dance floor. You were doing the twist or something?"

"Yeah," Marlee said. "Susie knows all these dances."

"So does Sam," Susie said, "but she's more of an upper-crusty ballroom dance kind of girl."

Sam smiled at her friend, knowing that the smile didn't reach her eyes.

"Hey, Cassie," Marlee said, "will we ever get to meet your new girlfriend?"

"Yes."

"Yes?" Susie said. "That was a definite answer."

"She wants to meet you guys." The sparkle of new love in

Cassie's eyes softened Sam's mood.

"When?" Lisa asked.

"Soon. Very soon. Good things come to those who wait." Cassie said cryptically. "Okay, women, we'll be at your private conversation spot in about two minutes. "I'm hanging up now to give you your privacy." She closed the tinted window between them.

Cassie parked the limo in an unofficial parking area near the west branch of the Gengo River and rolled the window down. "Hit that call button near Sam's knee when you're ready to head to the reception hall."

"Thanks, Cassie," Lisa said. She waited until the window was raised before saying, "Susie, last Saturday, you talked about the four of us as a family. We're kind of a family of our own making. A family of four."

"The Fam Four," Marlee echoed. "I like it."

There were nods of agreement all around. Even Sam thought it fit.

"So, okay, family," Lisa continued, "when one of us is hurting, we're all hurting." She took Sam's hand and gestured for Susie and Marlee to add their hands on top. "Let's talk." Lisa looked at Susie to begin. They had obviously gotten together and worked out a strategy. It felt like an intervention or something. Susie and Marlee sat back, leaving Lisa's the only hand holding hers.

"Sam," Susie said, "at the game on Tuesday, when you were up at bat. That catcher said something to you, and your knees buckled. She said something you haven't repeated."

"I can't, Sus," Sam said and looked down.

"I can respect that," Susie said, "so I'm not asking you to tell us. But then it happened to you again on first base and then a few more times later in the game, didn't it?"

Sam nodded.

Susie said, "You kept looking at me as if you wanted me to help you somehow, but when I asked what was wrong, you said, 'Nothing.' Why did you say that when it was obviously something?"

Sam inhaled deeply and let out her breath slowly. She squeezed the tissue in her hand, knowing she would need it. "Yes, I kept looking at you. I needed to ground myself in something that I knew was strong. All of you are strong. I'm not, but I thought I could handle their insults. I've heard insults my whole life and tuned them out. Mostly."

"I think you were tuning them out fine until...." Susie stopped. She probably hoped Sam would finish her thought.

"Yes. Until Bree knocked me down." She relayed briefly how Bree had kicked her leg out from under her.

"Sam," Marlee said and sucked air through her teeth. "I see the knot on your shin. That's an awful bruise."

"*Dios mio*, Sam. You never put ice on that after the game," Susie said.

"I was kind of numb and forgot about it."

Lisa reached for Sam's arm. "And look at this bruise on your forearm where that asshole grabbed you."

"Bree wasn't the only one hurt that day," Marlee said quietly. "Sam, you were hurt in a lot of ways."

"That girl is evil," Susie said.

"Stalkers suck," Marlee agreed.

"But even so, Sam," Susie continued, "your reaction to whatever Bree said to you was off the chain. You were a demon unleashed. I never saw such fury from anyone. If no one was there to stop you,

Sam, I think you might have done some serious damage."

Sam looked from Lisa to Marlee to Susie and said evenly, "Yes. I might have killed her."

The back of the limo got very quiet. No one said a word or even moved until Sam continued. "I understand now why my father gets so protective of my mother and me. There are real threats to my family all the time. Bree said—" Sam stopped herself. She had been about to tell her friends the filth that had come out of Bree's mouth. Instead, she pulled her hand away from Lisa's and clamped her eyes shut. She turned away from her friends and looked out the window at the peaceful scenery around her. She used the tissue to soak up the tears falling down her cheeks. Lisa put an arm around her waist.

Sam didn't look at her friends when she said, "Bree's teammates were attacking me, Helene, and my parents." She took a breath. "Those I could kind of handle. But then Bree ...." Sam turned toward Lisa. "Bree said things, nasty things, about you, Lisa, and I lost it. I lost my cool, my sanity, my...everything." She snorted an angry breath, trying not to relive the words. Her hands started shaking, and she knew her face and neck were beet red.

"You defended my honor, baby?"

Sam nodded.

"That's what this is all about?"

Sam nodded again.

Marlee shoved a tissue box between them, making everyone chuckle. Her timing was impeccable.

After dabbing her own tears, Lisa said, "You've suffered a lot of bullying in your life, Sam. At church, we always say that God never gives you more than you can handle."

Marlee chimed in and said, "Some people even say that we write our own life script before we're born. In each lifetime, we experience different things that our souls need to grow."

"I've never heard you talk in such a new-age manner, Marlee," Lisa said.

"I read. Too much, probably," Marlee said with a chuckle.

Sam had stopped crying and said, "But why would I choose for my mother to have cancer? Why would I choose to be publicly ostracized for coming out of the closet? Why would I choose migraines? Why would I choose to have no friends growing up until I met you guys? Why... just everything?"

"It's just a theory," Marlee said, holding both hands up in defense. "I don't know if I believe it either because why the hell would I choose for my father to die when I was in middle school? But if you believe this theory or Lisa's God theory, then you know that Lisa, Susie, and even I came into your life for a reason. We are three friends who can help you through these tough times."

"Marlee," Sam said, "you are very wise." Sam patted Marlee's knee. "Coach Gellar only gave me a one-game suspension, which I served on Wednesday. It should have been more. I was out of control."

"Did you at least get to go the game?" Marlee asked.

"No, I wasn't even allowed on the bus, so, Susie, you'll be happy to know that after my appointment with the family psychiatrist, I went home and studied for my AP Enviro exam."

"Oh, how did that go, you guys?" Marlee asked. Always the academic.

"Better than it would have if Susie hadn't been my tutor," Sam said.

"For me?" Susie said. "It went great. I think I'm going to major in Environmental Studies."

"Oh, yeah?" Marlee said, "I'll up you one. You can major in Environmental *Engineering* at Rockville."

"That's a thing?"

Marlee nodded. "We can check out the website tomorrow. And, you guys, did you ask Susie how her AP Calculus exam went on Wednesday morning?" Marlee puffed up like a proud peacock.

Before they could ask, Susie said, "Marlee is an amazing tutor." They shot each other a happy soulmate connection. With the ups and downs her friends had had recently, Sam was happy to see they had been able to work past them.

"You know when it feels like everything in your life is falling apart?" Susie said.

"Yes," Sam said. "Yes, I believe I do."

"Something always comes along to relieve the pressure." Susie looked thoughtfully at her friends. "Things will get better, Sam."

"You promise?"

Susie nodded and pulled Sam into a quick hug.

"I'm glad I have you guys," Sam said. "Fam Four." She put her hand out, palm up. Her friends, no, her family, put their hands on top and cheered, "Fam Four!"

"You know," Sam said. "Having you guys as friends is amazing. I also have Helene. I think she might stay for a while. Even after...." No, she didn't want to think about her mother's cancer treatments.

"Sam," Lisa said softly, "that would be great if Helene stayed longer."

Sam nodded. "But don't forget that I also have Dr. Boyle. Helene made me see him Wednesday. He told me that I had to find the anger behind my outburst. He's helping me recognize my triggers, so to speak." Sam turned to face Lisa. "Like my mother told her angel at the hospital the other day, I'm sensitive."

"And that's one of the many reasons why we love you," Lisa said.

"Honestly, I mostly just cried during Wednesday's session with Dr. Boyle. You know? I almost cried as much as Ms. Torres cries."

"I have overactive hormones," Susie defended herself.

"I'll say," Marlee said and shot Susie a smoldering look.

"Marlee!" Lisa put a hand over her mouth. "Geez, you always surprise me when you say things like that." She shook her head and added, "It's always the quiet ones."

"Get a room, you two," Sam said.

"Why thank you, but we've got one, and so do you two, thanks to Marlee's mom having her own sleepover at Bob's tonight."

"I'm so glad my mother is letting me stay over," Lisa said. "We have our room again, Sam."

"Finally, a proper prom night," Sam said. This time her smile did reach her eyes.

"Hey, Sam," Marlee said. "Does Dr. Boyle recommend that you punch a punching bag or something? I read about these things called rage rooms where people can throw fits and break stuff."

"No, no," Sam said. "Dr. Boyle is very much against that. He says that kind of thing will only condition my response to boil over into aggression. He says it's better to recognize my triggers and to respond to them with breathing techniques, calming thoughts, and whatever else. He wants me to be ever-mindful of how I'm feeling and to check in with myself on a regular basis." She stroked the necklace she was wearing. "Lisa gave me this. I touch it as a reminder that I'm okay and loved."

"Oh, baby," Lisa gushed. "That is so sweet."

"So, you guys," Sam said, lifting her head high. "I'm okay. Thank you for your little intervention, but I think all I want to do now is go to the dance and be with you guys."

She put her hand in the middle again. They cheered, "Fam Four," and then Sam hit the intercom, letting Cassie know they were ready to party.

Chapter Seventeen
Engaged

The summer beach theme at the Clarksonville High School prom was surprisingly well thought out and well-executed, even though Marlee kept insisting the committee had a small budget. A ton of aqua, blue, and white paper streamers hung overhead, simulating ocean water, and there was an actual boardwalk running the length of one side of the hall. A real lifeguard stand had been brought into the reception hall, and kids' beach toys on it. It was quite cute, actually.

Sam found herself having a good time right off the bat. After having their pictures taken in the lobby, Alivia dragged them toward a table that she and Jessica had claimed. Even though Jessica and Alivia had been pretty open about being a couple at the softball games, this was Jessica's first big outing with her own classmates.

"Oh, shit, baby," Sam whispered to Lisa as they followed Alivia to the large table. "This is your first Clarksonville event with me on your arm. Are you okay?"

"I'm trying not to think about that, Sam." Lisa grimaced. "Thanks for the reminder."

"Sorry."

Sam watched as Jessica looked over her shoulder and glared at

Susie. Thank God Susie didn't see it, but Sam got the clear message that Alivia had told Jessica about her make-out sessions with Susie. And Jessica, clearly, wasn't happy about it. Hopefully, Alivia had been honest.

They had reached the table, but before they had a chance to sit down, one of Lisa's classmates came sauntering over with an obvious entourage in tow. "You clean up nice, Lisa," the girl said. The brunette's hair was piled high on her head, and she was positively gorgeous. Sam figured she was one of those pretty girls that knew she was pretty. Could this be Lisa's infamous study partner?

"Sam," Lisa said, "this is Missy Matthews."

Ahh, yes, it was. Sam shook the hand offered her. "You are just as beautiful as my girlfriend said you were."

"Sam!" Lisa said, turning fifteen shades of red.

"It's okay," Missy said. "It's a compliment. I'll take it. This is my boyfriend, Brad. So, Samantha Rose, news travels fast in Clarksonville County. I heard you like to use your fists. Ever use them on Lisa?"

Lisa put a hand up to stop both Sam and Susie from advancing. "Missy, c'mon," Lisa said. "It's not like that."

"Oh, yeah? How do you like Lisa's new haircut, Samantha Rose? Kind of drastic, don't you think? Some people say you forced her to get it cut so she could be the butch one."

So, this is how it was going to be, Sam thought. Sam felt Susie take another step closer. Sam put a hand down to stop Susie's advancement. She was the one that had been thrown the challenge, so she stepped into the ring to go head-to-head with Missy Matthews.

"I don't force her to do anything," Sam said coolly. "In fact, I didn't even know she was going to cut her hair. But you do know why she had it cut, don't you?" Sam asked.

"No, Sam, don't—" Lisa tried to stop her.

"No, tell me. Did you give her lice or something?" Missy leaned back with an accusing smirk. She folded her arms across her chest.

"My mother has cancer," Sam said evenly, "and Lisa donated her hair to a foundation that makes wigs for people who lose their hair from chemo."

Missy's expression changed from night to day. She had tears in her eyes when Sam finished her statement. She looked at Lisa. "Why didn't you tell me? Why didn't you tell anyone?"

"I didn't want —"

"Oh, Lisa," Missy said, not letting Lisa finish. She pulled Lisa into a hug. "You are something else." She released Lisa, who frantically reached for Sam's hand and then clutched it like a lifeline. "All these a-holes around here," Missy continued, "they've been giving you such a hard time. Don't worry. I'll set the record straight, so to speak."

"Don't worry about—"

Missy didn't seem to hear because she was saying, "Samantha Rose, this is Marnie, and this is Collette. They have dates around here somewhere."

"Nice to meet you both," Sam said. Apparently, the pissing match with Missy was over.

"Holy shit, Jessica," Marnie burst out. "I never took you for a dyke. You've been hanging around these guys too much."

"Shut up, Marnie," Missy said. "Jessica can love whoever she wants." She turned to Jessica and said, "Introduce us to your date, please."

"Um, this is Alivia," Jessica stammered. "This is my *girlfriend* Alivia from East Valley High School." Jessica Myers was a strong, intelligent athlete but was withering under the scrutiny of Missy Matthews and her entourage. Sam didn't know what to do to help. Turned out she didn't need to do anything.

"I'm pleased to meet you all," Alivia said, stepping forward. "I love your gown, Missy. That blue really complements your eyes." She nudged Brad in the ribs. "And you're not too shabby yourself, handsome." She winked at him. His broad smile pretty much diffused the situation.

"Missy," Marlee interjected, "this is my girlfriend, Susie."

"Oh, believe me, I remember her from the winter formal," Missy said to Marlee. "She dance-shamed us all when she brought out her mad salsa-ing skills."

"It's nice to put some faces to names finally," Susie said.

Missy nodded and then said, "Okay, girls, we're making our rounds. We'll see you on the dance floor."

"You got it," Susie said and pulled a chair out for Marlee.

Lisa did the same for Sam. "What a gentlewoman you are," Sam said, looking over her shoulder at her girlfriend.

Lisa let out a long sigh at about the same time Jessica did.

"Oh. My. God." Jessica put her head down on the table. "I thought I was going to pass out." The words were muffled by the table but intelligible enough.

"I'm with you on that one," Lisa said. "But we passed inspection." Lisa's phone dinged with an incoming text. "Ooh, it's Julie and Marcus. They're heading our way."

"Oh, good," Sam said. "I haven't seen Marcus since those debates at the youth group meetings."

Within seconds Julie White and her boyfriend, Marcus Bryant, were giving hugs at their table. Julie and Marcus were as different as night and day. Literally. Julie was a dark-skinned black girl, and Marcus was a pale-skinned white guy. They had hidden their interracial relationship from other people until Julie came out to Lisa about it. Then, Lisa eventually came out to Julie about her same-sex relationship with Sam.

Lisa introduced Alivia to Julie and Marcus, only to be reminded they already knew her. Alivia had been on the opposing team's side of the youth group debates.

"How could I forget you, Alivia?" Marcus said with a smile. "You were vicious during those debates."

"I know," Alivia said. "And now look at me." She reached for Jessica's hand and kissed it.

"True love just finds you, doesn't it?" He kissed Julie's hand in the same fashion.

"So," Julie said once she could tear her eyes away from Marcus, "I see that it's opposite day in Clarksonville again."

"What do you mean?" Lisa asked.

"Uh, Missy Matthews gave you a hug, Lisa." Julie's confused expression was priceless. "Homophobic Missy Matthews touched, no, she embraced an out lez-been named Lisa Brown."

"That was my fault," Sam said. "I spilled the beans about why Lisa cut her hair. Apparently, it was a closely guarded secret." Sam turned to Lisa and said, "I'm sorry, baby. I didn't know you didn't want people to find out."

"It's okay, Sam. Really." Lisa shrugged. "It's just that it was my business, you know? My decision. It's okay. In Missy's hands, it'll be around the school in minutes." Lisa squeezed her hand and then looked away as if to say that the conversation was now officially closed.

Sam cleared her throat, searching for a new topic of conversation. "Hey, you guys, it feels like two of us are missing."

"Who?" Susie asked.

"Ronnie and Jordan."

Alivia perked up. "Oh, they're at Jordan's prom tonight in Southbridge." Alivia frowned as soon as the words were out. "Sorry, Sam. Sore subject."

Sam waved it away. "No worries. I don't hate all the Southbridge kids, just a chosen few. Tell the guys to send us pictures."

"Already did, and they already have." Alivia showed them pictures on her phone of the guys in their tuxes at Jordan's house and then in the lobby of the Best Western, where their prom was being held.

"Cool," Sam said. "Take our picture, and then we'll take yours to send them." Sam secretly wished she could ask Ronnie to find Bree and take a picture of her if she was even at the prom, that is. Sam wanted two things – to make sure she hadn't really hurt Bree but also to see if Bree had a black eye. She really, really, really wanted Bree to have a black eye. An eye for an eye, so the Bible saying went.

Instead, Sam busied herself taking pictures of Alivia and Jessica with Alivia's phone. While they were exchanging pictures with the guys, she noticed some familiar faces standing near the back wall. She handed Alivia's phone back to her and said to the group, "Hey, you guys, I'll be right back."

"Everything okay, Sam?" Lisa asked.

"Yeah, yeah. I just want to check in with the police presence Daddy hired." She nodded her head to the three police officers hovering nearby.

Sam walked over with her phone in hand. "Hello, officers."

"Hello, Samantha Rose," the cute female sergeant said. "Everything okay?"

"It should be, but I need you all to look at this picture." She scrolled through her pictures and found the one she was looking for. "His name is Alexander, and he's kind of been harassing my girlfriend, Lisa." She pointed toward Lisa, who was watching them. "I don't know if he's here, but if he shows up, can you keep an eye on him?"

"Has Alexander been physically violent in the past?" The sergeant asked.

"No, not that I know of. But I don't know what he's capable of. He's been stalking Lisa." The other officers looked over the photo, nodded, and then spread out to cover more area.

Sam came back to the table just as the infamous Kate and Rita were hugging Marlee and Susie as if they were old friends. So, these were the two girls who had harassed Marlee at the beginning of the school year. They were the self-appointed fashion police who had criticized Marlee about how she dressed and harassed her about not having a boyfriend. Marlee hadn't been out to anyone except Lisa at her school at that point, and Marlee had felt so backed into a corner that she lied to Kate and Rita, telling them she had a boyfriend. Sam had been so proud of Marlee for changing her mind and coming out loud and proud by bringing Susie to Clarksonville's Winter Formal. She had basically come out to her entire school at that dance. But, hey, how could she go wrong with a bombshell like Susie on her

216

arm? And, apparently, all had been patched up with Kate and Rita since then.

Sam was polite, shook the offered hands, and told each of them and their boyfriends that it was nice to meet them. Luckily a good beat came on over the sound system, and Susie leaped to her feet to herd them onto the dance floor.

"I Gotta Feeling," Susie sang along with the song title and whisked Marlee to the floor. Sam held out her hand. Lisa took it and let Sam whisk her off to the dance floor as well. The dance floor swelled with bodies, but that was okay. Sam had found her party mood and enjoyed moving to the beat with her friends. She was impressed at how well Jessica and Alivia danced together. The two seemed as smitten with each other as she was with Lisa. It was a good feeling.

After a while, the DJ played a slow song, and Sam put her arms around her tall girlfriend's neck and melted into her. "Time of My Life," Sam whispered the song title into Lisa's ear.

"David Cook," Lisa said. "You know, baby. We don't have an official song."

"Do you want this one?"

Lisa nodded. Sam chanced it and leaned up and kissed her girlfriend. But just once. They were at a school-sponsored function, after all. Thank God they had a place to go afterward for longer and much more intimate kisses.

"Lisa," Sam said in Lisa's ear, "You keep me hopeful when most of me wants to quit. This may be the last time I actually have fun for a long time."

"Why, baby?"

"Because of Mother." Sam sighed. "Lisa, I don't want to play cancer anymore."

"I know, baby. I know, but you know what?"

"What?"

"This is a waltz tempo," Lisa said with a grin.

"It is, isn't it?" Sam adjusted into a waltzing position. While the other couples swayed in a circle, Sam and Lisa waltzed around them. Lisa followed Sam's lead expertly, and they changed directions on a dime. Sam couldn't help her perma-grin. She loved the woman in her arms, and she loved being able to show the people around them that love.

When the song was over, Lisa reached down and kissed Sam once. "Let's go sit," she said and led Sam back to the table, but then she headed to the refreshment table constructed out of four surfboards. It really was quite clever. Someone on the prom committee was a carpenter or knew one, that was for sure.

Sam laughed when the music changed, and she heard Susie bellow from the middle of the dance floor, "Let's salsa." Sam's energy had waned a little, and she wasn't up for joining in on the sexy dance. It was fun to watch, though. She took a few pictures and sent them to Ronnie, Jordan, and Cassie. She pointed out the dance floor to Lisa when she returned with punch and cookies. The entire floor was filled with kids actually dancing well.

"I love this Ricky Martin song," Lisa said. "Geez, look at Missy go. It almost looks like she's leading everyone."

"Kate and Rita are out there, too." Sam laughed. "If it weren't for Susie, no one here in this quiet hamlet of Clarksonville would know how to salsa."

"Jessica's holding her own, too," Lisa said. "I think she learned how at your prom last week."

Sam enjoyed just sitting and watching her friends and Lisa's classmates having a good time. After the salsa and another slow dance, everyone returned to the table.

"What happened to you guys out there?" Susie said, wiping her brow with a tissue.

"I needed something to drink," Lisa said.

"Speaking of," Susie said. "Who wants refreshments?"

Susie, Jessica, and Marcus headed to the surfboard refreshment depot just as two teachers approached the table.

"Hello, girls," Coach Speers said. "Are you having a good time?"

"Definitely," Marlee said. "Thanks for being here."

"Is everything calm this time around?"

Marlee nodded. "No problems. Everyone seems to accept our little gay table."

"Let us know if it's not okay," Coach Spears said, including the other teacher in her statement.

"I'm glad your classmates are accepting you all," the stern-looking teacher beside Coach Spears said. "Marlee, not to bring up school work, but do you have everything you need for the AP Stats exam on Thursday?"

Ahh, this stern-looking teacher must be Mrs. Stratton, Marlee's infamous math teacher, Sam surmised. Marlee was right. She was a bit intimidating.

"Yes, thank you. I'll be fine." Marlee smiled at her teacher. She turned to her coach and said, "Guess what, Coach?"

"What?"

"My physics teacher, Mr. Burton, got the green light for me to take the AP Physics exam."

"But we don't teach AP Physics here," Mrs. Stratton said,

looking confused.

"I know," Marlee said, "but Mr. Burton thought I could handle the exam and was trying to find a way for me to take it. But, Coach, the exam is on Friday."

"What could possibly be happening on Friday?" Susie said with a grin as she handed a bottle of water to Marlee.

"Only the biggest game of the season," Lisa said and looked skyward as if she couldn't believe the nightmare unfolding.

"And it's in East Valley," Coach Spears said with a groan. "Marlee, please tell me your exam is in the morning."

"I don't know," Marlee said wide-eyed. "That's the problem."

Sam groaned. It would completely suck if Marlee had to miss the game. And if East Valley won, it would knock Clarksonville completely out of contention for the playoffs. Sam didn't think her own East Valley team deserved to go to the playoffs. Clarksonville was way better, by far.

Mrs. Stratton seemed to understand the gravity of the situation and said, "I saw Ralph here, Dottie. Let's go track him down."

"Okay," Coach Spears looked frantic. "Sit tight. We'll get some answers."

Before the girls and Marcus had barely had enough time to sufficiently razz each other about whose school would triumph in their next meeting, Marlee's physics teacher came to the table.

"Hello, everyone," Mr. Burton said. He was a middle-aged man with a slight paunch. His toupee was ill-fitting, and the color didn't suit his complexion at all.

"Hi, Mr. Burton," came the collective cheery answer from the Clarksonville students. It became immediately obvious to Sam that this man was loved by all, Marlee included. "Your coach was panicking, Marlee, but no need. The exam is in the morning."

Collective murmurings of "Oh, thank God" and "What a relief" went around the table from everyone, even those from East Valley. Sam was definitely relieved. Now the game would be fair.

"Oh, and Marlee," Mr. Burton said, pulling a small paperback book out of the inner pocket of his sport coat. "You've been so busy cutting a rug out there that I haven't had a chance to give you this."

"Ooh," Marlee said and ran her hand lovingly across the cover. "Gears." She held the book up for all to see. Yes, Sam laughed to herself. Her friend Marlee was a tried-and-true nerd.

Marlee's eyes lit up when her teacher opened the small book to a page and showed her a diagram about a reciprocating rack and pinion device, whatever that was. Marlee was riveted and nodded her head as he explained the diagram.

"That's my girl," Susie whispered. "Genuine science geek."

"Thanks, Mr. Burton," Marlee said as he was leaving. She sat down and, without looking away from the book, smacked Susie on the arm with the back of her hand. "Takes one to know one, geek."

Sam burst out laughing.

"So, listen to this," Marlee said, "Rack and pinion devices turn rotary motion into linear motion." She looked up from the book. "How cool is that?"

laughed again when Marlee said, "What?" when everyone stared at her with open mouths. "Science is cool. Right, Susie?"

"Yeah, but not at the prom."

"Okay, fine." Marlee slowly closed the book leaving it open an inch, so she could continue to read the page.

The loud crash of a chair hitting the floor beside them startled everyone at their table. Sam looked up and felt like she was in a horror movie. Alexander was standing three feet behind Lisa's chair. His greasy hair spilled over the collar of his brown velour tux and dingy white shirt. It looked like he had dragged it screaming from the seventies or maybe just from his father's closet.

"Why, Lisa?" he asked, his face contorted in anger.

Lisa's startled expression had turned to fear, and Sam leaped to her feet, hands already curled into fists. Marlee held Sam back by the arms as Susie positioned herself between Lisa and the lanky Alexander. Jessica moved in next to Susie, creating a wall between Lisa and her stalker.

"Why did you cut your hair, Lisa? You're a dyke like them, aren't you?" He huffed, and actual spittle flew out of his mouth. "Do you want to look like a man, Lisa? Do you want to *be* a man? Be with me, Lisa. I'll be your man."

Just as he took a step closer, one of the police officers grabbed him from behind. Alexander struggled for a moment and then calmed down when the officer tightened his grip. "I assume this young man is bothering you."

"Yes," Lisa said. A pained expression crossed her face, followed immediately by anger. She leaped to her feet behind the Susie/Jessica wall and scolded him. "Alexander Graves, I told you I didn't like you like that. Take a hint and leave me alone. All these people are witnesses, and they all heard me tell you to leave me the fuck alone."

"You don't like me?" He actually looked hurt.

Sam was relieved that he didn't struggle against the officer's hold anymore.

"No, Alexander," Lisa said. "I don't. And, besides, I'm engaged to be married."

"To a girl?" he asked meekly. It was clear by the tone of his voice that he knew he had lost.

"Yes."

"There's no chance for me? Ever?"

"None." Lisa crossed her arms over her chest and stood up even taller. "You should go home now."

"Okay," he said, defeated. "I didn't know. I'm sorry. And congratulations. The better person won, I guess."

"Yes, she did," Lisa said, her jaw set firm.

The officer led him away roughly, and as they watched him go, a collective sigh echoed across the table, followed by a stunned silence as everyone digested the news.

"Engaged?" Susie said to Sam, her eyebrows raised to the ceiling.

"Lisa?" Sam said, hoping she would explain.

"One day, baby. One day we'll be engaged, won't we?" Lisa's mischievous grin made Sam smile.

"Yeah, one day, but now I'm kind of disappointed." Sam laughed and said, "But that would have been the world's worst marriage proposal in the history of proposals."

"But it was unique, eh?"

"Hopefully, we are rid of that creep," Marlee said with a shudder.

"Here, here." Sam raised her glass of punch.

Lisa raised her glass and declared that fun was the order of the night. Rousing cheers of agreement followed. Sam echoed the sentiment but really just wanted to whisk Lisa away for some much-needed private time.

Chapter Eighteen
Mothers' Day

Sam helped Bridget out of the Brown family van after church, and together they raced up the walkway to the front door to see who could get there first. Bridget won, naturally.

"Do you have a key, Sweetpea?" Sam asked.

"No, Samtha," Bridget said with a giggle. She looked cute in her white tights and navy-blue Georgiana dress. "Papa has the key. Oh, look. A package."

"Who is it for?" Sam asked, knowing full well they were the flowers she had sent to Lisa's mother for Mother's Day. "Read the label." Sam picked up the package and pointed. "Sound it out."

"Less…" Bridget furrowed her brow in concentration and pushed her brown curls off her face. "Less…la, li, lee."

"Leslie," Sam pronounced for her.

"Brown," Bridget read the last name proudly.

"And who is Leslie Brown?" Sam asked.

Bridget turned and ran to her mother shouting, "Mama is Leslie Brown."

"Oof," Lisa's mother said as her youngest slammed into her.

"Mama, you have a white box."

"Let's go get it then, shall we?"

Sam handed her the box filled with Peruvian lilies. "Happy Mother's Day, Mrs. Brown."

"Samantha Rose, you didn't have to do that."

"I know, but I wanted to." Sam held the door open for the entire Brown clan, including Lisa. Sam was the last one in the house.

"All right, Brown clan," Lisa's mother said, "go change and then help Sam and Lisa in the kitchen with whatever surprise meal they're cooking up for Mother's Day."

Lisa's sister Lynnie was in the fifth grade and leaned over to Sam and whispered, "Supersonic Strawberry Supreme Pancakes?"

Sam nodded and whispered back, "That's the only thing I know how to make."

Lynnie laughed and headed to the room she shared with her brother.

"I'll be out in a minute, Sam." Lisa headed into the room she shared with Bridget.

"And I'll go ahead and get started in the kitchen," Sam said.

Lisa blew her a kiss when no one was watching. Sam caught it in the air and slammed it to her chest.

Lisa's mother came out of her bedroom after changing and met Sam in the kitchen. "Good, I see you found an apron." She opened the box of flowers and said, "Oh, Samantha Rose, these flowers are lovely. Thank you." She pulled Sam into a hug, and Sam thought, not for the first time, how wonderful it was to be part of a family that hugged all the time.

Once the flowers were in a vase, Sam said, "And now you have my permission to get out of your own kitchen, so you don't ruin the surprise."

"Thank you. I think I will." Sam's mother smiled at Sam and

then headed back into the living room with her vase full of flowers.

Sam got out the usual bowls and pans she used in the Brown family kitchen to make her pancake concoction and was pouring the dry pancake mix into a bowl when Lisa pinned her against the sink and kissed her silly.

"Lisa," Sam moaned, "you have to stop. You're turning me on."

"Good." Lisa pushed herself away. "That oughta hold you for a while."

Sam blew out a sigh and shook her head. The things her girlfriend made her feel. They'd gotten more sleep the night before at Marlee's house after the dance than they had the first time they'd slept over, but it still wasn't much.

"Hey, Sam," Lisa said a bit more seriously. "Those things Missy said about you using your fists. I'm sorry she said that to you. I don't think that."

"Every school has its share of mean girls, Lisa. And don't you ever worry. I would kill myself before I ever laid a hand on you in anger."

Lisa's breath caught in her throat. "Sam, don't say things like that."

Sam instantly regretted her choice of words. "I'm sorry. I didn't mean that to be so dark, baby. Just know that I won't ever hurt you. Not knowingly, anyway."

"I know that." Lisa pinned Sam against the sink again and kissed her gently.

"Oh, c'mon," Lynnie said with a groan as she entered the kitchen. "All you guys do is kiss. Blah!"

Lisa pulled away and tapped Sam on the nose with her index finger. "More later."

"Promise?"

"Yep."

"Okay, team," Sam said, "let's get most of this done before Lawrence Jr. and Bridget get here and slow us down." Sam gave instructions, and it wasn't long before they were sitting at the Brown family table serving up her famous strawberry pancakes with whipped cream, sprinkles, nuts, gummy bears, and whatever other assorted junk you wanted to put on them. It was kind of like dessert masquerading as breakfast.

Lisa's mother took a whopping four slices of bacon for herself. That was okay. Sam had made two whole packages. She knew from experience how much the Brown family could eat. During the meal, Lisa's sisters and brother filled Sam in on all the things they had going on in their lives, and Sam was particularly pleased to hear that Lynnie had been asked to play violin in a quartet with a bunch of sixth graders, even though she was still in fifth. A chip off the old block, Sam thought, proud of having introduced Lynnie to music.

"So, girls," Lisa's mother said, "what are Marlee and Susie up to today?"

Lisa wiped her mouth with a napkin and said, "Marlee is making dinner, meatloaf, I think, for her mother and Mrs. Petrov with help from Bob and Mr. Petrov."

"Oh, that should be interesting," Lisa's mother said. "Can you imagine this guy in the kitchen?" She pointed to her husband.

"Hey," Lisa's father protested. "I'm pretty handy in the kitchen. Those soup cans don't just open themselves, you know."

Sam and Lisa laughed, but Lisa's mother rolled her eyes and shook her head.

"Susie went home early this morning," Sam said. "She wanted to

227

start the prep on a meal she and Miguel are making for their mother when they get home from mass."

"And how are things going there?" Lisa's mother asked. "It must have been hard to have her father and grandmother leave in the middle of the night without so much as a goodbye."

"It *is* hard for her," Sam said with a sigh. "Susie's mother is in such a funk that Susie's had to take on the lion's share of responsibilities. She seems to be handling it all okay, though."

"Even with the challenges of going to AA and all of that?"

"She's doing really well with that, Mama," Lisa said. "I've been teaching her some of my new meditation techniques."

"Lisa's been teaching me those, too," Sam said, feeling her cheeks burn. It was hard to be vulnerable. Paytons usually hid that part of themselves, but with Lisa and her family, it was easier.

"Good, and how is your own mother doing? Your mother, Mimi." Lisa's mother amended with a chuckle. "This is going to be confusing, isn't it?"

Sam laughed. "It is. Well, Mother is scheduled to start radiation therapy two weeks from tomorrow. That is, if Dr. Kulkarni, the surgeon, says she's all healed up. If she is, she'll go five days a week for four full weeks."

"Wow, Sam," Lisa said. "That's twenty radiation sessions. I wish there were a better way."

"Me, too," Sam said. The three women sat in silence while the kids joked around with Lisa's dad. "You know, my mother doesn't eat well. She never has. She, uh, skips meals and barely eats when she does sit down for one."

"Does she have an eating disorder?" Lisa's mother asked bluntly.

Sam looked down. "Maybe. I don't know. How can you tell?"

"I'm no expert, but there are signs. Your mother did look a bit emaciated. Perhaps you can mention this to her. Or if you're not comfortable with that, talk to one of her doctors."

"That's a good idea," Sam said. "In the meanwhile, maybe you can help me figure out healthy foods I can try to get my mother to eat."

"Anything with antioxidants," Lisa said, "like blueberries, cranberries, pecans. Oh, and cruciferous vegetables like broccoli and cauliflower have cancer-fighting compounds. Around here, we try to avoid the dirty dozen."

"What's the 'dirty dozen?'" Sam asked.

"Oh, Sam," Lynnie said with a shake of her head. "And you're a senior in high school." Her grin let Sam know that she was teasing.

"Yikes," Sam said. "I must be one of the family now. Even Lynnie's giving me grief."

"Welcome, Sam," Lynnie said. "The dirty dozen are twelve foods you should buy organic because otherwise, they soak up a lot of pesticides and bad junk from the farms. Strawberries are on that list, you know."

"These were organic," Sam said quickly, pointing to the remnants of their breakfast. "I promise."

"What else is on the dirty dozen list, Lynnie?" Lisa asked.

"I memorized them alphabetically," Lynnie said. "Let's see. Apples, bell peppers, celery," she counted them off on her fingers, "cherries, grapes, lettuce, nectarines, peaches, pears, spinach, strawberries, and…." She looked down. "Oh, no. I forgot one."

"Potatoes," Lisa said.

"Oh, yeah," Lynnie said with a roll of her eyes. "Bridget's

favorite. Potatoes."

"So, all of those should be organic. Can you write those down for me, Lynnie?"

"Sure."

"I'll make sure Mrs. Tardelli buys these in organic form."

Lisa's mother looked up at the clock on the wall over the television. "Sam, isn't it about time you headed home to your own mothers?"

"Yes, it is." Sam stood up and reached for some of the dirty plates. "Let me get this cleaned up."

"No way, Sam," Lynnie said and stood up. "These three can help me clean up." She not only included Lawrence Jr. and Bridget in her hand wave, but she had included Lisa, too.

Lisa put a hand on her chest and said, "Oh, okay, taskmaster. Let me just see Sam out to her car."

Lynnie groaned. "Don't take forever kissing her goodbye." She made a gagging sound.

Lisa's mother hid a smirk behind her hand.

"C'mon, crew," Lynnie said. "Chop, chop, let's get these dirty dishes into the kitchen sink. March, march."

Lisa and Sam got out of the way of the Brown children assembly line and headed toward the front door.

"Oh, shoot, Lisa," Sam said, "I forgot my keys on your dresser."

"I'll get 'em." Lisa ran to her room.

As soon as Lisa was out of earshot, Sam whispered to Lisa's mother, "Are we all set for tomorrow?"

"All set. She doesn't suspect a thing."

"I'm going to drive here as fast as I can after my game. It'll take about an hour."

"Are you sure you don't want to do this another day when neither of you has a game?"

"Nope," Sam said, still whispering. "Tomorrow is our one-year anniversary, and it has to be special. How will you keep Lisa out of the house after her game?"

Lisa's mother didn't answer the question but moved back a step and said in full voice, "Remember, Sam, that hope is a state of mind. Hope is something you can choose."

Lisa must be on her way back. "Thank you, Mrs. Brown. I will meditate on that."

Lisa's strong arms went around her from behind. "Good," Lisa said in her ear. "Mom, I'll help the kids clean up, but I'm going to walk Sam out to her car first."

"Okay, but remember what Lynnie said."

"Mom!" Lisa groaned, handed Sam her keys, and ushered her out the front door.

"I'm so sorry I can't see you tomorrow, baby," Sam said, trying not to grin. "I wanted to be together on our one-year anniversary."

"Me, too. We had an amazing weekend, though, didn't we? And we picked our song." Lisa leaned back against Sam's Mercedes, effectively blocking Sam's departure. She pulled Sam against her. "I can't believe it's been one whole year since you kissed me in that dugout."

"I know. That was kind of ballsy of me, wasn't it?"

Lisa smiled and nodded.

"And one day, Clarksonville, maybe you'll make good on your proposal to marry me," Sam said.

"Maybe, East Valley, maybe."

Sam groaned. "I can't believe we have to play you guys on

Friday."

"Depending on what happens this week," Lisa said, "both teams might only have one loss."

"You guys shouldn't have that one loss."

"I know, but it is what it is."

Sam reached up and kissed her girlfriend. She felt instant tingles of desire settle low in her belly. "Oh, my God, Lisa," Sam said breathlessly. "I can't believe how you turn me on with just a kiss."

"Same," Lisa said and pushed off the car, still holding onto Sam. She grabbed Sam's keys, hit the unlock button, and opened the door. "Go on before I change my mind and make you drive me to that secluded spot by the Gengo River."

Sam smiled and got in. She lowered her window. "Thanks, baby. Thanks for your support this week. I'm sorry if I scared you and your parents with my Rambo imitation."

"We're just worried about you." Lisa stepped back as Sam started the engine. "Just keep breathing, my love. Just keep breathing." She leaned in and gave Sam one more goodbye kiss and stepped away.

Sam waved as she backed up the car. She hated this part. Leaving Lisa was always the worst feeling in the world. She wiped at the tears in her eyes as she pulled onto the street and drove away.

~~~

Sam reached into the trunk of her car and grabbed her overnight bag and the garment bag with her prom dress. It was an amazing spring afternoon. The temperature was perfect. It wasn't humid. The birds were flitting about, making nests, no doubt, and the bees were already buzzing. The daffodils had made their appearance in April, and the tulips were just starting to show their colors. Sam wondered if her mother had done any gardening yet. She'd make a point to ask as soon as she found her at home. If she was even home, that is.

No one greeted Sam when she entered the house, but then again, no one ever greeted her when she got home. Helene occasionally, maybe, but that was life in the mansion.

Sam laid her garment bag over the back of the couch in her living room and then went into her bedroom to process the things from her overnight bag. There was laundry, her cosmetic bag, and the corsage Lisa had given her to wear at the prom. She went back into her living room and tacked it on the bulletin board above her desk next to the others Lisa had given her.

She decided a shower was in order and took a long hot, soaking one, trying not to think about anything. She would not think about Alexander or Missy. And she would definitely not think about the raw feel of her fists connecting with Bree's cheekbones and nose. Nope, she would think about flowers. She'd normally let thoughts of Lisa intrude happily, but lately, thoughts of Lisa turned into concerned looks from Lisa and Lisa's parents. That was a place she did not want to go.

When her fingers pruned up, she knew it was time to stop avoiding the inevitable. She got out of the shower, dressed, and went to find her mothers to wish them a happy Mother's Day. The flowers she'd sent to her mother were in the tall vase on the table in the foyer. The flowers she'd sent to her *maman* were probably in her apartment. It was weird thinking of Helene as her *maman*, but this was the first Mother's Day that Helene would get to celebrate openly, so Sam would honor her by thinking of her as *Maman* instead of Helene.

Sam got out of the shower and put on a cheery sundress with sandals. She walked out of her rooms and began the hunt for one or both of her mothers. She guiltily thought about the fact that she'd made breakfast for Lisa's mother but hadn't planned on making any kind of meal for her own mothers. Surely Mrs. Tardelli had made something special for them.

Sam finally found them sitting on one of the stone benches in Mother's gardens. Helene, no, she wasn't Helene. She was *Maman*. *Maman* was listening to Mother's long-term plans for the spring, summer, and autumn gardens. Good, her mother was thinking about the future. Sam stood in the archway that would soon be bursting with climbing roses. She listened.

Sam's *maman* said, "Mimi, you've always kept your feelings close to the vest. You may think that's the way to be strong, but this is a scary time for you. For all of us. And you need to be open and deal with your emotions as they rise up. Express them. It doesn't have to be me, but…someone."

"I *am* frightened," Sam's mother admitted. "Gerald is a comfort. He listens."

"Good," Sam's *maman* said.

Sam's heart clenched as she heard her mother expressing vulnerability. This was new. Paytons didn't do this. Sam wasn't sure what she could do to alleviate her mother's fears. What *could* she do? Cancer was cancer, and it was a beast.

"I think the best thing you can do now, Mimi," Sam's *maman* said, "is use your energy to get strong. We don't know what lies ahead."

"No, we don't."

Sam's eyes clouded over with tears. She turned away and looked up at the brilliant blue sky. Susie would be able to tell her what those lazy puffy clouds were. It was funny how she often thought of her friends during stressful times. Maybe there was something to that whole Fam Four thing.

Sam sensed something had changed in her mothers' conversation and looked back. Both of them had turned and were looking at her.

"Sorry, mothers," Sam said. "I didn't mean to eavesdrop. I promise I wasn't standing here very long."

"Come. Sit," Sam's *maman* said and stood up. She patted the seat where she had been sitting.

"I can stand," Sam said as she walked over.

"No, no," Sam's *maman* said. "Come visit with your mother. I have some lovely flowers from my daughter that need to be put in a vase." She gave Sam a kiss on the forehead and pulled her into a hug. "*Merci beaucoup, Fille.*"

"*De rien, Maman,*" Sam said and smiled. It was the first time her *maman* had called her 'daughter' in front of her mother. "Happy Mother's Day."

"Thank you." Her *maman* then whispered in her ear, "I also got some lovely flowers from Lisa."

"You did?" Lisa hadn't told her she'd done that.

Her *maman* nodded and released Sam from the overlong hug.

Sam looked up to see her mother glance down quickly as if she'd been a voyeur, an unwanted spectator. Sam watched her *maman* walk back through the archway and head to the house. Sam sat on the bench next to her mother. She had no idea what to say.

"How was your school function last night?" Sam's mother said.

Oh, good. A safe, neutral topic. "It was lovely, Mother. Lisa's school had a beach theme, and the hall was nicely decorated."

"We had a benefit at the college reception hall once. I forget what it was for, but it was a nice space if I remember."

"It was." Sam was shocked that her mother even knew where the prom had been. That was new. Sam pulled out her phone and showed her mother a few pictures of her posing with Lisa and Lisa's family.

"Oh, no. Lisa cut her hair," her mother said. "Why on earth did she do that?"

Sam was confused. Her mother had seen Lisa right after she'd had it cut at the hospital. Could it be that her mother didn't remember calling Lisa her angel? Did her mother not remember telling Lisa all those other things, either?

"She donated her hair, Mother," Sam said calmly. "The salon at the hospital takes hair donations to be made into wigs for cancer patients. Lisa's was a record of twenty-four inches."

"I would imagine. That was a very noble thing she did, Samantha Rose. I hope you told her so."

"I did."

"They look happy." Sam's mother pointed to a photo of Lisa's smiling family members.

"They were. They were happy for us." Sam showed her a picture of Sam, Lisa, Marlee, and Susie.

"I should get to know your friends better." Sam's mother then frowned. "That Susie has too many muscles." Sam's mother pointed out Susie's biceps and strong shoulders. "No wonder boys won't date her."

"Mother!" Sam scolded but then thought better of it. She remained silent after that and wondered what 'defect' her mother thought she had that boys didn't date her either. Sam turned off her phone and put it in the pocket of her dress. Sam started to ask about her mother's plan for the gardens at the same time her mother started to say something. With her friends, Sam had been keenly aware of the smooth ebb and flow of their conversations, but with her Mother, there was no ebb and flow. It was as if both she and her mother were frantically searching for conversation points. Sam didn't care what they talked about, just that they did.

"Go ahead, Mother," Sam acquiesced.

"I started to say that Lisa sent me Mother's Day flowers, too."

"She did? She didn't tell me that."

"I put them in the conservatory near the piano table."

"I'll have to check them out when I go back inside."

"Dinner will be at four today," Sam's mother said and stood up. "I will see you then." She walked down one of the garden paths, leaving Sam sitting speechless on the stone bench.

Sam hadn't said she was heading back inside at that very moment to check out the flowers, but her mother had taken it that way.

"Happy Mother's Day, Mother," Sam called after her. "I love you."

"Thank you, dear," her mother said without turning around.

Chapter Nineteen
One-year-olds

Sam stood on third base and made sure her helmet fit snuggly. She hated being on third when her bestie was up to bat. Susie could rocket a line drive right through you, leaving a gaping hole where your intestines used to be.

"C'mon, Susie," Sam called. "Get a hit." *To right field*, she added silently in her mind.

The pitcher from the Adirondack Free Charter School put her hands together and exploded toward the plate.

Within seconds Sam's eyes grew wide as Susie's laser shot headed right for her. Sam leaped into foul territory and just missed getting hammered. Susie's line drive landed on the bad side of the line, just foul. At least it hadn't landed on Sam.

"Sorry, Sam," Susie called.

"My nerves, Susie. My nerves." Sam blew out a sigh and wished she could put on Baxter's catcher's equipment.

It was the top of the seventh inning, and East Valley was leading the game by three runs. A couple more insurance runs wouldn't hurt, and Sam prayed for a high pitch for Susie to hit over the fence.

Sam got her wish, and Susie rocketed the rise ball over the left field fence. Sam trotted in to score and waited for Susie and her oversized biceps to run the base paths. It was too bad Sam's mother didn't recognize Susie's strength and the amazing things she could accomplish with it. Some people never understood their own ignorance.

Sam held her arms out wide as Susie crossed the plate and engulfed her in a hug. "Way to go, bestie!"

Their teammates mobbed Susie and led her back to the dugout for more celebration.

The Adirondack Free team was from a small charter school located inside the Adirondack Park, but even though they were small, they were a scrappy team. Their pitcher, the same one they'd seen in their first meeting, was pretty good. An "up-and-coming" Coach Gellar had called her. The pitcher reminded Sam of Marlee back when they were in ninth grade. It was funny how back then, Sam had no idea that the young pitcher from Clarksonville would soon become one of her very best friends in the entire world.

Sam did her best to stay focused in the bottom of the seventh inning, but she was antsy to have the inning over so she could get on the road. She willed Mary to throw three pitches and get three outs, but it didn't quite happen that way. After walking the first two batters, the next batter hit a sharp grounder to Abby at short, who tossed it to Sam, covering second, who then leaped over the sliding runner and threw a bullet to Mae on first. A 6-4-3 double play had them one out away from winning the game. With a runner on third, Adirondack Free's clean-up hitter stepped up to the plate. She had beefy arms, almost as big as Susie's, and had already proven to be a power hitter.

The batter didn't waste any time and swung at Mary's first pitch sending a long fly ball down the left-field line. Darn, it looked like it was going to stay fair. Sam willed Susie to catch it for the third out, but it was too far away. Susie wasn't going to get it. Sam was about to be bummed, but then the most amazing happened. Susie launched herself into a head-first dive and caught the ball inches from the ground. The batter was out, and the game was over.

For the second time that day, Sam and her teammates mobbed Susie and escorted her into the dugout.

After the high-five line, Coach Geller called them together for their usual post-game meeting. They sat in a circle in left field with their coach in the center. Sam took off her cleats and gnarly socks and put on fresh ones and Crocs.

Coach Gellar talked about the good things they did that day and the things they needed to work on during tomorrow's away game against Racquette. She mentioned the upcoming potential "collision in the division" with Clarksonville on Friday and how they had to be mentally prepared to take on the state champs. All the while Coach Gellar was talking, she was holding one of the game balls.

Coach Gellar cleared her throat and said, "One last thing, ladies. I have had the privilege of coaching many strong and talented athletes, and it gives me great pleasure to give this ball to Susie Torres." Susie's confused expression was priceless. Coach Gellar said, "That homerun you hit set a new Clarksonville County record, Torres." Sam and her teammates cheered and smacked Susie on the back, arms, and whatever else they could reach. "Your name is now in the record books. I, for one, am proud of you." She patted Susie on the back and then said, "Okay, let's load that bus and go home."

And just like that, the accolades were over. Sam chuckled. Oh, well, at least Coach Gellar had acknowledged Susie's achievement.

"Way to go, bestie!" Sam hugged her friend.

"I had no idea there even was a record," Susie said. "Wait'll Marlee hears about this. I hit one off of her last year. Remember?"

"Grand slam," Sam said. "Of course, I remember."

"I'll tell her the reason I broke the record was because she served me up that meatball last year."

"Knowing her, she'll actually be happy," Sam said as they headed back to the dugout.

"I know. Hey, don't you have an anniversary dinner to head to?"

"Bye." Sam grabbed her bag and then raced to her car. Before heading out, she sent a text to Lisa telling her they had won. She got no reply which probably meant her game wasn't over yet. Then Sam sent a text to Lisa's mother telling her she was on her way and would be there in an hour.

Lisa's mother texted her back immediately and told her that Clarksonville was winning, and they were in the top of the fifth inning. She also said to park in her neighbor Mr. Muller's driveway at the end of the street.

"Isn't he your mean neighbor?" Sam asked. Lisa always referred to him as mean old Mr. Muller.

"Not since his daughter moved in. LOL. I'm heading home now. I will text you when the food is delivered from Le Bistro."

"Thank you so much," Sam texted and backed the car out of its spot.

Two more texts came in from Lisa's mother. Sam pulled onto the shoulder and read them quickly. The first text said, "I'll send Lisa to the store if you're not here yet. I will keep you posted. Drive safely."

The second said, "You and I need to talk about that other thing that got delivered and installed today. Later. When you get here,

Samantha Rose Payton."

"Uh, oh," Sam said out loud in the car as she drove out of the town park. "She used my full name." Lisa told her once that when her mother used their full names, they were in big trouble. Well, Sam thought, if giving my future mother-in-law a brand new dishwasher complete with installation would get her in trouble, then so be it. The Brown family needed it. Their old one was over twenty years old and had come with the house. They were overdue. Long overdue.

Sam did her best not to speed through the Adirondack Park, even though she desperately wanted to. The people who lived in the over nine-thousand square-mile park took their rules very seriously, and Sam didn't want to get pulled over and delay her arrival at Lisa's. About a third of the way to Lisa's house, Lisa texted and said that they'd won their game. It was a close one, she'd said, because no one on the Clarksonville team, including her, remembered how to hit.

Sam glanced at the package on the passenger seat. The one-year anniversary gift was supposed to be paper. Sam knew that Lisa kept a journal, so Sam had a custom-made journal created for her. The cover had a heart with an arrow running through it. The arrow itself was the word 'love' stretched out in ornate script. Inside the first page, Sam had written Lisa a love letter. Susie read the first draft and had tears in her eyes almost immediately. No surprise there. Despite her muscles, Susie was a bit of a softy. When she was done reading, she flashed Sam two thumbs up and said it was "beautiful" in a voice choked with emotion.

Sam patted the gift and waited to pass the "Leaving Adirondack Park" sign before pressing on the gas and punching her speed up to five miles an hour over the speed limit. Thank God Monday afternoons weren't high traffic times for logging trucks. Otherwise, she'd be having dinner with Lisa on Tuesday morning.

After what seemed like forever, Sam pulled into not-so-mean Mr. Muller's driveway and ran back down the street with her clothes bag. Lisa's car was nowhere in sight.

Sam knocked on the door, which was opened immediately by Lawrence Jr., who said, "Hurry, Sam." The excitement in his voice was infectious. He grabbed her hand and pulled her into the house.

Sam hugged everyone in Lisa's family except for Lynnie, who was placing two tall candlesticks on the table. "That looks so nice, Lynnie. Thank you, everyone."

"It was all Lynnie," Lisa's mother said. "She wanted control of it."

"I broke out the fine dishes for you guys, Sam," Lynnie said.

Sam hugged her and thanked her again.

"All you have to do," Lisa's mother said, "is take the salad out of the fridge for your first course, and then the rest of the food is warming in the oven."

"Okay. Easy enough."

"We, this noisy Brown clan, will make ourselves scarce in the master bedroom. We'll be watching a Supergirl marathon and doing our best to keep quiet." She glared wide-eyed at Lawrence Jr. and Bridget as she said the last.

"Excellent. Thank you. And about the dishwasher—"

"Nope. We'll talk about that later, young lady. Right now, you have to go change." Lisa's mother pointed toward the bathroom.

Sam nodded and did as told. She took a sponge bath and then put on a dress she knew that Lisa liked. She threw on flats and did a quick job with her makeup. At one point, when she was in the bathroom, she thought she heard Lisa come home, but it was only Lawrence Jr. loudly telling Bridget to be quiet. Sam chuckled and went about getting her eyeliner on just right.

She took a deep breath and opened the bathroom door. The coast was clear. She snuck into Lisa's room and stashed her gift under Lisa's pillow, where she would surely find it long after Sam was gone.

Sam went back into the main part of the house and turned off the overhead lights. Finding it was too dark, she lit the candles on the table. She went into the kitchen and turned the overhead light off, leaving just the light on over the stove. The combination created just the right mood. Her stomach growled. Okay, now she was really ready for Lisa to come home.

She didn't have long to wait.

The sound of Lisa's key scraping in the front door lock made Sam's heart race. She stood on the far side of the candlelit table and waited.

"Mama?" Lisa said as she opened the door, holding a paper grocery bag. "It's not quite cherry season, so I couldn't...."

Sam watched as a confused look crossed over Lisa's face.

"Sam?"

"Happy anniversary, baby," Sam said.

Lisa burst into happy tears, threw the bag down on the floor, and raced over to Sam to kiss her. "You did this?" She kissed Sam again. "I was sad all day because I wasn't going to see you." She kissed Sam again and again. "You're so sneaky." She kissed her again. She pulled Sam into a death-grip hug and said, "Where the heck is my family?"

Sam laughed and pointed down the hall to the master bedroom.

"Really?" Lisa grinned. "They're all jammed in there?"

"Your mom assured me they'll be fine while we dine on Le Bistro cuisine."

Lisa's jaw literally dropped open.

"Lisa," Sam said, taking charge, "go get cleaned up, and I'll put those groceries away."

"Okay," Lisa leaned down and kissed Sam again.

By the time Sam put the Brown family groceries away and had Caesar's salads on the table, Lisa came out wearing a short low-cut dress that almost made Sam forget about the meal.

"Oh, baby." Sam swallowed hard and then blew out a sigh. "With your short hair, that dress is even more stunning on you."

"Stay on that side of the table," Lisa warned as she made a wide berth around Sam. "Otherwise, my family might find us trying to make babies right here in the living room."

Sam burst out laughing. "Oh, God, let's not have it come to that."

During the entire hour of eating, Lisa couldn't stop reaching for Sam's hand to hold. Sam didn't mind. It was a little hard to cut the chicken cordon bleu, but she managed to steal her hand back for a few seconds now and then. During the meal, they talked non-stop about a myriad of topics, including the details from their respective games. Stuffed, Sam sat back and patted her stomach. Lisa did the same.

"I am so full," Lisa said.

"Me, too. And I was starving after the game."

"Sam?" Lisa reached for both of Sam's hands this time. "That song you played the other night at your Strings concert."

"Which one?" Sam knew which one.

"The one that made my heart glow."

"*Canto al Amor*. The Song of Love," Sam said.

"You looked at me the whole time you played it." Lisa searched Sam's eyes. "I felt you. I felt you deeper in my soul than I ever have before."

"You felt it, baby?" Sam said softly. "Why didn't you say anything before now?"

Lisa brought one of Sam's hands to her lips and kissed the back of it three times. She then held it to her cheek. "I wanted to keep it all for myself, for a little while at least. And, to be honest, I didn't know how to put my feelings into words."

"That piece always makes me think of you," Sam said. "More than think of you. I *feel* you in that song."

Lisa dropped the hand she'd been holding, put both hands on Sam's cheeks, and kissed her. They stayed locked at the lip until each one sat back breathless.

"Maybe we have two songs now," Sam said.

Lisa nodded.

Sam wished they could have continued the kiss but knowing they couldn't. ""Um, there's dessert. Sorbet."

"Oh, geez, there's no room. Hey, is there enough for...." She nodded toward her parents' bedroom.

"Absolutely. Great idea. I'll get bowls and spoons, and you call them in. How does that sound?"

"Perfect," Lisa said but made no move toward her family. "I like you." She pulled Sam onto her lap, and they spent the next five minutes kissing each other passionately.

"Dessert?" Sam said gasping for air.

"Yes, you are," Lisa quipped. She planted one last kiss on Sam's lips and said, "I'll go get them."

Within a minute, the tornado that was the Brown family descended on the kitchen table. Bowls of sorbet were scooped by candlelight, and the kids thought it was so cool. Lynnie wanted to know every detail of their romantic dinner, and Sam had the briefest thought that going-on-eleven-years-old Lynnie was growing up a little too fast. Lisa's parents were probably thinking the same thing.

While Lisa was giving her sister and brother G-rated details about their romantic dinner, Sam looked at Lisa's mother, hoping she could ask her a question.

"What is it, Sam?"

"First of all, how does everyone know what I'm thinking?"

"You are a very sensitive young woman," Lisa's mother said with a soft smile. "Your feelings are almost like tangible things."

"Mrs. Brown," Sam blurted before she lost her nerve, "how do I get to know my mother better? Mimi, I mean. I want her to understand that even though she isn't my biological mother that she's always been my ... my mother. She *is* my mother." Tears came to Sam's eyes, and Lisa's mother handed her an unused napkin.

Lisa's mother pointed to Lisa's father and said quietly, "He is her father."

Sam's eyes grew wide. Sam knew, but the three musketeers didn't know that the man named Mr. Brown was not Lisa's biological father.

"He knows it because she shows him."

"How?"

"Lots of ways. Hugs, their silly banter, exchanged smiles. And by saying it." Lisa's mother looked from Lisa to her husband. They were oblivious to their side conversation. "You need to say what you're feeling, Samantha Rose. Even if it's the scariest thing you've ever done, tell her you want to spend more time with her. Be honest because if you feel it, she'll know it."

Sam nodded, trying to absorb the advice. Sam's mother reached over and stroked Sam's forearm. "She'll know."

"What is it with you two?" Lisa said. "Somebody's always crying around here." She gestured to the napkin Sam was using to dab her tears.

"I needed some mothering, Lisa. But all that is going to change when your mother roots against East Valley in our game on Friday. Coach Gellar's calling it the 'collision in the division.'"

"Yeah," Lisa said, "but that depends on tomorrow's games. You guys should probably just go ahead and lose tomorrow, so you don't get your hopes up for Friday."

"Ooh, burn," Lynnie said. She had gone back to reading her book but apparently couldn't let that dig go.

"*Et tu, Brute*?" Sam said to Lisa's sister.

"How fast the love dies," Lisa's father quipped.

Sam looked back at Lisa and said, "Oh, yeah, wise guy? Did you forget that we have the home-field advantage this time? And, ready for this, we also have #7 Susie Torres, who, as of today, is the leading homerun hitter in all of Clarksonville County's history."

"Is she really?" Lisa said wide-eyed.

"Yeah, she had a homerun today, and Coach gave her the game ball."

"That's cool, but," Lisa pulled out a make-believe cell phone and said, "now I need to text Marlee and tell her to walk Susie every single at-bat on Friday."

"Don't you dare." Sam grabbed at the imaginary phone.

Lisa pulled her hands out of reach. "Nope. Not a single pitch to swing at," Lisa teased and made a face at Sam. "You, on the other hand. You've got one more shot at your dream of getting a hit off Marlee, you know."

Sam put her hands on her head and said, "Ahh, the pressure," as she rocked from side to side. Bridget copied the movement and echoed, "Ahh, the pressure." Lawrence Jr., not to be outdone, echoed it even louder.

Sam and Lisa laughed at the kids' antics, and then Sam said, "You know what? I think I'll hit a double off Marlee on Friday."

Lisa scoffed, "The only double you're going to get on Friday is a double knot in your cleats."

Sam clutched at her chest as if hit by an arrow. "Right in the heart." She groaned, closed her eyes, and sat still.

Naturally, the younger kids mimicked her reaction until Lisa's mother finally said, "Okay, Brown children, it's time for bed."

A chorus of whines followed her statement.

Sam sprang back to life and said, "Hey, Bridget? Can you give Lisa a big hug and tell her that you love her?"

"Yes." Bridget did as she was told.

Lisa said, "Bridget, can you give Sam a bigger hug and tell her that you love her?" Bridget did. Hugs really did make you feel good, Sam thought, feeling oh-so-warm inside. It was like the fire in her heart was being stoked by love.

"Bridget," Sam said, "can you go get ready for bed and then come back out and give us more hugs?"

"Okay." Bridget raced for her bedroom.

Sam spun on her chair to face Lisa's brother. "Hey, Lawrence

Jr.," Sam singsonged as if he were the next victim.

"I'm going. I'm going," Lawrence Jr. blurted before Sam could finish her request. He took off on the run for his room.

"Goodnight," Lynnie said. "Happy anniversary, you one-year-olds." She smiled and headed to the bathroom after giving them both hugs.

"You two are going to make great moms," Lisa's mother said once Lynnie was out of earshot.

"Mom!" Lisa said and covered her mouth.

"In the future, Lisa." The glint in Lisa's mother's eye was priceless. "C'mon, Papa, we're on nighty-night patrol. You've got the boy. I've got the girl."

"Will do, Mama." Lisa's father winked at Sam. "Happy anniversary, you two, and many more."

"Aww, that was sweet, Papa." Lisa stood up to give him a hug.

"Good night, Sam," Lisa's mother said. "We'll see you at Friday's game."

Once they were alone again, Lisa said, "I didn't know my mother could embarrass me so much."

Sam laughed, and together they cleaned up after their anniversary dinner.

"Hey, what's this?" Lisa said, just noticing the new dishwasher.

"A Mother's Day gift to your mother."

"Thank you, Sam, we needed one, but!" She folded her arms across her chest and frowned.

"But what, baby?"

"No more expensive gifts, okay? We've had this conversation."

"I know, but it was Mother's Day, and your mom helps me understand stuff, and your whole family is amazing to me, and sometimes I don't know how to say thank you or tell people how I feel, so buying things tells them that I love and appreciate them."

Lisa chuckled. "I don't think you took a breath in that entire run-on sentence. C'mere." She pulled Sam to her and rocked her gently. "I love you, Samantha Rose."

"I love you, too, Lisa Anne."

Chapter Twenty
Collision in the Division

You would think they were playing in the finals of the NCAA college world series based on the size of the crowd at Friday evening's game against Clarksonville. Sam didn't know where the news crew came from, but all of it made her kind of nervous. Sam was sitting on the bench in the East Valley dugout and smoothed down her jersey.

"Stop primping, Sam," Susie teased.

"This is way too much for me, Sus." Sam gestured to the overflowing stands. Marlee's mother and her new boyfriend were on the Clarksonville side of the stands. Helene was also there, sitting with Lisa's family. She and Lisa's mother had been talking and laughing nonstop. That was a good sign and made Sam's heart glow. Mother and Daddy weren't there, but she didn't expect them to be. Her father was in Albany on a business trip, anyway. No one from Susie's family was there either, not even her father, who had promised to go to as many games as he could. He hadn't been to a single one, and this would probably be the last game either of them played in high school. Susie hid her feelings well, but Sam knew she was disappointed. After a while, Susie stopped looking in the stands.

"Hey, once we get started," Susie said loud enough for her

teammates to hear, "we'll settle in and do what we do best."

"I hope so," Abby, the East Valley shortstop, said.

"This is crazy," Rachel, the center fielder, added. She and Abby were the other two seniors on the East Valley team.

"Listen up," Coach Gellar said from the other side of the dugout fence. "I don't have to remind you, but I will. This is the last game of the regular season for both of us. Whoever wins goes on to the playoffs next week. Clarksonville's got a good pitcher. You know that, and actually, she's not good—she's great. It's a real art for a pitcher to make the ball look big and fat coming down the alley, only to have you swing and miss in frustration as it bends just out of reach. McAllister has that ability. Her pitches are also frustratingly not easy to pick, either. She throws them all with the same motion with the exception of her screwball, but she doesn't throw that one often."

Sam's stomach knotted. Yikes, she was never going to get a hit off of Marlee. Better cross that dream off her bucket list right now.

"But don't get discouraged," Coach Geller continued. "You can hit this pitcher. Just find your rhythm, find your groove. She'll make a mistake. When she does. Pounce. And don't forget, we have the home-field advantage."

"Are you sure about that, Coach?" Sam looked toward the stands and saw an inordinate amount of Clarksonville blue.

Coach Gellar followed her gaze. "Well, at least hot dog sales will be up today."

Sam laughed along with her teammates. It felt good. Maybe a good laugh was what they needed at that moment.

"Now, let's get out there and play a good game. I'm sure our seniors will want a good one to remember."

Sam was instantly sad, especially when her teammates clapped her, Susie, Abby, and Rachel on their backs.

"Captains," the umpire called from home plate.

Sam leaped to her feet. "Captains' circle," she said to Susie. "C'mon."

Sam's heart dropped as soon as they walked out of the dugout. That troll of an umpire was back, and he was holding a mask which meant he would be calling balls and strikes. Sam smacked Susie on the arm.

"I see him," Susie said. "So does Marlee."

Marlee and Lisa were heading toward home plate as co-captains for the Clarksonville team. Neither was smiling.

They got to the plate, and the four athletes introduced themselves and shook hands as if they didn't know each other. Lisa hung on to Sam's hand a little longer than was socially appropriate, making Sam blush. The glint in Lisa's eye forced Sam to smile. She looked away and put a hand over her mouth to hide it.

The umpires went over the ground rules, not that any of them was really listening. At the end, they shook hands and said, "Good luck" to each other. Sam gripped Lisa's hand and said, "Let's play a fair game. Equal on both sides." Lisa knew, they all knew, that Sam wasn't telling Lisa. She was passively aggressively telling the umpires.

"Agreed," Lisa, Marlee, and Susie said in unison.

"Fam Four," Marlee said under her breath, but loud enough for each of them to hear.

Before returning to their respective dugouts, Lisa winked at Sam and smiled. Sam's heart warmed over.

"East Valley," the troll umpire called, "take the field."

Sam raced Abby to their infield positions and then took a few warmup grounders from Mae, the first baseman.

Baxter threw Mary's last warmup pitch down to second base. Abby caught it deftly and tossed it to Sam. "We've got this," Abby said.

"Of course we do," Sam said with conviction, feeling none of it. She tossed the ball to her third baseman, who tossed it to Mae, who then plunked it in their pitcher Mary's glove.

Sam smoothed out her already smoothed second base territory and pounded a fist in her glove. Johnna, the Clarksonville shortstop, stepped into the batter's box.

"And we're off," Sam said under her breath as the pitch headed toward the plate.

One slap hit later, Johnna was standing safely on first base. One pitch after that, she was standing on second, having stolen the base against Baxter. Baxter's throw hadn't been close. After that, Julie White, Clarksonville's first baseman and Lisa's good friend, put down a beautiful sacrifice bunt which sent Johnna to third. With one out, Jessica Myers stepped up to the plate.

"C'mon, bae," Alivia called from the East Valley side of the stands. "Swing your bat." Sam tried not to laugh out loud. Alivia still knew nothing about cheering at a softball game.

On the third pitch of her at bat, Jessica's mighty stroke sent a missile deep into center field. In an amazing show of athleticism, Rachel turned, ran toward the fence, and caught the ball with an over-the-head basket catch for the second out of the inning. The ball was so far out in centerfield, though, that Johnna tagged up and scored easily from third base. And just like that, East Valley was losing one to nothing.

With the bases empty, Lisa got up to bat and sent the first pitch right into Susie's glove in left field. With a grin, Lisa pointed at Susie as she ran in. Susie grinned and pointed right back. No words were exchanged, only mutual respect for each other's abilities and strengths.

Sam hustled into the dugout, grabbed her bat and helmet, and headed to the on-deck circle. Yikes, she thought as she watched Marlee warm up. Marlee's pitches were fast and had a lot of movement on them. Lisa said that sometimes Marlee didn't really get warmed up until the second or third inning. Great.

Rachel didn't swing at the first pitch, even though it was a perfect strike.

"Ball," the umpire said.

"What?" Sam blurted before she could stop her mouth from moving. Oh, no. The umpire was going to be an idiot again. What did he have against Clarksonville? No, it wasn't the whole team. When Kerry had gone in to pitch the day Clarksonville lost to Northwood, the umpire had called it much more fairly. No, this man had something against Marlee. What was it, and why?

Another strike went by for a called ball two. The Clarksonville fans roared their disapproval. Sam wished she could have been roaring with them.

"Swing your bat, Rachel," Sam called to her teammate at bat.

Rachel didn't and took the walk on four pitches. Sam wasn't happy about it, but she understood. She wanted desperately to get on base against the pitching powerhouse from Clarksonville, but she wanted to do it fairly.

Sam walked over to the batter's box in a foul mood, but it changed instantly when she saw the catcher's mask resting in the middle of the box. She picked it up and handed it to Lisa, who smiled and held Sam's eye. Sam nodded and took a deep breath to return her focus to the game. She turned to get the sign from her coach. She stepped back in and bunted the ball on the first pitch as instructed. The third baseman raced to field it and threw Sam out by half a step. It had been close.

On her way back to the dugout, Sam passed Abby heading for her at-bat and said, "Swing the bat, Abby. Swing the bat."

Abby took her stance in the batter's box and let the first pitch go by. It was clearly a strike, but the troll called it a ball. Abby stepped out of the box and took the sign from Coach Gellar. Hit away. With a runner on second base, Sam figured Abby would jump at the chance to swing her bat, but that didn't happen, not once, and she walked on four pitches. Four pitches that, in Sam's opinion, were all strikes. The Clarksonville fans were livid. They had already lived through two of these games with him and weren't up for a third.

Susie got up to bat and did what she usually did. She swung her bat. The result was a double into the gap in right-center scoring both Abby and Rachel. East Valley now had the lead, but Sam wasn't sure they had earned either of those runs.

"Hey, you guys," Abby said to Sam's teammates when she got back in the dugout after scoring. "The ump's got a tiny strike zone, so wait for a strike, okay?"

Sam wanted to say that the ump had an unfair strike zone for Marlee, but everyone on the East Valley team knew that Marlee was Susie's girlfriend and that Lisa was hers. They would think Sam was playing favorites, but she wasn't. The umpire was.

Keisha, the next batter in the East Valley lineup, heeded Abby's advice and walked. That fired up Sam's teammates. They were sharks smelling blood in the water. The batter after Keisha also walked. There was only one out, the one Sam had made, and the bases were now loaded.

"Baxter," Sam said as the next East Valley batter headed for the on-deck circle, "swing your bat, will ya?"

Baxter looked from Sam to Abby and back to Sam. She nodded. Sam wasn't exactly sure what the nod meant, but she had high hopes. Sam's hopes for Baxter were realized when she swung at all three pitches thrown to her. Even though Baxter struck out for the second out of the inning, Sam was relieved that at least three East Valley players out of nine had decided to play the game fairly and weren't going to take advantage of a cheating umpire.

Dara, the East Valley right fielder, walked on four pitches, forcing Susie to score from third base. Sam was surprised when Mary also let her bat rest on her shoulder and took a walk from Marlee. Sam thought that pitchers were kindred spirits. She thought Mary, at least, would understand that it wasn't fair to let the umpire take strikes away from Marlee. But Sam was wrong, and Mary's walk caused the fourth run to cross the plate, making the score 4-1 in East Valley's favor.

Susie grumbled, "C'mon, East Valley. We have to swing our bats. We have to make this fair. We are *not* earning these runs."

Only Baxter rallied. "She's right, you guys. It's not fair that this guy's giving Mary a fair strike zone but not Marlee. And you all know it's true because you cowards would rather walk than earn it." When no one acknowledged her plea except Susie and Sam, she groaned and turned away from her teammates. She smacked the fence with her gloved hand.

With two outs, Rachel got up to bat for the second time in the first inning, and Sam stepped into the on-deck circle. She was determined to do whatever she could to keep the game as fair as possible. She wasn't going to throw away her at-bat, but she would attack it like she usually did against Marlee.

Sam growled when Rachel let the four pitches go by with nary a glance. Sam watched Rachel trot down to first while Mary jogged to second. The most irritating thing of all, though, was to watch Dara walk, not jog, to third. It was disrespectful, and Sam hoped Coach Gellar gave her an earful about it.

Lisa still held onto the ball and fumed as she watched the runners advance. Sam took a few steps toward the plate but knew she had to wait until the umpire called time.

Sam jumped when Lisa fired the ball to Kym on third base. Kym tagged Dara.

"Out!" the umpire behind the plate called out.

Wait, what had just happened? Sam replayed it in her mind. Of course! Until the ball went back to the pitcher in the circle, the ball was still live. Even after a walk, runners can advance, and runners like Dara could be tagged out if they overrun or take a step off the base, which was exactly what Dara had done.

The Clarksonville fans cheered their good fortune, and Sam cheered inwardly. Maybe God or the Universe or whatever was trying to even things up. Either way, it served Dara right for being cocky, and now their half of the inning was over.

Marlee led off the top of the second inning with a double smashed in the gap between right and center fields. Good for her, Sam thought. And good for making stupid Rachel and stupid Dara run after it.

The Clarksonville team caught fire and batted around the order.

Sam laughed out loud when Marlee hit another double in almost the exact same spot. The bottom of the second inning ended with East Valley again on the losing side by a score of 8-5.

The East Valley team ran into their dugout, and Coach Gellar said, "This Cougar offense is seeing the ball huge right now. When you go back out there, Mary, just keep doing what you're doing. They're going to start getting cocky and going for more junk." Sam didn't think that was an accurate assessment of her friends' team. Yes, they had won the state championship the year before, but they were *not* a cocky team. They took each game and each at bat seriously.

Sam smiled on her way to the plate to lead off the bottom of the second inning. She picked up Lisa's mask and handed it to her. She didn't let go right away, making Lisa grin at its unexpectedness. Sam turned away from Lisa so she could somehow get the smile off her own face. She had to focus. There was no sign from her coach, which meant hit away.

The first pitch was a little too high for Sam, so she let it go by. It was definitely a strike, but he called it a ball, to no one's surprise.

Lisa sat frozen, her glove holding the ball in the exact spot she had caught it. She didn't turn around toward him when she said out loud, "Do you know how hard that pitcher out there works?" Sam wasn't sure if Lisa was talking to her, but then realized she wasn't. Lisa was talking to the umpire, but not directly. Sam firmly decided that her girlfriend had lost her mind. "She's not arrogant," Lisa continued. "We're not an arrogant team. We work hard. We *earn* everything. This batter up here also wants to earn it. She doesn't need anyone cheating for her. A strike is a strike. Keep it fair."

"Let's play ball, catcher," the umpire growled, a clear warning in his tone.

Sam blew out a sigh. She had seen Lisa hold pitches in the zone before but never like this. And she had never heard Lisa talk to an umpire like that either. Lisa had reached a breaking point, and it hurt Sam's heart.

Sam was determined to do something with the next pitch if it was anywhere close. She took a big practice swing to get out her nervous energy. She almost laughed when the third baseman took two steps back. Marlee's pitch came right down the center of the lane. Sam waited for the last second and brought her bat down, sending a bunt trickling down the third-base line. She leaped out of the box and raced toward first base. Her teammates' cheering fueled her feet.

"Safe!" the umpire in the field called.

"Yes," Sam said, pumping two fists in the air. She had finally gotten a hit off of Marlee. Okay, it was a bunt hit, but still, it would be recorded as a hit in the scorebook.

Her grin split her whole face, and when Marlee turned, She flashed Sam a genuine smile. Sam's heart melted. Marlee was happy for her. It was the first smile Sam had seen on Marlee's face since before the game had even started.

Abby was up next. When Abby walked up to the plate, a chant of "swing your bat" started in the Clarksonville section of the stands. Abby stubbornly ignored the pressure and took a walk on five pitches. By some miracle, the troll of an umpire had actually called one of Marlee's pitches a strike. The incredulous grin on Lisa's face was priceless.

There were now two runners on base with no outs as Susie headed into the batter's box. Susie hit a single to center field, which

Jessica had to run for. Sam put on her jet pack and flew around the bases to score. After that, she was pleased to see that a few more East Valley players weren't going to take the umpire's free ride and decided to swing their bats. By the end of the second inning, East Valley was still losing but had gotten closer with a score of 8-7.

Coach Gellar called a quick meeting when the top of the fifth inning ended. Sam circled up with her teammates outside their dugout.

"Don't let up," Coach Gellar said. "I want you girls swinging your bats and playing this game the way it's intended to be played." Sam wished her coach would just come out and say she didn't want them to take the walks. Or maybe her coach didn't mind if a few of them did. Sam wondered if her coach was capable of taking advantage of such blatant favoritism. "Listen, that team could explode at any time," Coach Gellar said, nodding her head toward the visitor's dugout. "They are not used to losing."

"Neither are we," Abby said firmly. "I don't want this to be my last game, you guys."

"Me, neither," Rachel said, appealing to her teammates.

"I don't either," Sam said, "but this umpire has something against Marlee, and it isn't right. Many of you played on the summer team with Marlee, and you know her. Come on, you guys, let's take honest at-bats. If you would normally swing at a pitch, then swing at it. If it's questionable, then don't. I'm not asking you to strike out or ground out or anything like that. Just have some integrity. Don't let that man cheat for us. It's not fair." Sam smacked the chain link fence and walked away from her teammates. "It's not fair to any of us," she said, her back to all of them, including her coach.

Apparently, Sam's appeal converted a couple more of her

teammates but not all. Keisha, Dara, Abby, and Rachel continued to take advantage of the umpire's bias and walked on clear strikes. Keisha's lone unearned run in the bottom of the fifth tied up the game making the score 9-9.

In the top of the sixth inning, Clarksonville answered the run when Lisa hit a triple down the right-field line sending Jessica in to score. Sam kept her smile to herself, thinking that Lisa probably chose to hit to right field because Dara, one of the holdouts, played that position.

"What goes around, comes around, Dara," Sam muttered to herself after the play.

East Valley was now losing by one run with a score of 10-9.

In the bottom of the sixth inning, Keisha had a change of heart and decided to play the game right. Abby did not, however, but since East Valley didn't score on Abby's walk, Sam's blood pressure didn't boil over too much.

Clarksonville didn't score in the top half of the seventh inning, and when Baxter stepped into the batter's box to lead off the bottom of the seventh, East Valley was still losing by the tight score of 10-9.

Baxter had the decency to take a real at-bat but struck out doing so. When she came back to the bench, she was upset about getting fooled by Marlee's off-speed pitch but not upset about striking out honestly.

Dara was up next, and despite her teammates and the crowd calling for her to swing, she didn't and walked to become the potential tying run on first base. Mary was the next batter up. She had been an original holdout but had seen the light and decided to try and earn her at bat fairly. Just like Baxter, Mary went down swinging for the second out of the inning. Rachel was now up. Sam walked out to the on-deck circle and didn't say a word. She let her teammates yell for Rachel to swing her bat at anything close. She didn't. Like Abby, she didn't want her season to end and walked. There were now runners on first and second.

Sam picked up the mask lying in the batter's box. As she handed the mask to Lisa, she said, "This whole thing sucks." She didn't care if the umpire heard her. He deserved to hear it.

"It does," Lisa said simply.

As expected with two outs, Coach Gellar gave her the swing-away sign. Sam dug into the batter's box and looked toward Marlee's hip, where the ball would fire from. She didn't dare look at her friend's face knowing her own nerves couldn't take it. It was torture watching Marlee get so obviously mistreated and discriminated against.

The first pitch was a strike but was too low for Sam to do anything with, so she didn't swing. The troll called it a ball. The second pitch skipped in the dirt toward the plate, and Lisa had to block it. Ball two. Sam decided to swing at the next pitch, no matter where it was. She fouled it off for her first strike. Sam let another ball in the dirt go by, and the count was up to 3 balls, 1 strike. She fouled off the next pitch for a full count. She had to swing at the next pitch, or the troll would call it a ball, and Sam would walk. That would load the bases.

Sam, and everyone in the stands, could predict what would happen after that. Abby was on deck, and Abby wasn't swinging. Her walk would force Dara home, tying up the score. Then the worst possible scenario would play out next. East Valley's best hitter, Susie Torres, would be up at bat with the bases loaded. Sam snuck a peek at her friend in the doorway of the dugout, bat in hand, helmet on.

She looked pale, as if all the blood had drained from her face. Susie understood what was about to happen. Susie wouldn't give away the game. Marlee wouldn't want that.

Sam would never forgive herself for allowing that impossible situation to happen. Her two friends had finally reconciled, and there was no way Sam was going to let anything to jeopardize that.

A pitch whizzed by her.

"Ball four, take your base," the umpire said and pointed toward first with his mask.

"No. Wait." Sam panicked. This couldn't be happening. Sam groaned when she realized she had been stupidly standing in the batter's box and hadn't asked for time.

Lisa held the pitch in the spot where she'd caught it. It was a strike. Sam should have been called out.

"Guess you gotta go," Lisa said coldly, still holding onto the ball.

"That was a strike," Sam said weakly to the umpire. Her voice sounded far away, even to her own ears. It was as if she was moving in an alternate reality. She stood in the batter's box and said, "Lisa, I didn't mean to. I didn't…."

Lisa had turned away from her.

Sam's heart crushed in on itself. What had she done? She had just set the wheels in motion to devastate Marlee and Susie both. Sam tossed her bat and headed toward first base as if in a dream. She watched Marlee trudge out of the circle to pick up a stray candy wrapper that had blown onto the infield. She put it in her back pocket and then took the throw from Lisa. Not once did she make eye contact with Sam or with anyone. Instead, her face was blank and showed no emotion. But Sam knew Marlee and knew this was killing her.

The more Sam thought about the game coming down to a Susie and Marlee face-off, the madder she got. She pounded her leg with her fist. There was nothing she could do to make an out.

She was a few feet from first base when Julie, the Clarksonville first baseman, said, "This is bullshit, Sam."

Julie was right, and Sam realized that there actually might be something she could do. It was worth a try. And she had to do it before Marlee stepped back into the pitching circle.

"Hey, Marlee," Sam yelled to her friend as she touched first base with her right foot and then kept going into the base path toward second. She trudged slowly toward second base. "Come tag me out. I should be out right now."

Marlee looked startled.

"What are you doing, Sam?" Abby called from the sideline.

"Get over here," Sam demanded to Marlee, her voice breaking with emotion. "Tag me."

"No, Sam," Marlee said. "I can't. It's not fair."

"This whole friggin' game hasn't been fair from the start, P." Her voice broke. Marlee didn't move, so Sam had to take a different tactic. She had to get Marlee to come to her. She softened her tone and said, "Just come closer."

Marlee, obviously not knowing what to do, walked toward her friend. Sam was breathing hard with emotion knowing that Marlee would hate her for what she was about to do, but she was going to do it anyway. Her East Valley coach and teammates might hate her, too, but she didn't care. She couldn't let this fall on Susie.

Marlee stood in the path from first to second base. Her back was to Dara, who was standing on third. "Sam, what are you doing?"

The crowd erupted, and Sam looked up. Shit, Dara had taken

off from third base and was heading toward home. The ball was still live. Sam couldn't let her score.

"Tag me out, Marlee." Sam rushed toward her friend, who stood frozen. Shit, if Marlee wasn't going to do it, then Sam had to before Dara touched home plate. "Hold it tight," Sam yelled and threw her knee up at the ball tucked safely in Marlee's glove.

"Out!" the field umpire called. "That run does *not* score. This ball game is over."

Sam fell to the ground, covered her face with her hands, and sobbed in relief.

Chapter Twenty-One
Strong and Capable

After the stupidest game of her life, Sam sat with her friends in the back of Marlee's van in the East Valley softball field parking lot. The game was over, but Sam still felt like she was in a dream world. She was shaking even though Lisa held her tight.

When the field umpire said the game was over, Sam had broken down only to be comforted by a crying Marlee. It wasn't long before both teams joined them in the base path between first and second. With tears in her eyes, Lisa helped Sam to her feet and then held her close. Susie did the same for Marlee. Most of Sam's East Valley teammates graciously shook hands with the Clarksonville team members. It wasn't exactly a high-five line, but it was a coming together in a difficult situation. And, really, it was all a blur for Sam. She was shaking from somewhere deep inside her core.

"What did that reporter ask you, Sam?" Susie said from behind Marlee, who was sitting in the well between Susie's knees. Susie also held Marlee tight in comfort.

"I don't remember."

"She's still shaking, you guys," Lisa said. "I think we should let her calm down first." She hugged Sam tighter, and Sam was grateful Lisa understood.

Susie reached over and squeezed Sam's hand. "I know why you did it, *gringa*. Thank you."

Sam took a deep breath and let it out. "I should have swung at that last pitch, Marlee, but I was overwhelmed with the whole injustice of it all, and then when I figured out Susie was going to have to get up to bat with the bases loaded, that just took over my brain, and I didn't realize I was still standing in the batter's box."

Lisa chuckled softly. "Run-on sentences are her new thing."

Marlee looked down as if ashamed. "I'm sorry I doubted you. You had your bat on your shoulder, and I thought you had joined Abby's crew and take the walk."

"Never," Sam blurted. "I'm sorry you thought that." She twisted around to look at Lisa. "And I know you thought that, too. I promise I was just lost in worry for them."

"She was definitely Marlee's champion tonight," Susie interjected. "Seriously, from the very first inning, she was urging people to swing."

"Marlee," Sam said, "are you mad that I tagged myself out?"

Marlee grunted. "Honestly, I didn't even know what you were doing. I was in a mental fog. Seriously, I didn't get it until the umpire yelled that you were out, and then the game was over, and you fell to the ground. You were crying. That was the only clear thought in my mind. I thought you were hurt."

"So, you're not mad?"

"No," Marlee said simply. "Sam Payton, you're my hero." She patted Sam's hand and said quietly, "Fam Four."

Sam felt the sting of a migraine starting. "Thank you, friend." She pressed on her temple.

"Close your eyes, Sam," Lisa said. "I'm going to give you

acupressure."

Sam nodded once and did as told.

Susie said, "Something has to be done about that umpire."

"Did you see my mom talking to Coach Speers about it?" Marlee said. "I've never seen her that upset."

"I have," Susie groaned.

Sam had her eyes closed as Lisa rubbed her neck with her strong hands, but she was sure Susie had grimaced or rolled her eyes.

"Yeah," Marlee said in agreement, "but you won her back. As you found out personally, my mom's kind of protective."

"I thought Jessica's father was going to kill that umpire," Lisa said. "He didn't let up on the guy until he drove away."

"I thought Abby was going to kill *me* after I tagged myself out," Sam said, eyes still closed. "I think I lost a friend today. A few friends." She thought of Rachel and Dara, too.

"Do you want friends with that kind of moral compass?" Susie asked. "Rachel and Dara are the ones that really surprised me." The back of the van was quiet until Susie added, "*Dios mio*, I can't wait for graduation."

"Thirty-five days for me," Marlee said. "Thirty-six for you guys."

Susie groaned. "That's over a month."

"I think this has been the longest day in history," Marlee said. "I started with a three-hour AP Physics exam—"

"How'd that go, *mi vida*?" Susie asked. "I never got a chance to ask you."

"Really well, I think," Marlee said, and then Sam heard Susie kiss Marlee. Sam smiled at the sound. Her friends were okay. And they were okay because she'd made sure of it. She breathed a little easier.

"That's it," Lisa said softly in Sam's ear. "Just relax." Sam hadn't realized how tense she still was until that very moment.

"And then," Marlee said, "I had to endure that asshole. What did I do to him to make him be so mean?"

"Mean people suck," Sam said. "I'm going to talk to Coach Gellar on Monday and see if we can get some answers."

"Thanks, Sam," Marlee said. "Lisa and I are going to do the same with Coach Spears. That shit shouldn't be allowed to happen. I mean, what if he umps one of the playoff games? A small strike zone is one thing, but out-and-out discrimination is another."

"Discrimination because of what?" Susie asked. The frustration in her voice was unmistakable.

"State champs last year?" Lisa offered. "Marlee's short hair? Marlee being gay?"

Lisa's last statement stunned them all into silence.

"It better not be that," Marlee said. "That's, like, illegal, isn't it?"

"And really hard to prove," Sam said, opening her eyes. She twisted her head from side to side. The migraine pressure had dissipated somewhat.

"You guys," Lisa said, "let's not go down that trail." Behind her, Sam felt Lisa gesturing to Marlee and Susie to drop it so Sam wouldn't get even more upset. "We don't know what his deal is, so let's not get an ulcer over something we can't prove."

Marlee sighed. "You're right. And you know what? All I want to do is go to Susie's room, take a shower, and snuggle for a while. Hang with us, you guys. I think we need each other tonight."

"Is that okay with you, baby?" Lisa said.

"Yeah. I need you guys, too," Sam said. "But I want to stop

home first. We can shower in my room—"

Lisa made a choked sound behind her, and Sam said, "Not together, baby. Separately. Even though I wish it could be together." Lisa laughed in her ear. "I want to go home and check in with Mother, and then we'll head over to Susie's. Sound good?"

"Sounds good," Lisa said.

"We'll stop for the snacks this time," Susie said. "I need junk food on a night like this."

"Puffy Cheetos," Marlee said, putting in her enthusiastic order. It was nice to hear her friend perk up.

~~~

Once at Sam's house, Sam and Lisa stopped by the kitchen to get a couple of bottled waters, and Sam was surprised to see the family cook still there cleaning up.

"Hello, Mrs. Tardelli," Sam said. "You're here kind of late. This is my girlfriend, Lisa."

"Nice to meet you again, miss." Mrs. Tardelli curtsied.

Having none of it, Lisa pulled the cook into a quick hug and then said, "Sam continues to tell me nice things about you. Sam is a fan, and so am I."

Mrs. Tardelli blushed, leaned in closer, and said, "She's a good girl, that one." And then she winked at Lisa making both Sam and Lisa smile.

"So, did Mother eat tonight?" Sam asked. Sam's mother didn't eat a lot in general, but lately, it seemed as if she had been eating less and less.

"I brought her up some soup earlier."

Sam hated how everyone tried to protect her from the truth. She was eighteen years old. She wished they would stop babying her.

"But she didn't eat, did she?" Sam said, her expression grave.

The family cook shook her head. "No, miss. Not even the crackers."

"Okay, thank you," Sam said. "And thank you for staying late. I'll make sure you're compensated."

Mrs. Tardelli waved Sam's statement away as if she didn't want to be paid for staying late. Sam didn't press it but would make sure it happened. Sam had known Mrs. Tardelli her entire life, and she was pretty much part of her extended family.

Sam and Lisa left the kitchen and headed up the stairs to Sam's wing. Sam wanted to check in with her mother immediately but decided to get cleaned up first. She didn't want her mother fussing over her softball uniform and how dirty it was. Sam guessed it wouldn't have mattered anyway, seeing as her softball season was over.

"What was the sigh for?" Lisa asked, following Sam into her rooms.

"Just that my season is over."

"Are you regretting—"

"Not for a second," Sam interrupted and turned to pull Lisa into her arms. "I'm just sorry you guys thought I had betrayed you."

"You know," Lisa rested her head on Sam's shoulder, "I knew you wouldn't, but when you didn't swing at that last pitch, I was very confused."

"Dizzy blonde," Sam said and pointed to herself.

"Never." Lisa picked her head up and kissed Sam square on the lips. "More later, Ms. Payton. Let's get cleaned up."

"You go shower first," Sam said. She led Lisa into her bedroom and then into the bathroom. "Here is a towel and washcloth. Use whatever else you need." She gestured around the whole bathroom and then said, "Call me if you, uh, need your back scrubbed."

"Mmm," Lisa said wide-eyed. "I wish. Helene's sense of impropriety would kick in, and she'd bust through that door."

Sam laughed. "You're probably right. *Maman's* spider senses are finely tuned, aren't they?"

Lisa pecked Sam on the lips and said, "Go. I need to wash this game off and move on with my life."

"Here, here." Sam headed back out to her living room. After stowing her softball gear, she used the intercom near her desk to contact her *maman*.

"How are you feeling, Samantha Rose?" *Maman* asked.

"Better. Much better with Lisa and my friends around me," Sam said.

"That was a noble thing you did. Lisa's mother explained the rule to me. She said it was your only option."

"I know. I hate playing against my friends. Next year maybe I can play on the same team with them. Susie and Marlee anyway."

"When is the deadline to accept a spot at Rockville?" Sam's *maman* asked.

"In two weeks."

"And the Wellesley deadline?"

"The same."

Her *maman* clucked her tongue. "You have time. Time for conversations with your parents."

"You mean my *other* parents, don't you?"

"Be respectful, Samantha Rose."

"I am. *You* are one of my parents, Helene. I mean, *Maman*. Don't forget that."

"You're right. I will talk to them about this, too. But only after you do."

"Okay, deal," Sam said. She heard Lisa coming out of the bathroom. "I have to go. I have to shower. Did you check in on Mother?"

"Oh, yes, as soon as I got home. Her soup was cold, and she said she wasn't hungry."

Sam relayed her brief discussion with Mrs. Tardelli earlier.

"Go get cleaned up, Samantha Rose. I'll meet you in your mother's room in a little while."

"Okay." Sam unclicked the talk button on the intercom and turned to admire Lisa. "Phew, woman. You look good enough to eat."

Lisa chuckled. "I don't think I'm on the menu tonight. We won't be alone."

"Gah." Sam felt her face flush. "That's not what I meant," she said in a tight voice, "but maybe we can find a way to be alone soon. I'm eighteen. Shouldn't I be able to, you know, have a sleepover?"

Lisa smiled and nodded her head toward Sam's room. "Go. At least we'll have a little privacy at Susie's and more room than your convertible." She headed over to Sam's floor-to-ceiling bookshelves and ran her fingers along the spines. "I, for one, am going to snoop around your room and try to find out more about you. I still haven't figured out the difference between this Samantha Rose Payton I hear so much about and the woman I know as Sam Payton." She raised an eyebrow in question.

"Look at anything you like. Open the drawers, cupboards,

anything. I'm an open book." Sam swept her hand to include her entire living room. "And if you figure it out, please let me know."

Lisa smiled and said, "I'll do my best."

Sam's heart was warm as she headed toward her bedroom. She was lucky to have such a strong, loving girlfriend. She stopped in her tracks when she saw the wrapped package on her bed. Sam looked back at her closed bedroom door. Lisa had obviously intended for her to open it up in private, so she did. She undid the red bow around the white wrapping paper, intending to save the ribbon forever. She carefully undid the paper and pulled out a frame. She turned it over to see what it was. Sam squealed. Lisa had found the sheet music with lyrics for their love song, "Time of My Life," and had it framed. Sam teared up and ran back out into the living room. She flung herself at Lisa and said, "Thank you, baby. That was so sweet. We're going to hang it up in our first house, wherever that is, and always remember the night we picked our song."

Lisa hugged her back and said, "The night I almost, but not quite, proposed to you."

"Yeah."

"Sam, the letter you wrote me in my new journal was amazing." Lisa kissed Sam on the lips. "I've never felt so special."

"It's how I feel, Lisa." Sam kissed her deeply and felt delicious tingles starting all over her body.

Breathless, Lisa said. "Better stop before we can't." She pulled back and cleared her throat. "It's so strong what I feel for you, Sam."

"I know." Sam sighed. "Me, too." She backed away from Lisa without losing eye contact. "I'd better go shower." She bumped into the door frame but felt around until she found the opening. "I love you."

"Same," Lisa said.

Sam backed into her bedroom. She shut the door quietly and let out an agonizing moan. One look from Lisa could turn her to jelly. She headed toward her bathroom, thinking she should make her shower a cold one.

~~~

Sam showered and dressed in record time but took a minute to apply some eyeliner. She knew Lisa liked it.

"Okay, my love," Sam said, remerging from her bedroom, "feel free to continue your snoopfest. I'm just going to say hello to Mother and maybe talk for a few minutes, and then I'll come get you so we can head out to Susie's."

Lisa nodded. "I've scoured the bookshelves already, and now I'm getting ready to rifle through your desk."

Sam reached over and opened all the drawers. "Have at it. I'll be right back."

Sam headed out the door wishing she was brave enough to bring Lisa with her to see her mother, but she wasn't quite ready for that step. Dr. Boyle said that Sam needed to minimize her stress, and the game that evening had basically destroyed every last one of her nerves. Bringing her girlfriend in to see her mother would have put her right over the edge in the nerves department.

Sam headed out of her wing and crossed the landing above the staircase. She knocked on the door to her parents' rooms. Her father was away on business, so her mother would be alone. Sam let herself in when she got no answer on the outside door to the suite. "Mother, I'm coming in. It's me, Samantha Rose."

The lights were out in the living room, but Sam saw light coming from under the bedroom door. Sam took a deep breath and knocked on the door to her parents' bedroom. Getting no answer, she knocked again and then called inside. "Mother? I'm coming in. I wanted to tell you about my game."

There was still no answer, so she listened intently at the door. Nothing. She didn't hear a sound. Sam's heart beat faster. Hopefully, her mother had simply gone downstairs for some reason. She knocked a third time and opened the door a crack.

"Mother? May I come in?" Sam peered through the one-inch crack and saw her mother's arm draped over the bedside stand. She wasn't moving. Was she sleeping? That made no sense. The lights were on full blast. Dread shot through her as she burst through the door. She rushed to her mother's side.

"Mother?" Sam shook her mother's arm. "Mother, are you okay?"

A din of confusion settled over Sam's brain. Isolated details permeated her brain. There was an open pill bottle. No, three opened pill bottles lying on their sides empty. An empty glass was on the floor near the bed. The carpet was wet. Her mother had spilled the water.

Realization hit her like a freight train. Overdose. She grabbed her mother's shoulders and shook gently. No response. She shook harder. Her mother flailed like a ragdoll. Sam heard her own wailing as if from afar. She needed help.

"Helene!" Sam yelled. "Lisa! Call 9-1-1. Help me."

Sam smoothed her mother's hair. "Oh, Mother, Mother, Mother. What have you done?" Sam raced to the intercom near the bedroom door and jammed the button to Helene's room. "Helene, call 9-1-1. Hurry. Mother's hurt." She jammed the button to her own room. "Lisa, I need you. Call 9-1-1. Hurry. Mother's hurt."

Sam raced back to her mother's bed, desperately trying to remember what she'd been taught in ninth-grade health class. "See if the victim is breathing," she muttered and leaned her ear next to her mother's mouth. The blood pounding in her own ears wouldn't let her hear. She groaned in agony. Where was everyone? She yanked open the drawer on her mother's bedside stand and grabbed the handheld mirror she knew would be there. She placed it to her mother's mouth and nose and waited. There it was. The mirror fogged up, not a lot, but enough to know that her mother was still breathing.

Lisa made it to her first. She was on the phone with someone.

"I'm in the room now." Lisa assessed the situation in seconds and said, "It looks like an overdose." She picked up the bottle and read the drug name into the phone. "It looks like she took three bottles of sixteen each." Lisa listened for a while and then took the mirror from Sam's shaking hand and held it up to Sam's mother's mouth. "Yes, she's breathing but shallowly."

Helene burst through the door.

"Yes," Lisa said into her phone. She rattled off the address. "Yes, okay. I'll go outside and wait. Yes, I'll lead them up to the room." Lisa listened again and said, "Okay, I was going to do that, but thanks for the reminder." She put a hand on Sam's back. "Yes, I'll stay on the line. Hold on."

Lisa looked past Sam and said to Helene. "Overdose. Sleeping pills. A lot. You stay here with Sam. Are you on the line with 9-1-1?"

Helene nodded and said into her phone, "Yes, that's the same person. I'm here with her. Talk to me about what to do." Helene listened and said, "On her side, in case she vomits. Okay."

Sam backed away while Lisa took charge and repositioned Sam's mother on her side. "Stay with us, Mother," Sam said like a prayer. "Stay with me."

Lisa squeezed Sam's arm as she headed for the door. "I'm going downstairs to let them in. The panel to the left of the front door opens the big gate, right?"

Both Sam and Helene nodded.

"Text me if you need to. I can get a text when I'm on the phone."

Sam nodded and patted her back pocket to make sure she had her phone on her. She did.

"Yes, she's still breathing," Helene said to the 9-1-1 operator.

Sam heard the distant sound of sirens. God, why did they have to live so far outside of town? She glanced out the window and saw the big gate opening. Good, Lisa found the right button. Sam saw Lisa outside. She had positioned herself on the top step under the brightest security light.

Helene put a firm arm around Sam's waist. The tears in Helene's eyes were scary. This was real. This was really real. Sam did her best to stay standing and not faint outright. Helene and Lisa already had their hands full and didn't need to worry about her. Coach Gellar once told her she was made of some pretty strong stuff. Damned if she could find it now.

After a million years, the sirens got louder and finally ended up in her driveway. She heard Lisa guide them into the house and then up the stairs. Sam and Helene moved away so the paramedics could get closer. Sam recognized the female paramedic from the winter formal. Lisa had given her a statement after Freddie's epileptic seizure.

The paramedics went to work immediately and asked Helene a dozen or more questions. They got Sam's mother loaded onto a stretcher, and Helene said she would go with them in the ambulance. Sam was to follow behind.

"Lisa," Helene said, "can you please drive? Sam looks pale."

"Yes, I will," Lisa said. "East Valley hospital, right?"

Helene nodded and then pulled both girls into one quick hug. "*Priez de toutes vos forces.*"

"I *am* praying," Sam said. "I am."

Sam raced to the window to watch them load her mother into the ambulance and then watched as the ambulance headed down the circular drive. Once it was on the main road, the sirens blared again. Sam physically recoiled at the sound.

The sudden quiet in the house startled her after the flurry of activity. She looked at her mother's empty bed; the sheets were so white. The water glass was still on the floor. Sam reached down and picked it up. She set it down carefully on the coaster. That was where it should be. Not the floor.

A strong arm went around her waist. Sam looked up at Lisa. Lisa was fighting her tears, trying to be strong for Sam, but Sam didn't know how to feel. She looked back at the empty bed. Her breathing turned shallow, and she shivered. Dizzy, she reached out for a handhold and found Lisa's arm.

Lisa turned them away from the bed and said, "Let's get out of this room."

Sam didn't respond but let herself be led out of her mother's bedroom. Lisa switched off the light, but Sam flicked it back on. Her mother needed that light.

"That's fine," Lisa said. "C'mon, let's keep going."

Sam groaned as dizziness overtook her. Her eyes darted back and forth as she tried to find her balance. She slammed her eyes shut and stopped walking. Her eyes continued to dart back and forth behind her lids. She was going to be sick. She pressed both hands over her eyes and felt her body go limp. Lisa pulled her toward her and dragged her somewhere. Together they slid down to the floor.

Lisa's strong arms had been around her the entire time, but this time Lisa moved them around Sam's head to hold it still. "Stop moving your head, Sam," Lisa said forcefully. Sam desperately wanted to stop; it was making her nauseous. After a moment, she was able to. Her head still trembled a little as she tried to catch her breath. Lisa relaxed her hold and moved to encircle Sam's core. "I have you, baby. I have you."

Sam groaned. She was so disoriented. She didn't know where she was.

A familiar voice said from far away, "Sam, you're having a panic attack. Relax into me, baby. Let your head fall back against me. I have you. Relax."

It was Lisa. At first, Sam couldn't find Lisa in the darkness, but the constant soft murmurs to relax her muscles and to breathe normally helped. Lisa kissed her cheek, and Sam reached up and touched the spot. She lay her head back on Lisa's shoulder.

"Relax your muscles, baby. That's it," Lisa said, her voice choked with emotion. "Now, breathe normally. You're okay, Sam. You're okay. I've got you."

Sam reached back and touched Lisa's face to let her know that she'd heard. Sam didn't know how long they sat there, but whenever she relived the events of her mother's overdose, Lisa would override it by saying, "No, baby, no. You're okay. Your mother is in good hands. Helene is with her. Relax your muscles. Breathe normally."

Once Sam felt good enough, she opened her eyes.

Lisa noticed and said, "I can't let you fall apart, baby. Not on my watch."

"Am I on your watch?" Sam choked out. Her mouth was incredibly dry.

Lisa kissed Sam on the crown of her head and answered, "Always."

"Don't leave me, Lisa. Don't *ever* leave me."

"Never." Lisa's voice was choked with emotion. She still held onto Sam tightly. She cleared her throat and said, "We're going to stay right where we are until you say you feel okay, and then we're gonna stay five more minutes after that."

"But Mother—"

"Your mother is in good hands, and you are of no use to her in this condition. You know how on an airplane, they tell the parent to put on their own oxygen mask before helping their child? That's you right now, Sam. You have to be strong and capable before you can help your mother."

Sam nodded. "Five more minutes then." She let Lisa hold her.

Chapter Twenty-Two
Walking the Path

It had been one week and one day since Sam's mother took the pills. She was home now, safe, and her spirits were up. But in true Payton fashion, no one had spoken to Sam about the events of that night. Her mother was talking to Dr. Boyle, of course. Every day. He had dropped everything that scary night and met them at the hospital. Thank goodness Sam's *maman* had the presence of mind to call him. Sam's mother trusted him like no other. And Sam, herself, had already had two sessions with him and was due for another next week. What Sam really wanted, though, was to talk to her mother about it, as scary as that was. Lisa's mother told her not to avoid scary stuff because avoiding bad things brings anxiety, migraines, and panic attacks. Lisa's mother said Sam had to learn how to deal with stuff.

Sam and Susie were in Susie's car driving home after Clarksonville's regional playoff win against the Champlain Valley League Champions, Our Lady of Mercy. Thankfully the game had been played close by at the Clarksonville Community College field. It would have been played at Clarksonville High School, but the High School Athletics Association wouldn't approve their poorly maintained and ill-equipped field. Lisa and Marlee's coach had quickly arranged the community college field, which was like having the home-field advantage.

"Marlee pitched a great game, didn't she, Sus?"

"Yeah, a two-hitter."

"Only two? That's fantastic. And they had a fair umpire today. I was so happy when Lisa told us that troll umpire is under investigation and won't be at any of their playoff games."

"That's good," Susie said. "So, with their win today, they move on to the quarterfinals."

"Next Saturday, right?"

"Yep. In Tupper Lake. That field right on the water."

"Cool. I like that field," Sam said, glad to have something to look forward to. "Mother will be done with her first full week of radiation by then." And just like that, Sam was back in the Mother-has-cancer/Mother-tried-to-kill-herself loop that had been playing in her head the entire week.

Susie was quiet for a moment but said, "Sam?"

"Yeah?"

"You have to prepare for the possibility."

"No. I don't want to think about it."

"In a tiny section of your brain, Sam, you have to store the thoughts. This way, you can pull them out and deal with them head on if you need to."

"You've had too many sessions with Dr. Austin, Sus." Her laugh was hollow even to her own ears.

"Maybe." Susie didn't say anything else, but Sam knew the conversation wasn't over.

"Did Lisa put you up to this?"

"No. Marlee did. She had zero time to prepare when her father didn't come home that night, Sam. Coach Gellar told me this thing about compartmentalizing. Put all of those thoughts in a box and tuck the box away. You can pull it out when and if you have to. And you may have to, Sam."

"I know," Sam said quietly. She knew Susie was just trying to help.

Susie moved into the center of the road as they passed a slow-moving Amish buggy pulled by a single horse. Two girls that looked to be in their early teens were heading to town with baskets to sell. They didn't look old enough to have driver's licenses. Susie moved back into her lane.

"So, Sam, what would life look like without your mother?"

Sam flinched as a spike of pain shot through her nerves. "Long before the cancer diagnosis, Mother used to talk about the funeral she wanted to have. I never took it seriously back then. I thought it was just Mother trying to stay in control or something. But this one thing stood out for me."

"What's that?"

"She kept rethinking the flower arrangements as if that was the biggest detail. Not the eulogy or who she would be leaving behind." Sam looked out the window. She didn't even have the energy to count birch trees.

"Do you think she's had, uh, self-harming thoughts before?"

"I don't know, Sus."

Sam didn't want to entertain Susie's new question, so she forced herself to think about Susie's original question. "Daddy would be lonely."

"And you?"

"Yes, of course, I would miss my mother," Sam said with more anger than she'd meant. She softened her voice and added, "Do you know that before this past week, my mother and I rarely saw each other? I mean, we didn't see each other every day."

"Really?"

"Sometimes we'd go weeks. No, seriously, Sus. Weeks would go by before I saw her in the house, which was often an accidental meeting in the hallway. I usually eat alone, or sometimes Mrs. Tardelli stays and eats with me. I think she feels sorry for me. On rare occasions, I eat with Daddy."

"And now?"

"Who knows what 'now' is, Sus. After Mother's incident, we've been trying to eat together in the dining room. Mother still only eats soup, but she's eating. Dr. Salazar and Stefan–"

"Stefan's your mother's exercise guy?"

"Yep. He, Dr. Salazar, and even Dr. Boyle advised my mother to be mindful of her nutrition. They all said that if she's going to have any fight in her during this radiation, she has to have the strength."

"Wow."

They had reached the Oak Tunnel on C.R. 62. Lately, it had become a sad landmark for Sam. It meant she was almost home and that she'd left Lisa far behind in Clarksonville.

"Mother wouldn't be at my wedding," Sam said, returning to Susie's question.

"Whenever that is."

"Exactly. I know who, but not when."

Susie shot her a genuine I'm-happy-for-you-and-Lisa smile. Sam couldn't help but smile back.

"You know, Sus, it sucks not knowing what's going to happen."

"Your life has had some big changes, Sam."

"Yours, too," Sam reminded her bestie.

"Still living it, and I'm not sure what's going to happen, either," Susie said pensively. "I think I need to move back into the house."

"Why?"

"It costs money to heat my room over the garage, and I have to find ways to save my mother money. I do the bills and now understand what living paycheck to paycheck means."

"What about your father's paychecks?"

Susie scoffed. "His lawyer advised him to stop making such big contributions—"

"Contributions? That's what he called it?"

"Our family income was basically cut in half, but the expenses are the same. Well, except that I can't get my mother to stop shopping."

"I'm so sorry, Susie." Sam reached over and rubbed her friend's arm. It was the best hug she could give from the passenger seat. "Hey, why don't you rent out your room over the garage? It really is an apartment. You could give the tenant a parking spot *in* the garage, too. You'd have to put in some kind of kitchenette, though."

Susie glanced at Sam. "How could I do all that?"

"I'll call my realtor, Marla Cohen–"

"*My* realtor," Susie mocked with a laugh. "Listen to you."

"She is," Sam said. "I own a house now, remember?"

"A huge one, too."

"Wait, wait, wait," Sam said and smacked her own leg. "Marlee's mother is a realtor. Get her involved."

"Hmm. That'll be a win-win, won't it?" Susie nodded in agreement.

"Speaking of Marlee and Lisa," Sam said. "What time are they coming over?"

"In about two hours."

"I'm so excited," Sam gushed. "I'm finally having friends over to hang in my room. Do you know that it was Mother who suggested it?"

"Maybe because you haven't left the house for one second since she's been home from the hospital."

"Probably," Sam said.

"And, Sam?"

"Yeah?"

"Don't forget what Cassie told us that time. Hope for the best, but plan for the worst. Thinking about that one possible future is you planning for the worst."

"I don't know if it's *planning*," Sam said, "but it might be a way for me to be ready for a change in my life. Change sucks. I hate it."

"Change can be good. You didn't always have Lisa in your life, and then that changed."

"Are you an optimist now, Sus?"

"I doubt it, but let's just say that I've had a lot of change thrust on me all at once," Susie's smile was grim. "And I'm trying to handle it *all* and stay sober. I can't wait to go to college and start over, to be independent."

"Be careful what you wish for, friend," Sam cautioned.

Susie pulled the car up the long circular driveway at Sam's house. "All right, *gringa,* get out of my car. I have to go home and check on the crockpot I set up for their dinner and probably run the vacuum. You're feeding us here, right?"

"Yep," Sam said. "Meatloaf and mashed potatoes."

"Marlee's favorites."

"That's why I picked them."

"You're a good friend, Sam," Susie said and pushed Sam toward the door. "Now get out."

Sam laughed and hopped out of Susie's car. She watched her friend drive down the driveway and head home.

Just as she was bounding up the steps, Dr. Boyle was walking out the front door. Even though it was Saturday, he wore a suit and dress shoes. He even wore an old-fashioned grey Fedora with a center crown crease pinched in the front. He was an older man, but in no way would Sam call him old. His hair wasn't even completely white yet.

He had dropped everything that scary night and was there when Sam's mother woke up after having her stomach pumped. He was an amazing comfort to everyone.

"How is Mother today, Dr. Boyle?" Sam asked.

"She is opening up," he said.

"Excellent." They both knew how difficult that was for every member of the Payton family. Before he got in his car, she yelled over, "I'll see you on Wednesday."

He nodded and tipped his hat in acknowledgment.

~~~

Once inside, Sam raced up the stairs as quietly as she could, just in case her mother was sleeping. It was now her habit to check in on her mother immediately upon coming home. No kitchen stops, no trips to her room.

She heard voices in her mother's suite, so she stood outside the door listening. She knew she should move away but couldn't. She desperately wanted to know what her mother's state of mind was.

"That's a good question, Helene," Sam's mother said. "What would I have done differently if I had known I would end up with breast cancer at age fifty-three? Well, many people say they wouldn't change a single thing. But I would have."

"Oh?" Sam's *maman* said. There was a distinct sound of a teacup settling back on a saucer.

"Oh, yes," Sam's mother said emphatically. "I would have spent more time with my baby girl. I would have gotten over my fears and hugged my sweet precious child. *Our* precious child."

"Thank you for giving me the gift of acknowledgment, Mimi."

"This is the way it should be." Sam's mother didn't wait for a response and said, "I would have let Samantha Rose have more quality time with her real mother. You. Maybe that way, I could have seen more smiles on her face as she grew up."

"Lisa makes her smile," Sam's *maman* said.

"That she does. She's become a cornerstone for Sam, hasn't she?"

"Mmm hmm."

"Just like you and Gerald are cornerstones for me, Helene. That rotten day when I called Sam at school to tell her I had cancer, she was surprised by my call. Why should a daughter be surprised when her mother calls? That's my fault—one hundred percent. But then I couldn't tell her. It was as if I was about to toss her a ticking hand grenade. You know how sensitive she is."

"Yes, she is."

"Well, thank you for this chat, Helene." There was the distinct sound of someone standing up. Sam's mother, no doubt. "Now, if you'll excuse me, I have to get changed. Stefano and I are walking the grounds today."

"This has been lovely, Mimi. We will do it again."

Sam heard her *maman* also stand up, so she high-tailed it to her wing. As quietly as she could, she entered her rooms and then hid in her bathroom. This way, her *maman* couldn't accuse her of eavesdropping, which she had been and now felt terrible about.

After a few minutes, Sam calmly walked out of her wing and found her mother heading down the stairs. "Working out, Mother?"

"Yes, join us, won't you?"

"Me?" Sam said, surprised.

"Yes, go get some good walking shoes on and join Stefan and me for a walk around the grounds."

"Okay." Sam bolted for her room. She threw on a pair of sweats, a t-shirt, and running shoes, although she doubted there would be any running.

Sam emerged on the front step just in time to hear her mother say, "Dr. Salazar said I need to get strong for all this radiation starting Monday. I'm going to try. I have not felt good in years."

"Let's change that," Stefan said. He was in his mid-thirties and wore his dark brown hair closely cut, not exactly a crew cut, but close. Sam didn't think he had ever been in the military, but he carried himself like he had and used precise movements. And he was fit, ooh, boy. He had muscles for days. No wonder her mother liked working out with him. He greeted Sam with a warm smile.

"We're going to do Samantha Rose's exercise path," Sam's mother said. "She trains there for her softball."

"That's great," Stefan said, letting Sam's mother lead them down the driveway. The late May mid-afternoon sun warmed Sam's face. It was a beautiful day to take a walk. "Let's warm up a bit, and then we'll get our heart rate up," he said.

They turned left at the gate toward the stand of woods. The woods extended beyond the Payton walls, but it was nice to have a small section of it on their property.

Mother set a good pace, one that Stefan approved of, and Sam found that her own heart rate was up by the time they hit the first corner.

"Looks like we'll have to turn around," Sam's mother said as she pointed to a low-lying wet area covered with damp leaves. "I'll have to have the gardener do something about this."

Sam had an idea. Now that softball was over, maybe she could fix up the trail a little at a time after school. Maybe Susie could help.

They turned around, Sam's mother still in the lead. She said, "Stefan, Dr. Boyle thinks restorative Yoga once a week will be good. When can we start?"

"Tuesday," he said enthusiastically. "I've been trying to get you to do yoga for years now, Mrs. Payton." His tone was both teasing and scolding.

"Oh, you know how stubborn I can be."

He raised an eyebrow as if to say, "Don't I know it?"

Her mother laughed at him and picked up her pace. It was really clear that Stefan genuinely cared for her mother and that they liked each other. They had a good relationship, and Sam was almost envious. No, not almost. She was definitely envious.

"The next three days are meditation days for your mother," Stefan said.

"Really?" Sam said. "Mother, you're going to learn how to meditate?"

"Mmm hmm. Stefan wants me to learn how to 'quiet my

mind.'" She used air quotes around the words.

"Yes, I do," he answered. "When those scary thoughts surface, and they will, she can push them aside. And then, Mimi, we'll work on visualizing yourself getting healthy."

"He wants me to use these techniques during my radiation sessions."

"That sounds like a great strategy, Mother." It sounded so simple to Sam, but she doubted it was. Well, good on her mother for trying.

They walked as far as they could around the property until another soggy area caused them to turn back toward the house. They stretched for a few minutes on the grass near one of Mother's rose gardens.

"Mrs. Payton, I'll go in and get the meditation space ready," Stefan said. "Take your time."

"Thank you, Stefan." After the front door closed behind him, Sam's mother said, "He is so grounded and calm. I have a lot to learn from him."

"I'm surprised you let him get close, Mother." Sam clamped her lips shut as soon as the words were out. What was she thinking saying something like that to Mimi Payton?

"It took a while, but remember, he's been my trainer for several years now."

Phew, her mother hadn't taken offense. "Mother, would you like to get to know some other people better?" A germ of an idea was springing up in Sam's mind.

"I suppose." Sam's mother wiped the sweat from her brow and took another drink from her water bottle.

"What if you took your daily walk with someone new every day?

You could start with Daddy, although we'll have to make sure it's scheduled in his planner, won't we?"

Her mother chuckled and then smiled at Sam. It was the best thing in the entire world. A week ago, they might not have had that moment. A pang of sadness went through Sam, but it didn't last long.

"You could walk with Helene, Stefan, Mrs. Worthington, and Mrs. Tardelli."

"Mrs. Tardelli?" Sam's mother's eyebrows shot up about as high as she could get them.

"Why not? How about the gardener, the maintenance man, and all the maids? Mother, you could even walk with Dr. Boyle, but we'll have to get that man some sneakers or something."

Her mother laughed. "True enough. I like this idea. I could finally get Mrs. Worthington to exercise."

"That's the spirit, Mother."

"And Lisa's mother. I would like to get to know her better. And Lisa, too."

Sam couldn't answer. Her voice was choked with emotion. She just nodded.

"And," Sam's mother continued, "there's one important person you haven't mentioned."

By this time, Sam had her emotions under control and felt she could trust her voice. "Who's that?"

"You."

"Oh, right. Of course, I'll walk with you, Mother. That will be fun." Sam was ecstatic. She had just heard her mother say she wanted to spend time with her. Yay.

Sam's mother put a hand on Sam's shoulder and said, "I'd better get in there."

"Of course, Mother. Enjoy your meditations."

She had already headed toward the house and simply waved in response without turning around.

~~~

An hour later, Sam's friends were walking the path with her. Sam was furiously writing down things she would need to do to get the path in tip-top shape. Raking the leaves and branches off the path seemed to be the biggest chore so far.

They came upon the muddy area at the first bend.

"See what I mean, you guys?" Sam said. "There's no good way around this."

Marlee and Susie walked closer to the wet and mucky area.

"I mean, it was dry the other day when I went for a run—"

"This is where you run, baby?" Lisa said.

"Yeah," Sam said. "Samantha Rose Payton can't exactly jog along the highway or in town, can she?"

Lisa narrowed her eyes and asked, "Can *Sam* jog along the highway? Can Sam jog in town?"

Sam locked eyes with her girlfriend. "I don't know." She looked down. "I don't really know," she repeated. The question had confused her a little. No. A lot.

"Hey, you guys," Marlee called to them, "c'mere. I have an idea for a bridge." She gestured toward Susie. "My colleague, the famous environmental engineer, Dr. Torres, agrees that it looks like this area is a low spot and is often filled with water."

"It is," Sam agreed. She slipped her arm around Lisa's waist.

"Okay, so if we build a beam bridge over this area, the problem will be solved. We'll have to build it up, though, so the bridge itself doesn't get wet.

"A bridge, Marlee?" Sam exchanged a concerned glance with Lisa. "Who's gonna build it?"

Marlee looked confused. "We are."

Sam looked from one friend to the next to the next. "Us? How?"

"Well, I was going back and forth in my head over whether a beam bridge or an arch bridge would be better. An arch bridge would—" Marlee looked up from her thinking and said. "You all look bored. Okay, I'll cut to the chase. For a beam bridge, we need a couple of stringers to run the length, and then we need cut planks to go across them." Marlee gesticulated with her hands over the space. It wasn't long before a far-off look appeared in her eyes. "No, wait, that's a pretty long distance to span. It might sag. You're right. We'll need additional planks along the sides to shore things up. Yes, of course."

Sam leaned closer to Lisa. "Is she still talking to us, or is she talking to herself now?"

"You've never seen her do this?"

Sam shook her head.

"She's having a conversation with herself," Lisa said. "The only thing we can do is wait for her to finish."

"Okay then," Sam said with a laugh.

"We'll use pressure-treated lumber because of the wetness, of course," Marlee continued.

"That's not environmentally friendly, Marlee," Susie said.

"What?" The look on Marlee's face was priceless. It was as if she realized there were other humans nearby. "Oh, you're right. Hmm."

Sam smiled. Marlee's 'hmm' was the most thoughtful she had ever heard.

"You know what? You're right." Marlee got that far-off look in her eye again. "We'll use cellular PVC or plastic lumber made from milk containers."

"There are still issues with plastic products, Marlee," Susie interrupted again. This time Marlee seemed somewhat ready for it. "The factories that manufacture that stuff have to be emitting God knows what into the atmosphere."

"I see," Marlee said. "We'll think on that together, okay?"

"Okay." Susie seemed surprised that her idea held merit with Marlee. Sam's heart warmed at the interchange between her two friends. They were getting better at communicating with each other.

"And we'll need concrete or stone blocks so the bridge itself won't be directly in the water." By the way she moved her hands over the space, it was obvious that she was designing the structure in her mind. She looked at Susie and said, "Concrete is pretty organic, Dr. Torres. It's just sand, limestone or clay or shale, gravel, and water. Hey, did you guys know that the stones of the great pyramids were made of an early form of concrete?"

Sam, Lisa, and Susie shook their heads.

"Yeah, the blocks were made of limestone, clay, lime, and water. Pretty cool, right?"

"Pretty cool," Sam said with a shake of her head. The knowledge her friend had in her head was astounding.

"Marlee," Sam said, "do you want to write any of this down?"

"Hmm? No, no, I've got it. Susie and I can go shopping tomorrow morning before we come over. We're doing this tomorrow, right?"

"Um, okay," Sam said.

"My van will hold everything. We'll need galvanized nails, or should we use screws? Hmm. Galvanized nonetheless." Marlee nodded her head once as if the decision on galvanized fasteners was final. Sam had no idea what the term galvanized even meant. "Lisa," Marlee said abruptly, causing Lisa to jump.

"Yes, Marlee," Lisa said with a laugh.

"How tall are you now?"

Sam looked up at the woman whose arm was still wrapped around her waist. She was finally going to get her answer.

Lisa's face turned bright red. "Six one."

Sam groaned. "Oh, baby, I knew you were getting taller. I just knew it."

"I couldn't tell you, Sam."

"You're the tower of Dubai," Sam said behind clenched teeth.

"Don't forget my bio-dad is six feet six."

Sam dramatically put a hand up to her head and squeaked, "I'm going to need a ladder."

Lisa bumped Sam with her hip. "That's why I didn't tell you."

Sam moaned and turned to watch Marlee size up Lisa and then move across the space as if her eyes were an actual measuring tape.

"Are you sure you don't want to write anything down?" Sam suggested holding out her pad and paper.

Marlee looked at her again as if confused. "No, I've got it. You guys, this is so exciting. We get to build a real bridge for a real purpose. Yay."

"Yay," Sam echoed sarcastically. "I get to be an engineer for a day, don't I?"

Marlee nodded. "How about I pay for the supplies, and then we can subtract the total cost from what I owe you for my bass equipment? Sound okay?"

"Perfect," Sam said.

Marlee nodded in agreement and took Susie's hand. She whistled as they made their way around the wet area and then down the path to look for more problems to fix. Marlee blathered on about the tools she would bring and how, oops, handrails would be a good idea, too. Duh.

Sam exchanged a look with Susie that conveyed the fact that they were both glad Marlee was happy.

Sam thought back to Lisa's question. Would Sam be able to jog out on the main road or in town like a regular person? She didn't know because even though she knew exactly who Samantha Rose Payton was, she was still trying to figure out who Sam was and how she fit into Samantha Rose's world.

Chapter Twenty-Three
Checking In

Cassie pulled the limo up to the entrance to the hospital. Sam, Lisa, Sam's parents, and Sam's *maman* stepped out of the car. It was Memorial Day, the day of Sam's mother's first radiation session, and they were all there in support.

"You guys go on ahead," Sam said. "We'll be right behind you."

"*Ne prends pas trop de temps,*" Sam's *maman* said as she and Sam's parents walked toward the entrance.

"No, we won't be long," Sam called after her.

Once her three parents were out of earshot, Sam and Lisa turned on Cassie. "So, how are *things*?" Sam asked pointedly.

"She's fine," Cassie said with a grin. A blush crept up her face.

"You've got it in a bad way. Don't you, Cassie?" Lisa said, smiling.

"Oh, you don't even know, you guys. She's so pretty. She's so freakin' smart; I can't stand it. We like the same books and movies. I'm head over heels, and I think she feels the same way."

"OMG," Sam said. "When can we meet her?"

"One day. One day soon."

"That's it?" Sam grinned. "That's all you're going to give us?"

Cassie nodded. "Yep." She opened the driver's door and got

back in. "My parents haven't even met her yet."

"Cassie," Lisa scolded.

"Soon. Soon. I don't want to jinx it."

Sam smiled and said, "I get that. Being in love is amazing, isn't it?" She shot a look at Lisa.

Cassie waggled her eyebrows as her blush deepened. "Listen, you'd better go in. I'll be hanging out right here in the parking lot. I have a good book on my Kindle app. Text me when you're ready to go."

They said their goodbyes, and Sam and Lisa hustled up the concrete walkway toward the entrance.

"Ain't love grand?" Sam said.

"Oh, yeah." Lisa reached for Sam's hand and then kissed it. "Did you see Marlee's face yesterday when we were building that first bridge? When Susie got hot, took off her outer shirt, and then stood there in a tank top?"

"Oh, my God, yes. I thought Marlee was going to throw Susie to the ground and make babies with her right there."

"I mean, I melt when I look at you," Lisa said softly, "but Marlee was an absolute puddle. And, to be honest, I don't think I knew how well-endowed Susie actually was."

"Uh, yeah, she usually keeps her girls strapped down pretty tightly."

Lisa bumped Sam with her hip knocking her a few feet away.

"Hey, watch it, Amazon," Sam scolded with a wag of her finger.

Lisa sent her a smoldering look. "Maybe later I can 'watch it?'" She bit her lower lip seductively.

"Don't get me worked up, woman," Sam said. "We're here for serious business, you know."

Lisa sobered up immediately. "You're right. I'm sorry. We need to focus on your mother right now. I'm sorry, Sam."

"Oh, baby, I wasn't reprimanding you." Sam pulled Lisa to the side of the hallway, waited for a nurse to walk by, and then said, "We'll find time for ourselves later. This is a rough day, and I'm definitely going to need your tenderness later."

"And you shall have it," Lisa said with a serious smile. She pulled Sam by the hand. "C'mon, let's catch up to them."

~~~

Sam stood in the waiting room and watched her mother follow the radiation technician through the double doors to wherever it was they were going to zap her. Knowing this was something her mother had to do on her own was hard. None of them could be in the room with her, and none of them could do it for her. Maybe this was a time in her mother's life that she had to learn to be strong all on her own. Sam hoped her mother was tough enough for the task. Sam wasn't sure she would have been.

The hug her father gave her mother before she went through the doors had brought tears to Sam's eyes. The love that passed between them was obvious. Lisa was teary-eyed at the sight, too.

Sam's *maman* reached for Sam's hand and squeezed. "We have to emotionally meet your mother wherever she is on any given day, Samantha Rose. We must be positive and hopeful even when she is not. We must allow her to be scared, too, though. If only for a little while."

"I'm scared now," Sam said. Lisa reached for her other hand.

"We all are, *mon petit hibou*. We all are."

Sam's father nodded his head in agreement. "But we're going to try to stay positive. And I, for one, am going to stay home more."

This time it was Sam's turn to nod.

After that initial exchange, they didn't talk much. Sam stood up and paced. She got water and looked at brochures but didn't see the words. She basically tried to remember how to breathe.

"With cancer, there's a lot of waiting," a woman with a scarf around her head said to Sam. The woman was very pale and very thin, and she was sitting in a wheelchair. "Your mind will go to some really unpleasant places if you let it." The woman smiled. "But don't let it."

Sam's face scrunched up as she tried not to cry in front of this stranger. She nodded and took a deep breath as the woman touched her sympathetically on the hand. "You have a good support system." She nodded toward Sam's family on the other side of the waiting room. "Use them."

"Yes, I will," Sam said, finding her voice. She wanted to tell the woman 'good luck' or something, but no words seemed right. She wasn't sure what to say to someone fighting to stay alive, someone who might not live to see the first snowfall next winter, the leaves change in autumn, or even the fourth of July fireworks next month. No, she didn't know what to say to someone like that, so she simply said, "Thank you," and headed back to her family.

Sam tried to stay out of her own head as emotion kept squeezing her chest tight. Never let them see you cry. That had been the unofficial Payton family motto ever since Sam could remember. It was a stupid motto and a hard one to keep anyway.

Lisa said, "I can't wait for everyone to see Marlee's bridges."

Thank God for Lisa. She knew how to bring Sam back from the

depths.

Sam cleared the emotion out of her throat. "I can't believe she didn't write a single thing down, and then she measured and cut all those boards and showed us how to put it all together. She saw it all in her head."

"I know. So, how did you feel using the circular saw, Sam?"

"Scared to death, and I only cut that one board. I was shaking the whole time. I think I'll leave the power tools to you guys."

"No kidding. I was a little scared, too," Lisa said. "Marlee's handrails were cool, weren't they? I mean, she used that router thingie to make a plain boring piece of wood look like it came straight from a factory."

"She's brilliant," Sam said. People always told her she was a virtuoso when it came to playing the violin, but Marlee seemed to be a virtuoso with her bridge project. Marlee had been so focused and so happy to see her mental designs take shape. It was an amazing thing to have been a part of. Sam hoped Marlee found that same joy studying engineering at Rockville.

Thinking about her friends heading off to Rockville without her stabbed Sam's already sore heart. She had only five days to mail in her acceptance form. The forms for both Rockville and Wellesley had to be postmarked by Saturday, and Sam still hadn't talked to her parents about it. The Payton family kind of had its hands full at the moment.

Lisa squeezed Sam's hand, probably sensing she was going somewhere dark, and said, "Those hybrid wood/plastic boards they found were such a good compromise, weren't they?"

"Yeah. Susie's happy the environment will be saved," Sam said, mocking her friend.

"And Marlee's happy the boards will stand up to the water."

"I, for one," Sam's father interjected, "can't wait to see these amazing feats of engineering on my walk later today with Mother."

"Oh," Sam said, "so you're the first victim on my 'Walks with Mother' campaign." "Be careful, Daddy. Mother sets a mean pace."

He chuckled and then patted his already trim stomach. "It may be time for me to exercise more, too. So, tell me, what exactly is restorative yoga?"

"No way," Sam said, her eyes wide. "Mother is making you do yoga with her and Stefan?"

He nodded. "And Mrs. Worthington. This should be quite a sight."

Sam grinned at the thought of Stefan leading those three in Yoga poses. "I wish I could see this."

"Join us tomorrow," he said. There was a pleading look in his eye.

"Oh, no," Sam said. "I'm pretty sure I have to be in school."

"I'll write you a note," he said with a twinkle in his eye.

Sam chuckled but thought it seemed a little disrespectful to joke around when her mother was probably in pain somewhere in the back. She looked down and then closed her eyes. Her grin faded.

Within minutes a large group of people came out from behind the double doors. An older gentleman seemed to be the center of attention. He held a colorful certificate with what looked like several official-looking signatures on it. One of the techs guided him to a gold bell mounted on the wall. A woman who was probably his wife stood by his side. Dr. Salazar was there too and stood next to the man's wife. The man reached up and grabbed the foot-long braided rope hanging from the bell clapper.

"Side to side," Dr. Salazar said.

He nodded and then yanked the rope left, right, and left. The clanging rang out in the waiting room. It was loud, but not louder than the cheers and clapping from the people surrounding him. Sam found herself caught up in the moment and clapped along with them. She shrugged at Lisa's perplexed look. She didn't know what was going on, either.

Once the handshakes and celebrations were finished, Dr. Salazar came over to them. There was a big grin on her face. "Mr. Dunham is eighty-eight years old and just finished his final round of radiation."

"That's what the ringing of the bell signified?" Sam's father asked.

"Yes, the bell ceremony is a tradition." Dr. Salazar brushed a strand of hair off her face that had escaped her bun. "He rang the bell to signal the end of his treatment here, but I also like to think that a bell signals a beginning, too. Like the way church bells ring to start worship or school bells ring to start class. Right, girls?"

Sam and Lisa both nodded.

"Cancer has a way of stealing hope," Dr. Salazar continued, "but I like to think the bell is a way of giving hope to others. It signals that there will be an end to the treatment."

"Thank you, doctor," Sam's father put his hand out, and the doctor shook it. She then shook everyone else's hand in their small group. She turned and headed out the doors of the radiation waiting room.

"That ceremony was nice," Lisa said.

"We'll have to tell Mother about this tradition," Sam said. Her spirits were lifted. Her own mother would be ringing that bell in four weeks' time, the day before Sam graduated from high school.

The waiting was the worst. Sam had just started her third tour of the waiting room when her mother emerged from behind the double doors. Sam rushed over.

"How are you feeling, Mother?"

"All right," Sam's mother said. "A little tired from all the nervous anticipation, I suppose." By this time, Sam's father, her *maman*, and Lisa had gathered around.

"Four weeks of this, Mother," Sam's father said.

"I'd better get used to it then, haven't I?" Sam's mother laughed resignedly and said, "Let's go home."

"Gladly," Sam said, making everyone laugh. "I'll text Cassie to meet us out front."

Once in the limo, Sam asked, "Mother, will you tell us what it was like? I mean, if you want to."

"Your mother is tired—"

"No, it's okay, Helene," Sam's mother said. She turned to look at Sam. "It wasn't what I thought it would be. The tech walked me back to this big room and had me put on a hospital gown. In the center of the room was this hard table. Along the back wall were these big machines. That's where the radiation was going to come from. They had me lie on the table and strapped me in."

"They strapped you down to the table?" Sam said. "I would have panicked."

"They have to do that, so I don't move."

"Because of the radiation beam," Lisa said. "It has to hit a very precise spot."

"You read too much," Sam said to Lisa with a grin. Lisa smiled back.

"Lisa's right. They continuously reminded me not to move. I used Stefan's meditation techniques which calmed me immensely. I thought it was going to take longer, but then it was over, just like that." Sam's mother snapped her fingers. "Over the intercom, the tech told me to put my arms down, and then they came back into the room to help me off the table."

"The technicians weren't even in the room with you," Sam mused. "Did you feel like a lab rat?"

Sam's mother chuckled. "Kind of, but I knew they were helping me and will continue to help me for the next four weeks."

"Four weeks," Sam muttered in a dejected tone. She was appalled when she realized she had said the words out loud. She cleared her throat and, even though she already knew the answer, asked, "Who will be your walking partner this afternoon, Mother?"

"Oh, this handsome fellow that I know. I met him at a cotillion. He was the most handsome boy in the entire room."

Her father returned the smile Sam's mother sent him. Sam's heart warmed to see the obvious affection they had for one another. She hoped Lisa would still look at her that way when she was fifty-three. A tear comes to Sam's eye. All of this was hard on her father also, but he was hiding it well, putting up a strong front. Sam made a mental promise to visit with her father now and then and check in with him. Yes. Checking in with each other. That was something the Payton family had never been good at. Maybe it was time for that to change.

~~~

Five full days had come and gone since Sam's mother's first

radiation treatment. It was late Saturday morning as Sam strolled with her mother in one of the back flower gardens. Later on, Susie was coming by to pick her up for Lisa and Marlee's playoff game in Tupper Lake, an hour and a half away.

"Samantha Rose," Sam's mother said, "where shall we revisit this morning?"

"How about the Gardens in Versailles?" Sam suggested. "We can start at the *Statue de la Marne au parterre d'Eau du Château de Versilles.*"

"Your favorite spot," Sam's mother said. She pulled some dead leaves off of one of her plants and put it in the bag Sam held out for her. "You always wanted to go back for one last look."

"I'd love to bring Lisa to Paris and the gardens one day," Sam said wistfully. As soon as she said it, she realized it was the first time she'd ever spoken to her mother so casually about her girlfriend.

"And one day you will," Sam's mother said, dumping an entire handful of dead clippings into Sam's bag. "But I don't want to revisit Versailles this morning."

"Oh, no? Where would you like to go?" Sam and her mother had begun reminiscing about places they'd been together in the world. It had been Sam's idea, but her mother loved it. So far, in their daily talks, they'd been to the Swiss Alps, Central Park in New York, and the Syracuse Performing Arts Center.

"I would like to go to Phoenix."

"Arizona?"

"Oh, yes. Where a certain little one was born a little over eighteen years ago."

"Almost eighteen and a half, Mother."

"That much?"

Sam nodded. "What was Phoenix like?"

"Lovely in the winter months. I hear it gets dreadfully hot in the summer. Your father and I rented this lovely home. It looked like one of those Adobe houses. Even the McDonalds was made to look that way."

"Really? Maybe I'll take Lisa to Phoenix, too."

Sam's mother smiled. "We lived together—your father, Helene, and me. She had her own room, of course, and I always stayed back at the house when your father took her to doctor's appointments. I didn't even go to the hospital when you were being born."

"Oh, Mother, you didn't? Was that terrible for you?"

"Agony. I wanted to be there to comfort Helene, but it would have been too hard to explain who I was. She was so young and so brave taking on this surrogacy role. What a sacrifice she made for our entire family."

"But, Mother, she's family now," Sam said quietly.

"Mmm hmm. She is, Samantha Rose. She is." Her mother sat down on one of the many stone benches in the gardens, so Sam did the same. "When we let her go right before Christmas, we weren't kicking her out, as you may have thought. In my mind, I was giving her tough love. I was allowing her to get out from under the Payton finally hold we had on her. I wanted her to go have her own life. Fall in love. Settle down."

"Is that what she wanted, Mother?"

"I thought so at the time, but we never asked."

"You just assumed."

"We did, but now that she's back, I see she belongs here."

"And what will happen to her when I go away to college?" Sam asked, hoping she could direct the conversation toward her college choices.

"This is her home as much as any other. She's doing us a favor by caring for me for now, but later? That'll be her decision. She is welcome to stay as long as she wants. Forever, if she wants, but let's keep this between you and me because I haven't had this conversation with your father yet."

"You'll be sure to ask my *maman* her opinion, won't you?" Sam deliberately used the French word for mother. She used it as a reminder.

"Of course, we will. Ahh, you were, and still are, such a beautiful child. You were this tiny little thing. Your fingers were like little matchsticks, and your eyes were so blue. We couldn't get enough of you. You were so needy. You needed to be fed every few hours. There were so many diaper changes, burping, wardrobe changes."

Sam laughed. "Wardrobe changes for you or for me?"

Sam's mother chuckled. "All of us, dear. You were constantly spitting up on yourself or us. Laundry was a way of life. It became routine after a while, but I never could get the hang of holding you. You always cried when it was my shift to take care of you. You must have felt my nervous energy."

"I'm sorry, Mother."

"Helene asked if she could try, and I gladly handed you over only because you were so miserable. Helene knew what you needed."

"I love you both, Mother." Sam wanted her mother to understand that it wasn't a competition.

"Thank you for the reassurance. I have loved watching my daughter grow into a beautiful young woman willing to play her violin for her old mother's garden meetings."

"Mother," Sam scolded, "you're not old."

"Do you know what other day stands out for me?"

"What day is that?"

"Meeting Lisa for the first time. At that little pool party you had with your friends last summer."

"Oh, yeah?" Sam prayed it was a *good* standing-out moment.

"Samantha Rose, she is strikingly pretty, you know."

"I know." And she did know. Sometimes she still couldn't believe Lisa let her kiss her in that dugout on their first date.

"With her height, she could easily be a model, but the day I met her, there was something about her. I didn't know what it was then, but I think I do now. Stefan talks about the aura around people."

"Getting meta-physical on me, Mother? You've been hanging around Stefan too much."

Her mother smiled. "Stefan says that a person's aura emanates from their very being. He says I must have sensed hers."

"You talked to Stefan about Lisa?"

"I didn't set out to," Sam's mother said. "We were talking about auras, and I told him about the strong feeling I got from Lisa that day. I felt, and still feel, that Lisa is an old soul. I believe she has uncanny wisdom, a great ability to love and to be loved." Her mother closed her eyes for a moment lifting her face to the sun. Sam did the same. "Lisa knows herself, but I think she's trying hard to know *you*. Make sure you let her in, Samantha Rose."

"I'm trying." Sam wasn't sure she knew who she really was yet, though.

"Don't get me wrong. I see the connection you two have. It's ethereal. It's otherworldly. It's almost like you've known each other in past lives and waited to meet each other again in this life."

Wow. Sam tried to digest her mother's observations, but it was too much. Instead, she said, "Do you believe in reincarnation, Mother?"

"I don't know, but it sounds nice, doesn't it? I may be finding out soon, won't I?"

"Mother, don't talk that way."

Sam's mother patted her on the knee and smiled. It was a smile that said Sam was too young to understand. "Your friends are genuine and authentic, and they love you. Your father and I couldn't have wished for better companions for you."

Helene walked into the garden and cleared her throat. "Samantha Rose, Susie *est ici.*"

"Thank you, *maman.* I'll be there in a minute."

Helene nodded and turned to go back into the house.

Sam was instantly sad, not because Susie was there to pick her up, but because it meant her time with her mother was over for the day. Sam was finding out that she liked spending time with her mother and said so.

"And I'm glad we're finally getting to know each other, Samantha Rose. I love you more than words can express."

Sam waited for her mother to turn and hug her. When she didn't, Sam stood up and hugged her mother first. She said goodbye and headed back into the house. She hadn't found a moment to bring up her college decision, and they still hadn't talked about that fateful night two weeks ago, but her mother had been quite fatigued from the five consecutive days of radiation sessions, so Sam didn't push either subject.

Her *maman* was waiting for her in the foyer. "Wish the girls good luck for me," she said to Sam.

"I will." Sam hugged her *maman* and grabbed a light jacket

from the foyer closet.

"The deadline is today, Samantha Rose."

"I know."

"Did you have that talk with your parents?"

Sam didn't answer the question directly. "I have the acceptance form in my pocket, and Susie already knows we're stopping at the post office on our way." Truth be told, Sam had two stamped envelopes in her back pocket, one for Wellesley and one for Rockville. She was going to make the decision at the post office.

"Which did you choose?"

I don't know yet, came the answer in her head. Instead, she said, "I haven't spoken to Mother or Daddy yet, so I'd rather not say."

Sam's *maman* frowned. "I will respect that." She hugged Sam and said, "Just be happy, *mon petit hibou.* Be happy."

Chapter Twenty-Four
Depraved

Susie parked in the grassy field that served as a parking lot for the Clarksonville quarterfinal playoff game. Sam loved this part of Tupper Lake. The ballfield sat right on the actual lake, and she wondered how many foul balls went into the water.

Clarksonville was out on the field taking their infield and outfield warmup. Marlee was walking toward the dugout; her part in the warmup finished.

"So, before we get to the bleachers," Susie said carefully, "are you going to tell me which envelope you mailed?"

Sam hesitated. When she first got back in the car after the post office stop, she'd told Susie she didn't want to talk about it, and they both artfully avoided the subject of colleges and choices and parent opinions. But now Susie wanted to talk about it.

Sam sighed and stopped walking. She turned toward her friend. "I'm a coward, Susie."

"Why?"

"I decided not to decide."

"What does that mean?" A perplexed but caring expression crossed Susie's face.

"I mailed them both."

Susie's eyes got wide. "Both?"

"I figure I'll call one of the schools and cancel my acceptance once I get my head out of my ass and talk to my parents. We're just so focused on Mother's illness right now, and my mother and I have been talking more and getting to know each other, and she almost killed herself, and I still don't know why, so I don't want to rock the boat, upset the apple cart—"

"Stop, stop." Susie pulled Sam into a hug. "You have a lot in that head of yours. Let's talk about it on the way home, okay? You can practice what you want to say to your parents. You know? Run it by me."

Sam stabbed at the stupid tears in her eyes. If she had any backbone, she wouldn't be in this predicament. She pulled back from Susie's healing hug.

"Samantha Rose would be merrily heading off to Wellesley in the fall," Sam said. She pulled a tissue out of her jacket pocket and blew her nose. Gah, she hated crying, especially because Lisa would see her and worry, and Lisa needed to focus on the game.

"What about the girl named Sam?" Susie asked softly.

"Sam would be excited to be heading to Rockville University with her friends."

"Is that the only reason you'd want to go to Rockville? To be with Marlee and me and eventually Lisa?"

"Not the only reason, no. They have a great school of music, and the softball team seems like a good fit. I like Coach Greer and the assistant coaches. It just feels right for me."

"It feels right for 'Sam.'" Susie tugged on her arm, and they continued walking toward the bleachers. "It must suck having multiple personalities."

Sam was dumbfounded by Susie's statement. Multiple personalities? She showed different faces to different people, yes, but was it that severe? Bridget came running toward Sam and slammed into her legs.

"C'mon, Samtha," Bridget said, pulling Sam by the hand. "Mama saved you guys a seat."

Sam let herself be led to the home side bleachers. Alivia was on the far side of the bleachers sitting with Jessica's parents. She waved at them but made no move to get up. Sam waved back. Susie just looked at her shoes. They, or at least Sam, would go say hello later. She and Susie went over to greet Marlee's mother and her boyfriend, Bob. Marlee's mother was very nervous for her daughter, and Sam was glad that Bob seemed to be a calm and steady influence.

When they climbed up on the bleachers, Lisa's mother hugged Sam and said, "Good to see you, Samantha Rose. How is your mother feeling?"

Sam didn't answer right away. Lisa's mother had called her Samantha Rose. Was she 'Samantha Rose' to Lisa's family, or was she 'Sam?' All this time, she thought she was Sam. Did they see her as a wealthy socialite? One that lived frivolously and bought expensive gifts just because she could?

Sam cleared her throat. "She's fine," she said automatically. Sam blinked and came back to the present moment. "She and I are spending a lot of time together. Talking, getting to know one another."

"That's wonderful," Lisa's mother said, a nurturing smile on her face.

Sam greeted Lisa's father and siblings. True to form, Lynnie was reading a book on her Kindle. That was Lynnie, bookworm extraordinaire. Lawrence Jr. was already squirming in his seat.

"Mama," Lisa's father said, "I'm going to take these wiggle worms to the playground. Get out some of this pent-up energy." He pointed to a playground just on the other side of the right field fence.

"An hour in the car has them antsy," Lisa's mother said. "Go on. You can see the game from there."

Once they left, Sam and Susie excused themselves to go greet their girls. They waited near the home team dugout. As soon as Clarksonville's warmup was done, Lisa and Marlee made a beeline toward them.

"You made it," Lisa said to Sam.

"We did," Sam said.

Susie and Marlee broke off into their own private conversation.

"Good luck." Sam stuck her fingers through a hole in the chain-link fence.

Lisa grabbed the fingers and seductively swirled her index finger over Sam's palm. "Which one did you mail?"

Sam laughed. "Both."

"Whoa, you couldn't make a decision, eh?" Lisa said with a laugh.

"Yeah, but at least this way, I'll have a spot at Rockville if I ever work up the nerve."

"You will," Lisa said with confidence.

"I'm glad you're so sure," Sam said sarcastically.

Someone called for Lisa and Marlee to join the team.

"Gotta go," Lisa said. "ILY."

"Same," Sam called after her. "Good luck."

Back at the bleachers, Sam settled herself in between Lisa's mother and Susie. Lisa's bio-dad William and his wife Evelyn walked over.

"Hey, you two," Sam said. "How are you?" Sam's eyes grew wide when she looked at Evelyn. "Are you?"

Evelyn nodded, and William put a protective arm around her.

Sam squealed and leaned over Susie to give them both hugs. "Does Lisa know?" Sam glanced over at Lisa, walking behind the plate for the start of the game.

"Not yet," Evelyn said. "There's no hiding it now." She lovingly rubbed her baby belly.

"When are you due?" Lisa's mother asked.

"End of October," William said. "Lisa will have another—" He cut his statement short and glanced at Lynnie. He must have remembered at the last second that Lisa's siblings did not know he was Lisa's bio-dad. He cleared his throat. "Lisa will have another long game ahead if this umpire is like that one at East Valley."

Good save, William. Good save, Sam thought.

"Samantha Rose, what an incredible thing you did in that last game," Evelyn said. "You threw yourself down on your sword in the name of fairness. You did the right thing. I'm proud of you."

Susie clapped Sam on the back. "She's a keeper, this one."

Sam didn't really register the praise. She was stuck on the fact that Evelyn had called her Samantha Rose. Not Sam.

"We have news about that particular umpire," Lisa's mother said. "Coach Spear's friend, Anne, came by and told us that he was 'relieved of his duties' by the umpiring association while they investigate."

"Oh, really?" William said. "What made them come to that decision?"

"It turns out he had an issue with Marlee herself."

"Are you kidding me?" Susie clenched her firsts. "What issue? What could he possibly find wrong with Marlee?"

"Apparently, his niece is a ninth grader at Clarksonville High, and the night she came home from Clarksonville's Winter Formal, he just happened to be visiting his sister. When asked about the dance, she told her family how much she admired the bravery of the short-haired blonde pitcher on the softball team who had gone to the dance with another girl. Apparently, this man took exception to his darling niece being exposed to such depravity. Those were his words, according to Anne."

"Depravity?" Sam muttered. "He's the depraved one. Why can't people just let you live your life?" Sam felt a mixture of anger and profound sadness pushing itself up from the very depths of her soul. "Excuse me." She flew off the bleachers, afraid she would make a fool of herself sobbing, and ran into the parking lot. Once she found Susie's car, she sat down on the grass, leaned back against the front tire, and sobbed. Sadness, anger, frustration. It all burst out from somewhere deep inside. She pounded a fist into the grass. It was not satisfying at all, but she didn't want to punch Susie's car. She wished she could punch that umpire. She wished she could punch cancer in the teeth, but most of all, she wished she could punch the coward named Samantha Rose.

"Sam," Susie called from behind the car, "are you okay, *gringa*?"

Sam couldn't find her voice and simply shook her head. Susie sat down on the grass next to her. Susie's hip touched hers as she reached over to hold Sam's hand. The wordless gesture let Sam know she was loved and cared for.

"I can't handle life, Sus," Sam said without looking up. "Why do people have to be so stupid? Why do people want you to live a life that's not true to who you are? Doesn't that troll of an umpire understand how difficult it is to be gay, how hard it is to want an authentic life, to live honestly? Who the hell is Marlee hurting? Marlee is the sweetest and most innocent person I've ever known. She happily built two damn bridges for my family without a second thought, without expecting a reward or praise. She does things out of love. She isn't worldly, Susie. She's almost childlike sometimes. Like that time at our winter formal? Remember? Marlee had just put a cookie in her mouth, and that asshole Ryan grabbed his crotch and asked if she had room for his dick? My heart broke, Susie. Marlee didn't react other than to look down and wad up the half-chewed cookie into a napkin. She went inside herself. She didn't know him. She didn't know why he had targeted her. She doesn't have that hard armor that we do. Well, that you and Lisa seem to have. If he'd said those things to you or me or Lisa, we would have shrugged it off as a comment from a jerk, but Marlee is innocent, Susie. She's completely innocent."

"I know. I'm pissed." Susie let go of Sam's hand. "Lisa's mother said the team doesn't know any of this yet. Coach Spears will tell them a watered-down version of it and then pull Marlee and Lisa aside later to tell them the whole story. I told Lisa's mother I wanted to be there when that happens."

"Marlee was targeted for being who she is," Sam said. "That's a hate crime." Sam looked up at her friend, seeing a mixture of anger and compassion battling over Susie's face. "Susie, why do people feel they can judge you? Judge who you are. Judge what you want. Force you into doing what you don't want to do?"

"We're not talking about Marlee anymore, are we?"

Sam shook her head.

"Sam, a lot of people would like to see the Payton empire fail."

"Why?"

"Jealousy, maybe? I don't know, but your parents have had to be over-protective of you. But you're eighteen now, heading off to college somewhere, and you want independence. Going out with Lisa was a form of rebellion, you know. They hadn't met her. They knew nothing about her, and then, all of a sudden, they find out she's in your life. They hadn't approved her or vetted her or had her checked out."

"Actually, my father has had all of you and your families checked out."

Susie raised an eyebrow but didn't respond.

"But, you're right. My parents didn't know she was special to me."

"And they probably would have had the same reaction if it had been a guy," Susie said. "Well, a similar reaction. Your mother was kind of thrown by the whole lesbian thing. Which boggles my little mind because how could she not know? You're the biggest, butchiest dyke I've ever—"

Sam lifted her arm and pushed her friend away weakly. "Am not." She smiled at her friend's teasing.

"No, actually, you're not," Susie said, "but they should have known. I knew."

"You did?"

"Yeah, you were quiet and shy when I met you at softball in ninth grade, but I could tell you were *family*."

"Everyone else thought I was stuck up and arrogant," Sam said.

"They didn't really look, Sam. They saw the surface, and they believed the legend."

Sam laughed. "Legend?"

"The Payton family is big beans around Clarksonville County. You know that. Paytons drive around in limousines."

Sam sighed. "And Samantha Rose would never do something so contradictory to the perfect Payton image like being a lesbian."

"Samantha Rose and Sam are the same person," Susie said softly. "The point I was making about you going off to college is that you have to figure out what *you* want. We play so many roles in life, but you are still essentially you, Sam. Stop trying to please everybody. That's impossible. You know who you have to make happy?" Susie didn't wait for a reply. "You. You have to make *you* happy."

"Yeah," Sam said, "but I don't know how to do that."

"Listen, it sounds like the game started, so let's head back, okay?" Susie stood up and reached a hand down.

Sam took the offered hand and stood. "Lisa's family must think I've lost my mind. Again."

"Lisa's mother understands," Susie said. "She knows you're on fragile ground right now."

"Fragile is the right word," Sam said. She touched the necklace that Lisa had given her. It helped her feel grounded.

As they headed back toward the bleachers, Susie said, "*Dios mio,* I didn't tell you what Lynnie said when William and Evelyn walked away."

"What?"

"She asked her mother who William was."

"What did Lisa's mother say?"

"That she had gone to high school with William and that

William and Evelyn were friends of the family."

"True statements, but Lynnie is very smart," Sam said. "She's going to figure this thing out."

"Maybe."

When they returned to the bleachers, Lisa's mother gave Sam a wordless but meaningful hug. She said, "Marlee struck out the first three batters."

"That's my girl," Susie said. "Who are they playing anyway?"

"Whickett High School from Albany," Lisa's mother answered.

"Oh, no," Sam said. "That's the same team they played last year. They have that rocketball pitcher."

"Anne said the pitcher added a rise ball to her repertoire," Lisa's mother said with a frown.

"They're good hitters," Susie said, gesturing to the Clarksonville team getting ready to take their turn at bat. "They'll be okay." It almost sounded like Susie was trying to convince herself of that fact.

Watching the first three Clarksonville batters strike out in turn made Sam nervous. This was going to end up being a pitchers' duel, with the winner taking advantage of mistakes by the other team.

After five innings of perfect ball by both pitchers, neither team had managed to get a single baserunner, and the game was still scoreless. Sam got a little antsy and hopped off the bleachers saying she was going to stretch her legs. She walked past the Clarksonville dugout as the team was getting ready to head onto the field for the top of the sixth inning.

"Marlee," Lisa said in an exasperated tone, "to elevate your fastball, you have to use the change-up. You can't overpower them with every pitch, so stop thinking and just do it."

"Okay," Marlee said.

Wow, Sam thought, that was easy. Marlee was in her own head a lot, but Lisa pulled her out just like that. Sam headed toward the concession stand, wishing that Lisa or someone—anyone—would tell her what to do. Tell her who to be.

"Why do I have to figure out *who* to be?" Sam muttered as she got on the end of a long line. "Why can't I just *be*?"

"Excuse me? Did you say something?" A girl around her own age turned around. She wore a Watertown softball t-shirt.

"Oh, no. Sorry," Sam said, embarrassed. "I'm just muttering to myself."

"I know you," the girl said. "You were on the news."

"Me?"

"Yeah, the Watertown news. That game. Yeah, it was you," the girl said. "Jo, come here. This is that girl."

"Oh, shit," the girl named Jo said. "You are my freakin' hero."

"What did I do?" Sam said, bewildered.

Jo exchanged a glance with her friend. "That umpire was a weasel. So unfair. The news camera showed that girl's pitches." She pointed to Marlee, who was on the field pitching. "That girl there. Clarksonville. Her pitches were strikes, but he kept calling them balls. They even showed her last pitch to you."

"It was a strike," the first girl said. "You looked so confused, and then when you made that pitcher tag you out. Oh, my God! It was classic!"

"You really stuck up for that pitcher in your interview, too," Jo said. "And she was on the *other* team. I could tell you wanted to call that umpire an asshole, but you were very diplomatic, saying he was being unfair and cheating or something like that. It's all over YouTube and Instagram and Facebook," Jo said. "Look it up. You're famous."

"Wow, who knew?" Sam was incredulous. The last thing in the world she wanted was to be in anyone's spotlight. "Thanks. I, um, I gotta go." She turned back toward the bleachers, the concession stand forgotten.

"I bet Ellen has her on her show," Jo said to her friend as Sam was leaving.

"God, I would have killed myself if I was that pitcher," the other girl said.

Sam cringed as she heard the words. They had been spoken so casually. There was nothing casual about killing yourself. Anger flashed through her, igniting already frayed nerves. It took all her strength not to turn around and give the girl a piece of her mind. Instead, she took a deep breath and pulled out her phone. She sent a quick message to her mother, filling her in on the game and asking how she was. She didn't get an immediate reply but hadn't really expected one. She knew she was being needy, but maybe she'd ask her mother to text back more quickly in the future.

Sam was quiet when she got back on the bleachers. Lisa's mother and Susie picked up on it but didn't make a big deal about it.

"Whickett got two runs, Sam." Susie pointed to the scoreboard.

"Errors," Lisa's mother added.

Sam's heart sank. This was turning out to be a truly rotten day.

Marlee struck out the last batter to end the top of the sixth inning. Clarksonville was losing 2-0 going into their half of the sixth.

"That catcher is rock solid behind the dish," one of the people in the stands said, pointing to Lisa in the dugout.

"Yes, she is," Sam said to Lisa's mother. Lisa's powerful legs could withstand two hours or more of constant squatting. And her throws down to second base, you'd have to be crazy to try and steal on her. And the way she took charge of Marlee and the way Marlee accepted the role were exceptional. The duo was doing what they did best. They were going to work, and no one was impeding on that. At least not in this game. The Clarksonville team was a well-oiled cohesive team that deserved to be in the New York State playoff games. Sam was glad she had made sure of it, even if it was at the expense of losing three people she had called friends. Abby, Rachel, and Dara still weren't talking to her or Susie. They didn't even look at them in the hallways at school.

"We've got six outs to get back in this," Lisa said to her teammates. "Let's do it."

"Keep your head in there, Julie," Sam called to her friend heading up to bat. "You can do it." Sam forced herself out of her own head to be there for her friends.

Julie smashed a searing line drive through the three-four hole on the right side of the infield and was safe at first base with a single.

Jessica, a good power hitter, surprised everyone by bunting the ball down the first base line. The Whickett first baseman took a chance that it would go foul, but it didn't. The ball died right at the edge of the chalk line in fair territory. There were now two base runners on with no outs, with Lisa heading up to bat.

"Go, Lisa," Sam shouted. "Do what you do best, b—" Oops, she'd almost shouted, "baby." Sam clamped her lips shut. Maybe there were people around her who thought her relationship with Lisa was "depraved." She didn't have the energy to open that can of ignorance right now.

Lisa laced the first pitch foul down the left-field line.

"I love her swing," Susie said, watching Lisa. She looked away and then said, "Whoa, what is that team doing?"

"Oh, my God." Sam could not believe her eyes. "They're putting on a shift. Look! Their right-fielder is practically in center field."

"Oh, they are about to get so burned," Susie muttered low, so only Sam could hear.

No truer words were spoken as Lisa sent the next pitch screaming down the right field line. The Clarksonville fans leaped to their feet, roaring their approval. The race was on. Julie scored, then Jessica. Lisa booked around second and headed toward third. Holy crap! Coach Spears was sending her home. Lisa got part way, pulled up, and sprinted back to third. The cutoff player rifled a perfect one-hopper to the Whickett catcher. Lisa would have been out at the plate.

"Good idea, baby," Sam called. Oops. Oh, well. Too bad. The bigots were just going to have to get over it.

"*Aay*, that team got scorched," Susie said, plopping down hard on the bleachers.

"Skee-orched!" Sam echoed and laughed.

The score was now tied 2-2, and Clarksonville still had no outs. Marlee stepped up to the plate and smashed a double straight up the middle, almost searing the pitcher in half. Lisa scored easily, giving Clarksonville the lead.

The rest of the Clarksonville lineup couldn't get Marlee past third base, and the inning ended with Clarksonville ahead by a score of 3–2.

"Hold 'em now, Clarksonville," Susie called out. All they had to do was get three more outs and hold Whickett scoreless, and the quarterfinal game would be theirs.

Lisa's father, who had wandered back to the bleachers at the beginning of Clarksonville's at-bat, shouted, "You have a championship defense behind you, Marlee. Just do your thing."

Susie leaned over to Sam and said low, "Marlee's been using the rise /drop combination with a few fastballs and off-speed pitches thrown in for fun. I know Lisa's going to switch them to a curve/screw combo. I just know it."

Except for an off-speed pitch, Sam still couldn't really tell what pitches were being thrown. Even at bat, she never knew. She either hit them or didn't. A thought occurred to her. Maybe softball wasn't her calling. Maybe she shouldn't count on playing ball in college. Maybe Wellesley was the better place for her if softball wasn't going to be part of her college life. Maybe her parents knew that and were waiting for her to realize it, too.

"Come back to me," Susie said.

"Hmm?" Sam said. "Oh. Sorry."

Susie slapped her friend on the knee. "Stay out of your head, Sam."

"Okay." Sam smiled. She sounded the way Marlee had earlier when Lisa told her what pitches to throw.

Susie's prediction came true, and Lisa and Marlee literally threw a completely different game plan at the Whickett batters. Whickett didn't know what hit them, not literally, and Marlee got three quick strikeouts to end the game.

"That team got McAllistered," Lynnie said quietly under the din of the screaming Clarksonville fans.

"That's exactly right, Lynnie," Sam said and then hugged Lisa's mother.

Lisa grabbed Marlee in a bear hug keeping her protected from their mobbing teammates. After the high-five line and a Clarksonville team meeting, Lisa and Marlee walked over to William and Evelyn. Judging by Lisa's squeal and the big hugs she gave them both, she now knew she was going to have another brother or sister. After saying goodbye to them, Lisa and Marlee headed toward the bleachers. Lisa's parents and siblings said their goodbyes and dragged a tired bunch to the family mini-van. Marlee's mother was still teary-eyed, and Marlee just hugged her and laughed. Apparently, it was a common occurrence. It was nice watching Marlee hug Bob, too. He seemed like a good man.

After Marlee's mother and Bob left, Marlee said, "Oh, man, for a minute there, I thought our season was over." She had a massive bag of ice tied down on her right shoulder and held another in her hand.

"Sit," Lisa said, and Marlee did. "Ice." Lisa pointed to Marlee's crotch. Sam would have raised an eyebrow but knew about Marlee's groin injury. She hoped neither injury would be an issue in the semi-final game the following weekend.

"You guys are a fantastic team," Susie said. "You not only have the best pitcher but the best-looking one at that."

The blush that spread across Marlee's face was priceless. She bit her lower lip and smiled at Susie in a way that sent a very private message to her girlfriend. Sam looked at Lisa, who was rolling her eyes.

Lisa leaned closer and said, "You'd think she'd be too exhausted to even think about, you know, that."

"Are *you* too tired, my love?" Sam said, reaching for Lisa's hand.

"Never," Lisa said with a suggestive raise of her eyebrow.

"See? Love never gets tired."

"Excuse me, Samantha Rose?"

Sam turned at the sound of her name. Lisa and Marlee's coach stood right behind her.

"Hello, Coach," Sam said. "Great game. A nail-biter."

Coach Spears rolled her eyes. "No kidding. Listen, I just wanted to say how much I admire your sense of fairness and honor at our game last week. I was at my wits' end trying to figure out how to get through to that man. And then to find out that he—" She stopped herself short and looked at Marlee, who was in an animated conversation with Susie.

"Coach, I heard the whole story," Sam said. She felt Lisa's eyes on her. "I'm sorry there are people like that in the world."

"Me, too," Coach Spears said. She sighed. "I have a challenging task ahead. Would you and Susie sit with Marlee and Lisa while I tell them?"

"Of course," Sam said.

"Tell us what?" Lisa asked. She must have read the concerned look in Sam's eyes because she said, "I'm going to have to sit for this, aren't I?"

Sam nodded.

Coach Spears told them about the troll umpire with the same details that Lisa's mother had used. Lisa pounded the metal bleacher with a fist.

The confused and hurt expression on Marlee's face broke Sam's heart. Marlee lowered her eyes and put her hands in her lap. "How can loving someone be depraved?" She said it quietly. She didn't look up.

Chapter Twenty-Five
From This Point Forward

The end of the school year was fast approaching, and the East Valley High School awards ceremony was a testament to that fact. The ceremony was over, and Cassie pulled the limo out of the parking lot. She headed toward the Payton family estate. Sam, all three of her parents, and Susie sat in the back.

"Thank you so much for allowing me to tag along, Mr. and Mrs. Payton," Susie said.

"We're happy to have you," Sam's father said with a smile.

Susie smiled back, but the smile didn't quite reach her eyes. She looked down and then looked out the window. She was clearly uncomfortable with the fact that her own mother hadn't shown the slightest bit of interest in going. When Sam heard that, she invited Susie to go with them.

Sam felt the need to lighten the mood and said, "Ronnie was a shoo-in for Best Thespian. Don't you think?"

"No kidding," Susie said. "And Alivia got Best in Choir."

"She's a songbird, that one," Sam said.

"Hey, let me see yours again, Sam," Susie said.

"Only if I can see yours." Sam reached across her *maman*, who was sitting between them, handed Susie her awards, and then took a plaque and a large envelope from Susie. She read the plaque out loud, "Best AP Environmental Science Student."

"We're very proud of you, Susie," Sam's *maman* said.

"Oh, yes, we are," Sam's mother echoed. "You girls are coming home with many accolades this evening. And, Cassie, that was sweet of you to stay and watch the ceremony."

"I wouldn't have missed it, Mrs. Payton," Cassie said. "Thanks for inviting me. Now, if you'll excuse me, I'll put the window up and give you privacy."

"Leave it open," Sam's mother said in an uncharacteristic move. "You're a part of this family now."

"Oh," Cassie said tentatively, clearly moved. "Okay, thank you."

"Hey, you guys," Sam said, wanting to continue her quest to cheer up Susie, "I'm not done reading all of Susie's awards." She pulled two certificates out of the envelope. "Best Scholar-Athlete. Who knew you were smart, Sus?"

Susie reached across Sam's *maman* and swatted Sam lightly on the thigh.

Sam's mother clucked her disapproval, but the smile on her face told a different story. It was obvious to Sam that her mother was glad she had a friend to pal around with.

"And," Sam continued, "a New York State scholarship for high-achieving students. Susie, there's obviously been a mistake. You should check into this."

Susie laughed but then said, "I guess you should check into yours, too. Why they ever gave you that Best Strings award is beyond me. The sounds coming out of your violin are like cats crying in the moonlight."

"Ahh, ha ha," Sam said with a fake laugh, reaching across her *maman* to swat Susie back.

"You had them all fooled, Sam," Susie continued. "Most Accomplished Music Student, too. When I heard that oboe player tonight, I knew he was better than you could ever hope—"

Susie couldn't finish her statement because she had to defend herself from Sam's physical assault.

"*Filles, comportez-vous*," Sam's *maman* scolded. "Do I have to put you both in time out?"

"She started it," Susie said, trying not to laugh.

"Did not."

"Did so."

"Gerald, Helene," Sam's mother said, "I think I'm glad we didn't have more than one."

Everyone in the limo chuckled, including Cassie.

"But I am so very glad we had that one." Sam's mother reached across the space between the seats and patted Sam on the knee.

"I am, too," Sam's father said. The twinkle in his eye made Sam smile.

"I don't want to say that having cancer has been a good thing," Sam's mother said. "It has not, but it has woken me up. I'm learning to cherish the people I love. And I'm taking better care of myself. Mrs. Tardelli has been trying to get me to realize this for years, but I was stubborn. If I had only listened to her—"

"Mother," Sam said, "remember what Dr. Salazar told us. There's no sense second-guessing anything. She said the best thing to do is to think from this point forward." Sam pushed both of her hands away from her body to indicate forward.

Sam's mother reached over and squeezed Sam's hands in hers. "The day I felt that lump was the day my old life ended, and a new one began. I have since learned that it is crucial for me to live for each and every moment. I'm sorry your father and I haven't been very supportive of your softball, Samantha Rose. It was important to you, and I wish I had that to do over again."

"Thank you, Mother," Sam said. She never expected to hear such words from her parents.

Sam's mother sat back. "A few weeks back, I had a weak moment. A fragile moment." She looked down at her hands and said, "I was scared. I still am, but I mistakenly thought it would be easier on all of you if I weren't around anymore. I figured I wasn't necessary since Samantha Rose now had her maman full-time. And with this whole cancer nightmare, I didn't want to be a burden." She paused for a moment and looked up at Helene. "I'm also afraid of the disease itself. How it might eat me alive from the inside." She turned to face Sam's father. "Since then, I've had a lot of help from my wonderful family and so many others in my life." She looked at every person in the car, including Susie and Cassie. She focused back on Sam when she said, "I want you to know that I am sorry about my confusion. I've made a commitment to live now, to truly be present. And, as you said, Samantha Rose, I'd like to start living from this point forward."

Sam whipped off her seatbelt, dove across the space, separating them, and hugged her mother with all her might. Sam's father joined the hug, as did Helene.

The hug ended, and Sam sat back and put her seatbelt back on. "Mother, you've taken care of me my whole life. You've given me a very real and meaningful life. When you found out I was in love with Lisa, it surprised you and Daddy, I know, but I think you both found your footing fairly quickly. We found a new equilibrium which became our new normal. And now our *normal* is being redefined again." Sam looked at each of her three parents in turn.

"Mother," Sam continued, "you are powerful and stoic. You are my pillar. I didn't come from your body, but what does that matter? You are my mother. Please don't ever think any less, and please don't think I don't need you. We all need you." Sam couldn't help the tears that were brimming over. "I can't imagine my world without you. I can't imagine knowing you weren't somewhere in the house or—" Sam had to stop as emotion choked her voice.

Sam's mother wiped at her own tears, "I didn't know you had all that bottled up inside you, Samantha Rose."

Sam chuckled around her tears. "Communication hasn't always been our strong suit. Has it, Mother?"

Susie pointed past Sam to the tissue box tucked in the door. Sam laughed and pulled it out. She took a tissue and handed the entire box to Susie. What a softy Susie was, Sam thought with a chuckle, even as she wiped away her own tears.

It wasn't long before the tissue box made the rounds of the back area. Everyone laughed when Cassie stuck her arm through the open window demanding one.

"Helene," Sam's mother said, "I'm not sure I ever truly appreciated your kind and giving spirit. Not until my uninvited illness. You are a bright soul, dear. Your energy and compassion know no bounds. I am proud to call you my daughter's mother. I'm sorry I was bullheaded and tried to send you away. You are family, Helene. I won't forget that ever again."

"Here, here," Sam's father said, raising his plastic water bottle in salute.

"Thank you, Mimi," Helene said, dabbing at her tears. "I

appreciate your honest candor." The two women smiled at each other, and Sam's heart beat happily at the sight.

"Mother," Sam's father said, "are you going to tell her?"

"Tell me what?" Sam said as silent alarm bells rang in her head.

"Ah, yes, of course," Sam's mother said. "We're having a graduation party for you, Samantha Rose."

"You are?"

"Oh, yes. We're opening up the mansion, so invite as many of your friends as you want. We're going to have a cake with the Wellesley College seal on it. It's already been ordered."

Sam tried not to blanch at the word Wellesley. It was so obviously a done deal in her mother's mind that Sam didn't have the heart to protest, especially not after all the soul-bearing and sharing they had done in the back of the limo. She would have felt like a spoiled brat demanding to go to Rockville. Sam felt Susie watching her but didn't dare look over. Susie would see her for what she was. A coward.

"I've invited a few of the gals from the alumni association," Sam's mother said, her eyes lighting up in anticipation. "I want you to meet them, Samantha Rose. This will be the start of some serious networking for you."

Sam watched her Rockville dreams slip away as she heard Samantha Rose dutifully say, "Thank you, Mother. That sounds like an exceptional opportunity."

Sam's mother chatted happily about the party arrangements, but Sam heard little of it. She was relieved when Cassie finally pulled into the estate.

Once they were all out of the limo, Cassie said, "I will see you on Saturday, Mrs. Payton."

Sam was alarmed. "Mother, what's going on? Is everything all right? Do you have an extra radiation session?"

"Everything is fine, Samantha Rose," Sam's mother said calmly. "Cassie and her new love interest are my walking partners on Saturday."

"Ooh," Sam gushed, her interest piqued. She turned to Cassie, "So, I finally get to meet her?"

"Nope," Cassie said with a teasing grin. "Apparently, you'll be in Binghamton at a softball playoff game that day."

This was some kind of cruel joke. "You two are colluding," Sam accused. The twinkle in her mother's eye gave away the truth of Sam's statement. "Mother, you'll need to give me a full report. We can't get anything out of this one." Sam pointed to Cassie, who just stood there smiling.

Sam's parents laughed and then walked up the steps. Sam called after them, "Mother, at least get a name, a description, anything!" Sam's mother didn't turn around but simply waved in acknowledgment.

"*Maman*," Sam appealed to her other mother, "take photos. Come on. We need to know."

Sam's *maman* just laughed and shook her head. "Don't stay out here too late. You two have school tomorrow." Her gaze included Susie.

"*Oui, Maman*," Sam said with a dejected tone. "I don't want to get put in time out now, do I?"

Sam's *maman* laughed and headed into the house.

"And you!" Sam whirled on Cassie. "You are so mean."

Cassie gave an evil laugh, hugged both Sam and Susie, and then drove away, all without saying a word.

"I can't believe my parents get to meet Cassie's girlfriend before we do." Sam sat on the top step at the edge of the landing.

Susie sat next to her. "Something's weird about that whole situation. You'd think Cassie would have at least shown us a picture by now."

Sam shrugged. "She said she didn't want to jinx it."

An incoming group text from Lisa dinged on both their phones, halting any further musings over Cassie's love life. Oh, good. Marlee and Lisa's Clarksonville High School awards ceremony was over, and they wanted to know if Sam and Susie's was finished, too.

"I'll text back," Susie said.

SUSIE: Yes, we're done. Video chat?

LISA: Yes. Have Sam call my phone.

Within seconds the four friends were video chatting on Sam's and Lisa's phones.

"Wow," Sam said, looking at her friends across the miles, "you guys clean up nice."

"You, too," Lisa said. "I love when you put your hair up like that, Sam." Lisa's voice almost sounded wistful.

"It'll grow, baby," Sam said, referring to Lisa's uber-short hair.

"I know." Lisa reached up and ran her fingers through her hair. "I'm still not used to it. Okay, so tell us how your awards ceremony went."

Sam gave them a summary of the awards they'd been given and added that all the scholarship money Susie had gotten was going to help out big time for college. She then said, "I need my Fam Four right now, you guys. It seriously looks like I'll be going to Wellesley next year."

"Oh, no, Sam," both Lisa and Marlee said simultaneously. "That sucks," Marlee added quietly.

"I heard the conversation," Susie said. "Sam's mother is so excited about Sam following in her footsteps at Wellesley."

"All right, look, people," Lisa said, taking command. "It is what it is."

"And that's what it is," Sam muttered in agreement. She needed a change in focus. "So, tell us about the Clarksonville awards ceremony. Hey, wait, where are you guys sitting? It looks weird behind you."

"We're on my front porch," Marlee said. "It has a lot of clutter on it. We never use it. I've been meaning to clear this out."

"You've been a little busy, Marlee," Sam said with a laugh. "I guess I've never looked closely at your porch before. We're sitting on my top step. It's a beautiful June night, isn't it?" The cicadas humming in the background made the evening feel peaceful. It was exactly what Sam needed. "I wish we could all be together."

"Me, too," Sam's three friends echoed.

"So, Lisa got the Best Anatomy and Physiology student award," Marlee said.

Sam and Susie clapped and cheered for her. "I knew you were going to get that one, baby," Sam said.

Just then, Susie's phone dinged. Out of sight of the FaceTime screen, she flashed Sam the screen. It was a text from Marlee's mother.

MRS. MCALLISTER: SOS. All hands on deck.

Have you talked to Marlee yet?

SUSIE: On the phone with her now.

MRS. MCALLISTER: Text me once you hang up.

SUSIE: OK.

Susie's eyes were wide with wonder.

During the time of the brief texting exchange with Marlee's mother, Lisa had been talking about something silly that Bridget had done when Lisa went up to the podium to get her award from her teacher, but Sam hadn't heard it because she'd been reading Susie's texts from Marlee's mother. To cover, she said, "Hey, Marlee, did you get anything?"

"This one?" Lisa pointed to Marlee. "No, not a thing. She's not a very good student. Oh, wait, let me think about it for a minute. There was the Best AP Statistics student award. You could say she was in a class by herself."

Sam and Susie laughed. Marlee's school had run out of math courses for her to take, so she was enrolled in an online statistics course. She was the only one in her school to take it.

"There was the best AP Computer Science Java something-or-other award." Lisa held up her hand and started ticking off Marlee's awards on her fingers. "The AP Latin award. The Physics award."

"Wow, Marlee, you—" Sam was cut off as Lisa continued.

"Oh, geez, you guys. We're not done. She got the Scholar-Athlete award, a New York State Scholarship for high-achieving students, a Lion's club scholarship, and a few other scholarships I can't remember."

Sam was stunned. She knew her friend was smart, but wow.

"You cleaned up, *mi vida*," Susie said, proud of her girlfriend.

Marlee shrugged. Even sitting on the dark porch, Sam could see Marlee turning crimson from all the accolades and attention. Sam knew how much Marlee hated to be singled out.

"No English award, I see," Sam teased. "We all knew she was illiterate."

"Marlee," Susie said, genuine concern in her voice. "Are you okay? You look like you're turning purple or green or something."

Marlee didn't answer but hid her face behind Lisa's back.

"Oh, you guys," Lisa said with a grin, "we're still not done."

"What else?" Susie said. "Marlee looks like she's going to pass out."

"She just might," Lisa said. "They announced the valedictorian tonight."

"No way," Susie and Sam shrieked at the same time.

Lisa nodded. Her smile practically split her face. Marlee stayed hidden behind Lisa.

"Marlee," Sam scolded, "come out so we can see you. That's excellent news."

"She has to give a speech," Lisa said matter-of-factly.

"Oh, no," Susie said. She exchanged a look with Sam. They now understood the text from Marlee's mother.

"At graduation," Lisa said. "In front of a million people."

Susie said, "*Aay, mi vida*. What can we do to help?"

Marlee peeked out from behind Lisa's back. She simply shrugged but didn't say anything. Her expression turned into a frown, and she started crying. There was some shuffling as Lisa pulled Marlee into her arms and rocked her back and forth like she might her little sister Bridget.

"Aww," Sam said. "Marlee, you'll be fine. We'll help you practice, okay?"

Marlee nodded but didn't say a word.

"You're breaking my heart, *mi amor*," Susie said. "Do you want me to drive out there? I will." Susie pulled her keys out of her pocket and showed Marlee.

"No," Marlee choked out, her voice thick with emotion. "I'll be okay. Maybe. It's a shock."

"All hands on deck," Sam said, borrowing Marlee's mother's words.

Marlee laughed, and so the others did, too. Poor girl, Sam thought. Public speaking was a big fear for most people.

"You guys?" Lisa said, still cradling Marlee in her arms. "I need my Fam Four, too."

"What's up, baby?" Sam tried not to let her mind go toward a million different things that could be wrong in Lisa's world.

"Mama thinks it's time to tell the three musketeers about William."

"Oh, wow," Sam said. "That's big. When?"

"Soon. They're planning a family dinner. An extended family dinner."

"Lisa," Susie said, "a lot of people already know the truth, and the kids really should hear it from your parents first."

"You're right," Lisa said. "I didn't think about it that way. I'll keep you posted."

Marlee sat up, and the two of them changed roles as Marlee gave Lisa a quick, caring hug.

"You guys? I need you, too," Susie said and burst into tears.

Sam looked at her friend in shock just as Marlee said, "Susie, what's wrong?" Sam put an arm around her. "Yeesh, we're all falling apart tonight," Sam said, giving Susie a moment to catch her breath.

Susie swiped at the tears in her eyes and blew out a sigh, obviously trying to find her voice. "My mother and brother are moving to Brooklyn. They're going to live with my mother's younger brother until she can find a nursing job, and then they'll get their own apartment. *Tio* Emilio thinks an apartment might open up in his building soon."

"Susie, this is huge," Sam said.

Marlee and Lisa agreed.

"But what about you?" Marlee asked gently. "You said your mother and Miguel were moving."

"I wasn't invited," Susie said, her voice high and tight.

The four friends remained silent except for Susie's quiet crying. Sam held her close, Susie's head resting on Sam's shoulder. Susie covered her face with her hands.

Once Susie caught her breath, she said, "Mami figures because I'm going to college, we don't need to burden *Tio* Emilio's family with me." She was so choked with emotion that she couldn't finish her thought.

Sam had mixed feelings swirling through her head. She was angry at Susie's mother for being so insensitive, and at the same time, her heart was breaking for her friend.

"According to my father's lawyer," Susie said, "the house is an 'asset.'" She used air quotes around the word asset. "My mother wanted to keep the house, but my father's lawyer says the house has to be divided equally. Since my mother can't afford to buy out his half, they're selling it and splitting the profit."

"Susie, this sucks," Marlee said. "When is your mother moving?"

"You'd think they'd wait until I actually head off to Rockville in August, but no," Susie said. The anger on her face was scary. "They're leaving as soon as school is out for Miguel."

"Susie," Marlee sat bolt upright, "that's in two and a half weeks."

"I know."

"Where are you going to go?"

"I don't know. Maybe I can stay with my father and *Abuelita* in Vermont."

"Your mother will hate that," Marlee said.

"Who cares?" Susie said. Her expression had gone from anger to indifference. That indifference scared Sam the most.

"Susie, you'll come to my house. No question," Marlee said. "I mean, sure, we can visit your father and grandmother in Vermont, but you'll have all your stuff. I mean, you'll have, like, all the stuff from your whole life." They all seemed to understand the seriousness of the situation after Marlee spoke the words. "Susie, we'll make room for you here."

"And we always have room for you here, Susie," Sam said. "You can store some of your stuff here, too. You know that."

"Susie," Lisa said, "we don't have much room at my house, but we can always make some. I've always wondered what bunk beds were like."

"See, sweetie," Marlee said, "anyway it pans out, you'll have a place to go. We are not turning our backs on you."

"Thanks, you guys. Marlee, can you tell your mother about all of this for me? I don't think I can retell it without falling apart again."

"Of course, I'll tell her once we get off the phone." Marlee paused and said, "Do you want me to come out there? I will." Marlee held up her car keys.

"No, *mi vida*, but I'll call you when I get home so you can help me fall asleep."

"Okay, call me later, no matter what time."

The four friends smiled at each other sympathetically. Sam patted Susie on the back.

"Anything else, friends?" Sam said.

"Yes," Susie said. "Dirk's trial is in July at the courthouse in East Valley. I have to be there for it."

Sam was hopping mad. "Your parents can't put aside their differences until after that?" Sam pulled her friend into another hug. "We will all be there for you, Sus. All of us."

Lisa nodded her agreement and then shook her head. "Divorce sucks. I'm sorry, Susie."

"Thank you, family. I didn't know they could be so mean to each other. You guys may be the only family I have left."

"Family hug," Marlee called from her side of the phone. She put one arm around Lisa and extended the other to include Susie and Sam. The others did the same.

"I love you guys," Susie said. "And I hate to say it, but I have to get home. I have to go over Miguel's homework with him." She and Sam stood up.

"Family," Sam said, "we're all in this together from this point forward. Let's keep checking in with each other. And don't be afraid to ask for help."

There were murmurs of agreement as the friends took an extra ten minutes saying their goodbyes. Marlee ended her goodbye to Susie by spreading her fingers over her heart and then holding her hand toward the screen toward Susie. Susie did the same. It almost looked like they were high-fiving each other with spread fingers, but Sam had seen them do this before. They were silently sending each other love directly from their hearts.

Once Sam hung up her phone, she said to Susie, "I am so sorry your life is caving in on you, friend."

"It is what it is."

"It still sucks." Sam hugged her and walked to her car. "Sus, I know you have that AA sponsor person you can call if things get too overwhelming, but don't forget that you can call me, too. Any time. Day or night. You can't go back to—"

"I won't. Thanks, Sam."

"Hey," Sam said, "you have to text Marlee's mother."

"Oh, right." Susie sat in the driver's seat with the door open. Sam rested one hand on the door frame, the other on the car itself.

Susie typed into the phone and sent the text. She smiled when Marlee's mother responded immediately.

> MRS. MCALLISTER: Now, do you understand? Susie, are we up for this?

Susie murmured out loud as she texted the words.

> SUSIE: We have to be, don't we?

> MRS. MCALLISTER: Let's PLEASE check in with each other to make sure our girl is okay.

"I think Marlee's mother may be more nervous than Marlee is," Sam said.

"True," Susie said.

Susie thumbed her reply.

SUSIE: Okay. Thanks for including me.

MRS. MCALLISTER: How could I not? You're very special to Marlee. And to me. Thank you.

Marlee's mother's response tugged at Sam's heart. "Aww, Sus," Sam gushed. "Looks like you're back in with the mother-in-law."

Susie nodded, but her smile was a sad one. Susie seemed lost in thought, so Sam didn't interrupt.

"My life moves on, Sam," Susie said and then finally looked up. "From this point forward."

"Yep." Sam nodded. "I love you, friend."

Chapter Twenty-Six

Again

On Saturday morning, three days after Sam found out Susie was going to be homeless, the two of them sat together on the highest bleacher at the Binghamton Softball Complex. Clarksonville's semi-final game against Chenango River High School was just about to begin.

The Clarksonville team had gotten out of school early the day before to travel to Binghamton to settle into their motel and then to practice on the field. Sam wished she and Susie could have stayed overnight, too, but Susie needed to stay home and take care of things there. Sam had gone over and helped Susie pack up her stuff. There were a lot of tears and the occasional throwing of objects by Susie, but they successfully got it all done. The For-Sale sign on the front lawn seemed to upset Susie particularly and had been used for target practice for a few well-heaved rocks. According to Susie, once her mother decided to move, she sprang into action and was back to barking orders.

Sam knew why Susie wanted to sit on the highest bleacher, far away from everyone. It was so she could watch the game unbothered by questions and sympathy. Susie's life was kind of falling apart, and she didn't want to talk about it. Sam didn't blame her.

"C'mon, Marlee," Susie shouted to her girlfriend. She was laser-focused on the game. "Show 'em what you've got."

Clarksonville won the coin toss and ran onto the field to start the game. The first Chenango River batter slapped the ball, and it bounced high in the infield. She beat out the throw from the Clarksonville shortstop.

"Damn it," Susie spat. She slapped her thigh in anger.

Sam pointed to the next batter heading toward the plate. "She'll bunt the runner over." And true to her prediction, the second batter bunted, but then Corrie, Clarksonville's second baseman, dropped the throw from Julie, who had charged in to field the ball.

"Fuck!" Susie cursed, earning her a few looks from people in the stands. Susie didn't even notice them.

The third batter took a McAllister pitch and rocketed it over Jessica's head in center. Two runs scored, and the batter stood on third, looking pretty smug.

A string of Spanish flowed quietly out of Susie's mouth. Sam knew some of the words but hoped the people in the stands didn't.

Coach Spears called a time-out and gathered the entire team, outfielders included, into the circle with Marlee. It was a long meeting, longer than umpires usually allow, but by the time Coach Spears turned to leave, the entire team was laughing and high-fiving each other.

"Coach Gellar would have reamed us all new ones," Sam said, pointing to Coach Spears walking off the field.

"No kidding," Susie said. "Marlee told me once that Coach Spears makes them feel like they can do anything, no matter how bad things are. Their coach says they have all the tools and all the smarts they need to get out of whatever mess they're in."

"Sounds like your life, Sus," Sam said. And a little like her own.

"Yeah, but I don't know if I have all the tools and smarts to figure it out."

"You do."

Susie slowly turned to look at Sam. Tears rimmed her eyes. "It doesn't feel like it."

"What do they say in AA? One day at a time?"

Susie's laugh turned into a sigh. She went back to watching the game.

Clarksonville got out of their bad start when Marlee struck out the next three batters to end the top half of the first inning. They headed back into the dugout, losing by a score of 2-0.

"Marlee's mother keeps looking up here, Sus," Sam said.

"I know. I'll talk to her when the game's over."

"She's just worried about you."

"I know."

"Unless maybe she wants to talk to you about Marlee's big speech in two weeks."

"There's that, too," Susie said with a sigh. A sigh that said her already overflowing plate was getting too heavy.

Sam knew that her friend dreaded having to talk to Marlee's mother. It would be the first time Susie would talk to her face-to-face since she'd agreed to let Susie move into the guestroom. Sam lightly punched Susie on the thigh with the side of her fist, letting her know that she understood how difficult and awkward the conversation would be. She also tried to convey to Susie that she was tough enough to handle it.

Using a game plan similar to the Chenango River team's, Clarksonville got their first two runners on base. Jessica then smashed a double to right field, scoring one run. Alivia, sitting in the third row, cheered the loudest of all.

Lisa stepped into the batter's box with runners on second and third. "Go, Lisa," Sam called. She was nervous for Lisa but tried not to let it show in her voice. "Take your pitch."

Lisa must have heard her because her at-bat lasted for eleven pitches before she walked, loading the bases for Marlee. When Marlee walked up to the plate, Sam felt Susie sit tall and visibly stiffen.

"Relax, Sus," Sam said with a laugh.

"I can't," Susie said without mirth.

They both leaped to their feet when Marlee swung at the first pitch sending it over the right fielder's head. It skipped all the way to the fence. Marlee pulled up on third base with a bases-clearing triple. Clarksonville was now in the lead by a score of 3–2 with no outs.

The Clarksonville batters played inspired ball after that, and by the time the first inning was over, they had batted around the order and were leading 7–2.

Over the next five innings, the Chenango River team threatened but couldn't push another run across the plate. When the seventh and potentially last inning rolled around, Clarksonville had extended its lead 12–2.

Susie rose to her feet when Kerry walked out to the circle instead of Marlee. "Something's wrong." Susie leaped up and scrambled over Sam in a near panic. She took the bleacher steps two at a time. Sam had no choice but to follow.

The dugout was made of cinder blocks so that you couldn't see into it. They made their way to the far side of the dugout, farthest from Coach Spears.

"Marlee," Susie whispered at the dugout wall. "Marlee, what's wrong?"

"Hey, Marlee," someone inside the dugout called out, "you've got company."

After a few seconds, Marlee said, "Yeah?"

"It's me," Susie said. "Are you okay?" They couldn't see each other through the cinder blocks.

"Yeah, my shoulder hurts," Marlee said. "Coach says it's 'inflamed,' so I'm icing it to get ready for the next game."

"Are you okay?" Susie put her palm to the concrete wall and spread her fingers. She was sending Marlee love. Sam smiled at the sight.

"Yeah, I'm okay. Go sit with my mom," Marlee said. "Tell her I'm okay. She's probably worried."

"Okay," Susie said. "ILY."

"Me, too," Marlee said gently. "I'm okay, Susie. Really." She must have known that Susie was on the verge of panic.

Susie and Sam made their way over to the second row of bleachers and sat between Marlee's mother and Lisa's mother. Bridget climbed onto Sam's lap and asked her where Marlee was. Bridget said she was "so worried."

"Marlee's resting her shoulder for the next game," Sam said. She squeezed Lisa's little sister for her extreme cuteness. "She's okay."

Marlee's mother let out an audible sigh. Bob put a reassuring arm around her from the other side.

"She's fine, Mrs. McAllister," Susie said. "I just talked to her."

"Susie?" Mrs. McAllister said tentatively.

Susie stiffened.

"Marlee's eighteenth birthday is in six days," Marlee's mother said. "On Friday, I've got dinner planned with all her favorites."

"Pizza, meatloaf, mashed potatoes, and corn on the cob?"

Marlee's mother laughed. "You got it. And since she's on this no-sugar kick, I might make her a grilled cheese sandwich *cake*, but I'll play that one by ear. Marlee's in charge of inviting her friends. Lisa's family is invited as well as the Petrovs from next door and Dr. and Mr. Aldwell. After dinner and cake, all the adults will be leaving. I'm staying at Bob's that night. In the morning, you and Marlee can take both your cars to East Valley and bring all of your things back to the house."

"Thank you for...." Susie started, but emotion closed her lips.

"Yes, yes, I know," Mrs. McAllister said softly. "Now, Susie, bring everything. Please don't be shy about it. If there's anything you're not sure about bringing, bring it anyway. No regrets later. We have a ton of room in the basement. And if you have to make seventeen trips, do it."

Bob leaned over and said, "Call us if you need our help. We'll be showing some properties that day, but one of us can break away."

"I don't want to inconvenience you," Susie said.

"Hey," Bob said, "Marlee and Susie come with the Marge McAllister package. Oh, and there's this little fuzzball named Patches comes with the group, too." He shook his head and widened his eyes. "I am so outnumbered by females."

Marlee's mother grinned and said, "And don't you forget it, mister!"

Sam smiled at their teasing. She wondered if Marlee's mother and Marlee's father had teased each other like that.

Sam heard Susie trying to swallow her tears. A sharp breath let her know Susie was losing the battle. Marlee's mother pulled Susie into a healing hug. "Shh, shh, shh," Marlee's mother said and rocked her gently. "You're okay. You're going to be okay. I won't let anything happen to you."

Susie tried to pull away and say something, but Marlee's mother held her tight and said, "Nope, you're mine for a few more minutes."

Sam reached over and held one of Susie's hands to let her know she was there. Lisa's mother reached behind Sam and rubbed Susie's back.

"See?" Marlee's mother said. "We've all got you."

Susie's eyes were closed as she cried in the arms of her girlfriend's mother. She finally gathered her composure just as the game ended on the field. The Clarksonville fans broke out into wild cheering.

Sam pulled Susie to her feet as they continued to cheer for the Clarksonville team's win. Susie wiped away her tears. Sam knew there would be more at some point, but for now, Susie was smiling at the win.

After the high-five line and a brief team meeting, the Clarksonville players poured out of the dugout. Anne, Coach Spears's friend, divvied out Subway subs for them to regain their strength.

After greeting her family and bio-dad William, Lisa made her way to the bleachers. She plopped down next to Sam. They hugged but didn't kiss, even though Sam wanted to. They were probably both remembering the troll umpire and his bias toward Marlee. Sam didn't want to chance it. You never knew what went on in people's minds.

"What a game," Sam said.

"No thanks to me," Lisa said. "I struck out twice." She took a bite of her sandwich. "I'm so hungry. Geez."

Sam chuckled. "You were saving your hits for the next game."

"Oh, yeah," Lisa said. "I forgot." She rolled her eyes. "Oh, geez, would you look at that?" She pointed to Bridget making her way into Marlee's lap. "I think my little four-year-old sister has a crush on a certain blonde pitcher."

Sam covered her mouth. "It sure looks like it. That is so cute."

"Did you text Helene? I mean, did you text your *maman* yet?" Lisa took another huge bite. "Don't tell her I suck at hitting."

"I won't, and you don't." Sam looked toward Susie. She whispered, "I didn't want to text Mother and *Maman* in front of Susie."

Lisa looked confused for a second, but then it must have dawned on her. "Because Susie has no one to text. Anyone she would have texted about the game is here."

"That's why I love you," Sam whispered. "You get it."

Sam took a brief moment and texted her mothers about the result of the game. She told them they were going to watch two more games. The winner of the next game would determine who would play Clarksonville in the finals at four o'clock.

"Hot off the press," Lisa's father said, handing Sam a newspaper. He held several more copies in his arms. He gave one each to Lisa, Susie, Marlee, and Jessica. He said to them, "Sports section. Page three. You're all in there."

Sam opened the paper and shrieked with happiness. "You guys," she gushed. "Look at that."

"I see it," Susie said. "Wow."

"I can't believe we all made first-team all-county." Lisa touched each of their photos in turn. "All of us. Oh, and look, Jessica, you made second-team in batting."

"Me?" Jessica extricated herself from Alivia's hold and looked at her picture. "I hate that picture. I am not photogenic at all."

"Oh, yes, you are, sweet thing," Alivia said. Jessica got pulled back into Alivia's embrace and was forced to listen to a stream of compliments from her girlfriend. There could be worse things.

"First-team second base," Marlee read, "Samantha Rose Payton. First-team outfield, Susana Torres. First-team catcher Lisa Brown. First-team pitcher, me." Marlee grinned, her aching shoulder and groin muscle forgotten.

"Good girl, Marlee," Bridget said.

Sam and Lisa burst out laughing.

"Hey, Bridget." Marlee held her hand up like a high-five. "Hit me high." Bridget reached up and smacked her hand. Marlee moved her hand right in front of Bridget's chest. "Hit me medium." Bridget smacked her hand. Marlee moved her hand down by Bridget's knee. "Down low." As Bridget lunged to smack the hand, Marlee pulled it away and burst, "Too slow!" Both Marlee and Bridget burst out laughing. Others turned to see what was so funny and got caught up in the mirth. A ripple of laughter went through the Clarksonville fans as Marlee and Bridget repeated the game.

Lisa leaned over and whispered in Sam's ear, "Marlee's going to make an amazing aunt to our babies." Lisa pulled back and looked Sam in the eye. She bit her bottom lip. "One day."

Sam looked into the depths of Lisa's eyes. Oh, how she wished she could kiss her girlfriend silly. "One day," she agreed.

"Sam," Susie said, breaking the moment. "Looks like you came in third for base stealing in the county. "And Lisa came in third for homeruns."

"And you came in first, Sus," Lisa said. "And it says you're the new homerun record holder. Oh, geez, Sam, look at this. You were first in fielding percentage for second basemen. This says your 0.982 is a new county record."

"Score!" Susie said, high-fiving Sam. "Record holders. Right here. In the stands." Susie did a slow but rhythmic version of the whacking arms dance. She made sure to whack Sam with every movement of her arms.

"Cut it out, doofus." Sam fake-slapped Susie back.

"You two need a serious time-out," Lisa's sister Lynnie quipped from where she sat in front of Lisa's mother, Kindle in hand.

"She started it," Sam said with a grin.

Lynnie just shook her head.

The other playoff game started in front of them while they sat in the bleachers. The winner would play Clarksonville for the title. It didn't take long to see that the Forest Brook team from somewhere downstate was going to win. Their players had hit three homeruns already—one in the park and two over the fence.

"Forest Brook is the top homerun hitting team in the state," Lisa said. She leaned over Sam and Susie and said to Marlee, "That's okay, though, because we're going to use that homerun-hitting mentality against them."

Both Marlee and Susie nodded their understanding, but Sam wasn't sure what Lisa meant. But she didn't have to; she wasn't pitching. She just hoped it worked.

It wasn't long before Coach Spears called her team off the bleachers for a meeting. Sam's heart was full, but it was also breaking a little. Lisa had another year of high school ball to play and would be playing in college. Susie and Marlee were going off to Rockville to play, both being recruited to do so. Sam hadn't been recruited. Sam wasn't on anyone's softball radar. She sighed big as she realized her softball-playing days might be over. Done. She might have to hang up her cleats forever.

Sam watched quietly as the predicted loser lost and then exited the dugout. The Clarksonville team took its place.

"What?" Susie said, her tone making her sound a little defensive.

Sam looked over, thinking Susie was talking to her, and then burst out laughing when she took in the sight. Bridget was standing next to Susie, hands on hips, staring at her as if sizing her up.

"Are you Marlee's wife?" Bridget asked innocently.

Susie smiled. The smile reached her eyes and her very soul. "Not yet, kiddo. Not yet."

Bridget climbed into Susie's lap and said. "Mama says June weddings are best."

Susie exchanged a glance with Sam. Sam said as seriously as she could muster, "It's still June, Sus. Plenty of time left."

"You could get married tomorrow," Bridget said seriously and then laid her head down on Susie's chest.

"Aww." Susie cradled the four-year-old in her lap.

On the field, the game started and remained scoreless, heading into the top of the fifth inning. It wasn't exactly a pitcher's duel since both teams had made good contact at the plate—it was that both teams were making amazing defensive plays. Marlee caught a line drive up the middle that would have surely broken her jaw if she hadn't reacted. Susie got up and paced for a full five minutes after that one. Lisa dove in foul territory to catch a popped-up foul ball.

And Julie made an over-the-head wide-receiver type catch in shallow right field for the third out of an inning in which Forest Brook had been threatening to score.

In the top of the fifth, Lisa led off with a line drive in the gap between center and right. Forest Brook's center fielder made a diving catch robbing Lisa of a double, maybe more. After that, Marlee popped up to the first baseman for the second out. Her swing had been a little weak. Her shoulder or groin muscle must have been talking to her. The next Clarksonville batter struck out, and just like that, the inning was over. The game headed into the bottom of the fifth inning, still tied at 0-0.

The Forest Brook center fielder who had made the diving catch led off. Sam heard Lisa say from behind the plate, "Nice catch out there."

The batter looked startled that the catcher had spoken to her. "Oh, thanks. That was a nice hit. It kind of hurt my hand." The girl grinned at Lisa. "But just a little."

"Just a little, eh?" Lisa teased back.

The batter laughed and then struck out on three McAllister pitches. She was one of the batters that had hit a homerun in the last game, so whatever strategy Lisa and Marlee were using to combat those big hitters was working.

"I can't hit Marlee's stupid drop balls, either," Susie said.

"Oh, those are drop balls," Sam muttered to herself. See? She didn't know the game as well as her friends. Yeah, the writing was on the wall. Go to Wellesley and focus on the violin. Minor in finance so she could take over the family business one day. Her future was carved in granite.

The sixth inning came and went with neither team scoring nor getting a single runner on base. Bridget had moved on and was now playing monster trucks in the dirt at the bottom of the bleachers with her brother, Lawrence Jr.

Julie led off for Clarksonville at the top of the seventh inning and got on base when the Forest Brook first baseman made a fielding error. Jessica stepped into the batter's box next.

"C'mon, honey, hit that softball," Alivia yelled in her high-pitched girly voice.

"Yeah, *honey*," Sam echoed. "Hit it." That earned her a smack on the arm from Alivia.

"Don't make fun of me," Alivia said, sticking out her lower lip.

Sam was about to apologize, but then Alivia smiled. "Gotcha."

Sam rolled her eyes and turned back to the game. Alivia might have been misguided in the whole Susie-kissing incidents, but she really was a fun person to be around. Maybe one day they could all be good friends again.

Jessica squared to bunt, and Susie said, "Good idea." Jessica sacrificed herself and moved Julie over to second base.

"Oh, no," Alivia cried. "What happened?"

"No, it's a good thing," Sam said. "Julie's on second base now. She's the go-ahead run."

"I don't know what that means, Sam," Alivia said emphatically. "All I know is that my bae didn't get on the base, and now she'll be in a foul mood."

"You'll just have to work to get her in a good mood."

Alivia narrowed her eyes. "Right. That's easy enough to do." She raised one eyebrow, lost in thought. "She does have those certain fun spots."

Lisa stepped up to the plate. It was Sam's turn to sit up taller and visibly stiffen with worry.

"Relax, Sam," Susie said with a laugh.

"I can't." Sam's whole insides were trembling; she could only imagine what Lisa was feeling.

Lisa watched the first pitch sail over the catcher's head for ball one. Julie took third on the wild pitch. Sam leaped to her feet, joining the other Clarksonville fans who roared their excitement.

Lisa got ready for the next pitch and sent another rocket into the same gap in right-center. This time the center fielder didn't dive, and Lisa cruised into second with a standup double. Julie scored from third base, and Clarksonville was now up by a score of 1-0.

"*Dios mio*," Susie said. "I can't take this." Her eyes never left Marlee, who was digging into the batter's box.

"We both need to breathe, Sus," Sam said. Before the pitch, Sam saw Marlee's bat dip a little. "She's bunting? Why isn't she hitting away?"

"What do you mean?" Susie asked.

How had Susie not seen that? Sam pointed as Marlee lowered her bat and bunted the pitch into the infield. Her placement was good. The catcher leaped out from behind the plate and fielded the ball. Marlee was running to first, but she was limping. She was an easy out. Lisa, meanwhile, had taken off on the throw and was safely standing on third base.

Marlee half-jogged and half-walked across the infield to the Clarksonville dugout when the play was over.

"Oh, no," Susie said. "She's hurt. Her groin muscle. It has to be."

Sam didn't say what everyone in the Clarksonville stands was thinking. "I hope she can pitch."

Kym was the next batter in the Clarksonville lineup, and she worked the pitcher to a full count. The ball skittered in the dirt on the next pitch, and the catcher couldn't handle it. The ball ended up at the backstop behind the catcher. Lisa sprinted home and slid even though there was no throw to the plate. The pitcher hadn't moved fast enough to cover. In the confusion, Kym quietly stole second base after her ball four walk to first. The dam broke after that, and Clarksonville scored two more runs. They were leading by a score of 4–0 when their half of the seventh inning ended.

"It ain't over 'til it's over," Lisa called to her teammates as they ran back onto the field.

The Clarksonville fans held their collective breath watching Marlee warm up. Her graceful movements seemed normal. Sam knew her friend was in pain but was putting on a brave face.

Marlee was indeed in good form, and she struck out all three Forest Brook batters in the bottom of the seventh inning. Sam leaped to her feet. The Clarksonville Cougars had just won their second straight state championship. The crowd erupted, and Sam was sure their cheering could be heard all the way in Clarksonville, over two hundred miles away.

Sam and Susie hugged each other as they bounced up and down on the bleachers.

"Again," Sam said in Susie's ear. "They did it again."

"New York State champions," Susie yelled in a booming voice.

The trophy ceremony was quick. Marlee was given the Most Valuable Player award for the second year in a row. She limped out to get her trophy. When she got back to her teammates, they nearly crushed her with enthusiastic hugs and back slaps.

Susie growled kind of low.

"They're not hurting her, Sus."

Susie grunted. She obviously wasn't convinced, and Sam wondered if her friend was becoming too overprotective.

After much celebrating, Coach Spears asked her players and their parents to gather on the farthest set of bleachers away from the general crowd. Sam sat behind Lisa, who leaned back into her. Sam rested her hands on Lisa's shoulders. Marlee did the same with Susie. Marlee had a big bag of ice on her groin muscle and another taped down to her hurting shoulder. Bridget sat on the bleacher next to Marlee, holding her pitching hand.

Coach Spears congratulated them again on their amazing set of wins throughout the playoffs, an amazing season, and the resilience they showed during trying times.

"On a more somber note," Coach Spears said, "I have news about that umpire. Unfortunately, he won't have any kind of official or formal hearing." She gestured toward her friend Anne and said, "We contacted several lawyers, and each one said that even though his bias did seem to affect every game he umpired for us, there really is no way to charge him with anything in a court of law."

A few of the parents grumbled their disapproval. "I know. I know," Coach Spears said, putting her hand up to halt the grumbling. "We talked to the lawyers about the Hate Crimes Act. Some people know it as the Matthew Shephard Act, which says that if someone negatively targets a person because of the belief that the person is of a certain race, color, national origin, ancestry, gender, religion, age, disability, or sexual orientation, even if it's not true, then that is a hate crime."

"So, it *was* a hate crime," Sam said.

"Yes, but even though this man was targeting Marlee, there is no real way to prove it."

Marlee's mother spoke. "Didn't Anne tell us he admitted it to his supervisor?"

"Yes, and his thirty-year umpiring career ended that day. His supervisor fired him. Every single one of the lawyers we talked to said that in court, the umpire would simply deny his statement to the supervisor, and it would quickly become a he said/ he said/ she said circus with no tangible proof."

There were more grumblings until Coach Spears said, "Look, I'm mad, too."

"So am I," Anne said. "But it saddens me because I'm also an umpire, as many of you know. He was a mentor of mine. I learned a lot from him. It's too bad he couldn't see past his own bigotry." Anne looked at Marlee and said, "I know it's not the same, but his hearing is actually being played out on social media. There are over twenty thousand views of the news footage video and Sam Payton's interview, and the numbers are climbing. The comments, I must say, are not kind to this man."

"We really tried, girls," Coach Spears said. "We really did. We just have to let the court of public opinion try and convict him."

Marlee moved the ice pack from her lap onto the ground and stood up. Bridget stood up with her. Marlee raised her hand and made the traditional Clarksonville Cougar paw with her ring finger tucked, the other four fingers bent. Her teammates also made the symbol. "Coach, in spite of him, we won it all anyway." She pointed to the state championship trophy sitting momentarily forgotten on the bottom bleacher.

A relieved cheer rose up from the bleachers.

"Yes, we did," Lisa said.

"Good overcame evil, eh?" Lisa's father said.

Coach Spears smiled at Lisa's father, and then her cheeks turned pink. "And do you know what else happened?" she asked the crowd. "This whole situation has made me so mad that we decided to do something rash." She reached over and took her friend Anne's hand in hers. "We've decided to get married."

The whole team whooped and hollered their approval. "Sorry if this is a shock to some of you," Coach Spears said, "but I've watched these brave girls live their true lives not afraid of what anyone said or thought." She gestured to Marlee, Susie, Lisa, Sam, Jessica, and Alivia. She looked at Anne. "We're done hiding. We're done lying by omission. Never again. From now on, we are going to be our true selves."

There were calls of congratulations, and the players physically held each other back from springing up and giving their coach hugs. "All of you are invited to the ceremony in July." With a grin, Coach Spears announced, "This meeting is done."

Marlee reached their coach first, and it wasn't long before the entire Clarksonville team had surrounded their coach and her new fiancée in a crushing Clarksonville standing dogpile.

Chapter Twenty-Seven
Don't Settle

Two weeks after the Clarksonville softball team won their second state championship, Sam stood in Marlee's living room for a pre-graduation gathering for Marlee's friends, family, and well-wishers. Lisa and Marlee were in one corner of the room, talking and laughing with Ronnie and Jordan, Alivia and Jessica, Julie and Marcus, and Karl. Lisa's little sister Bridget held tightly onto Marlee's hand as the friends talked. It seemed that Bridget's crush on Marlee was still going strong, and it was adorable. Lisa's parents were in the kitchen talking with Marlee's grandparents and the Petrovs.

Sam pulled Susie aside to find out if the dust had settled in Susie's life yet.

"How's life in Clarksonville?" Sam asked Susie. Susie had officially moved into the spare bedroom in the McAllister's home six days before, the day after Marlee's eighteenth birthday.

"Marlee said it was the best birthday present ever." Susie's smile was genuine, but it was obvious that she was tired and under a lot of stress. "Mrs. McAllister is awesome. She's putting up with all my stuff, including my weights and bench, in the basement."

"There was room down there, right?"

"Yeah, but it's like my stuff is taking up that whole space. But I am making myself useful, Sam. I've made dinner twice, and Marlee and I cleaned the whole house for this little shindig. And I'll have you know that I'm keeping my room clean."

"That was Lisa's and my room, you know," Sam said with a fake scowl.

"I know. And Marlee's grandparents flew up from Florida. That was always their room."

"Where are they staying?" Sam asked.

"At the Gengo River Bed and Breakfast."

"That's a nice place, but how do they feel about having to stay there?"

"I don't know." Susie shrugged. "But, hey, I'm the one paying rent, so the room's officially mine now." She grimaced.

"Marlee's mother is charging you rent?" Sam asked, incredulous.

"No, I had to fight her about it. I told her that she might later regret her decision and that I didn't want her mad at me, so at least she'd have some compensation for the inconvenience and burden of me."

"Susie, I doubt she sees you as a burden."

"Sam, I have nowhere to go. I have to tread carefully."

Sam started to remind her friend that she did, indeed, have other places to go, but Susie interrupted her retort. "It's been a long commute to school from Clarksonville every day, but that is officially over as of today."

"You get to drive out there one more time for graduation tomorrow."

"Yeah, one last time, *gringa*."

"Are you going to stop at the house? Your house, I mean."

"Hell, no," Susie said. "I moved out. Thanks for helping with that, by the way. I helped Miguel sort out what he was keeping, and I took six-thousand trips to Goodwill and to the dump for my mother's cause. She would rather give the shit away than let my father profit from it."

"My *maman* loves the piano you gave her. Now she can play in her apartment."

"Excellent," Susie said. She took a deep breath and let it out. "Their moving truck is coming tomorrow, Sam."

"Tomorrow is graduation, Sus."

Susie shrugged. "She doesn't care, I guess."

Sam's heart broke again for her friend.

Susie stood taller when Marlee's mother and her boyfriend Bob wandered over.

"How are you holding up, Mrs. McAllister?" Sam asked, almost glad for the change in focus.

Bob answered instead. "She is doing the best she can be considering that her shy and introverted only child is about to give a speech in a huge auditorium in front of hundreds of people in about an hour."

Sam laughed. "Bob, I don't think that's helping."

"You may be right, Sam," Bob said. He looked at Marlee's mother with adoration in his eyes. She looked back at him in much the same way. It was cute seeing them so in love. And brave, too. It was the first time Marlee's grandparents were meeting the new man in their daughter-in-law's life, the man who was possibly replacing their son. That had to be nerve-wracking for everyone.

The thing that stuck out for Sam, though, was that Bob had

called her 'Sam.' So many other people, Lisa's parents included, called her Samantha Rose. Sam was having an epiphany as she stood half-listening to Bob tell a joke. Maybe the others only called her Samantha Rose because it was the name they'd known her by before actually meeting her. Maybe they weren't really thinking of her as Samantha Rose, rich debutante. Maybe Susie was right. Maybe Sam and Samantha Rose were, in fact, the same person.

Susie laughed at the punch line, so Sam did, too, having no idea what the joke had been about.

"Marlee's been a little preoccupied with her speech," Marlee's mother said to Sam. "She hasn't filled me in on your mother."

"Happy news. Mother had her very last radiation session this morning."

"That's wonderful," Marlee's mother said.

Marlee's mother's friends, Paulie and Joan Aldwell, walked over and exchanged greetings. Joan was the doctor who had helped Susie out with some urgent medical needs after Susie's first major blow-up with her mother. It was touching to watch Susie hug her. And Paulie was Marlee's boss at the auto repair shop where Marlee was going to work every day during the summer. He was, in fact, going to pay for her to get certified in, like, eight different areas of automotive repair. Marlee had been crazy excited when she heard that.

The crowd around them grew. Cassie and her father, Big Joe, Marlee's mentor at the shop, and Eddie, one of the guys Marlee worked with, wandered over. Sam and Susie shook hands with them.

Eddie was a young guy, about twenty years old or so, and according to Marlee, was a good mechanic. He shook hands with Sam again and pointed toward Lisa in the corner. "Is that your magnificent other?"

Cassie rolled her eyes and stifled a laugh.

Sam squelched her own laugh. "Yes, that's Lisa." And she most certainly is magnificent.

"Listen," Eddie said, "I could care less what you lesbians do—"

"Manners, Eddie," Big Joe growled, his bald head turning as red as his daughter Cassie's hair. The way he growled at Eddie made it seem as if reminding Eddie about his manners was an everyday occurrence.

"Oh, sorry," Eddie said. "Look, I'm not a wolf in cheap clothing or anything, but she is smoking hot." He looked back over at Lisa longingly. "If you guys ever, you know, break up…."

Big Joe scoffed and said directly to Sam. "I'm sorry about him. I will now take him into the kitchen." Big Joe grabbed Eddie's elbow and led him away. "What did I tell you, Eddie?"

"What?" Eddie said, clearly not getting it. "You pacifically said to mind my manners. I was complimenting her."

"Do you even know who you were talking to?" Big Joe asked him.

"No, why? Is she a princess or something?"

"Uh, yeah, she kind of is, Eddie. She kind of is."

Paulie cleared his throat and said, "Please excuse us. We may need to rescue the folks in the kitchen." Paulie steered his wife Joan toward the other room.

After they left, Cassie said, "Sorry, Sam. Eddie is Eddie."

"Sam," Marlee's mother said, "you were telling us about your mother's last day of radiation."

Sam's heart fluttered. Marlee's mother had called her Sam. She used to call her Samantha Rose.

"Right," Sam said. "The smile on her face was huge when she rang that healing bell this morning."

"She was so ready to be done," Cassie said. She held up both hands with two sets of fingers crossed.

Sam mimicked the gesture. "Yep. Here's hoping it worked."

"The great news," Cassie said, "is that your mother seems to have taken all that radiation amazingly well."

Sam nodded. "Yeah, she did have to cut a few of her walks short, but one of them was with Mrs. Tardelli, who I think was kind of happy about it."

Cassie laughed. "I think your mother faked fatigue that day just so Mrs. Tardelli wouldn't pass out from the workout."

"I didn't think about that angle," Sam said with a laugh. Sam was glad that Cassie and her mother had seemed to hit it off so well. "My mother's blood work showed no anemia, and she's had healthy counts all around. She has, in fact, gained a little weight."

"That's wonderful, Sam," Marlee's mother said. "I am so relieved."

Sam nodded and added, "I mean, she'll continue to have regular scans and everything, of course."

"Tell them what Dr. Salazar told your mother after the bell-ringing ceremony this morning," Cassie said.

"Oh, this is so funny. Dr. Salazar told my mother to go live her life and live to be an old lady. My mother laughed and said she couldn't wait to get old."

Marlee's mother and Bob chuckled along with Sam, Susie, and Cassie.

"Will she have any kind of reconstruction surgery, Sam?" Susie asked.

"Oh, yeah, she will. In a little while. They want Mother to get a little stronger after all that radiation, and then they'll reconstruct the breast." Sam felt a little weird talking about her mother's breast in front of people, but then again, she didn't. That was life.

The conversation turned to a different topic, and after a while, Marlee's mother excused her and Bob, saying they might need to rescue her mother-in-law from Eddie. Cassie followed them into the kitchen.

Sam and Susie joined their friends. Sam hadn't seen Marlee's old teammate and friend, Jeri D'Amico, walk in, but there she was, standing next to Marlee. Jeri was holding the hand of some good-looking guy.

Sam exchanged a look with Susie that said, "Jeri found love. Good for her."

"Why didn't you play softball at college, Jeri?" Marlee was asking when they walked up.

"My parents needed me for the restaurant," Jeri said. "Sometimes family expectations come first." There was, however, a hint of disappointment and regret in her voice.

Sam wondered if Jeri's words were a sign from the heavens. Maybe it was time to commit to her parents' wishes and fully accept her fate. Going to Wellesley might not be such a bad thing. To be fair, she hadn't really given it serious consideration. And maybe, just maybe, she could unhang her mental cleats and play softball there, too.

Sam missed some of the conversation while she mused on her future, but Marlee was now saying, "I think it's time to go to my graduation ceremony, you guys."

"We're going to head out, Marlee," Jeri said and hugged her

friend. "Good luck with your speech. Good luck in college. And keep in touch, okay?"

Marlee nodded. "Thank you. I will." Once Jeri and her boyfriend left, Marlee looked at her East Valley friends. "You guys, I don't have enough tickets for all of you."

"Oh, darling princess," Ronnie said. "We have our ways." He grabbed Jordan's arm and pulled him closer.

"Oh, he has a way about him all right," Karl quipped, earning him a smack on the chest from Ronnie.

"Ow," Karl said to Ronnie.

"We'll see you there," Jessica said, her arms wrapped tightly around Alivia, who hadn't spoken a word to Marlee. None that Sam had seen anyway. Good. Alivia was giving Marlee that courtesy. Jessica added, "We're all going to sit in the way back center section, Marlee, so look for us there."

Julie reached for Marcus's hand and said, "We'll be in the back with them."

"The gays, the blacks, and the token straights to the back of the bus," Ronnie said in his booming theater voice.

"Ronnie," Sam admonished.

Julie, the only black person in the group, burst out laughing. "You are a treasure, Ronnie. I like you so much."

Ronnie let go of the grip he had on Jordan's arm and held his bent arm out for Julie to take. "My ebony princess, allow me to escort you." She took his arm, and then they all laughed when her boyfriend Marcus offered his arm up to Jordan, who took it with a smile. "When in Rome, as they say," Marcus quipped.

~~~

Once settled in their seats in the back of the school auditorium, Sam looked around at the people who had come out in support of Marlee. The entire back two rows of the center section were filled with Marlee's friends and family. Sam's heart was full, but she found herself getting nervous as the Clarksonville high school graduates in their blue caps and gowns processed into the auditorium to *Pomp and Circumstance*. And if Sam was this nervous, Marlee must be catatonic. Sam exchanged a glance with Susie, who took a deep breath and let it out slowly. Susie was anxious for Marlee, too. Marlee hadn't taken them up once to practice her speech in front of them. No one, except Marlee, knew what was in it.

Once the graduates were seated on the large stage, Mr. Wilson, Clarksonville High School's principal, greeted the audience and welcomed the honored guests. He then asked them all to stand for the pledge of allegiance. Following the pledge, he introduced Marlee as the valedictory speaker.

Marlee stood up from the sea of Clarksonville blue and walked up behind the podium. The tassel on her cap swung back and forth. She cleared her throat and said, "Man, there are a lot of you out there."

Sam laughed along with the people in the audience.

Marlee looked toward the back of the auditorium until she found the face she was looking for. Susie's. She lifted one corner of her cap and pulled out a thin piece of folded notebook paper. People chuckled as they realized like Sam did, that this was Marlee's speech.

Marlee cleared her throat and began. "Good evening, honored guests, administrators and school board members, teachers, friends and family, and my fellow graduates. I am beyond privileged to be the lucky one to give this valedictory address. Any one of these awesome graduates behind me could be up here giving this speech. They are amazing people, each in their own way, and every one of them could impart great wisdom on us all."

She paused for a moment and smiled. "But you're stuck with me." The audience chuckled.

When Marlee looked away from Susie, Sam exchanged a glance with Susie. They both let out sighs. So far, so good.

"But first, let me address my fellow graduates." Marlee turned to look at her classmates. "What a journey. Can you believe we made it?" Her classmates whooped their relief. "We survived Mrs. B's eleventh-grade American History class." The students behind her laughed. "Honestly, I think I still have six more chapters of reading to do." There was more laughter, and Sam began to relax. Marlee had this. She had the attention of these people and was keeping them interested.

"We survived the wrath of Stratton." There were genuine groans behind her. Marlee looked at her math teacher sitting on the stage with the faculty. "You *are* kind of scary, Mrs. S." The audience laughed.

Marlee looked at one of the administrators and said, "And who hasn't trembled at Mr. Braun's permanent scowl? See it? He's the very definition of 'tough love.'"

"Don't I know it," Lisa muttered. Falsely accused of cheating by a fellow student earlier in the school year, Lisa had to visit him in his office. She was exonerated and lived to tell the tale.

"And graduates," Marlee continued, "one more thing, and I mean this sincerely, I think we are the best looking class—" She had to wait for the laughter to die down before continuing, "to have ever graduated from Clarksonville High."

Marlee turned her full attention to the audience. "So, I finally turned eighteen. Last week, as a matter of fact. I can buy a lottery ticket now, although I won't. The probability of winning is so low that I won't bother. See, Mrs. S, I used math in the real world. And I can buy cigarettes, too." Marlee looked to where her mother was sitting. "Don't panic, Mom. That won't happen. I sincerely wish cigarettes weren't a thing. They're kind of ridiculously stupid if you ask me.

"Anyway, I have mixed emotions about this point in my life. You know, turning eighteen, graduating, this whole high school thing ending. For a whole year, we were the top grade. We ruled the school." A few of the graduates whooped their agreement. "But that's over. We're starting over. All of us. Moving on. Some of us are going to college, some to trade schools, some to the armed forces, and others right into a job or starting families.

"But wherever you go or whatever you do, remember to be *who* you are. Be *where* you are. Be present, and don't contort yourself into becoming something you're not. It won't work, so stop trying." Marlee had to wait for the applause to die down before continuing. "Trying to live up to someone else's expectations of what your life should look like? Man, that is hard. No, it's not hard. It's impossible. You have to be yourself. But who are you? People spend a lot of time trying to figure that one out. But, you know what? You know who you are. You wake up with yourself every morning. You're the first one you greet and the last one you're with when you go to sleep. People always say they're trying to 'find themselves.'" She used air quotes around the words. "Maybe they're just trying to figure out where they fit into other people's expectations of them.

"I was guilty of the same thing recently. At one time, I was afraid of offending people or making them mad if I held the hand of the person I am hopelessly...." Marlee paused for a moment and cleared emotion from her throat. "...the person I am hopelessly and madly in love with."

Sam and the rest of Marlee's friends clapped Susie on the back and cheered. Once it died down, Marlee continued, "But I got over that fear after a while. Now I hold hands with her all the time." There was a smattering of applause. "But that whole thing makes me wonder what other things I'm afraid to do because I'm worried about what others think. But, you know what? Don't let anyone make you scared to be who or what you are. Don't ever ever *ever* give anyone that much power over you. What other people think is their own business. Don't make it yours."

Marlee seemed surprised by the sudden burst of applause from the entire audience. The whole back two center rows were on their feet cheering.

"It's okay to be different," Marlee continued once the applause died down. "Because we're all different. You have to judge people by who they are, on a case-by-case basis, and not by a perceived prevailing stereotype. You'll miss out on some amazing people if you judge them too quickly with potentially wrong information."

Marlee glanced back at the graduates. "Follow your passions. I got into Cornell, but I'm not going. It didn't feel right for me. I'm going to Rockville University to play softball, study engineering, and be with my girlfriend, who has become part of my family. If you haven't already, find what's right for you, and don't apologize for it. Are you afraid? Fear comes from your own brain, you know. *You* make the fear. It feels real, I know. But, listen, if you want to be a carpenter, do it. A stay-at-home mom? Do it. If you want to be one of those chefs that makes tiny little food—do it!" Marlee chuckled as the audience laughed with her.

"Demand respect! Don't let anyone or anything stop you from living the life you were given. It's your life, by the way. You're the one that's living it. And you get to live it the way you want to. Stand up for yourself. From personal experience, I've learned that I'm made of tougher stuff than I thought. And so are you. Listen, everyone feels lonely at times. Everyone gets confused. It makes you human, but never sell yourself short. Don't settle."

Sam looked down at Lisa's hand making its way into hers. Settle. That's exactly what she had done by letting her parents choose her college for her.

"Cherish the moments you have with the people in your life right now. Take care of them, look out for them. You've probably learned this already, but people continuously enter and leave your life. Love them while you've got them because you never know when they'll be gone. And who knows where you'll be five or ten years from now. Seven years ago…." Marlee paused, clearly choked up. Marlee's mother grabbed Susie's forearm. Susie placed her hand over Marlee's mother's.

Up on the stage, Marlee cleared her throat. "Seven years ago, I never would have thought in any possible version of my world that my father…." Marlee paused again and looked down at her paper for a moment. When she spoke again, her voice was high and tight. "I never thought my father wouldn't be here to see me graduate." She cleared her throat. "Crap, to see me give a speech!" She inhaled sharply and blurted, "Oh, sorry, Mr. Wilson." Tension-relieving laughter filled the auditorium.

"But what do I expect in the five years? To be graduated from college. To be married." Marlee's eyes grew big, and she zeroed in on Susie. "Oh, shoot, sweetie. I just asked you to marry me in front of all these people." There was a mixture of laughter with quite a few "Awws" thrown in. Marlee muttered into the microphone, "I did not mean to do that so publicly." The general laughter seemed to ease Marlee's sudden discomfort.

Sam whispered to Lisa, "I want to go up there and hug her."

"Oh, geez, me, too," Lisa agreed.

Right at that point, a couple of little kids about Bridget's age ran up the aisles toward the stage. They stood in front of Marlee and looked up at her. Principal Wilson got up and said, "It's okay. They're okay."

From behind the podium, Marlee waved at the kids and smiled. They all waved and smiled back shyly. A few more little kids ran down the aisles to join the ones up front.

Marlee laughed at her unexpected cheering section and then said, "So, where was I going with all of that? Oh, yeah. Of course, you should plan for the future, but you must live now. Don't be so rigid that you break. Learn to bend. Adjust to the ever-shifting tides of life. A good friend reminded me once to hope for the best but plan for the worst."

Marlee waved to the kids, who had been frantically but quietly trying to get her to wave back at them. She looked at the audience. "And, please, forgive sincerely. No matter how frickin' mad you are, if a person makes an honest and sincere apology—forgive them. Watch how fast your own anger dissipates. Watch how fast you realize how stupid you've been to hold a grudge. Watch how fast your relationships repair."

Marlee turned toward her classmates. "Graduates? It's time to make it real. I hope each of you finds true happiness and success in whatever ways you define it. And remember to thank your parents. Sure, they bugged us to eat our veggies and gave us tough love when we needed it, but they have our best interests at heart. They love us. And us growing up like this? Graduating? This is really hard on them. My mom can't stop crying. See?" Marlee pointed to where her mother still held onto Susie's arm but had a tissue wiping at her tears in the other. The audience politely chuckled.

"And thank your teachers, too. Thank the administrators. I bet they never get thanked. Maybe Mr. Braun would smile more if we had thanked him for giving us detention." The biggest chuckle came from the graduates behind her. Mr. Braun smiled. Even Sam got the idea that this was a rare occurrence.

"Let me wrap this thing up." Marlee held up her hand with her thumb pointing up. "One. Cherish the people in your life and thank them." She kept her hand up but tucked her thumb and held up two fingers giving the peace sign. "Two. Follow your passions but bend when you need to. Adapt." The little kids in the front mimicked her hand gesture; they all flashed Marlee the peace sign. She smiled at them, and Sam thought the whole thing was endearing. She noticed that a few people in the audience and some of the graduates behind Marlee were also holding up peace signs. Sam, Lisa, and Susie shrugged and did it, too.

Marlee switched her fingers to the 'I love you' sign language sign with her thumb, index finger, and pinky extended. "Three. Stand up for yourself. Demand respect."

She added a fourth finger by popping up her middle finger and then bent the fingers forward, making the Clarksonville Cougar claw. The entire sea of graduates behind her echoed her movement and roared in true Cougar fashion. Sam smiled when Lisa did it beside her. "Four," Marlee said. "Forgive sincerely."

Marlee popped up her ring finger and then spread all her fingers out. The audience did, too. "Five. Be who you are, and don't ever apologize for it. Ever." The audience had no way of knowing, but Marlee was sending them her secret symbol of love that she and Susie shared. Sam was amazed that she could feel the love from Marlee at this distance. At this point, most of the audience, Sam included, and the kids up front spread their hands toward Marlee. Sam hoped that Marlee felt the love directed right back at her, even if the audience didn't know what they were sending.

Marlee looked at her hand and then back at the audience and waved. The audience waved back and laughed. "Thank you, everybody. Thank you." Marlee looked down at the kids waving frantically in front of her. She was focused so intently on the little kids that she hadn't noticed that the audience and her classmates were on their feet applauding. When she looked back up, she seemed taken aback by the standing ovation and put her hand over her heart and mouthed, "Thank you."

Marlee folded up her speech, tucked it under her cap, and then waved one last time. Her face was bright red as she returned to her seat in the middle of the row of M last names. Her classmates patted her as she went by them.

"Thank you, Marlee," Principal Wilson said. He turned to look at her. "That was a very thoughtful speech." He gestured at the sea of kids on the floor in front of the stage. "And you seem to have a growing fan club." The audience laughed as they took their seats. "Ladies and gentlemen, I think we may have just met the future mayor of Clarksonville."

The wide-eyed deer-in-the-headlights look on Marlee's face was priceless. Clearly, she was not used to getting so much direct attention.

After the graduation ceremony and a bajillion people shook Marlee's hand and told her how great her speech was, Sam finally had Marlee all to herself. She hugged her friend. "Your speech was great."

"Thanks, Sam."

Sam felt shy all of a sudden. "You said some things in your speech about not settling and about sticking up for yourself." Sam swallowed hard at the sudden emotion bubbling up inside her. "Marlee, can I read your speech before I go home?" She pointed to Marlee's cap.

Marlee grimaced. Sam didn't know what to make of Marlee's expression as Marlee reached under her cap for the folded notebook paper. She handed it to Sam without a word.

Sam's mouth fell open as she unfolded the paper. It was blank.

Chapter Twenty-Eight

Sam

It was ten o'clock at night by the time Sam pulled into her garage after Marlee's graduation ceremony. She sat in her car for a full five minutes going over the speech she had mentally prepared to give to her parents. She didn't care how late it was. She had the nerve now and was going to give her parents, all three of them, a piece of her mind.

She made the Clarksonville claw and roared. There was no stopping her now. She headed into the house, knocked on her *maman's* apartment door, and asked her to meet her upstairs in her parents' suite in ten minutes. After a quick trip to her own rooms to get her nerves under control, she knocked on the door to her parents' suite.

"Come," her father called.

She opened the door. They were sitting in their well-lit spacious living room. Her father had spreadsheet printouts on the coffee table in front of him, and her mother held a gardening magazine in her hand.

"How was Marlee's speech?" Sam's mother asked.

"She did an amazing job. Everyone laughed and cried at the right times."

"Cried?" Sam's *maman* said from behind her.

"She mentioned her father's passing."

"Aww, *pauvre petit*," Sam's *maman* said and sat down in the empty chair next to Sam's other mother.

"She did a great job, though. She didn't seem nervous at all." Nervous like Sam was at that very moment. She looked down and shuffled her feet, not sure how to begin.

"Samantha Rose," her father said. "It's late, and your mother's a bit tired. What's on your mind? There's obviously something."

"I want to go to Rockville University," Sam blurted, not wasting time. "Mother, I know you have your heart set on me going to Wellesley, but that doesn't feel right. Rockville does." She needed to get it all out before they interrupted and derailed her train of thought. "You know how hard it is for me to make friends. Susie and Marlee are going to Rockville. I'd have built-in friends there. And the softball team, I'm not being recruited, but I might be able to walk on. The coach knows me from that winter softball camp."

Sam's father stacked his spreadsheets into a neat pile and leaned forward. Sam had to keep going before her father took over.

"Rockville's music school has produced amazing musicians," Sam continued. "Opera singers Bartulli Encanardo and Valentina Ricci. And musicians like cellist Ru Shi Chen, pianist Victoria Spellman, and violinist Arthur Prax who's with the London Symphony Orchestra. The list goes on." She wanted to put her hands on her hips in an aggressive stance but didn't want to press her parents' buttons.

It became clear that her parents were going to let her continue to speak, so she did. "Mother, Daddy, *Maman*," Sam said, looking at each of them in turn, "when I've gone to Rockville for those all-state music concerts, it felt right. Like I fit. It was like the air was fresh, and I could breathe. Maybe you can let me have one year at Rockville, and if it's not all I thought it would be, I'll tell you honestly that it isn't. And then I will dutifully transfer to Wellesley."

Her three parents exchanged glances, but Sam couldn't read what the messages were.

"Parents, I do not want to be resigned to a fate that isn't of my own choosing. I don't want to end up resenting you. I'm not trying to be a brat, but I really don't ask you for much." She paused for a moment and then said. "But I'm asking you for this. Let me go to Rockville." She paused and added, "If I ... If I don't have your blessing, then I won't go."

Sam stopped talking and braced herself for the onslaught. They would probably call her ungrateful, disrespectful, selfish, and whatever else they thought she was. And all of it was probably true.

An entire minute ticked by before her father said, "We've heard what you've had to say, Samantha Rose. You can go on to bed now."

And just like that, all the rehearsing and sticking up for herself was done. Sam's *maman* gave her a sympathetic smile, but Sam's other mother wouldn't look up to meet her gaze. That was not a good sign at all.

She bade her parents goodnight and turned on her heels to go. At least now she could hold her head high and say she hadn't wimped out. At her graduation ceremony in the morning, it was going to read Wellesley College next to her name in the program, but she didn't care. At least she'd had her say.

~~~

Sam felt bone tired when Cassie pulled the limo up the driveway following the East Valley graduation ceremony. Sam didn't have quite as many well-wishers at her ceremony as Marlee did, but then again, most of her friends had been graduating with her. The night before, Sam had tossed and turned and tossed some more. She had to use a little extra under-eye cover to hide her dark circles that morning.

At breakfast, she had hoped for some kind of response from her parents, but she got none. Nor did any of them say a word about Rockville or Wellesley in the limo going to or coming home from the ceremony. And now the mansion was about to be inundated with a million people celebrating her graduation, and there would be no time for family chats. Her parents hadn't taken her seriously. Talk about stealing hope. Her chat with them the night before had meant absolutely nothing.

Defeated, Sam let Lisa pull her out of the back of the limo. She let Lisa embrace her.

"Are you okay, baby?" Lisa asked, knowing she wasn't.

"I'll live."

"C'mon." Lisa pulled her up the steps to the front doors. "It's a party."

"Yep. You're right," Sam said. "Let me put my game face on, and let's do this thing."

They scurried to her rooms so she could put away her cap and gown and freshen up. She looked out the window toward the pool deck and veranda. A million balloons in East Valley red, white, and black dotted the scene. The early afternoon June sky was a beautiful blue with a smattering of floaty cotton candy clouds.

"Look, Sam." Lisa pointed. "There's a clown."

"A clown?" Sam said, surprised.

"Just kidding," Lisa said. "But now that I have your attention, please kiss me."

"I bet you say that to all the girls."

"Nope." Lisa wrapped her arms around Sam's waist. "Only the ones I'm going to marry one day."

Sam smiled big and pulled Lisa closer for a kiss. The kiss was unsuccessful because her smile wouldn't go away. Lisa finally laughed and said, "I want this summer to last forever. I am going to miss you so much, Samantha Rose Payton-Brown."

"Are we hyphenating, Lisa Ann Brown-Payton?" Her forehead was pressed to Lisa's.

"Maybe. Maybe not, Samantha Brown."

"Maybe not, Lisa Payton," Sam said. She tilted her head back in invitation. Lisa accepted, and they kissed until they were both breathless.

"We'd better...." Lisa blew out a sigh. Her breathing was heavy. "Oh, geez. I need a minute."

"C'mon," Sam said and led Lisa by the hand toward the door to her suite, "this is my graduation party, after all, so I'd better get down there. Mother has these Wellesley alumni women coming, and I have to make a good impression."

"Maybe I'll play softball at Wellesley," Lisa blurted and stopped walking.

"What do you mean?"

Lisa shrugged. "I doubt I can afford Wellesley, but maybe they give scholarships or financial aid or something. Anything." She pulled Sam toward her. "Sam, I can't do four years away from you. That is just not going to work in my world. I'll visit you at Wellesley in the fall and talk to the softball coach there. Maybe...." Lisa sighed.

"Baby, that would be amazing." Sam reached up on her tippy toes and, with a little stooping help from Lisa, kissed Lisa on the forehead. "Let's think about it later, okay? For now, let's party." She led Lisa out of her rooms, down the stairs, and through the maze of hallways that finally led them to the pool deck where the party was.

"There she is," Ronnie gushed and pulled her into their group of friends. He handed Sam and Lisa each a glass of sparkling cider. "Congratulations to us." He raised his glass.

"To us," everyone echoed.

Sam rolled her eyes. "Can you guys believe we're done? No more classes, no more cafeteria."

"No more PE," Jordan said with a disgusted look.

"Well, I don't know," Ronnie said. "PE was kind of a hunk fest."

"Ronnie!" Sam said. "You're so bad."

Sam looked for corroboration in her assessment of Ronnie from Jordan or Karl or Alivia or Jessica or Julie or Marcus or Susie or Marlee, or even Bridget, who was holding Marlee's hand. She got none. Instead, they were all staring wide-eyed behind her.

"What?" Sam turned around. Her estranged teammates Abby, Rachel, and Dara were right behind her. Sam turned and said, "Hi, you guys. Glad you could make it." That wasn't how Sam really felt, but she had to play the part of a gracious host.

"Sam, Susie," Abby said, taking a step forward. It looked like she was going to be the spokesperson for their little group. "I'm sorry." She gestured toward Rachel and Dara behind her. "*We're* sorry. We watched that video about the umpire going around on Facebook and everywhere. You were so right, Sam. That umpire was an ass—" Abby noticed Bridget and caught herself.

Abby turned to Marlee, who was gripping Susie's arm for dear life. "I owe you and the whole Clarksonville team the biggest apology of all, Marlee. *I* was an even bigger ass. I couldn't see past my own need to win at all costs. I was selfish. I didn't stop to look at the fairness of it all. I hope you will forgive me."

All eyes turned to Marlee, who looked from Abby to Rachel to Dara. "I have to admit; it grated my cheese when you guys didn't swing." She looked back to Abby. "What made you change your mind?"

"We didn't know the guy was a bigot," Abby said. "I honestly thought he was just trying to even up the game a little. You know, Mary isn't a great pitcher like you are, so I thought maybe he was trying to give us a leg up. I thought Sam and Susie were overreacting. I thought they were being too protective. I didn't mean to be such a jerk. But to answer your question, I changed my mind when I read some of the comments that said he was gay bashing you. That made me want to crush his soul." Abby pointed to Sam, Susie, Ronnie, and Alivia. "I watched these guys get harassed and bullied at school for it, and I realized the umpire had been doing the same thing. And I, with my selfish blinders on, did nothing to stop it. I was part of it." She shook her head. "Marlee, Lisa, Jessica, and awesome first baseman whose name I don't know."

"Julie," Julie said.

"And Julie," Abby continued. "We almost messed everything up for Clarksonville, and I am truly sorry. You can stay mad at me, but I wanted you to know that I'm an idiot, and I'm sorry." Abby's eyes were brimming with tears.

Marlee let go of her two best girls and said, "C'mere." She held out her arms for a hug.

Abby stepped into them and said, "Thank you." When she pulled back, she said, "You're not like most people, Marlee."

Marlee chuckled. "Is that a good thing?"

"Yes. A very good thing," Abby said. "Now, Sam, if you want us to leave your house, we will. The invite said the whole softball team was invited, so that's why we came."

"Stay, stay, stay," Sam said. "Any friend of Marlee's is a friend of mine."

"Thanks, you guys," Rachel said contritely.

"Yeah, thanks," Dara echoed.

The three of them headed for the refreshment depot.

Marlee blew out a sigh. "When someone offers you a sincere apology—"

"Forgive them," Lisa finished.

"I never thought I'd have to use my own advice so soon," Marlee said, making everyone in the group laugh.

"Hey, look," Karl said. "Ms. Armstrong's here."

Sam looked over her shoulder. "Oh, wow. Mother told me she invited my teachers."

Their AP Enviro teacher looked pretty in her yellow sundress and white sandals. It wasn't exactly school attire, but then again, they weren't at school. And her hair was down, too. Relaxed. That's it, Sam thought. Ms. Armstrong looked like she was officially on summer vacation. The East Valley students waved, and their teacher's face lit up. She headed over to the group.

"Bae," Jessica said softly to Alivia, "you were harassed at school because of me? Because of us?"

Alivia nodded. Sam and Susie exchanged a glance with Ronnie. None of them had known that. Sam looked at Karl. His expression also said he hadn't known.

"Why didn't you tell me?" Jessica asked.

"They were jerks. And I didn't want to upset you," Alivia said. "It's okay."

"It's *not*." Jessica wrapped Alivia in a tighter hug and said, "Tell me more later, okay?"

Alivia nodded and melted into her girlfriend.

"Congratulations, all of you," Ms. Armstrong said, giving hugs to the East Valley graduates.

"Ms. Armstrong," Sam said, "this is my girlfriend, Lisa. And this is Susie's girlfriend, Marlee, Alivia's girlfriend, Jessica, and Ronnie's boyfriend, Jordan. Julie plays softball with these three, and Marcus is her boyfriend."

Their teacher greeted each one in turn and said, "I hope there won't be a quiz later. Actually, I'm pretty good at memorizing a lot of names, now that I think about it." The group chuckled.

Their teacher turned to Lisa, "You have your hands full with this one, I imagine." She pointed at Sam.

Sam laughed, and so did Lisa. "Yes, I do." Lisa rolled her eyes skyward.

"Hey," Sam protested. The smile on her face told a different story.

Ms. Armstrong looked from Marlee to Susie and said to Susie, "So, this is the young woman who has stood by your side the entire time?"

Susie nodded.

Marlee said to Susie, "And this is the teacher who tough-loved you into getting help?"

Susie nodded again.

Marlee turned back to Ms. Armstrong. "Thank you." Marlee gave her no choice and pulled her into a hug. "She can be stubborn sometimes."

"Hey," Susie protested. "Aww, who am I kidding? It's true."

Everyone laughed, and it wasn't long before their laughter attracted Cassie.

"What's happening, graduates?" Cassie said, walking over to the group. "I'm so proud of all of you."

"Thanks, Cassie," Sam said. "Oh, Cassie, this is one of my teachers, Ms. Armstrong."

"We've met," Ms. Armstrong said.

"You have?" Sam wondered how they'd met.

"In fact," Cassie said, moving closer to their teacher, "Erin Armstrong and I know each other quite well." She leaned over and kissed the teacher on the lips.

The entire group erupted in excited shouts.

"Aah," Susie screamed. "This is your mystery woman?"

Cassie and Ms. Armstrong were now holding hands. Ms. Armstrong's blush reached the roots of her hair.

Sam backhanded Cassie on the arm. "No wonder you wouldn't tell us."

"I wanted her to wait until you were all officially graduated and no longer my students," Ms. Armstrong said. "And that day is today."

"Congratulations, you guys," Susie said. "It's nice when two amazing people find each other."

"That was sweet, Susie," Ms. Armstrong said.

"She's mostly sweet," Marlee said, "with a dash of stubborn." It was Susie's turn to blush.

Just then, Coach Spears walked up with her fiancée, Anne. Seeing Lisa and Marlee's coach holding hands with another woman was weird. She knew it shouldn't seem weird, but it was.

"Coach, we didn't know you were going to be here," Lisa said.

"I asked Mother to invite them," Sam said. She made introductions, and a few hugs were exchanged.

Coach Spears smiled and then said, "Where's my softball team? I have news."

"About that umpire?" Marlee said, hopeful.

"No, I wish. No, it's bigger than that. Someone, and I don't know who, has made an anonymous donation."

"For what?" Lisa asked.

"For a new fully funded state-of-the-art softball field at Clarksonville High School. Dugouts, lights, PA system, a real fence, everything."

"You don't know who?" Julie asked wide-eyed.

"Nope," Coach Spears said. "The groundbreaking will be Monday. They want the state championship team there for the ceremony."

"That would be us," Jessica said with a grin.

Lisa turned toward Sam and narrowed her eyes.

Sam put her hands up in defense. "Hey, not me. I buy dishwashers, not state-of-the-art softball fields. I promise, Lisa. It wasn't me. I wish it were, but it wasn't. And I know it wasn't my parents. They've been, uh,...." Sam didn't exactly want to relay her father's recent anxiety over the family finances, so she clammed up.

Lisa squeezed her hand as if she understood. She probably did. "This is unreal," Lisa said and turned the attention away from Sam. "Sorry, Marlee. A new field doesn't do *you* any good."

Marlee sighed dramatically. "I'll just have to remember my humble beginnings."

Coach Spears patted Marlee on the arm and then asked her about her injuries. Sensing it was a somewhat personal conversation, the group broke up and scattered.

After a few minutes, Coach Spears and her fiancée excused themselves and made their way to where Marlee's mother and Bob were talking with Lisa's parents.

"Fam Four meeting in five minutes," Sam whispered to Marlee and Susie. "Right-side changing hut."

Sam pulled Lisa by the hand to greet a few of her mother's friends, and then she and Lisa slipped away. Sam shut and locked the changing room door behind her.

"You guys," Sam said to her friends, trying not to let her emotions take over, "we're going in different directions in a couple of months. Well, except you two love birds." She nodded toward Susie and Marlee. "But I wanted us to make more memories together before that, so I asked my parents for a special graduation present. Mother wanted to gift the four of us a shopping spree in New York, but I asked her for something slightly different." She pulled out four white envelopes. She kept one for herself and handed one to each of her friends.

They opened their envelopes, and Sam jumped when Marlee squealed and then sat down hard on the chaise lounge.

"Marlee, are you okay?" Sam asked with a laugh.

"Sam, Sam, Sam." Marlee put both hands over both eyes. "Evanescence? Are you serious?"

"Yep," Sam said. "It's in two weeks. Fourth of July. Central Park. You and Susie have to get two days off." She whirled around to face Lisa. "And we're going to have to break the news to your mother that I'm stealing her babysitter for two days." She looked back at Susie and Marlee. "We're staying overnight at the Ritz Carlton overlooking the park."

"In New York City?" Marlee said. "I've never been."

Sam was taken aback by that. "Never? Not even to Flushing, Queens?"

"I wish," Marlee said. "My dad and I always planned to go to a Mets game there."

Sam pulled out four more tickets and held them up. "These are tickets for a Mets game. The next day. July fifth."

Marlee practically swooned.

Sam looked at Lisa with as innocent an expression as she could muster. "Apparently, it's some kind of subway-series game."

"No way. Let me see those." Lisa grabbed the tickets. "Yankees at Mets. Oh, geez. Oh, geez. I can't wait to tell my father about this."

"Which one?"

"Mr. Brown. He is going to flip out. He's the reason I'm a Yankees fan." Lisa turned to Marlee and said, "Isn't this awesome? Sorry we have to root for different teams, though." She turned back to Sam. "So, you don't buy softball fields, but you do buy a lot of tickets."

"I can't help it. I love you guys."

Marlee leaped to her feet and threw herself at Sam. "This is the best day ever. Thank you, Sam." Marlee pulled back and wiped at the tears in her eyes. She seemed to sober up and said, "Sam, it's too much. I have to pay you for all of this."

"Oh. My. God," Sam said. She heard the annoyance in her own voice. "Would you guys please let me and my parents do this for you? For us? Okay? Once school starts, I'm not going to see any of you until Thanksgiving, and then that'll only be for a few days." Her face scrunched up as tears started. She couldn't help it. She had finally found friends and happiness, and now it was getting ripped apart.

Her friends surrounded her in a group hug until Marlee pulled back and said. "I am honored to be your friend, Sam. Thank you for the generous gifts."

"Yeah, thank you, *gringa*," Susie said.

Lisa didn't say anything. She just kissed Sam on the cheek and looked into the depths of Sam's soul. It was a look that said Lisa would always be there, no matter how many miles separated them.

"Oh, by the way, you guys," Sam said, trying to lighten the mood, "how do you feel about small planes?" Sam cracked up at Marlee's stricken expression.

Susie coddled her and said, "You'll be okay, *mi vida*. It's just basic physics. You know that."

"Aerodynamics," Marlee said, letting out a long sigh. She seemed to relax a little. "Bernoulli's principle."

"Exactly." Susie kissed the hand she was holding.

Sam and Lisa chuckled as the two would-be engineers began talking seriously about the physics of flight. They were two peas in a pod, that was for sure.

"Sam?" Sam's *maman* called and knocked on the outside door. "It's time to bring out the cake."

"We're coming," Sam said, wondering how her *maman* knew where they were. She opened the door, hugged her *maman*, and said, "*Merci pour tout ce que vous faites, Maman.*"

"You're welcome for, err, 'everything,'" her *maman* said with a grin. She hugged Sam again and then excused herself.

"Uh, oh," Sam said, pointing to the group her *maman* had walked up to.

"Our mothers are talking," Lisa said. "That cannot be good."

"It would have been five if my mother cared," Susie said without passion. "Good thing Papi gave me that car out of guilt before they both lost their minds."

Sam didn't know what to say to her friend. She just patted her on the arm, letting her know she sympathized.

The mom group broke up, and Sam's *maman* beckoned for her to approach the giant sheet cake. Sam's guests gathered around her.

"Shh, everybody," Sam's *maman* said. "Read the writing on the cake out loud, Sam."

Sam waited until the conversations died down and then, resigned to her fate, looked at the college seal. She tried to make it read Wellesley, but it wouldn't. As if in a dream, she felt Lisa's hand squeeze hers. The word Wellesley didn't start with the letter R. At that moment, she realized the seal wasn't Wellesley College. It was Rockville University. She gasped her understanding and spun around to face her parents. She didn't dare smile in case it was some cruel joke.

Sam's father nodded. "It's real, kitten."

Sam flew into his arms. "Thank you, Daddy. Thank you." Her tears flowed freely as she hugged her mother and hung on longer than usual. Her *maman* was next. Sam's sobs poured from her as she squeezed her *maman* tight. All of her hopes and dreams flooded into her mind. She would be with friends at college, and not just any friends. They were her besties. And soon Lisa would join them there. It would be an entire year later, but that was better than four years later. They would be the Fam Four instead of a splintered group.

Still crying but no longer sobbing, Sam pulled back. She noticed Lisa's parents and Marlee's mother wheeling the cake and moving the guests to the other side of the pool deck, asking them to give the family privacy. Sam loved them even more at that moment.

Sam wiped at the tears on her face. "What made you change your minds?" Sam rubbed her temple. A headache was coming on, but it was a good headache if such a thing existed.

"Kitten," her father started, but Sam interrupted him.

"Oh, Daddy, you called me that in front of everyone." Sam groaned. "I'm never going to live that down."

He laughed and pulled her into a quick hug. "Sam," he amended with a grin, "it was your tenacity last night. You stood tall and told us what you wanted. You also respected what we wanted for you, as well. It was clear that you would sacrifice and go to Wellesley if we made you."

Sam's mother joined in. "Sam, you said you would *dutifully* transfer to Wellesley after a year."

"And I will, Mother if Rockville isn't right for me."

"That wasn't the point I was trying to make," Sam's mother said. "It was the word you used. 'Dutifully' meaning out of duty. I don't want you to feel like you have to do anything out of a sense of duty to us, to your parents." She paused for a moment and then said, "I think you've done enough of that already for this family. It's time for you to figure out your place in the world. We will help you, of course, but we are going to let you take the lead from now on."

"Thank you, Mother, Daddy, *Maman*." Sam hugged them all again. "I won't disappoint you."

"How could you, *mon petit hibou*?" Sam's *maman* asked. "Now, there is one more matter."

"There is?"

"Yes, there is," Lisa's mother said from behind her. She had her arm around Lisa. Lisa reached for Sam's hand, looking as bewildered as Sam felt.

They weren't going to make her break up with Lisa, were they? Was that the condition for being allowed to go to Rockville? Dread crept up Sam's spine. The only thing that kept her grounded was the twinkle in her *maman's* eye.

"We've talked," Lisa's mother said, "and we collectively realized that you two are in a serious relationship and that you are old enough to conduct yourselves maturely and with dignity."

Sam exchanged a where-the-hell-is-this-going glance with Lisa.

Sam's *maman* said, "You're both mature young women, and to cut to the chase, as they say here in America, Lisa is welcome to stay here."

Sam's eyes widened. Were they saying what she thought they were saying?

"In your rooms," Sam's *maman* continued. "With all the doors closed. Overnight."

"Overnight," Sam repeated. The meaning of the words hit her like a Susie Torres line drive. They were giving her permission to have sleepovers with Lisa. "With no one walking in?"

"No one," Sam's *maman* said. "Complete privacy like I expect you to give me and like we give your parents."

So far, Lisa hadn't uttered a word. She just stood there wide-eyed, looking at the people around her.

Lisa's mother said, "Lisa, I packed an overnight bag for you. It's in the van."

Lisa turned slowly at first and then lunged to hug her mother. Sam heard her whisper. "Mama, are you sure?"

"Does Lynnie read books?"

Lisa laughed. "Yes, she does."

"Yes, we are sure," Lisa's mother said. "Your father and I know how much Sam means to you, and we know she's leaving in a couple of months. We all remembered what new love was like, and we want to give you two the space you need."

"Now, go on," Sam's mother said. "Go be with your friends."

Sam grabbed Lisa's hand, and they giggled all the way back to where her friends were eating cake.

Susie bear-hugged Sam and lifted her off the ground. "Teammates again."

"Sam," Marlee said, "I'm stoked to go to college with you and play on the same team. This whole living far apart has sucked."

"I'm still shocked by the whole thing," Sam said. "My head is spinning."

"Maybe you need some cake, *kitten*," Ronnie teased.

"I knew you guys heard that," Sam said with a groan.

Her friends laughed and teased her mercilessly for a few more minutes.

Marlee held up her plate for Sam to see. "Your *maman*...did I pronounce that right?"

Sam nodded.

"Your *maman* said she knew I was sugar-free and had a pretzel made for me." Marlee pointed to a table near the cake. "Look, Sam, it's a pretzel shaped into the letter R for Rockville. Where all four of us are going." She held her plate high and did a happy dance.

"To Rockville!" all of Sam's friends cheered.

"So, what else went on after Lisa got dragged over there?" Susie asked.

"Oh, geez," Lisa said, keeping her voice low. "It was embarrassing, but our collective parents basically gave us permission to have all-night sleepovers."

A series of "Oh, my God," and "That's amazing," and "I wish my parents would do that" followed Lisa's announcement.

"Kitten," Ronnie teased, "is your Amazon princess staying over tonight?"

"Oh, you'd better believe it," Sam said and wrapped herself around Lisa. "And I'm never letting her go."

Sam's parents had done an enormous thing that evening. They had respected her choices and her relationship. She knew she would always let them protect her, that was their job as parents, but it was time to make her own way. She would let them guide her, of course, but she felt ready to take on life and all its challenges.

It wasn't until hours later, after all the guests had gone and she was leading Lisa up the stairs to her rooms, that she had an epiphany. It was then she realized all three of her parents had called her Sam.

~~~ The End ~~~

Helpful Resources

<u>988 SUICIDE & CRISIS LIFELINE</u>
The 988 Suicide & Crisis Lifeline is a national network of local crisis centers that provides free and confidential emotional support to people in suicidal crisis or emotional distress 24 hours a day, 7 days a week in the United States. We're committed to improving crisis services and advancing suicide prevention by empowering individuals, advancing professional best practices, and building awareness.

988 is now active across the United States. This new, shorter phone number will make it easier for people to remember and access mental health crisis services. (Please note, the previous 1-800-273-TALK (8255) number will continue to function indefinitely.)

https://988lifeline.org/ Call 988 or 1-800-273-8255

<u>SURVIVORS OF SUICIDE (SOS)</u>
The purpose of the Survivors of Suicide website is to help those who have lost a loved one to suicide resolve their grief and pain in their own personal way.

http://www.survivorsofsuicide.com/

<u>SUSAN G. KOMEN FOUNDATION</u>
Mission: Save lives by meeting the most critical needs in our communities and investing in breakthrough research to prevent and cure breast cancer.

www.komen.org 1-877-465-6636

THE AMERICAN CANCER SOCIETY

Mission: At the American Cancer Society, we're on a mission to free the world from cancer. Until we do, we'll be funding and conducting research, sharing expert information, supporting patients, and spreading the word about prevention. All so you can live longer — and better.

www.cancer.org 1-800-227-2345

PANTENE BEAUTIFUL LENGTHS

Our real-hair wigs help women fighting cancer feel like themselves again.

https://pantene.com/en-us/beautiful-lengths

LOCKS OF LOVE

Locks of Love is a public, non-profit organization that provides hairpieces to financially disadvantaged children under age 21 suffering from long-term medical hair loss from any diagnosis.

https://locksoflove.org

WIGS FOR KIDS

Mission: Helping Children Look Themselves & Live Their Lives

https://www.wigsforkids.org/

Newsletter Signup

Sign up for Barbara L. Clanton's newsletter to stay on top of new (and revised) releases. She also likes to provide writing tips for newbie (or oldbie) writers and recommend books to read (other than her own, of course).

Sign Up on Barbara L. Clanton's Official Website:

www.BLClanton.com

About the Author

Barbara L. Clanton

Barbara L. Clanton is a native New Yorker who left those "New York minutes" for a slower-paced life in central Florida. While in middle and high schools, she played any sport she could find—softball, volleyball, basketball, and field hockey. During high school she could even be found in the upstairs gym playing handball with her friends. She played softball at Princeton University and was the team captain during their Ivy-league champion senior year.

Her career has been spent teaching mathematics at college preparatory schools in both New York and Florida. She also coached softball and basketball in both states as well. She was inducted into the ASANA's (Amateur Sports Alliance of North America) Hall of Fame as an amateur softball player.

Somewhere in adulthood, she picked up a new hobby. "Dr. Barb" plays the bass guitar and has been in several pop-rock bands, playing such notable events as Gay Days Orlando.

When asked why she started writing, she said she was writing the books she wished she had in high school to help her make sense of her "differentness." Although the world is evolving, it's still not easy to come out to yourself or the world. She hopes her books will help.

Barbara L. Clanton's Website:
http://www.blclanton.com

Barbara L. Clanton's Instagram:
https://www.instagram.com/barbara.clanton14

Barbara L. Clanton's Facebook:
https://www.facebook.com/BassGuitarGirl

Barbara L. Clanton's Goodreads Page:
https://www.goodreads.com/author/show/3072442.Barbara_L_Clanton

Barbara L. Clanton's Author Page on Amazon:
https://www.amazon.com/Barbara-L-Clanton

Books by Barbara L. Clanton

THE CLARKSONVILLE SERIES (Young Adult)

The Clarksonville Series follows four high school girls in upstate New York as they maneuver the difficult process of coming out to themselves, each other, and their families. And it doesn't always go well. The four friends have a mutual love of softball which helps them bond and find love. Each book is from a different character's point of view, but all four main characters are present in each book. There are currently eight books in the series.

Out of Left Field: Marlee's Story
(Book One in the Clarksonville Series)

High school junior Marlee McAllister lives and breathes softball. She's the pitcher for the Clarksonville Cougars in the North Country of upstate New York. With the season opener approaching, Marlee and her best friend, Jeri D'Amico, go to scout their rivals, the East Valley Panthers. The Panthers' star pitcher, Christy Loveland, took the All-county pitching title the preceding year. It is a title Marlee covets. Marlee and Jeri settle in for the game, but as the Panthers take the field, Marlee finds herself staring at Susie Torres, the Panther left fielder.

For reasons Marlee doesn't understand, she's drawn to Susie. Over the next few weeks, Marlee and Susie will slowly act on their mutual attraction. But suddenly, Susie pulls away without explanation, and Marlee realizes it has to do with Christy. Susie won't explain the bond she and Christy share, but whatever it is, it threatens Marlee's burgeoning relationship with Susie.

Struggling to maintain her grades, dealing with the ever-increasing estrangement from her best friend Jeri, and handling the pressures of the All-county pitching competition, Marlee also has to confront the bittersweet realities of what it might mean to be gay.

ISBN: 978-1-953734-04-4 (eBook)
ISBN: 978-1-953734-16-7 (Paperback)

Tools of Ignorance: Lisa's Story
(Book Two in the Clarksonville Series)

Lisa Brown is the starting catcher for the Clarksonville Cougars High School softball team, and she has a major crush on her pitcher Marlee. Lisa continues to carry her torch for Marlee, even when Sam, a rival softball player, flirts sweetly. However, Lisa becomes more confused than ever when Tara, the first girl she ever kissed and the first girl who ever broke her heart, resurfaces. Since Marlee doesn't know Lisa's alive, should Lisa give up on her once and for all?

Sam seems to have secrets of her own, but Lisa wonders if she should overlook them and allow her fledgling attraction to grow for the pretty blonde, or should she fan the tiny flame still burning in her heart for Tara? Lisa faces these problems and deals with society's tools of ignorance in her quest for love and acceptance.

ISBN: 978-1-953734-06-8 (eBook)
ISBN: 978-1-953734-17-4 (Paperback)

Going, Going, Gone: Susie's Story
(Book Three in the Clarksonville Series)

Susie Torres planned to spend most of the summer before her senior year of high school with her girlfriend, Marlee McAllister, but that's proving to be quite challenging. Marlee works at D'Amico's restaurant, and Susie babysits for Mrs. Johnson, her mother's boss. Susie hates the job because she not only works like a slave but almost gets paid like one. Susie is desperate to take her physical relationship with Marlee further, but she knows she has to go at Marlee's slower pace. Complicating things is the attention that a pretty blonde softball player from another team shows Marlee, and Susie falls into a funk when Marlee seems to enjoy it.

On top of that, nothing she does seems to be good enough for her summer softball coach. Frustrated with life, Susie accidentally, on purpose, comes out to her mother. It would be an understatement to say that her mother didn't take it well. Can Susie deal with a girlfriend whose head has possibly been turned by another, an employer who treats her like dirt, a coach who doesn't respect her, and a mother who tells her she is unnatural? Can she get her life back on track before senior year starts?

ISBN: 978-1-953734-05-1 (eBook)
ISBN: 978-1-953734-18-1 (Paperback)

Stealing Second: Sam's Story
(Book Four in the Clarksonville Series)

Samantha Rose Payton likes girls, but her parents don't know that. And Sam would like to keep it that way because her parents are ultra-conservative Republicans. They live in a mansion and have servants and chauffeurs. However, instead of playing the dutiful debutante who plays the violin and still has a nanny at age seventeen, Sam would rather watch ice hockey on TV and play second base on her summer softball team. Having to hide her relationship with her girlfriend, Lisa, from her parents is becoming an agonizing struggle. Not only are her friends pressuring her to come out to her parents, but they are also trying to convince her to attend a very public gay pride festival at the local college.

At least she has her nanny Helene to confide in, but for how much longer? Sam is acutely aware that the time for Helene to move on may be fast approaching. And if that isn't enough, Sam's summer softball coach gives her no end of grief after an error-filled game and isn't afraid of making an example out of her. Will Sam remain the perfect princess her parents expect? Will her beloved nanny leave her forever? Will her girlfriend get fed up about being kept hidden? Will her friends continue to pressure her about coming out? Will Coach Greer make her life miserable? All of these questions are answered in Stealing Second: Sam's Story.

ISBN: 978-1-953734-07-5 (eBook)
ISBN: 978-1-953734-19-8 (Paperback)

Out at Home
(Book Five in the Clarksonville Series)

Marlee McAllister just wants to fit in. She didn't know she didn't fit in until Kate and Rita - the prettiest girls in the senior class - pointed it out. Even Marlee's grandmother declared that Marlee's too old for "this tomboy nonsense." All the other girls at school have long hair except Marlee. All the other girls wear something other than jeans, a t-shirt, and sneakers to school every day. Except for Marlee. All the other girls fit in except Marlee.

Marlee decides to grow out her short hair, buy femmy girly clothes, and pretend she has a boyfriend named Ronnie. Really, though? She has the most amazing girlfriend in Susie Torres. Susie is everything Marlee hoped for - sweet, sexy, kind, athletic, pretty. And best of all? She loves Marlee as much as Marlee loves her. Although their parents know about their relationship, not many other people do.

Marlee is out at home but not to anyone else. And if anyone else finds out she's into girls, Kate and Rita especially, the entire school and her grandparents will know within a day. Life as she knows it will be over.

Out at Home is the story of Marlee McAllister's life-altering struggle to fit in.

ISBN: 978-1-953734-20-4 (eBook)
ISBN: 978-1-953734-24-2 (Paperback)

Tools of the Devil
(Book Six in the Clarksonville Series)

Seventeen-year-old Lisa Brown loved going to church. Oh sure, sometimes she'd rather sleep in, but she liked the calming and empowering strength of her faith. Sundays revitalized her spirit when she thanked God for the wonderful things in her life, like her loving family and amazing girlfriend, Samantha Rose. One day she hoped to marry Sam, have a house and yard, and have babies together. One day.

But then it happened. That fateful Sunday, the guest preacher stepped behind the pulpit and spoke four words that would change Lisa's world forever. "Homosexuality is a sin," he said. Had she heard him right? When her mother put a hand on her forearm, she knew she had. Every muscle in her body tensed, and she forgot to breathe. What was happening?

The church she'd been baptized in, grown up in, and wanted to get married in had, in one instant, turned against her. Still not quite believing what she'd heard, she mumbled, "Ignorance is a sin, Reverend." Never one to back down from a challenge, she scanned the congregation but didn't find a single soul who looked upset by his statement. On the contrary, many nodded in agreement. Under her breath, she muttered, "Game on, people. Game on."

ISBN: 978-1-953734-21-1 (eBook)
ISBN: 978-1-953734-25-9 (Paperback)

Going Under
(Book Seven in the Clarksonville Series)

Susie Torres is a second-semester senior with devoted friends and an amazing girlfriend in Marlee McAllister. Susie's father has the kind of job that takes him away from home on frequent business trips, but lately, his trips seem to be longer and more frequent. Tensions rise at home when Susie's mother challenges him about that. At first, Susie and her younger brother Miguel hide in her room when their parents' frequent squabbles elevate to out-and-out yelling matches. But as her parents' war escalates further, Susie finds other ways to escape the tension.

A fake ID becomes a clear and easy way to anesthetize herself with alcohol. Her crumbling home life becomes momentarily forgotten whenever she swims in a sea of peaceful drunken bliss. Unfortunately, Susie doesn't realize that she is alienating everyone around her with her attempts to cope with her parents' possible divorce. Including Marlee. Her best friend Sam tries to warn her that her excessive drinking is driving away all of her friends, but Sam's well-meaning advice isn't heard. Will Susie finally realize that it is her own actions that are making her life fall apart around her? That her new love of drinking is getting in the way of everything good in her life? That her amazingly patient girlfriend isn't going to put up with much more?

ISBN: 978-1-953734-22-8 (eBook)
ISBN: 978-1-953734-26-6 (Paperback)

Stealing Hope
(Book Eight in the Clarksonville Series)

Sam Payton is a high school senior with a bit of an identity crisis. Raised in a well-to-do family, she dutifully plays the role of Samantha Rose Payton, the wealthy debutante. Now, almost one full year into her life-changing relationship with Lisa Brown, Sam is hit with many life-challenging events. Her best friend, Susie Torres, struggles with alcohol addiction and a wrecked home life as her parents go through a bitter divorce, and Sam tries to help her friend keep her head above water. In another struggle, two friends cross the line between friendship and intimacy—a line that should not have been approached. Sam finds herself trying to make them see how incredibly egregious the transgressions are for all involved. And to top it all off, Sam's mother is diagnosed with a serious illness.

Through the love of her parents and her girlfriend, Sam navigates these challenges the best way she can, all while trying to fulfill everyone's varying expectations of her. Sam struggles to break free of the preconceived roles she seems to be bound by to figure out who she really is. It ultimately comes down to whether Sam can make everyone see that she is both a softball-playing ice-hockey-loving lesbian named Sam as well as a classically-music-trained debutante named Samantha Rose.

ISBN: 978-1-953734-23-5 (eBook)
ISBN: 978-1-953734-27-3 (Paperback)

THE WHICKETT SERIES (Young Adult)

Art for Art's Sake: Meredith's Story
(Book One in the Whickett Series)

High school senior Meredith Bedford is a social outcast. Her family recently moved from the Catskill Mountains to the sprawling suburbs of Albany, the capital of New York State. Shy and self-conscious about her acne scars, she stays to herself and tries to remain invisible. Her twelve-year-old brother, Mikey, has Down Syndrome, and she tries hard not to blame her troubles on him. Despite verbal and sometimes physical harassment, she survives because she has her art. She was selected to be part of the elite Advanced Placement art class and is quite good at capturing the emotions of her subjects in her portraits. Besides her family, art is the one thing that helps her cope with her outcast status.

One day, at a senior class meeting, she sees Dani Lassiter, president of the senior class and captain of the lacrosse team and knows that she must paint this enigmatic young woman. One class period later, Dani manipulates things to have Meredith as her partner for a history project. Meredith is suspicious of Dani's motives but takes a chance. And it pays off. Meredith slowly sheds her invisibility cloak and allows Dani in - a little at a time. They explore an old Victorian house for their history project and become close with Esther and Millie, the two older women who own the house and who've lived together for about forty years. But, when Dani reveals to Meredith that she is gay, Meredith simply can't deal with the news. How had she not known? What is it that won't allow her to come to terms with this unexpected news? Will Meredith control her own homophobia, or will she reject the one person who had taken a chance on her and made her feel human?

Dani's Story
(Book Two in the Whickett Series)

< Coming Soon >

THE GRASSE RIVER SERIES (Young Adult)

Quite an Undertaking: Devon's Story
(Book One in the Grasse River Series)

Devon Raines, a sixteen-year-old journalism nerd, was happily minding her own business when wham, her life was turned upside down. She struggled with grief when her grandmother died from a sudden heart attack. But it was at her grandmother's wake that she locked eyes with the most beautiful black girl she'd ever seen. No, Rebecca Washington was the most beautiful *girl* she'd ever seen, period. Would this beautiful dancer freak out if she knew Devon was gay and attracted?

Enter Jessie Crowler, Rebecca's basketball-playing best friend. Or were they only friends? Devon tried to hide her attraction for the ebony dancer, but would fate allow Rebecca to look her way? Would Jessie get in the way? Would the difference in skin color keep them apart? All this adds up to quite an undertaking in Devon's formerly quiet existence.

Rebecca's Story
(Book Two in the Grasse River Series)

< Coming Soon >

THE GIRLS' SPORTS SERIES (Children's Books Ages 9-12)

Bases Loaded

Sixth-grader Mackenzie Kelly's first love was soccer until her best friend talked her into playing summer softball. Now Mack is eager to be on her school's softball team and dreams of playing in the Olympics with her idol, Cat Osterman. But first, she needs to bring up her failing English grade to stay on the team. When she learns softball has been cut from the Olympics, she's determined somehow to get it back into the Olympic Games so she can fulfill her dream.

"I just wanted to let you know I received the book and I think it is FANTASTIC!"
– Jessica Mendoza, *US Olympic Softball Team*

ASIN: B0094IT3RK (eBook)
ISBN 978-1-934452-79-0 (Paperback)

Side Out

Seventh-grader Dina Jacobs feels like she's landed on another planet when her family moves from Long Island, New York to Indiana. She tries out for the seventh-grade volleyball team, and her new friend, Christine, introduces her to Olympic volleyball. Now Dina dreams of playing in the Olympics like her newfound idol, Logan Tom. Indiana doesn't seem so bad until Dina's Jewish faith crashes against her coach's win-at-all-costs attitude. Miserable, Dina is torn between staying true to her religious customs or putting them aside to play the game she loves.

ASIN: B005HM9CUU (eBook)
ISBN 978-1-934452-65-3 (Paperback)

Live, Love, Lacrosse

Addie Coleburn, fresh out of the sixth grade, is spending the summer at her grandmother's house in Syracuse with her mother and brother. Kimi Takahashi, a girl who lives up the street, invites Addie to go to the park and play lacrosse. Addie hasn't the first clue what lacrosse is and would rather sit on Grandma's front porch eating potato chips, drinking sodas, and reading books. But then again, spending the summer dealing with her younger brother isn't that appealing, either, so she goes to the park with Kimi. Within a week, she's hooked on lacrosse. She's overweight and can't keep up with the faster, stronger girls. She has to find a way to lose her excess weight quickly or risk getting cut from the team.

ASIN: B09GPYMHDK (eBook)
ISBN 978-1-943837-50-2 (Paperback)